FORESHADOW

Also by Emily X.R. Pan

The Astonishing Color of After

Also by Nova Ren Suma

Imaginary Girls

17 & Gone

The Walls Around Us

A Room Away from the Wolves

Co-created by Emily X.R. Pan & Nova Ren Suma

FORESHADOW: A Serial YA Anthology (foreshadowya.com)

FORESHADOW

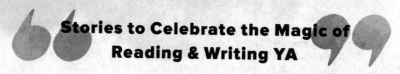

**Stories to Celebrate the Magic of
Reading & Writing YA**

Created and edited by

Emily X.R. Pan & Nova Ren Suma

Algonquin   2020

Published by Algonquin Young Readers
an imprint of Algonquin Books of Chapel Hill
Post Office Box 2225
Chapel Hill, North Carolina 27515-2225

a division of Workman Publishing
225 Varick Street
New York, New York 10014

Short stories and introductory blurbs were originally published online in slightly altered form by *FORESHADOW: A Serial YA Anthology* (foreshadowya.com), edited by Emily X.R. Pan & Nova Ren Suma.

Printed in the United States of America.
Published simultaneously in Canada by Thomas Allen & Son Limited.
Design by Carla Weise.

Library of Congress Cataloging-in-Publication Data
Names: Pan, Emily X.R., editor. | Suma, Nova Ren, editor.
Title: Foreshadow : stories to celebrate the magic of reading and writing YA / created and edited by Emily X.R. Pan & Nova Ren Suma.
Description: First edition. | Chapel Hill, North Carolina : Algonquin Young Readers, 2020. |
Audience: Ages 12 and up. | Audience: Grades 7–9. |
Summary: Presents an anthology of thirteen short stories by contemporary young adult authors, ranging from fantasy to the experience of Mexican Americans living in border cities. Each story is followed by an author's note, commentary by one of the editors on such topics as voice, imagery, and mood, and some, with story prompts.
Identifiers: LCCN 2020025236 | ISBN 9781643750798 (trade paperback) | ISBN 9781643751238 (ebook)
Subjects: LCSH: Young adult fiction. | CYAC: Short stories.
Classification: LCC PZ5 .F747 2020 | DDC [Fic]—dc23
LC record available at https://lccn.loc.gov/2020025236

10 9 8 7 6 5 4 3 2 1
First Edition

For the writers waiting to share their voices with the universe,

who trace fingers along shelves,
dreaming of spines with their own names,

who scrabble and dig for words
in the dark and unholy hours,

who know their hearts are full of tales,
and are just beginning to hope—

we can't wait to read your words.
The world needs your story.

**And for Michael Bourret,
incredible friend and human and advocate.**

CONTENTS

FORESHADOW

INTRODUCTION

by Emily X.R. Pan

STORIES ARE THE BEST KIND OF SPELL. THERE'S NOTHING LIKE CRACKING OPEN a book and being magicked away to a different time and place, giving your heart over to characters who will live forever in your mind. What's remarkable about the *short* story is how an author manages to sharpen that experience, condensing it into something powerful.

This is why a short story is so difficult to write: How do you make someone fall in love with your characters in the span of so few words? How do you pull your reader in fast enough and make them feel the hum of a deeply resonant emotion? There's also the question of structure, the style of the prose. In a short story, all the things that make a good novel have to be compressed into a neat little package.

Tell the blank page a story, and it will tell you who you are. It will shine back at you the quiet undercurrents of your mind. Peer into those waters, and you'll see your swells of confidence, your sleep-stealing fears. Storytelling, if you think about it, is the most human thing we do. It's a universal language. It's so instinctive, baked into our way of surviving and connecting, that we do it without even thinking about it.

Whether or not you've ever tried to catch a story and pin it to the page, you are a storyteller. I'm sure, for example, that you could easily tell me about the time you got into such trouble that people who love you wheeze with laughter to remember it. The hilarious thing that happened to you some weekends ago. The best moment of your life so far. The most devastating way you've ever had to say goodbye.

This is how we connect. We share experiences. We tell of what happened. Many of us even conjure our stories up out of nothing.

There was one time, a handful of years ago, that writing a short story changed my life.

I had sent a fantasy novel out to agents, crossing every bone in my body, hoping-wishing-praying . . . but what came back were only rejections. I felt fragile; I needed to rebuild my confidence. That was when I turned to a short story I'd written years earlier. The execution had never been right, but I still loved the idea. With new characters and new stakes, I rewrote the whole thing from scratch.

That was a turning point for so many reasons. First, it offered the reminder that I could finish something, that *I was capable of it*. Those agent rejections had not destroyed my love or my creativity. Second, the process of rewriting something so thoroughly and successfully turned me bold. It takes a great deal of bravery to scrap existing words. From that experience I learned to trust myself. I learned that returning to the blank page isn't truly starting over, because all the earlier sentences make for crucial scaffolding. It changed the way I think about the revision process.

But most importantly, that story—weird and sad with a touch of the fantastical—carried me back to my instincts and helped me pin down the kind of writer I wanted to be. My excitement for it was electricity crackling in my veins.

People often ask me about the process of writing *The Astonishing Color of After*. I explain how I rewrote it again and again. How I found new angles, how the premise morphed. The book wouldn't exist if I hadn't first developed the courage to rewrite from scratch.

When I read short stories now, I find myself searching for similar sparks in the works of other writers. Sometimes you can see them wrestling with creative questions on the page. Sometimes you can see the first few bricks being laid for works that came later. Always, there's something of the author preserved like a fossil in amber—you can see it so much more clearly because a short story is sliced so thin.

FORESHADOW was originally born as an ode to the short story, and it was our way of finding brand-new writers whose voices we wanted to champion. We wanted to celebrate young adult stories by authors of many different backgrounds in an online format of our own invention.

And since our love for the short story came from our devotion to the craft of writing, here is a book with a sprinkling of exactly that. We've added commentary to go along with each piece, a peek behind the curtain as we discuss the various facets of storytelling. Like an orchestra with its many instruments, the individual elements of fiction—voice, world-building, stakes, just to name a few—must work together and take their turns being loud and soft.

So please: Drink these stories in. Taste the words on your tongue. Relish the worlds that have been built here. After all, what's the point of storytelling magic if it isn't shared?

FLIGHT

Tanya Aydelott

I

SHE REMEMBERS THE FIRST TIME SHE SAW THE UNICORN TAPESTRIES. Mama had just moved them to New York City, piling their weathered brown suitcases in the foyer of an apartment almost too small to be called a home. On a sticky August afternoon before Mama started her new job on TV, they took the M4 bus, crowded and noisy, up to the top of Manhattan. She sat in Mama's lap, watching the other passengers: the teenager with the headphones so much larger than his ears, the tired woman with thick ankles and stretched shopping bags, the older gentleman with a checkered hat tugged low over his bushy white eyebrows. She couldn't see his eyes. There were young twins, their hair bound up in braids, babbling to each other in a language she couldn't understand, and an older brother watching them with exasperation. Maybe she wasn't the only one who didn't know their language.

"We're here," Mama said gently, and pried her loose.

She hopped down the big step of the bus and looked up at the imposing building, this place Mama said was important for her to see. Mama said that about many things, and usually the girl wasn't sure why they were important, even after she had seen them.

The museum was fairly large, with narrow stairwells and hushed, cool rooms. She felt her heart leap when Mama pointed out that one entire archway had been brought over from Spain, dismantled and reassembled to look exactly as it had in its original location. She thought, *This is what I am, too. Brought here like a stone and expected to fit.* She reached out to touch the pitted arch, but Mama gently tugged her back.

Outside, there were spindly dwarf trees and a small herb garden laid out by the curators based on a medieval plan. Mama pointed out the fruit that was beginning to grow, the small glossy bodies rounding into recognizable shapes. The girl watched butterflies and squirrels dart in and out of the greenery. The air was scented with herbs and flowers, nothing like the greasy gas smell of the city. She wanted to stay here, away from the cold stone walls that had been stolen from their homes, but Mama took her hand and moved them back inside.

They stayed for a long time in the room with the unicorns. Mama had told her stories, but nothing looked the way she had imagined. Instead of gentle, sloping heads, the unicorns had beards, and their mouths were turned down as if they were sad or worried. And they were being hunted, first by dogs and then by men. The final unicorn was captured and enclosed, its body torn by sharp spears. The cage around it was low, but the unicorn could not escape it.

Mama touched her cheek, and she realized she was crying.

"Yes," said Mama, "we should cry for them."

"But they're not *real*," she remembers saying, her young voice high and hot.

"Things can be real even if we never see them," Mama said. "Most things are. Don't say a thing isn't real until you know for certain."

She remembers being bewildered and afraid. "Why is there a belt around its neck?"

Mama let out a breath. The dark shadows that had begun to ring her eyes seemed to have moved lower, into her voice. She said, "Things that are unexplainable—these are things that people feel they must control. Magic. Beauty. Art. Creatures like the unicorn, which they aren't even sure are real. Even in their imaginations, they cage them."

Her eyes moved from the unicorn to Mama. This was something important, something she needed to know. "People, too?" she asked, her voice hollow like a shell.

Mama passed a hand across the girl's head, smoothing the stray hairs at her temples. "Oh," she said softly, and, "Yes."

Someone came into the room then, feet slapping against stone, and bumped up against Mama so she had to move to the side. "Hey," the voice said, and then, "*Hey*, I know you—you did the desserts on that morning show! Let me get a picture with you."

Mama demurred, as she always did, and they left very soon after.

On the way out, the girl had wanted to buy a postcard—one of the ones showing the unicorn with its horn in water, before it was brought down by the hunters. But Mama said no, the magic was in remembering the unicorn, not in owning it.

II

MAMA'S NEW COOKING SHOW WAS NOT, INITIALLY, A SUCCESS. THAT CAME later, after the producer suggested she wear low-cut blouses and skirts that flared and heels that made her stand differently. She became someone else. The makeup crew curled her hair and threw red on her lips and splashed dark paint across her eyelids and eyelashes. She and the girl laughed about the transformation; they called the TV version of her "Marlena," after an actress Mama had admired when she was young. Marlena would smile and the live audience would thrill to her; she would bend over in one of her new blouses to reveal a soufflé, and the producer would promise her champagne. "The camera loves you!" he would crow every time the ratings came in.

"It won't last," Mama would say in her throaty Marlena voice, fluffing her skirts and patting her dark hair. "We'll leave here soon and do something else. But for now, this is fine for us."

The girl spent afternoons in the studio watching her mother become Marlena, and nights watching Marlena turn back into her mother. There were trips to restaurants and museums, evenings at literary salons where the adults talked for hours in smoky, dull-scented rooms, weekend out-of-town trips to go antiquing and pick through racks of fashionable old stoles, and jaunts to toy stores where they bought puzzles and paints.

There was one place Mama wouldn't take her. When her class had a field trip to the Prospect Park Zoo, Mama drew her out of school for the day and they went across the city to the Museum of Modern Art. The girl remembers protesting; she had wanted to spend more time with the other children in her class. But Mama was adamant. "Bodies are cages already," Mama said, something dark and pained in her eyes. "There's no need to see cages inside cages."

At the MoMA, Mama stood for a long time in front of Willem de Kooning's *Woman I*. "Can you see?" she finally asked, one hand so tight around her purse strap that her knuckles showed white as bone. "Look how she escapes her body. Look how he's given her wings." She led the girl through the exhibit, stopping before Picasso's *Two Nudes* and *Les Demoiselles d'Avignon*. "Look how their bodies are and are not, at the same time."

There was a wistfulness to Mama's voice that was all hers, with none of Marlena's brass.

"They're ugly," the girl said. She remembers how she had hated the way the artists smudged the women's bodies so they looked small and vulnerable. She remembers how her own body felt as though its edges were smudging into curves. Some days, it had felt like she was becoming a stranger to herself. "They don't look finished."

"They're in the wrong skins." Mama's cheeks were pale, like the blush roses she sometimes received from fans and left with the studio's doorman. "Being trapped inside the wrong skin can feel like a curse. The moment you find the right one, you can't wait to live in it."

Her gaze grew faraway then, as though she were looking past the paintings, and the girl turned away from *Les Demoiselles*, uncomfortable.

When they got home, Mama poured so much rosewater into her coffee that the air was nearly pink with it. She drew from her oracle deck that night, and the first card she pulled was *Grief*.

Mama stopped using the subway soon after that, saying that more and more people recognized her; she was uncomfortable with their attention. "New York is fine," Mama would say. "There's no need to go national." Her producer was upset; he wanted to send Marlena on tour across the US, not just giving cooking lessons but interacting with local chefs. Mama had loud phone arguments with him, her sharp heels clicking against the hardwood floors of their second New York apartment—slightly bigger than the first, with an armoire they'd found at an antiques shop in Hudson and a sideboard and mirror from Essex. It seemed like home always reflected cities or towns they visited and left, never the city they walked every day. "I know what I want," Mama would tell her producer, "and I know what I don't. Stop trying to change my mind."

One night, Mama hurried them home from the studio without even taking off her makeup. She stank of grease and had an angry splotch of red at the base of her neck. Once the door was closed and locked behind them, she brewed and drank two cups of tea scented with rosewater, then met her own eyes in the mirror over the sideboard. "Don't ever put yourself on display," Marlena said in Mama's voice, her eyes heavy with liquid eyeliner and exhaustion. "They'll never give you back."

The girl knew their time in New York was up when Mama stopped using rosewater in Marlena's desserts. It wasn't because the rosewater was running out—Mama was careful to have three bottles in the cupboard, always, just in case. But the bottles disappeared from the television kitchen, and then the three bottles at home became six, and then nine. Mama began staying up late to check and recheck the numbers in her bank account; one morning, the girl found a fistful of cash tucked inside one of the tea caddies. She began putting her favorite books into a suitcase and deciding which of her clothes to bring with her and which to donate, and when Mama said they needed to go, she already had one bag packed and was nearly finished with a second.

The week before they left, they went to see the unicorns again. This time in a taxi, with a driver whose music jangled and slurred, and who eyed Mama again and again in the rearview mirror. Mama tipped him so he would not wait for them.

They did not walk through the gardens of the Cloisters. They did not spend time looking at the Spanish archway or the French chapels, even though she ached to see that Spanish stone again, to reassure herself that it was still there.

They went straight to the unicorns and stood for a long time with them. This time, she noticed that the colors on the tapestries were faded and whole sections were coming loose, but the majesty of the creatures was still there in each thread. The unicorns were beautiful, or perhaps a word beyond beautiful. They were calm, exaltation, peace. And for their otherworldly beauty, they were hunted.

"Remember them," Mama told her. "It will be a long time, I think, until we are here again."

Mama squeezed her hand then, so tightly her bones squeaked, and stepped away.

The girl stood alone before the unicorns. She felt her body move with every cold breath, her ribs and skin and lungs stretching to keep her alive. She looked at each unicorn in turn, counting them, memorizing them. And for a lonely, chilled moment, she was sure they looked back.

III

THEY MOVED SOUTH. MAMA'S HAIR BECAME GOLD, THEN BLACK, THEN auburn. She darkened and lightened her eyebrows, changed her shoes from heels to flats to sandals to boots. Bracelets appeared on her arms, became watches, then disappeared. She had four earrings, then none, then two. A beauty mark rose high on her right cheek, but was gone one morning and reappeared days later by her clavicle. Her smile widened and shrank, grew brittle, grew edges. Marlena came back only once, for a television commercial for a cooking oil, and then Mama threw out all of Marlena's dresses and makeup. They wouldn't even watch the real Marlene's movies, Mama said; they were done with that name forever.

She bought a car, threw their books and clothes into the trunk, and locked it tight. Sunglasses to hide their eyes; haircuts to frame their faces differently. Mama said she was enrolling the girl in the school of life, and bought an entire set of encyclopedias for her to read. She sent postcards to New York and Chicago and places the girl did not remember, mail that never had a return address. When they checked into new hotels and found messages awaiting their arrival, Mama did not read them aloud.

One night, the girl woke in a dark, sterile hotel room to the sound of Mama weeping. It was a wrenching noise, no less horrible for being muffled in the overstuffed hotel pillow. She crept from her bed to her mother's, placing her hand on Mama's elbow. Mama's skin was hot, too hot, and she snatched her stinging hand back.

"Mama?" She remembers the fear, the worry.

"It hurts." Her mother's voice was tight and scratchy, and the girl realized that it was Mama's whimper that had woken her. "It *hurts*."

The girl knew what to do, or at least where to start. She boiled water in the electric kettle they always carried, filled a mug, and poured in enough rosewater that the air above the mug was fragrant and wet. She carried the steaming mug back to Mama and tried to get her to sit up. "Here," she said, and reached around her mother's shoulders.

Something pricked at her palm. Hissing, she bent over Mama to see. Something was on her skin, or maybe in it, something sharp, something trying to grow—

Mama sat up quickly, rubbing her hands across her face. She took the mug from the nightstand and gulped down the hot rosewater. As she drank, the color returned to her face. "I'm sorry," she said when she had emptied the mug. Her voice sounded almost normal. "Did I wake you? You should go back to sleep."

"Mama," the girl asked, "what's wrong with your back?"

Mama looked at her for a long moment. She pulled at the neck of her nightgown, easing it down and baring her shoulder blade. There was a dark red blotch, like a burn or a bruise that hadn't yet realized it was supposed to purple, and Mama let out a quick breath when the girl gently touched its edge.

Nothing poked out from her skin. It was still hot to the touch, but it was smooth.

"Are you okay?" The girl didn't know what else to say.

Mama nodded. "Could you—would you put some cream on it for me?"

The girl brought three of her mother's creams to the bed. As the months had gone by, she'd noticed the growing collection of bottles and lotions and wondered why they were all suddenly necessary. When she was little, Mama had only kept one or two bottles on her dresser. Now there were so many that they had their own case, a zippered bag embroidered with swans. Mama kept it in her suitcase with her cards.

Mama touched each of the bottles in turn and chose the one she wanted. It was made from rose hips, and when the girl unscrewed the lid and released the scent into the room, Mama sighed and her face gentled. "Thank you," she whispered. "I don't know what came over me."

They left the next day. Mama's face was still swollen from crying, but they said nothing to each other about the tears, the red blotch on her right shoulder, or the one she had revealed, after the girl had spread the cool white cream on her skin, on her left.

When they checked into their next hotel, Mama said she was taking a bath and locked the bathroom door. She was inside for a long time, and when she finally emerged, the steam that billowed out of the room was tinted pink and smelled like roses. She drew her cards before bed, and the first card she pulled was *Deception*.

It was in Knoxville, Tennessee, that it happened. They were coming out of a department store, Mama slicking on a new lipstick, when a shout stopped her. "Hey—*hey*, Lianne! Lianne, *wait*."

Her face froze. Her foot, about to lift and propel her into the next step, paused; her heel was already off the ground. It would have been comical, except that when she turned, her face was ashen, and the lipstick color, which had been so perfect just moments before, was suddenly all wrong for her.

"Lianne, I *knew* it was you," the man said, striding toward them. His face was deeply tanned, flat and grooved like the back side of a hatchet, but his hands were steady on Mama's wrists. He shook her, very gently, as though he were afraid movement would cause her to disappear. "Where did you *go*?"

He caught sight of the girl, and his eyes widened.

"Lianne?" he whispered, and Mama seemed to crumple, right there, so that he was holding her wrists but somehow also holding her heart.

"I can't, *I can't*," Mama said, but of course they did.

IV

THE MAN'S NAME WAS TED, AND HE KNEW MAMA FROM—BEFORE. BEFORE everything, it seemed. Before the television program, before New York City, before D.C. and Chicago and Savannah. Before she learned how to paint her face and talk into spotlights. He knew her when she traveled alone.

A few days after he found them, they accompanied him to Nashville. Mama was careful to tell the girl that they would be staying with Ted for a time, but she was also careful not to say when they would leave.

In Ted's house, she helped her mother take down the heavy, dark drapes and replace them with lighter fabrics; hang bright paintings and prints in place of the mirrors he had on every wall; and lay richly colored carpets on his cold floors. It was like doing magic, the girl thought, the way Mama transformed his house from a mausoleum into a home.

And there was another new school for her. Mama refused to let Ted pay for it. "Some things," she said testily when he offered, again, "we can manage on our own." The girl did not feel brave enough to ask Mama which things they couldn't manage.

"So she had dark hair when you met her?" the girl asked him once.

"And she was skinny," he said, shuffling a deck of cards. He was teaching her to play gin rummy. "Bones, mostly. I used to feed her pancakes with extra syrup and milkshakes with three cherries on top, and still she was just this bitty thing. My momma thought she must be half-noodle."

The girl laughed, thinking of the desserts her mother made with thin noodles curled around one another, fragrant fruits and syrups nestled in their curves.

He flashed his teeth at her and dealt. "She was skinny as a rose stem," he drawled. "Like a line of paint down a highway. I kept feeding her and feeding her, and that line didn't get any wider." He looked at his hand and reordered the cards. "And then she wasn't skinny anymore, and then she wasn't *here* anymore."

"Was that because of me?" the girl asked, lifting the top card from the deck. She paused, looking tightly at the eleven cards in her hand, trying hard to concentrate only on which card she would trade back.

He put his cards down—facedown, because he wouldn't let her win easily, not even like this—and looked at her. She liked this about him, that he could look directly at her without flinching, that his eyes were patient and did not judge. He simply met her gaze and waited.

"No," he said after a quiet moment. "But I've been missing you all these years, even when I didn't know it." His gaze touched her eyebrows, her cheekbones, the light glinting on her middle part. "Even your hair is like mine."

She lifted the end of her braid and looked at it. Her hair was brown; his hair was brown. But Mama's hair could be brown, too, any shade she wanted. If he'd said that her eyes were like his, she might have agreed. Or her height—she was going to be tall, just like him, probably at least four inches taller than Mama. If he'd said the shape of her chin, the way her big toe edged ever so slightly to the side, the way her nostrils flared when she got angry—any of those would have convinced her. But he said *hair*, the thing she was most sure was changeable.

"Mama's hair is brown," she replied.

"It's the curl," he said, and picked his cards back up. "The curl in your hair doesn't come from your momma."

There were days she was glad she didn't look very much like her mother. She'd seen how Marlena tried to dodge but could not escape the people around her, how the eyes on her were a constant weight she struggled against. But she'd also spent days wishing she had the same grace, the same smooth-milk skin, the same casual wave and flip to her hair. When she was little, she had tried on her mother's lipsticks and frowned when they didn't look good on her; clipped on earrings and grimaced to find them too big for her face. She'd once tried styling her hair with her mother's hairbrush, and then had to ask to be unsnarled from its bristles.

"It isn't—I'm not—" she said, and blushed hotly when Ted looked at her.

"Of course not," he said mildly, and waited for her to play her card.

She played; he played. The hand continued for a few more moments, and as she drew close to making her third set, she asked, "Do you hate her for any of it?"

Ted's answer was swift. "No." He chewed for a moment on the next thought. "How could I? Even when I missed her, even when I was confused and hurt, even at the lowest point, she was always—Lianne." He played his final card, facedown, laying out a perfect hand, ace to the ten of spades. "One day, hopefully, you'll see."

The girl considered this. She wasn't sure how she felt about getting romantic advice from Ted, particularly when he was winning. "What about me?" she asked. "Are you mad she took me away from you?"

Ted sighed. "I didn't know why she left, not at first," he admitted. "And I didn't know about you, so how could I be mad about that? If anything, I was hurt. But then—well, she had her reasons."

The girl's nose wrinkled, and she gathered the cards to shuffle and deal. The deck was well-worn and slick; the design on its back was a loon, the patterned feathers carefully reproduced in dark blue ink.

"Reasons?" She thought about where they'd lived, the things they'd seen. She wondered what would compel her mother to leave. "Like being on TV?"

Even as she said it, she knew it wasn't right.

He laughed, low and wary. "Sure," he said, "we can say that." But then he shook his head. "No, it wasn't that. It was—well, she lost something important, and I couldn't help her find it. Maybe she's spent all this time looking for it."

The girl thought about the trips she and Mama took, the antique stores and vintage clothing shops, the auction houses and flea markets and midnight bus rides to cities she could barely pronounce. She wondered what a search would have looked like if Mama had stayed in one place.

Mama had rolled her eyes when Ted started teaching the girl gin rummy. "It's a game we can all play with my mother," he said by way of explanation, winking at the girl and dealing Mama into the game.

"Your mother never liked me," Mama reminded him, pressing her fingers against the backs of the cards. She was wearing white, a color she had never worn as Marlena, with a string of jet beads around her neck. She looked young and happy and helpless.

Ted only laughed, saying in his solid, confident way, "Having a grand-daughter will change things."

"She'll spoil her, just to spite me."

"Your daughter?" Ted had a broad voice; it took up space, smoothing corners and making lights brighter. He filled rooms with the grin his words always seemed to carry with them. "She wouldn't dare."

On Tuesdays, they went to visit Ted's mother in her retirement community, just a short drive from his house. Ted called her Ma, and Mama called her Nancy, or Mrs. Holland. When they met, she instructed the girl to call her Nana Nancy. She styled her hair in tight golden curls, always brushed to shine, and wore three rings on each hand. She liked to talk about her jewelry when Mama was in the room, and about Mama when she wasn't.

The girl overheard Mama and Ted once, when she was supposed to be doing homework in another room. She wanted Ted's help with math, which was her least favorite and hardest subject. She had come looking for him, and heard him arguing with Mama. Or maybe it was Mama arguing with Ted.

"I swear she watches me, Ted. She watches me like a—" Mama stopped short.

Ted's voice was smooth, unhurried. "She's just curious, like a magpie."

"I hate that she watches me. I hate that she knows so much about me."

"Just that you were in New York," Ted said. He sounded uncharacteristically grumpy. "*I* didn't even know that. She only told me when you'd left and it was too late for me to come find you. That's when I learned you'd been on TV."

Mama was aghast. "She watched my show?"

"She found your recipes online," Ted told her. He hadn't heard the tremor in her voice. "I'd been eating your desserts for months and I didn't even know it."

The girl was careful to make no sound as she returned to the living room where her textbooks were waiting, the shiny white pages splayed open.

The retirement community was a series of small bungalow homes with tight little yards and a larger central building that served as the social hub. Nana Nancy liked them to come to the little café at the social building so she could show them off, her Ted and his marvelous daughter, what a beauty she was going to grow into, and her mother, that one. Mama would be all smiles for the residents, her laugh full of rosewater and honey.

But when they returned to Nana Nancy's for a final sit-down with tea, Mama would grow quiet and restless. She'd take her teacup and roam the house, touching photographs and nudging the Lladró bird figurines Nana Nancy collected out of their dust-roughened places.

One afternoon, when Nana Nancy was relating her plans for her eightieth birthday party—"The women in my family usually don't live this long, so it's special," Ted had said—they heard a small thump and a muffled cry.

"Why," said Nana Nancy, her painted eyebrows rising, "I think that was from the guest bedroom. Teddy, go see what she's knocked over."

Ted was only half out of his chair when Mama burst in. There was a splash of tea on the edge of her skirt, and her hands were full of something dark and glossy. Her cheeks burned red.

"What is this?" she asked. Her voice was flat, like a freshly cut board. It shoved splinters into the air. "I've been looking—*How long have you had this?*"

Nana Nancy's eyes were hard as opals. "It's not polite to go through another person's things." She coughed once, delicately, and touched a napkin to her thin, spidery lips. When she spoke again, her voice was casual, but the girl saw that her hands were shaking. "I picked it up at an estate sale, but I haven't worn feathers in at least a decade. I was thinking of giving it away." Something bright and birdlike moved in her eyes. "Why, do you like it?"

Mama moved swiftly into the room, shoes striking the floor. The scent of rosewater scorched the air around her. "It's not yours," she seethed. "It was never yours. How *dare* you."

Nana Nancy lifted her chin. Goose bumps rose on the loose skin of her neck. "Teddy, be a dear and get her a glass of water," she said. The white rims of her eyelids flashed. "There's no call to go flying off the handle."

"I am taking this," Mama said, her eyes raking over Nana Nancy's thin skin, perfectly coiffed hair, wrists just beginning to darken with liver spots. She looked down at the thing she was holding. "You will never get it back. You will *never* use it again."

The girl only realized she was standing when her shin smacked into the coffee table and set cups rattling. One of the crane figurines—one of the more expensive ones, Nana Nancy had said—wobbled and she reached out, gasping, to catch it before its graceful neck snapped. When she straightened, she caught the flick of Nana Nancy's eyes.

Mama noticed, too. "*How dare you*," she said to Nana Nancy. She said it again, and it sounded as though the hinges of her voice had broken: "How dare you."

Ted put his fingers over Mama's, over the thing she held in her trembling hands. "Lianne," he said, his voice trying to bring brightness back into the cramped sitting room, "I'm sure she didn't mean—"

"*No*, Ted," said Mama, and she jerked around, grabbing for her purse. "We're leaving."

"So soon?" asked Nana Nancy, her six rings winking. "There's still tea and meringues. They're your recipe."

But Mama was at the door, fumbling to wrench it open, and Ted murmured something to his mother and Nana Nancy purred back, and then they were outside in the shocking sunlight, and Mama's breath was a shudder, then a sigh, then a wail.

V

WHEN THEY GOT BACK TO TED'S HOUSE, MAMA SWEPT HER UPSTAIRS AND shut the door against any interruption.

Mama was breathing hard. Her eyes were wild. There was something frightened and frightening living inside them. "Do you remember the unicorns?"

The girl nodded. Of course she remembered the unicorns. She remembered the stolen stone walls, too, and the fruit trees twisted for human pleasure. She remembered the bus and the babbling twins, and the taxi driver's greedy eyes.

"Sometimes the things you've been waiting for and fearing, they just *happen*," Mama said, moving to the window and shoving it open. Cool air blew into the room and rumpled the sheer curtains. "Do you understand?"

The girl shook her head.

"I wish—I *wish* I'd never found it." Mama's voice dropped; it wasn't clear if she meant to be heard or not. "I wish it didn't hurt so much. I wish we'd never been discovered." Her breath was a tight gasp. "I wish Ted had never found us, but oh, I'm so happy he did. For *you*."

"Mama?"

Mama turned and pressed her hands hard against the curve of the girl's face. "I love you," Mama said, bending to place a fast kiss in the center of her forehead. She smoothed her thumbs across the girl's cheekbones. "I have loved every minute with you."

The girl was bewildered. "I love you, too," she answered breathlessly, confusion taking the space of air in her body. "What's happening? What's going to happen?"

"I am so sorry, baby," Mama said. "I am so sorry."

Ted knocked on the door, saying something that the door held back.

Mama unwound the jet beads from her neck, pushing them into the girl's hands. "Remember," she said. "Remember I love you."

The knocking was louder now. Ted's voice was impatient.

The girl felt the unyielding shape of the beads against her skin, her palms, her thin fingers. A shudder started in her knees and she said, "Mama, please." She wasn't sure what she was asking, just that she needed to put words into the space between her body and her mother's. "Mama, *don't*."

"I have the best daughter in the world," her mother said, tearing her earrings from her ears and pulling her shirt out of the wide belt of her skirt, "the best and most wonderful child I could have ever asked for. I have lived a good life; I have seen amazing places, and it has been the best adventure to share those places with you. And I love you. *I love you.*"

Mama was nearly naked—just her slip was left, covering her bra and panties, as if she knew the girl didn't want to see that last stretch of skin. Rosewater scented the air, and the air felt sticky with promises and secrets.

"Mama," said the girl again, hating the rough note in her voice.

Mama opened her fingers on the thing she had brought back from Nana Nancy's house. Her eyes met the girl's, the dark liquid of her irises swimming suddenly with shadows and branches, and then the glossy thing was up over her head and her bright eyes were gone. Ted crashed through the bedroom door, splinters falling onto the carpet and a noise like a train whistle rushing out from his body. "Lianne!" he cried, voice cracking like glass, and the beautiful black bird before them flapped once, twice, and disappeared out the open bedroom window.

VI

SHE REMEMBERS ALL OF THIS. SHE REMEMBERS THE UNICORNS, THEIR HOOVES protected by little skirts of hair, their mouths downturned. She remembers their eyes, wild and mocking, which seemed to know her the second time she came to visit. She remembers the Spanish arch, torn from its home and brought across the world to be an example to schoolchildren and art historians. She remembers the fruit trees, planted to human design, pruned and shaped for the benefit of the gardeners. And she remembers her mother, beautiful and glossy, free until she wasn't, untethered until the cage was shut around her.

Nana Nancy didn't live long after that. She fell in her garden and never came home from the hospital. The EMTs said that when they got to her, they found two glossy black feathers near her feet. Ted refused to take them. And the girl couldn't bring herself to touch them.

Ted bought a black suit for the funeral and a black dress for the girl. She wore her mother's jet beads to the cemetery and threw a single skinny rose onto the dirt over the casket.

"Well," Ted said, hands deep in the pockets of his stiff suit, and they watched as people slowly made their way out of the cemetery. Everyone had driven, and the line of black cars stretched bleakly to the gates. Ted said it was the way his family had always done it: no one ever walked if they could drive somewhere.

"Will I still go to school here?" the girl asked, because she hadn't known what else to say. Her mother had never mentioned boarding school, but she knew it was a thing that existed in Nana Nancy's world and, therefore, in Ted's.

Ted drew her to his side, dropping a long arm around her shoulders. "Yeah," he said roughly, his voice a small fire in the gloom. "And we'll visit museums whenever we can. She would've liked that."

They never needed to say who *she* was.

They traveled in Ted's reliable sedan, or bought tickets for the train or airplane. She tucked vials of rosewater into her backpack, pouring them into sweetened boiling water and, later, when Ted said she was old enough, into her morning coffee. Something eased inside her with every sip, something she hadn't realized was clenched and tense.

Ted watched her drink, his mouth curling gently at the sides; he said she reminded him so much of her mother, even though her height was coming in, and they told each other stories of how she lit up rooms and stages and sidewalks. "She *was* here, wasn't she?" he asked her once, when he was tired from a long day's drive, almost stumbling when they finally made it home. "I didn't imagine her?"

They went to see the McNay, the Getty, the San Francisco Museum of Modern Art. One summer, they spent two weeks in Washington, D.C., visiting all the national museums and memorials. She liked the still exactness of Andrew Wyeth's paintings, especially the one of Christina in the meadow, looking toward a farmhouse with her face turned away from the viewer. They traveled to Pennsylvania and Maine to see Wyeth's studios and the paintings on permanent exhibition. Ted wanted her to "contextualize" his work, and they went to exhibits of N. C. Wyeth's paintings in New York and Massachusetts and North Carolina; he wanted her to see how the son took what the father taught him and turned it into something new, something of his very own, and how his own son did the same. They ambled through famous and lesser-known museums, tracing light and shadow and reading plaques posted on chalk-gray walls.

She knew what he was doing, and she loved him for it. He was giving her reasons to stay, finding her beautiful things to feed her starving heart.

Ted never minded when she sat for hours in museums, sketching. He hung her paintings throughout their house. When she said she wanted to draw a mural on her bedroom wall, he nodded; a week later, there were paints and brushes waiting. After he saw her design of roses and wings, he gave her a book on historic rose cultivation and offered to help her plant a garden.

She knew he meant well, but her designs weren't rooted in the world around her. They came from the stories her mother had told, from the faces of the cards she didn't quite dare to pull for herself, and from the shapes woven into the tapestries she remembered seeing so long ago.

On her thirteenth birthday, Ted watched as she unwrapped her last gift. It was the crane figurine from Nana Nancy's house—the expensive Lladró she had almost broken that last day. Her startled eyes met Ted's; he smiled at her and said, "She would have wanted you to have it."

Later, when she knew he was out of the house, she crept outside and smashed the figurine into shards with a hammer and, when that wasn't enough, stomped them to dust.

Ted promised her a trip to Spain and France for her high school graduation, a chance to visit the museums there. "And the churches," she murmured, thinking of the stone museum at the top of Manhattan. What would it be like to see those walls in the places they had been meant for? Would it help her feel settled, or would it just be another stone wall?

She did not ask Ted these questions.

They never spoke about the thing her mother had found or how she had left. The only time they came close was a bright spring Sunday, when she was sketching a swan and worrying over the arch of its tender neck. "She lived longer than anyone expected," Ted said from the doorway, and for a scalding moment the girl thought he meant her mother. "It was something of a miracle."

She was fifteen when they did a unit on mythology in her English class, reading about men who turned themselves into monsters to conquer the world and women who became beasts to avoid their men. She gave Ted a draft of one of her papers, and he brought it to breakfast, his cheeks drawn and eyebrows low. "This is a good paper," he told her, watching her sip at her rosewater coffee, "but the books never tell you what's true. She didn't become a monster, you know. All she did was leave everything monstrous behind."

The girl promised herself to never fabricate reasons for why her mother chose to leave her: she already knew the most important one. *Being trapped inside the wrong skin can feel like a curse. The moment you find the right one, you can't wait to live in it.*

But knowing something does not mean making peace with it, and she ached deep in her bones.

At a party when she is sixteen, West Benson pulls her aside and tells her she is the prettiest girl out of all the girls there, or at least the prettiest one not wearing makeup. His hand is slick and insistent against her skin.

Later, once he has taught her that her body is filled with holes, she finds herself shaking in front of an open window, looking up at a sky dark as feathers, dark as an unhealed heart. The air smells like rosewater and salt. She can't get warm.

"What," says West Benson, his voice thick with something she doesn't like and has never liked. "You wanted it."

She doesn't turn. Her mind is full of stones and fruit and creatures in pens.

She hears the clink of a belt buckle fastening, and then West Benson is standing behind her and breathing hard on her shoulder. "Huh," he says, and reaches out. There's a black feather on the windowsill.

She slaps his hand away. "That's mine," she says.

She can hear his pout, even though she doesn't turn her head.

She thinks of the unicorns, of hunters, stone archways stolen and moved across oceans, ripe fruit waiting for someone else to come pluck it. She thinks of de Kooning, erasing his women in order to draw and redraw them. Picasso pointing women toward and away from each other, their individual bodies misaligned. And Wyeth, who gave Christina a canvas but hid her face. She thinks of bodies that exist as prey instead of promises, of girls who see unicorns until they can't anymore. She thinks of her mother, who said the body was a cage and who colored hers in with paints and clothes. She thinks of the last card she watched her mother pull, the night before she disappeared: *Courage.* And she thinks of West, with his clammy words and sharp hands, who would have carried a spear and attacked stone churches and turned Christina around to face him, and only him.

She thinks of all the ways there are to give up.

She thinks of all the ways there are to escape.

Inside her ribs, her heart thuds. She feels too many places on her body where her skin has failed to provide cover. She aches for a sip of rosewater, for something to ease the hurt that gathers inside her bones. Her shoulders flex; for a moment, she thinks she has wings.

In her fingers, the feather stretches into a cuff, something that can be tied around a wrist or a waist or a neck.

She thinks of all the ways that giving up and escaping are the same, and all the ways they are each other's opposite. In her mind, she shuffles a deck of cards and pulls the ones she needs. *Grief. Deception. Courage.*

"Here," she says, and throws the glossy thing at West Benson's face.

VII

LATER, WHEN THE PARTY IS OVER AND SHE IS BACK HOME AND THERE IS A shrieking turkey out in the front yard and West Benson's parents are calling around to find their son, she says what she says about her mother: "Yes, he was there. He was until he wasn't."

Ted, bewildered, will wonder aloud what to do about the turkey. She will tell him to keep one feather, and then shoo the bird away.

One day, perhaps, she will want the feather for herself.

AUTHOR'S NOTE

I've long been unnerved by selkie tales, as the stories seem to strip the selkie of any agency: either she's trapped by the person who has stolen her skin, or she's compelled to return to the sea the moment she finds her pelt. Neither of these actions is based on a decision she makes—and that strikes me as a terrible and lonely gap in the tradition. When I started writing FLIGHT, I intended to write a selkie story where the selkie finally got to make her own decisions. But I found I was more concerned with *how* she decided to act: What moments and memories did she draw on to make her choices? Who did she look to as she learned how to be herself? As I wrote, she slipped from seal to bird, from water to air. She remembered how to breathe, and she is learning how to fly.

CHARACTER CONNECTION IN *FLIGHT*

by Nova Ren Suma

WHAT KEEPS YOU READING A STORY? WHAT MAKES YOU CARE ENOUGH TO believe in the otherwise unimaginable and stay committed to the last word? FLIGHT offers us an answer. The story may whirl through cavernous museums and scattered cities, imaginative and mysterious, but the magic is tied to the characters who command this story's glorious, beating heart: Mama and the daughter she ultimately leaves behind, called "the girl." How is it possible to form a bond with a character who is kept unnamed, and to feel the gaping wound the girl must feel as Mama takes to the window? It's because we've come to understand the girl's longing. The story has allowed us to feel the girl's desires and the weight of her unanswered questions.

The story introduces this right away, when Mama takes the girl to see the unicorn tapestries and, in the reverent hush at the museum, reveals a taste of secrets that must stay hidden. It's here that Mama offers up the first piece of a puzzle: She cryptically tells the girl to remember the unicorns but is unable or unwilling to say why. Don't forget: "the magic was in remembering the unicorn, not owning it." Each scene that follows elevates the mystery. We empathize with the girl because we seek the same answers she does. Don't we want to know why Mama is so concerned with creatures who cannot be caged?

Like the mythical unicorn, like the selkie that inspired this unique story reinvention, Mama is the perfect enigma—a character we cannot know, not fully, not ever, even as she lights up the corners of our imaginations. When Mama is gone, the girl must live with what she's learned, what she's lost, and what it means for her future.

Once a character comes to life in my mind, seeming alive because I understand and feel their desires, I'll never be able to let go. We may have assumed this was a story focused on the mystery of Mama, but in the end, the mysteries point inward: In the final moments of the story, the girl is at last able to recognize herself.

No matter the extraordinary worlds a story may travel, when we're connected to a character's inner desires, we're more likely to become deeply invested—all the more so because of the strange creatures revealed under their skins.

RISK

Rachel Hylton

RISK is a jaw-dropping, powerful story of transformation. I raced through it on the first read, stunned by Rachel Hylton's imagination. The second time I read it slowly, savoring the plot twists and the brilliant language. You're going to love this one!
—Laurie Halse Anderson, author of *Shout*

We, the sophomore girls of Carol Moseley Braun High School, would like to set the record straight.

We were there for Marnie Vega long before she became a lobster.

You think that we are interchangeable, that we are two-faced and faceless, that we don't say what we mean and you can't understand us anyway. You can't distinguish what makes a girl *in* from what makes a girl *out*. But Marnie was in, okay? She was one of us. We were there for her in seventh grade when her dad kept getting deployed, like, over and over. We would crowd onto her twin bed and play songs from before Taylor Swift got bangs and flip through the book her dad sent her of pictures of Korean shrines, brightly colored against red leaves. "It looks so calm," Marnie would say to us. "Don't you think it looks so calm? Don't you think it's probably so calm there?"

And we were there in eighth grade when she got her first period *during* first period. One of us ran to her locker for gym shorts. One of us handed her tampons under the stall door. One of us sat cross-legged on the counter and coached her—at least until she refused to try, removed the applicator, and pushed it in like an o.b.

We were at Lara's birthday party, too, on the night Marnie wasn't in the group photo. During Ghost in the Graveyard she hid on *that* side of Lara's house, the one with all the serial killer bushes, so of course we didn't search there. Did we realize when we lined up for the photo that we hadn't found her? Did she realize we hadn't searched? Does it matter? She probably just hid there for attention.

If we noticed her slip in, eyes downturned, just in time for cake, we didn't comment. We forgave her. We reabsorbed her.

And she didn't *turn into* a lobster, no matter what Evan Brockwell says. There was no *changing*. At the exact moment in Math II when he turned around and said, "Hey, Marn, wanna graph *my* natural log?" Marnie just *was* a lobster. She held up a huge claw—beetle-black with an iridescent wetness of purple and teal to it, like fresh nail polish. She said, in that dreamy Marnie way, "You want me to what?" and she shut it with a *snap*.

Nobody was scared—well, *Evan* went green, but nobody else. The lobster was just so obviously Marnie. After class, we gathered around her in the hall. Her eyes were all pupil; her mouth had no lips, just little arms that clenched and unclenched over a hole. After that first thing she said to Evan, all her words came out in a rattle, not like human speech at all. *Marnie*, she said. *Marnie*. Her own name, over and over. She held up her claws and opened and closed them.

We told her no one would notice. We tried not to look at the stems that held her eyes onto her head.

"Marnie, Marnie Vega." We parted for Slidell Williams. Sly was basketball All-Conference and baseball All-State and the editor of the paper, all in one. He had a tight Afro and gray eyes, and he was a junior. And Marnie, like the rest of us, had wanted him. And Marnie, like the rest of us, had walked the halls with hair dipping into her face, mouthing *Hey, Sly* to the floor because she was afraid to say it out loud.

And now, in her worst hour, Sly was saying *Marnie, Marnie Vega* like he'd always known her name.

One of us stepped forward to head him off. "Marnie's having a hard time, Sly," she said, tilting her head, her hand on her hip. "You shouldn't put this in the paper. I mean, if you want to talk to one of *us* about it, that's fine, but Marnie—"

"You're a lobster," said Sly, looking past her at Marnie.

Marnie put up her claws.

It took us a minute to realize she was shrugging. *It happens*, she said.

"Can—can I have a quote for the *Spectator*? How do you feel about it?"

About the Spectator?

"About the . . . lobsterness."

I am luxurious, said Marnie. *I am unsettling.*

"Do you mean you feel unsettled?"

Marnie spread her claws again, chattering her legs against the tiled hallway. *No.*

That's when we realized the awful truth. Marnie Vega *liked* being a lobster.

She *admired* herself. She spidered sideways, holding each leg up daintily for her own inspection. She examined the white-tipped nubs on the inside edges of her claws, coronated like the top of a conch shell. She twisted her eyestalks and looked down her own hard-plated back.

And okay, we did think she was *kind* of beautiful, with her shell sometimes blue-green, sometimes black, mottling into purple and tan at the edges.

What? No, we didn't.

Like, a *little* lovely. The interlocking armor of her tail. Its delicate, feather-tipped fan.

But that wasn't the point. Here we were, the same as always, with our eyebrows too skinny or our ankles too thick or our hair that we had to straighten or steam or curl or relax or highlight or dye or braid or bleach—and Marnie was a *lobster*. And she didn't even *care*.

The *Spectator* published a feature and an editorial. The feature was meant to educate us so we'd know how to relate to her. Her shell was called a *carapace*. Her mouth-arms were *maxillipeds*. A group of lobsters is called a *risk*. It's rude to ask a lobster why she's not red, because crustaceans only turn red when you boil them.

Slidell called the editorial "The Bravery of the Homarine," and he went on for three hundred words about high school and experimenting and diversity and being yourself. But come on, what was brave about being a giant lobster? It wasn't like Marnie chose it. And it wasn't like she could unlobster. She was kind of stuck with it.

But no, according to Sly, Marnie was *different*—she wasn't *fake*, she was *authentic*.

Her parents, at least, understood the absurdity. One of us was working as an office aide when they came to see Mr. Jeffress. One of us was waiting to be picked up for the dentist. We heard them through the principal's door.

"Someone should have stopped this," her father complained. "This is ridiculous. People should have been informed about this district, about the possibility of turning into a—a—una pinche langosta."

Her mother murmured, "Tom, cuida tu lenguaje."

"Something is wrong with her. She has *whiskers*. She has a *shell*."

"Exoskeleton, Tom."

Mr. Jeffress had clearly been prepped by the guidance counselor. The school, he said, can't be held liable for astakosyntosis in individual students. And honestly, shouldn't the Vegas be relieved? At least she's not drinking. At least she's not pregnant. There are worse things to be, after all, than a lobster. She isn't shooting heroin. She isn't spreading STDs.

"Isn't she, though?" one of us said, hearing the story. It was clever; it got repeated. Did you hear about Marnie Vega? She has the *worst* case of crabs.

We were tired, all right? We were over it. Marnie was a Brave Homarine who didn't care. She went on scuttling through the school, spraying down her body with salt water during homeroom, hanging out in the bio lab during lunch, writing weird poems that Ms. Ingram called *transcendent*.

> *Cut-crush-glide*
> *I*
> *devour myself, I*
> *armor my own*
> *bite*
> *I bite*

So at first it was just YouTube videos. "How to prepare a live lobster." The thick knife slicing cleanly through the *carapace* between those stalky eyes and halving it clear to the *maxillipeds*. "GRAPHIC! 5 Ways to Cook Live Lobsters!!!" A *risk* of them tossed into a giant pot.

Just at sleepovers—it wasn't like we were watching them at school. Marnie never came to sleepovers anymore.

Did we ask her?

Well, she couldn't—she slept—

But we didn't know that yet. We didn't know anything about her.

I mean, we didn't even know if there was any girl left in her brain. Remember? We all started carrying lobster crackers just, like, out of *caution*, to *protect ourselves*.

So then there was Jaclyn's party. We were all running up and down the synthetic wood deck between the pool and the in-ground hot tub, with Jaclyn's parents somewhere pretending we were wholesome, and Evan tossing a freshman girl into the pool, and seniors intertwined in every corner of the hot tub, and somebody's mobile speaker playing "Mala Gente," and Jaclyn dancing salsa by herself with her vodka lemonade, eyes closed, only the *occasional* look at the guys to see if anyone was buying. And the reach and shush of the waves below on the beach, and the basketball guys playing flip cup on the edge of the wet bar, and the freshman girl crying because her phone was soaked and she couldn't post anything to her story, and past the pool loungers, Marnie, like Grendel's mother in that poem, watching from the shadows.

Of course we were curious. *Everyone* was curious. Everyone at that party was looking at Marnie, wondering why she was there and whether *that* would happen—even just a little bit—if she got in the hot tub. Maybe Marnie wondered, too. Maybe she'd been trying to figure out what was *her* and what was *it*.

So all we did was ask her to join in—we, her friends. So she wouldn't be, like, *lurking*. "C'mon, Marn, don't you want to get in?"

We came around behind her (there were no serial killer bushes at Jaclyn's, only bougainvillea). She turned.

"Lobsters are marine animals, right?"

"You mean *ho*marine." The basketball guys were laughing.

Her legs made funny noises on the plastic wood as she backed up. She said nothing—no giggling, no appealing to the guys to save her like any of us would have done. But she couldn't have been worried—not about *us*. Not when she was a giant *lobster*.

Marnie edged back, and back, and back. People were laughing and clearing out of the hot tub because *Oh my god lobster bisque*, and then Marnie's tail touched the surface of the water and curled up fast—so fast that she fell backward, legs scrabbling—*splash*—

Her body thrashing. Her tail pumping, throwing her armor-first into the tub's wall. Again. Again. Again. Too small. Too steep. Again. Again.

"What the *hell*?" Sly raced out of the open game room door and plunged into the water. He latched his arms around Marnie, slinging her into the air. Marnie landed on the deck and whirled toward us. Her claws were wide and high and open, her eyes taut and bulging, her mouth-arms outspread in a high, raw, throbbing scream.

We didn't move.

Marnie wheeled and lashed at Evan and wheeled and lashed at someone else, and all the time that scream, like skin burning, like steam.

"*Marnie, stop.*" Sly threw himself into the space between her claws, right at her eyes, and wrapped her around his shoulders with her claws flat against his chest. He ran out of the house lights, over the white-pebbled path and across the sod lawn, straight through the canna lilies toward the beach.

We streamed after him. Sly took a flying leap down the dune stairs and thudded onto the sand, his legs churning, his hands clamped tight to his chest. And Marnie on his back like a barbed cape, like a dragon taking out a horse, riding him all the way down.

Sly hit the waves, and his knees buckled, and he dove down, down into the surf under the flat, shimmering track of the moon. We saw his head break black through the silver twenty yards from us. Saw an armored splash and then churning.

Sly's voice, carrying over the water: "Are you okay? Are you okay?"

Another splash, the curve of her.

"Let me take you home."

If she replied, we couldn't hear it, just the wash of Sly treading water and the pulse of the surf.

Finally he stumbled onto the sand, blood and ocean streaming off him—his chest, his neck, his legs. "You almost killed her."

"Lighten up, Sly," someone said. "It wasn't hot enough to hurt her."

Sly swept his hand across his chest, flinging drops into the sand. "Lobsters drown in fresh water, assholes."

No one got back into the hot tub after that.

People clustered on the pool deck.

"She's, like, not human anymore."

"I thought she was going to *kill everyone.*"

We stood with everyone else, but we were watching the water. Sly drove his Denali down onto the beach and sat for an hour on the tailgate, waiting, but Marnie never came out. We didn't know if she'd swum out to sea or just up the beach. We imagined her crawling out to the road, scuttling along the asphalt, her shadow doubled in the streetlights. Creeping into her own house. Waking her dad with her noise on the stairs. She was still alive, right? She hadn't been in the hot tub long enough to drown.

On Monday, her mother called the office to say Marnie was sick. Well, anyone in their right mind would be. That scream, the kids watching, Sly bleeding just from holding her.

But then she was sick on Tuesday, too, and someone posted a video of her thrashing in the hot tub and set it to "Rock Lobster" by the B-52s, and someone else turned it into a sex meme, and someone's parents called to complain that she was a threat to student safety, and someone else's parents stormed in to demand that the school shut down all this animal porn.

And all day, Evan kept creeping up behind us, playing audio of the scream, and every time we heard it, the colors of it changed like a bruise: she was angry, she was scared, she was hurt.

But she hadn't made us stop pushing her. Her claws had been down, her mouth had been closed. She'd just kept going backward and backward and backward.

When she wasn't at school on Wednesday, we went to her house.

"We moved her to the basement," her father told us. "Careful—the stairs are wet." We filed past photos of Marnie—Marnie in kindergarten, pink-painted fingernails against her cheeks; Marnie gap-toothed and swim-capped, holding up her wiry bicep to kiss it. Marnie in the cream-and-coral bloom of her quinceañera dress, eyes lowered toward her clasped hands.

Her door gaped into darkness. We stepped down onto the polished concrete floor.

Her twin bed had been replaced by a giant tank with a ramp at one end.

Marnie lay curled on her side with her back to us, her claws limp over her head.

We gathered around the tank. The dim blue glow of the water reflected on our faces.

"We came to say sorry about the hot tub."

Marnie didn't answer, didn't even move. There was only sand around and underneath her, nothing else. What did we expect? Green and purple pebbles, plastic trees, a castle?

"We didn't know it would be that dangerous. Sly told us afterward about the fresh water."

The tank, humming. The water filter, bubbling in the corner of it.

"Don't you kind of think that, you know, lobsters shouldn't be in school? Like, maybe you would be way happier somewhere else. The ocean. SeaWorld. Something like that."

The room, breathing.

"Marnie?" we said.

I'm not sorry.

She wasn't sorry what? She wasn't sorry we'd forced her into the hot tub? She wasn't sorry for going to school?

I'm not sorry.

The words were like one of those ocean currents, the ones you can't tell if they're warm or cold.

Her lower legs rippled. The shell of her back—her *carapace*—pulled slowly away from her body, like the hood of a car. Underneath we saw the same shape, but different, somehow—soft, like the skin of a dolphin, and darkly freckled under a cloud of membrane.

She lay still. The tank murmured. The room smelled like iodine and fish and oranges. On Marnie's desk, a candle glowed.

Marnie's legs twitched again, and her tail shivered. We could see her side rising, falling. The carapace was still, but her soft new back crept out and out. Tugging itself away from the armor.

She was leaving behind her claws. She was leaving behind her *head*.

Then, white tissue, something throbbing underneath. Eyes—her eyes, scrabbling on their stems, groping, breaking free. The tissue, floating away in diaphanous wisps. Marnie nodded sharply, dragged her head out of the carapace. Her new antennae, inch by tawny inch. Her maxillipeds, striped and shiny where they pushed through the papery film.

We pressed up against the glass.

Marnie curled and then *yanked*, a frantic thrust-thrust-thrust. She paused, her sides swelling and shrinking, swelling and shrinking. We could see her arms trapped under the carapace.

Would they band her claws when she came back to school—dangerous, aggressive, obscene?

"Come on, Marnie," one of us whispered.

The old top half of her body lay motionless, like some strange, dead refraction. She yanked again, then faltered.

Come on, Marnie. We were all saying it. *Go, come on, go.*

Marnie gathered herself, coiling her body from tail to eyes. She unfurled. Membrane ballooned out like smoke and dissolved, and then— faster, faster, coiling and unfurling, out, out, *free*. Blue elbows, speckled claws, triumphant tips of antennae. Marnie shot backward in a zooming loop. Then she danced, showing us, waving to us with every barbed leg, every claw, every graceful inch of her feelers.

Look, she said, *look*.

We waved back with fragile fingers, light and dark. We pumped our short arms, our clenched fists.

She'd grown by at least a foot, her claws wider and longer. She was remade. She was newborn. She was soft and hard and strong.

Marnie surveyed her old shell, her locust protein husk, her *exoskeleton*, Tom. She circled it. Her mouth-arms fastened on to it.

And *oh*.

Oh.

We heard the *crunch*.

Unsettling.

Unseating.

Unyielding.

No one *turns into* a lobster, no matter what Evan Brockwell says.

You simply *are*.

We were.

We were

one

by one

lobsters.

Sliding into the water, the cool of it on our plated backs, our fanning tails. Piling into a tangled hug. Saying our names, *Sarah, Maeve, Aisha, Alicia.* Tasting brine and cold and Marnie.

We were there for Marnie Vega long before she became a lobster.

We are her risk.

We are *our* risk.

AUTHOR'S NOTE

I am hesitant to say more about either Marnie or her crustacean-aeity. Lobster is as lobster does. If you're a lobster, you know it.

But the story of a girl is never just one story about one girl. A girl is an aspen tree—however solitary she appears, she is always linked (through intimacy or jealousy, careless exclusion or intentional expulsion) to her colony.

Outsiders don't understand this. I, typing this, do not understand it. We tend to depict groups of girls from the outside—as opaque and sexy and shallow and ruthless and all the other things we've decided they are.

Marnie Vega *liked* being a lobster. As soon as I knew that, I thought of Jeffrey Eugenides's *The Virgin Suicides*, how the neighborhood boys narrate the lives of the Lisbon sisters. We are always watching girls. I wanted RISK to feature girls who were not gazed-upon but gazing. Is this possible? I don't know. But I wanted the feeling of being in the wonderful, fearful, intimate center of a girl group, looking out at the one who isn't afraid. We will always need that person more than she needs us, and isn't that frightening?

Franz Kafka's *The Metamorphosis* and Alan Cumyn's *Hot Pterodactyl Boyfriend* both gave me further insight into Marnie. Would her metamorphosis set her apart or bring her into community? The answer, I am pleased to report, is *yes*.

So this story goes out to the lobsters, the ones who take the risk.

VOICE IN *RISK*

by Emily X.R. Pan

VOICE. WHEN IT'S THERE YOU CAN *HEAR* IT.

Any character who is speaking has *a* voice, of course. But when editors and agents talk about "*the* voice," they're referring to the author's narration, the distinct rhythm and style shaping the sentences. Sometimes these do intersect—if a story is told in first person, the character's voice doubles as the narrative voice. But even in third person, the voice can and should be just as clear and strong. It brings to life a specific and vital narrator. Let's look at how quickly RISK succeeds at doing that:

> We, the sophomore girls of Carol Moseley Braun
> High School, would like to set the record straight.
> We were there for Marnie Vega long before she
> became a lobster.

The first-person plural "we" is a bold choice, unusual and intriguing. The second line immediately demands that we readers suspend our disbelief. Quick and sharp and funny, its confidence makes us trust the narrator even as we're given far-fetched details: her eyes, all pupil; her little arms that clenched and unclenched; her rattling speech; those stems that held her eyes onto her head.

Then there's Marnie's dialogue, spoken "in that dreamy Marnie way": *I am luxurious*, said Marnie. *I am unsettling.*

Marnie has a character voice that's quirky, distinct from the narrative voice. Her statements are declarative, her vocabulary sensuous and sophisticated. In contrast, the group narrating the story has a collective personality that sounds completely different. Plus the first-person plural design of this narrative voice gives the writer a chance to have a little fun: the girls telling the story are not entirely in agreement. It's clear that people see Marnie a bit differently:

> And okay, we did think she was *kind* of beautiful,
> with her shell sometimes blue-green, sometimes black,
> mottling into purple and tan at the edges.
> What? No, we didn't.

Voice is the key to humor, too—when a story is funny, it's at least partly because of the voice. The matter-of-factness in RISK becomes a vessel for exactly that kind of deadpan delivery, allowing for more layers of absurdity:

> "And honestly, shouldn't the Vegas be relieved?
> At least she's not drinking. At least she's not pregnant.
> There are worse things to be, after all, than a lobster.
> She isn't shooting heroin. She isn't spreading STDs.
> "Isn't she, though?" one of us said, hearing the
> story. It was clever; it got repeated. Did you hear about
> Marnie Vega? She has the *worst* case of crabs.

RISK is voiciest in its first half. Until we care about the characters and have suspended our disbelief, Hylton's main tool to keep us reading is that distinctive voice. Once we're sucked in, the priority shifts—it's less about the girls deciding what to make of Marnie's transformation, and more about trying to understand the lobster. The sassy human narrative voice also makes a subtle transition as they, too, become dreamy, become a risk of lobsters.

STORY PROMPT:
BUILDING CONFLICT

Part I: As you figure out who your main character is, ask yourself what they want. (Maybe they want multiple things; for the sake of this exercise, go ahead and pick just one big-picture item for now.)

———◆———

Part II: How can you use your character's setting and circumstances to make it more difficult for them to get what they want?

———◆———

Here's an example:

- **Part I:** Your character wants to be with the person they love.
- **Part II:** The person they love is plugged directly into the core of the planet and single-handedly powering all existing life, and as long as they are doing so, they will be asleep and unreachable.

SWEETMEATS

Linda Cheng

> Such a delicious tale—SWEETMEATS is Grimms' 'Hansel and Gretel' flavored with Guillermo del Toro and a dash of Miyazaki, all wrapped up in a modern-day setting and served with a distinct and compelling voice. I absolutely devoured it.
> —HEIDI HEILIG, AUTHOR OF *FOR A MUSE OF FIRE*

THE MARK IS ON THE INSIDE OF OUR ELBOWS. MARLIE'S ON THE LEFT, MINE ON the right. Stacked triangles inside a semicircle. The police can't figure out how we got the brand and neither can the doctors. We weren't cut or burned or tattooed, but the black outlines on our skin appear to be permanent. The reporters have their own theories—everything from satanic cults to sex traffickers. Most of the headlines say that Marlie and I were taken from our bedrooms.

That's not what happened.

We weren't kidnapped. We ran away. Right before summer vacation started, right after I screwed up my audition for Interlochen Arts Academy and my mother asked me in front of my violin teacher why I was wasting his time and her money if I couldn't even bother to try.

We were running away to New York. I had a plan, and years' worth of red pocket money collected at Chinese New Year dinners from aunts who told me to save the money for plastic surgery. You should at least do your eyelids, Mei, and maybe your nose, such a shame you didn't get your mother's face. The plan was to busk in the subways. While other little girls played house, we played opera. I had to practice violin after school every day, and Marlie would sit with me, harmonizing while I ran scales and drilled études. She didn't need any sheet music; she did it all by ear. She hates getting on stage even though she's the best singer in her church choir, but there won't be any stages in the subway, no spotlights, no one watching for our mistakes, just me and her performing our opera for non-judgmental commuters. Someone might film us and we could go viral. People get famous like that all the time.

We didn't even make it to the Greyhound station before the witch got us.

"You keep referring to your abductor as a 'witch.' Why do you say that?" The detective taking our statements squints at me after every question he asks.

"Because that's what she is," I tell him. "A witch who eats girls. She kept giving us cake and candy to fatten us up."

"You said there were other girls with you. What happened to them?"

"I told you," I repeat, "the witch ate them."

He squints harder. "How did the two of you escape?"

"The door wasn't locked that day. We ran out of the cabin and through the woods until we got to the road."

I tell him the truth, exactly what happened, but the detective looks to Marlie and waits. She stares at the floor tiles and scratches at her elbow, at the mark. She says nothing.

"What did the witch look like?" the detective asks.

"The most beautiful woman in the world," I answer.

They tell us we've been missing for weeks, but I swear we were only gone for a few nights. We sit next to each other in the police station until our parents show up. Marlie's father thanks God over and over; mine is silent. Her mother cries and cradles her; mine can't look me in the eyes.

Marlie and I have been neighbors our whole lives. Literally since birth. We were born on the same day in the same hospital. Our bassinets were side by side in the nursery, and we were wrapped in matching pink muslins. My mother hosted a joint Zhuazhou ceremony for us when we turned one. It's this birthday ritual where you line up a bunch of stuff in front of the baby, and whatever they pick up predicts their future. Stethoscope for doctor, textbook for teacher, paintbrush for artist, spatula for chef. Allegedly, Marlie's parents loved it. They make a point to tell us all the time how they find Chinese traditions "so charming." I don't think they realize how many hurtful comments they've made about our food—How are you supposed to eat fish that's looking up from the plate with those giant open eyes!?—or the fact that we don't go to church. During the Zhuazhou ceremony I went for the toy violin and Marlie started chewing on a karaoke microphone. Born to be musicians, my mother would say when she talked about it at block parties. I've probably heard it hundreds of times, but I never get tired of watching my mother tell that story, the way her face glows with pride.

Neither of us has siblings, but it doesn't feel that way. We have each other. Boys would pick on Marlie for her large ears, her freckled face, the baggy corduroy skirts her mother dresses her in, and I would get in trouble for kicking those boys in their knees. She's a few hours younger than me; it's my job to look after her.

Marlie hasn't said the words *It's your fault*, but New York was my idea, and if I hadn't come to her window that night, she never would have put on her backpack and climbed out.

It's the first week of high school and there are rumors about us spreading all over campus.

"Aren't those the girls who escaped from some serial killer shack in the woods?"

"Someone should make a movie about them, they're like, real-life Final Girls."

"My cousin said they were being auctioned off to rich pedophiles in Russia."

"Did you see the satanic symbol on her arm? They were totally supposed to be human sacrifices."

I don't care about the gossip, but Marlie shrinks whenever someone looks her way. She wears long sleeves all the time and waits for me outside of my classes so she won't have to walk down the halls alone.

"Don't listen to those assholes," I tell her on our way home. We still hold hands when we cross the street. Her fingers are always freezing.

"Mei," Marlie says, clinging to my arm, her nails digging in through my sweatshirt. She's staring at something on the other side of the road. I look, and my breath stops in my throat.

There's a woman standing across the street. She's in a white dress that reaches past her ankles. Long black hair falls over her face. I can't see her eyes, but I know she's looking at us.

I take a step forward, and the woman does, too. I take another step, and the woman follows. Marlie's grip on my arm tightens, and I start walking quicker, pulling her with me. Across the street, the woman breaks out into a run after us. Marlie screams. I grab her hand and we sprint, our feet slamming against the pavement, our schoolbags swinging, we run for our lives, the way we did when we fled from the witch's cabin, all the way up the front steps of my house.

"Hurry," Marlie gasps, "the door!"

I scramble for my keys and pull them out of my bag, but my hands are shaking so much I can't fit them into the lock. I look over my shoulder. The woman is standing on my lawn now. She reaches a hand up, and pulls all of her hair off.

It's Bryan Haywood. He grins and holds up the wig.

Bryan is a year older than us—rich, handsome, and heartless—a trifecta of qualities that have kept him popular since nursery school. He never got over the fact that I gave him a black eye in the fifth grade for making Marlie cry. His dad is a cop; he must have heard about the witch from him.

Bryan's girlfriend, Clara, pulls up in Bryan's new car, a shiny Bimmer he got for his sixteenth birthday. "Quick, get the door before the witch eats you!" Clara calls out, snapping her gum. Three boys from the lacrosse team lean out of the back seat windows and chant: "Run, run, run!" Bryan whips the wig around over his head like a helicopter propeller and jumps into the car with his friends. They're all laughing so hard they can't sit up.

The next weekend I spot his car in the mall parking lot, and I run my keys down the entire driver's side from mirror to bumper.

Marlie goes to her pastor for counseling twice a week, but my mother doesn't believe in therapy. She doesn't believe in post-traumatic stress disorder or witches who eat children.

She doesn't believe me.

She thinks if I go back to my routine everything will be normal again. She sits with me as I practice, counting aloud to the metronome, but all I hear are the hard clacks of her shoes as she walks out of my ruined audition. My hand cramps up and I trip over the same series of arpeggios like they're raised road spikes on the page.

"Again, from the beginning," my mother says. "Again. Again. This is your favorite concerto—why can't you play it right anymore?"

It's not my favorite, I think. *It's yours.* I lift my bow, inhale, and mess up at the same spot.

My father was married to someone else once. He was still married when he met my mother. They were both soaring on their respective rising stars, my father an assistant conductor to the city symphony, my mother the lauded prodigy. When I was little my father called me baobei—precious—and sat me on his lap while he worked. We'd share a pair of headphones, one bud each, the cord dangling between us, music pumping like blood between two halves of one organ. He was my refuge when my arms grew weak from stretching in order to reach my mother's expectations. Until I overheard him yelling at my mother, accusing her of having me despite their "agreement." Afterward, I noticed he sometimes looked at me the way a child looks at the sheets they've soiled. A dirty mistake. I stopped going into his study to sit with him, stopped our ritual of sharing compositions we enjoyed, stopped smiling at him, and then one day we stopped talking altogether. Now he gives all his attention to Xiao Long, the dog he purchased from a breeder in Australia and treats like the son he never got to raise.

I try to tell him what happened to me.

"Mei, there is no cabin in that part of the woods," he says. "The police searched the whole area." He picks up Xiao Long and coos at him as if he's trying to comfort the dog instead. "You were taken by a bad person, but you're home now."

He doesn't believe me.

I still dream about the night we ran away, the night we met the witch. I dream about me and Marlie walking down the dark sidewalk, hand in hand. It's almost midnight and we're heading to the bus station when we hear singing coming from the woods just beyond our neighborhood. A tune we've never heard before but that somehow sounds familiar, innocent and nostalgic, like the childish melody we had once cobbled together and performed for our stuffed animals. The song reaches out and lovingly pulls us in, until we're standing at the edge of the trees. I see the witch so clearly in my dreams, singing to us, a delicate paper silhouette against the jagged black shapes of the underbrush. Long raven hair falling over white lace sleeves. Little pearl buttons along her throat. Her eyes are hidden behind her hair, her pretty pink mouth smiling.

No more tears, little ones, the witch sings. Come with me, I'll take good care of you.

We follow her into the woods, the branches closing up the path behind us. She leads us farther and farther into the darkness until we forget about the bus station, forget about New York.

Do you smell that? Marlie asks, her icicle fingers curling against my hand.

I close my eyes and breathe in. I smell fresh-baked cookies and cotton candy.

The witch leads us through the woods to a little cabin with ivy growing along its brick walls all the way up to the crooked chimney pipe. There's a layer of white dust coating the roof and sprinkled on the banisters of the front porch. It can't possibly be snow, because it's May.

When I get closer I see that it's powdered sugar and frosting.

The witch opens the door for us. Come in, come in, she sings. We step through the threshold. There's a wood stove burning, and the fire smells like warm vanilla and cinnamon apples. We sigh deeply and breathe in again. This time we smell spiced cocoa and caramel kettle corn. Our mouths water. There are confections everywhere, stacked high on platters, overflowing from bowls, stuffed into colorful jars.

Eat, rest, the witch says, poor things, you look exhausted.

We take off our shoes and lie down on the plush cushions spread out on the floor. The witch tucks us in under knit blankets and feeds us chocolate soufflé with blackberry soda. The carbonation tickles the back of my throat. There are other girls there, stretched out on more pillows, some of them eating, others sleeping. The witch takes one of the girls by her honey-drenched hand and leads her out of the parlor and into the room beyond. They don't come back.

I look over at Marlie, and she's eating candied cherries, her mouth and fingers dripping with red syrup. I always wake from those dreams starving.

Ms. Wilde lets us have lunch in the art room after she sees us eating by ourselves under the bleachers. She tells us about her kitchen renovation project and shares adventures she had backpacking through Iceland. She shows us YouTube compilations of babies getting scared by their own farts, and Marlie laughs for the first time since we came home.

"If anyone says something to make you uncomfortable, let me know, all right?" Ms. Wilde tells us.

After lunch, we walk along the grove of trees that marks the border between the school and the neighborhood. We still haven't talked about any of it. Marlie doesn't bring it up, so I don't either, even though all I want is to ask if she has those dreams too, if her stomach churns so loud it wakes her, if she sees moving shadows in the spaces between trees, if she feels like a part of her never walked out of those woods, if she'll ever, ever forgive me. Watching her light up with laughter made me brave, so I take the leap.

"Everyone thinks I made it up. Do you think Ms. Wilde would believe us?" I ask, picking at the frayed and split ends of my hair. "She's probably the only grown-up who will. She doesn't treat us like we're freaks."

"She doesn't actually care. She's only acting nice because she's obviously desperate to be a mother."

I pause in the middle of a step and turn to Marlie. "What?"

It doesn't sound like something Marlie would say, because Marlie doesn't say nasty things about anyone, not even about the spineless bullies who torment her.

Marlie shrugs and veers off the path, kneeling to study something in the tall grass. I walk up behind her and cringe when I see the quivering body in the bushes. It's a baby rabbit. Most of its fur has been stripped off and left hanging like an unzipped bodysuit, pink flesh and white tendons exposed. The rabbit twitches, still alive.

"Mittens strikes again." I frown. The tabby cat that hunts around the school grounds is relentless in her massacre and happily leaves the mangled remains of her victims for students to find.

Marlie gathers the skinned rabbit into her coat, holding it to her chest.

I scrunch my nose. "Should you be touching that with your bare hands?"

Marlie whispers something into the rabbit's furless ear. Then she breaks the rabbit's neck in one smooth twist.

I jolt back like I've been slapped. The shock leaves my mouth in one sharp gasp. Marlie has trouble looking at a paper cut. She sheds tears watching animal shelter commercials. I've never seen her crush a trail of ants, stomp a spider, a house centipede, anything.

She looks up at me, her face remorseless, and for a chilling instant I'm staring at a stranger. The moment passes. Marlie blinks her clear green eyes. "It was in pain," she says. "I freed it."

I dig a hole under the bushes and we drop the rabbit inside. Marlie stands over my shoulder and watches as I push dirt over the body, her gaze boring into my back.

My playing worsens. My fingers are clumsy and inarticulate, like they've been snapped and healed back wrong. The sounds I make aren't music, just angry screeches and sad wailing.

"Stop it, you're hurting my ears," my mother shouts.

At night, my mother moves swiftly through the house, relentlessly organizing the already spotless rooms. I stand in the doorway of the practice room and watch as she takes everything off the shelves and tidies them into boxes. Plaques and trophies, certificates and ribbons. She pauses, holding up a framed photo of us together on stage at my first competition. My first win. The moment is crystalline in my memory. Her hand on my shoulder was the only thing that kept me from coming apart with joy. My daughter, she proclaimed to the crowd, as if anointing me, laying her crown on my head.

I watch as she traces her fingertips over the photo, her shoulder blades sharp against the back of her shirt. "Where have you gone?" she whispers.

Violin is the only thing I'm good at. It's the only thing that makes my mother happy. If I can't play anymore, then what good am I?

I rush up to my room and dig out my phone, desperately willing Marlie to pick up before the tears come.

"Oh, hello, Mei," Marlie's mother answers. "I'm keeping an eye on Marlene's phone, she's been getting unkind messages and I don't want her to see things that could be . . . upsetting. You can speak to her at school tomorrow."

"Right. Of course," I mumble, swiping my hand across my eyes. "Sorry to call so late."

I drop out of orchestra and fill my elective period with Ms. Wilde's art class. Ms. Wilde compliments my brushstrokes even though they're hairy and uneven. Marlie switches to the same class and has an easier time than me commanding her paintbrush. She fills her canvases with large swatches of color and bold lines.

Ms. Wilde nods in appreciation. "What are you expressing with your piece, Marlie?"

"Hunger," she answers, and my gut rumbles.

After class, I run to the vending machine and put in every dollar I have. I tear through bags of chips, stale cookies, mushy honey buns, and two bottles of neon sports drink. Everything tastes like chalk.

Two weeks before midterms, we're working on a still life, the class sitting around the display in a circle of easels. I'm concentrating on drawing the curve of a vase when Ms. Wilde's scream pierces the room. Pencils drop and chairs screech against the floor. Everyone looks up.

Ms. Wilde stumbles away from Marlie's station, cradling her wrist. Blood drips from the cracks of her fingers onto her pants. Marlie is holding an X-Acto knife, the tip of the blade red.

"You stabbed Ms. Wilde!" June Bickel shrieks. The class erupts into panic.

"I'm okay," Ms. Wilde says, "everyone sit down, please, I'm okay." Her face is pale.

Nobody sits down, they're all looking at Marlie, a room full of wide eyes and pointing fingers. I rush to her side and throw my arms around her, shielding her from the stares. She doesn't let go of the knife.

"Should we call nine-one-one?" someone finally asks.

Ms. Wilde is taken to the hospital, and Marlie is sent to the counselor's office. Security escorts me back to class after I screamed in the counselor's face when she wouldn't let me stay with Marlie. By the end of the day, the whole school is talking about it.

"That girl who was kidnapped tried to cut off a teacher's hand!"

"Oh my god, what if she starts attacking us in class?"

"Maybe she's having traumatic flashbacks."

"Maybe she needs to not come back to school. Ever."

Marlie is suspended for a week. Her parents try to fight it, but in the end it seems fair for the amount of stitches that Ms. Wilde needed. Ms. Wilde says it's not Marlie's fault and she isn't going to press charges. I bring Marlie her homework and notes for our midterm exams.

"Thanks, Mei. You want something to drink? We only have diet soda, Mom's trying to cut down on sugar." She spreads her notebooks and binders out across the kitchen table, like this is just another study session we're having, like she isn't suspended for slicing a teacher's wrist open.

"Marlie, if something's going on with you, if something's wrong"—I lean in toward her—"you'd tell me, right?"

"Of course I would." She looks up at me. "I tell you everything."

"Why did you do it?" I ask. "Why did you hurt Ms. Wilde?"

She sits back, perplexed. "I didn't. It was an accident."

"But June said she saw you, she said that you—"

"It was an accident. You believe me, don't you?"

No one believed me when I needed them to. I want to believe her. I have to believe her. I nod my head.

"Ms. Wilde only wants to fix us." Marlie reaches out and rests her hand on top of mine. "But we're not broken. We don't need to be fixed."

She laces our fingers together. Her skin is much warmer than usual. "Besides. We have each other."

I look down at our joined hands and nod again. "We have each other."

After the incident with Ms. Wilde, I don't dream about the witch and her candy cabin anymore. I dream about Marlie. I dream of her running through the woods. She's all alone, zigzagging through the trees, sharp pebbles and broken sticks cutting her bare feet and slicing between her toes, but she doesn't slow down, doesn't look back.

There's a shadow chasing her through the darkness. Hunting her. Her hair falls out of its usual neat braid, her breath escaping in erratic pants. She stumbles over an outcropping of roots and nearly trips.

The shadow gains on her, something massive and animal, moving on all fours. The sounds of wet breaths and snapping jaws are right behind her. She looks over her shoulder and sees only teeth.

The shadow leaps forward, and Marlie's face twists into a silent scream. Claws tear into her chest, and teeth close around her neck. There's red everywhere, the smell of it sticky sweet.

In those dreams, I'm never there to save her.

Exactly one year after the witch led us into the woods, the mark appears on the trees behind the neighborhood. It's carved into tree trunks, the same mark that's on our arms—stacked triangles inside of a semicircle.

"It's just Bryan messing with us again," I assure Marlie.

I honestly think the carvings are another one of Bryan Haywood's sadistic pranks, but then the first girl disappears. A fourteen-year-old from Montgomery Middle School. Then a second girl from Wynter Heights Elementary goes missing. Marlie has a panic attack in biology when our classmates start discussing the Amber Alerts. She gets sent home early, and stays home the next day. I stop by her house after she misses school again.

"Marlene's been very anxious lately. We think it's best for her to stay home for a bit, in case she, well . . ." Her mother kneads her plump hands together. "How about you, Mei? How are you doing?"

Marlie's mom is short and round, her cheeks always bright red. I still can't tell if it's a skin condition or too much blush. Her life's purpose seems to be to orbit Marlie's world, providing never-ending warmth and a constant supply of casseroles. The opposite of my mother in every way. My mother who's stern and frighteningly tall, angular and radiant, like she's made from shards of stained glass. My mother who sacrificed her career as a violinist for an illicit love that turned out to be unremarkable. My mother who hasn't once asked me how I was doing since that night she picked me up from the police station.

"I'm okay," I say. "A little stressed about finals."

"Bless your heart. Are you going to try out for that music school in Michigan again this year?" she asks.

"No," I tell her. "I'm not going anywhere."

I head upstairs and knock four times on Marlie's door—three hard knocks and a light one, the entry password—and push inside. She's sitting on the windowsill bench, her legs pulled up against her chest. Her bedroom hasn't changed since we had our first sleepover. Her walls are still painted yellow and covered in pastel butterflies; her army of stuffed animals still stands guard over her bed. Marlie doesn't move when I sit down against the other corner of the window.

Her eyes are skimming the treetops beyond the cul-de-sac, her fingers scratching at the crook of her elbow where the mark sits under her sleeve.

"The witch is back," Marlie says. "She's going to hurt more girls."

"Hey." I reach out and grab her hand, pulling it away from her arm. "Listen to me. No matter what happens, I'll protect you. No one's going to hurt you, not while I'm around."

She yanks her hand back. "You think I'm pathetic, don't you? It makes you feel good to know that you're so much braver and stronger."

Outrage and hurt boil in my stomach. "Of course not," I snap. "Why would you say that?"

There's that stranger again, the Marlie who kills rabbits and cuts teachers and says cruel things. Where did she come from?

"I'm sorry." Marlie looks down, the stranger slipping back into the crevices of her kind face. "I'm just tired of everyone acting like I'm this sad victim all the time." She glances at her elbow. "My mom is this close to ordering an exorcism to get rid of this 'devil's mark.'"

"You're not pathetic, Marlie. And you're not a victim," I tell her. "You're a survivor."

She lets out a small, dry laugh. "Can we pretend that just this once I'll be the one to protect you?"

"... Okay." I nod. "Promise you'll keep me safe?"

"I promise," she vows.

I come home from school the next day to the smell of fire. Thick black smoke billows up from behind the house, and I race into the backyard to see my mother standing in front of a raging bonfire. I cover my mouth and cough against the acrid heat. There are bits of burnt debris floating up from the flames, fluttering around in the hot breeze. I reach out and pull a piece out of the air. There's part of a staff and ascending sixteenth notes on the half-charred paper. My mother stands with her back to me, tossing stacks of sheet music and theory books into the fire.

"Mama, what are you doing?" I storm up to her. "You can't just burn stuff in our yard like this, it's totally against the law!"

"Gone, she's gone," my mother mutters and feeds another song into the fire. Vivaldi's Violin Concerto in A Minor.

"We have to put this fire out before our neighbors call the cops," I tell her.

"My baby is gone, ran away in the night," she mumbles to herself like I'm not there, and throws another piece in. Paganini's *Le Streghe*, op. 8.

"Mama, please," I plead, "you're scaring me."

She picks up the black case sitting at her feet and pulls my violin out by its neck. "I pushed her to it, my sweet plum left because of this." She raises the violin high above her head.

"No!" I shout, but it's too late, she hurls my instrument into the blaze. Its defenseless wooden body is eaten alive.

I grab my mother's arm and twist her toward me. "Why did you do that?!"

She blinks at me several times. "You're not my daughter," she says, her lower lip trembling. "Who are you?"

"What are you talking about, Mama?" My hand slips away from her arm.

"Who are you?" she demands, her voice cracking with hysteria. She reaches out and grabs me by the shoulders. "*What* are you?"

It's me, it's me, I repeat, but I see no recognition in her eyes, only the reflection of the towering flames as she pushes me toward the fire. The heat claws at the back of my neck, the smoke makes my eyes tear. My mother screams in my face, "What are you? *What are you?!*"

I shove her, hard, and she falls back onto the grass. "Somebody, please," she sobs, "help me find my baby!" I turn and run as fast as I can away from her, away from the symphonic pyre, across the street to Marlie's house, and pound on the door with both fists.

Marlie opens the door and I fling myself forward, clinging to her. I try to explain what happened, what I saw, but nothing comes out right, just incoherent sounds, my teeth and tongue refusing to form words.

I stay at her house till nightfall. After the fire truck leaves, Marlie's mom sits me down in their kitchen and tells me that my father took my mother to the hospital.

"Do you have any relatives nearby you can stay with?" she asks.

I shake my head.

"Well, you know Marlene hasn't been feeling well, I'm afraid you being here might not be the best for her . . . let me call our pastor, maybe you can stay with his family—"

"She's staying here," Marlie says from the doorway.

"Heaven's sake, Marlene, cover that up!" her mother gasps, and I see that Marlie's wearing short sleeves—she hasn't this whole year—her thin arms hanging at her sides, the mark on full display.

"She's staying." Marlie sounds so sure of herself; there's no room for compromise in her voice. She's standing with her back and shoulders pulled completely straight, no sign of her habitual slouch. I'm shocked to discover that she's actually taller than me.

Marlie's mom opens her mouth, but Marlie walks right past her. She takes my hand and leads me upstairs, leaving her mother dumbstruck in the kitchen.

We wash our faces and brush our hair, then climb into her bed together, pulling the blanket over our heads. We're sound in our cocoon, shut off from the world, from mothers as mean as witches, and witches who pretend to be mothers.

"Do you get the feeling that we're supposed to be somewhere else right now?" Marlie's voice echoes in our cushy cave.

"This is exactly where I want to be," I tell her. "With you."

"Then why did you try to go so far away?" she whispers.

Under the blankets, only the whites of her eyes are visible. I can hear the still-fresh wound in her voice.

"It was important to my mother," I whisper back.

"You didn't even tell me you were auditioning." She sounds miles away. "I tell you everything, and you never told me."

"I didn't say anything, because . . ." I shut my eyes. "It doesn't matter now. I messed it all up. I got up on that stage and Mama was watching and I couldn't stop thinking that even if I played perfectly, even if I did get in, Baba still wouldn't want me, and Mama still won't get her career back, and you'd never forgive me for leaving you behind, and I choked, I couldn't remember the first bar, I couldn't . . ." My fingers clutch the sheets. "I just wanted her to be proud of me again."

Marlie leans in and kisses the tears from my eyelashes. "It's okay."

"I'm sorry I made you come with me that night, I'm so sorry . . ."

"Shh." She smooths a hand down my hair. "You think I'm the one who needs taking care of . . . but you're the one who's terrified of being alone. I couldn't let you go all alone."

Marlie sings to me quietly, and I drift off to the humming, a tune I can't place and yet it sounds so familiar.

I jerk awake in the middle of a fitful, shallow sleep and reach out for Marlie. Her side of the bed is empty, the sheets cold. I sit up. The room is silent; stuffed rabbits and porcelain dolls stare down at me, unblinking, from the bookshelves.

The window is open.

I jump out of bed and climb out without a second thought, without putting on a jacket or shoes. I flip over the backyard fence and trample Mrs. Parker's petunias to get to Bishop Ave, racing through the sleeping neighborhood. A fog gathers over the neatly manicured lawns, dimming the glow of the streetlights and settling over the oversized SUVs parked in every driveway.

I know exactly where I need to go.

The woods lie just beyond the blue house at the end of the street. As I run past the last stop sign, I hear it. A ghostly song floating down the sidewalk, calling out to me through the mist. I remember it now. It's the song the witch sang to lure us to her cabin made of sweets.

Except this time it's not the witch singing. It's Marlie's voice.

"Marlie? Marlie!" My feet leave the hard asphalt and step onto wet earth. I follow Marlie's voice into the maze of white pines. The fog is so thick I can't tell left from right; all I have is the singing guiding me forward. I grasp on to the song like it's the end of a thread winding its way back toward the spool.

Up ahead, I see the hazy outlines of two people moving through the fog. I catch a flash of Marlie's blond hair in the moonlight. It looks almost silver. She's leading someone behind her, the two of them winding in and out of the shadows, like playful sprites heading to a midnight garden party. The woods grow less dense, and the fog starts to clear. Marlie and her companion slow to a stop in a clearing, long enough for me to catch up, long enough for me to see that the other person is Bryan.

I'm about to step out toward them when Marlie turns to face him. They're both wearing pajamas: Bryan in a T-shirt and loose pants, Marlie in her thin nightgown. Marlie stops singing. She sinks down to the ground, onto her hands and knees. Bryan doesn't move, doesn't speak, just watches Marlie, entranced, and so am I, I can't look away, my eyes peeled so wide they burn at the corners.

Marlie's back bows up. Her neck twists. Her elbows bend inward; the ridges of her spine jut out from between her shoulder blades. *Pop, pop, pop.* The shape of her distorts into something not human. Her nightgown rips and instead of fair, freckled skin, there is a tough leathery hide. Her face stretches like taffy, her ears and nose pulling longer and longer. A bony tail unfurls between her legs. Her fingernails grow into knives. Her mouth is so, so wide.

Bryan hasn't moved from his spot. His expression is pleasant; he sways a little from side to side like he can still hear the song in his head.

The creature that was Marlie digs its claws into the dirt and springs forward on sinewy legs. Rows of teeth descend on the tyrant prince's crown of golden curls. There's a heavy crunch, and Bryan crumples to the forest floor, his puppet strings cut. The beast bites down and eats like it's been starved for days. For months.

For a whole year.

I don't turn. I don't run. Slowly, I step into the clearing. The smell is overwhelming, and suddenly I'm famished. I reach my hands out, my fingers aching to grab at the gleaming treats spilling from Bryan's belly. My foot lands on a branch, breaking it in half. The monster lifts its head.

It has Marlie's green eyes.

The primal hunger in my gut forms a tight fist and squeezes. I let out a hoarse cry and fall to my knees. It feels like I'm being pulled apart at the sockets. My body is clay and it's molding into something else, meat and organs twisting into different configurations. My mouth drops open as extra incisors push through my gums. My skin wraps taut over my new skeleton.

When I stand again, it's on all fours.

I join Marlie's side, reveling in the power of my muscles, the steel in my bones.

Bryan's still alive under her jaws, half-skinned and peeled open like a ripe pomegranate. He smells so good. I lean in and sink my teeth into the pulsing candy apple in his chest.

We finish our meal down to the last bite, and when we look up, she's there, smiling at us, a shepherdess who found her precious lost lambs.

"My darling little ones." The witch glides over, her toes skimming over the grass. She reaches down and strokes our faces. "You've grown lovelier than I could have hoped."

I can see her eyes now, as black as the woods, as black as the sky, an endless swirling void. Eternity.

The witch runs her fingers under our ears and down our backs. "I've loved you since the moment I saw you. I heard your broken little hearts crying out to me. If you love something, you set it free, and when it comes back, it's meant to be." Her hands trace over the joint of our elbows, where we still bear her mark. "I planted the seeds and I let you go, and here you are returned to me, fully blossomed."

Marlie nuzzles her snout into the witch's palm.

"This is what you're meant to be," she says. "Mine."

Her words cinch around my neck like a leash. "We'll be together, forever."

When she turns, I'm yanked along. The witch walks back into the trees, humming her song. We follow, her bound pets. My will slips with every note, replaced by her voice commanding me to obey. Beside me, Marlie strides forward, the arch of her back confident. Her body brushes against mine. She slides up to the witch, graceful and silent, a sleek line in the dark.

In an instant, she lunges. She grabs the witch by her neck and tears her down.

The witch's screams sound like roaches scurrying inside my ears. "Stop," the witch howls, but her shackles hold no power over Marlie.

Crimson ribbons spray across her white dress and onto the trees in long arcs. Marlie rips at the witch until there is nothing left but tattered lace and bloody clumps of raven hair.

The chains shatter. My sense of self pours back into my veins, flushing out the parasitic spell congealed in my blood. The gruesome shell encasing me cracks and splinters, my limbs breaking through, emerging from the prison. My arm is bare—all traces of the witch's mark gone. Marlie crawls toward me, claws becoming knuckles, snout becoming nose, she sheds the beast in pieces, until she's a girl again. She reaches out and pulls me against her.

"I promised," she says.

She holds me there, at the edge of the precipice, where the inferno nearly swallowed us both. My monstrous angel unfurls her wings and draws me in, where I'm safe, where I'm needed. Where I'm home. Nothing can hurt me, not while she's around. Her face and hands are dripping red. Her eyes are bright and feral. There's flecks of bone on her shoulders, blending into the constellation of freckles.

She's beautiful.

"Hey," I murmur against the curve of her neck. "Do you still want to go to New York?"

"If we can find some pants first," she says.

I wrap my arms around her and laugh into her hair. We huddle together in the grass, naked and glistening, newly born.

I lick at my teeth, at the wetness still coating my mouth.

It tastes like candied cherries.

AUTHOR'S NOTE

Ever since my first haunted house experience ended in tears and my mother had to carry me out because I was too scared to walk, I've had a masochistic relationship with all things spooky. I still scare easy, but most of my favorite books and movies are in the horror genre. The undercurrent of terror in fairy tales is something I'm especially drawn to—cannibalism, body horror, twisted parental figures juxtaposed with knights, princesses, and happy endings. With SWEETMEATS I wanted to explore these familiar tropes, subvert them, and inject them into a modern setting. The mother-daughter relationships reflect both issues I faced growing up in the West raised by a traditional Eastern mother and my own anxieties as a new mom. Shortly after this story was first published online I went through a very difficult period of my life, and despite having our challenges, my mother was by my side to support me through it all. Thank you, Mama, for holding my hand as I made my way through the darkest part of the woods.

SUSPENSION OF DISBELIEF IN *SWEETMEATS*

by Emily X.R. Pan

SWEETMEATS IS A MODERN-DAY FAIRY TALE, SET IN A WORLD LIKE THE ONE we know, but with a few deliciously weird twists and a dash of creepy. To pull all this off, Cheng has to convince us to set aside our disbelief, that skeptical part of the brain that goes, "Hey, wait—that's not real. This would never happen."

The first few sentences hook us, getting us to ask, *What mark? What does it mean?* But they're short so that we can quickly reach this piece of information: "The police can't figure out how we got the brand and neither can the doctors." This mention of police and doctors and, later on, real things and real places, gives us some of the basic rules and boundaries of this world. Dropping these details at the beginning of the story functions as a shorthand to confirm: Yes, this is a world the reader already knows. With that established, Cheng can begin to play around with the rules:

> "You keep referring to your abductor as a 'witch.'
> Why do you say that?" The detective taking our
> statements squints at me after every question he asks.
> "Because that's what she is," I tell him. "A witch who
> eats girls. She kept giving us cake and candy to fatten
> us up."

Learning this information through conversation, we get the detective's skepticism and the narrator's conviction all in one thrust. Because the detective feels antagonistic, we're inclined to side with Mei. We are on her side, so we believe her.

In asking the reader to suspend disbelief there's strategy, too, in how much information to give and when. For now it's enough to tell us there's a witch; Cheng waits for us to fully swallow each new piece before she feeds us more. She shifts the focus to Mei and Marlie's relationship and sets up the emotional stakes.

Things grow more bizarre as the story zooms in on Marlie, who has been affected by the witch in a way that Mei doesn't understand. While Mei still seems human and—for lack of a better word—normal, Marlie's perspective is more unsettling: Her chilling calm as she breaks a rabbit's neck. "Accidentally" stabbing a teacher.

The dominoes are falling, gaining speed: There are marks on the trees again; girls are disappearing; Mei's mother rejects her; Marlie sneaks out the window in the middle of the night.

The reader isn't pausing to consider what to believe anymore—we're just desperate to know what's going to happen, and we can't turn the pages fast enough. We're all in. It hardly even feels weird when Marlie and Mei transform into four-legged beasts. We see the witch, and have no doubt of who she is.

GLOW

Joanna Truman

> I loved Joanna Truman's GLOW so much! Knockout writing and romantically suspenseful. Truly reminds me of those caged butterfly feelings when you're bursting to tell someone they're your favorite person and the soaring glee when you finally get it off your chest.
>
> —ADAM SILVERA, AUTHOR OF *INFINITY SON*

IF YOU DIDN'T KNOW BETTER, IT MIGHT SEEM BARREN OUT HERE. SKY, SAND, pavement. Mountains patched with scrappy weeds and scattered stones. Wind turbines blinking lonely red lights as they turn like vinyl on a record player, soft and lilting.

Beth knows better.

She knows that the desert can grow things from little more than gravel, that stillness on the surface often means turmoil underneath. That once you kneel down and have a look, you can't unsee it, can't forget what's there.

That's why they picked this place, after all.

It's past midnight by the time they start driving down the 10, the highway stretching for thousands of miles like a belt buckled loosely around the country. No matter the hour, there's always someone on the road. The later it gets, the more the commuters distill into grizzled truckers piloting eighteen-wheelers and bleary-eyed college kids who can't afford to lose a day to travel. Beth watches the shadows blur outside the passenger window until her eyes focus on the reflection of the inside instead, where she sees Naia in the driver's seat, steering with one hand while the other taps staccato on the doorframe.

Beth allows herself a moment, a single breath, to be selfish. She watches Naia angled in the glass, her form silhouetted. In that breath, she can almost forget where they're going.

Beth looks away and sips from her drive-through coffee, grateful to have something to do with her hands. Beside her, Naia has to constantly press and release the gas pedal to stay with traffic. The hand-me-down station wagon is a warm cocoon huddling them together in the middle of the night, but luxurious it is not; before Naia inherited it, cruise control and automatic locks were merely the stuff of imagination.

Heat blasts from the air vents. It gets freakishly cold at night in Arizona. Once they're in California, though, something will change in the way they breathe. Out there at the end of the line, they will share the air only with the ocean.

Beth wonders if now is the right time.

The space between them is abuzz with the sound of traffic and the heater and the low hum of the radio crackling from the nearly busted speakers. Beth tries to imagine what she'd say. How she'd start. How to puncture the quiet without bursting it like a balloon.

Beth opens her mouth and wills the words—any words, anything at all—to come out.

"You can change it if you want," Naia says, nodding at the dial. A crooner belts out timeless tunes from the oldies station. "If the whole horror movie feel isn't doing it for you."

Beth raises an eyebrow. "Horror movie?"

"Yeah, you know. In movies, when a girl is driving with a creepy guy down the highway at night, there's always some old-timey song playing on the radio. To set the mood."

"The . . . murder mood?"

"Exactly."

"And you're the creepy guy in this scenario, correct?"

"Well," Naia says with the tip of her tongue between her teeth as the dashboard glow turns her smile red, "I am driving."

Beth can't help but snort. "You creep."

The clock reads nearly four in the morning. Naia never changed it during the last round of daylight saving time, just waited until it rolled back around and the clock was correct again. She taught herself to think one hour back, in both the present and the past at the same time, waiting and waiting for the future to catch up.

Beth knows that sometimes you can wait forever and it still won't be right.

There are moments.

Moments when, amid the endless chaos of the world, Beth feels like there's—*something*.

Something more.

Something on the other side of the veil, a crack in the universe that lets you see everything inexplicable all at once if you reach out and touch it. The bridge between what's real and what simply can't be, but somehow is.

It's all Beth can think about the first time she ever sees Naia—flying through the air on the volleyball court, arms outstretched, long legs bent in a wild and frenetic burst of energy, the atmosphere around her practically singing as every dimension hits all the right frequencies. Naia spikes the ball with fluid power, and it's gone, rocketing to a corner on the other side where no one can save it, and everyone is cheering, and Naia lands light-footed on the ground, and Beth wonders—*Did everyone see what I just saw?*

Naia's gaze sweeps over the crowd, not really landing on anything as she hugs her teammates, laughing and smiling and shining under the lights. But when that gaze flickers over Beth, Beth *feels* it, sure as a shock—like the first spark of coming back to life.

Later in the parking lot, as the sun casts the long lacrosse fields in shades of pink and green, Beth pops the hood of her car to stare dumbfounded at the exposed innards, trying to figure out why it won't start, when she hears a voice behind her.

Naia is there, her hair wild and cheeks still red from the game. She smiles.

Beth feels the engine of her heart ignite.

The world is brighter, bolder, stranger now that she's noticed Naia. Now this girl, who must've been walking these halls before while Beth was oblivious to her, waits at Beth's locker after French class, greeting Beth with a terribly accented "Tu es ma joie de vivre!" and a slow sweep of her eyelashes across her cheeks. It's a whirlwind, this feeling, and Beth cannot quite find a name for it; she only knows that it's spelled the way Naia's fingers draw hearts on the fogged-up windows of the station wagon on a frosty morning. It's shaped like handwriting, messy and true.

Beth has never kissed anyone before, but when she looks at Naia, she thinks: *Yeah. It could be you.*

And then: *It could ruin everything.*

You could ruin me.

They are lying on Naia's bed, curled up shoulder to shoulder, when Naia tells Beth about her plan to break open the world.

"It's in the canyons," Naia says. "Near Palm Springs." She's wearing the T-shirt Beth likes best, the faded red one with the fire department logo. The box fan murmurs from the window, sending strings of cool air into the dry heat. It makes Beth feel like they've created a world here in this room that no one can touch, one that's made up only of quiet sunlight and breathing and the feel of ribs under cotton T-shirts.

"What is?"

"The fault line." Naia leans in closer. "Where we can unmake the world."

Beth presses her cheek to the soft sheets. She takes a deep breath.

She opens her mouth to ask Naia what she means, what this is, what they can do—but nothing comes out.

Maybe there aren't words yet for what she wants to say.

"The fault runs all over the canyons, but there's one spot where you can stand directly on top of it. A place where the earth cracks open. That's where we'll do it," Naia whispers.

Beth becomes aware of the sheen of sweat across her brow, her own shirt sticking to the sheets, the fan not quite enough anymore. It's a bold and terrifying thing to realize: she *believes* Naia. She believes that Naia could bring the world to its knees, because she also believes that Naia could save the world if she wanted to, could take this broken place they're growing up in and change it into something better.

Instead, Naia wants to tear it down.

You could ruin me.

You could ruin everything.

Beth's heart kicks in her chest, the same familiar strike as when she first locked eyes with this girl, but this time it feels like the engine has stalled, her heart running on fumes. There's a word rattling around inside her, something that sounds like *fear*, but that's not quite right.

"You think we can do that?" Beth tucks her hair behind her ear and looks at Naia, serious and steadfast, but Naia breaks into a smile.

"Of course we can. Girls are *magic*." Naia emphasizes the last word, murmurs it like a spell she's written into the air. "*We're* magic."

Beth's heart rumbles again. She's not sure if it's love or the end of the world.

So she says, "Let's do it."

Naia's eyes widen. "You'll be there? With me?"

"I'll be there," Beth whispers. "I'm with you."

Beth is too close to her to see all her facial features at once; her gaze flickers between Naia's eyes, where the world spins back at her, gold half-buried in the earth, and her smile, huge and mountainous and wide, wide open.

You could ruin me.

Beth knows it's true, knows that she would give herself over to this girl no matter the consequences, whether it ends with them standing on top of the world or the world swallowing them whole.

The gas station is a lonely, flickering thing, stuffed at the base of a small valley past an exit. Beth glances at the map on her phone; they're less than an hour away from the canyon. As they're pulling off the road, Beth notices a sign: STATE PRISON 1 MI. DO NOT PICK UP HITCHHIKERS.

Beth thumbs in the direction of the convenience store. "Want anything?"

"A winning lottery ticket," Naia calls as she presses the faded keypad on the gas pump.

"Yeah? And what would you do with it?"

"Nothing." Naia grins. "But how cool would that be?"

As she sets two bags of chips and two water bottles down on the counter, Beth looks out to watch Naia, who leans against the car as she waits for the tank to fill. It reminds Beth of family road trips, long car rides up and down mountain passes and hidden switchbacks and plains without a bump on the horizon for miles. Trying to drown out her parents singing along to the radio with an audiobook on her phone. Unable to keep a smile from her face when her dad caught her eyes in the mirror and danced.

Her parents, asleep at home, none the wiser.

It has become so easy to sneak out that Beth has begun to wonder if her parents actually know what she's doing and just don't bother to stop her.

She wonders if they know that even if she is sneaking out, she'll only be with Naia. She wonders if they trust Naia too.

The thought makes her hands shake when she picks up the bag from the counter.

She has to tell Naia.

Before they end things this way, with something so huge locked up inside her that Beth can barely breathe sometimes. After all, there are some things that can't be undone, that can't be rewritten once they exist in the universe.

Maybe two of those things will happen tonight.

The bell on the door jingles as Beth heads back outside. The wind has picked up and brought a chill with it, sending trash skittering across the parking lot like something in the shadows.

"Did you . . ." Beth swallows. "Did you do anything to . . . prepare for tonight?"

"Listened to the new Shawn Mendes album on repeat." Naia sighs. "Just in time, thankfully."

"I mean like . . . I don't know. Say goodbye." Beth can't help herself—she searches for the slightest chance that Naia gave something—someone—any last considerations.

Naia's eyebrows knit, but her expression smooths over quickly. "To who?" she murmurs.

And then Beth sees it—something she has never seen in Naia's eyes before, at least never directed at *her*.

Doubt.

Beth tries to read Naia's face, desperately hoping she's seeing it wrong, that Naia's eyes aren't saying *Maybe I chose the wrong person*, that the way her lips are slightly parted and her chin is set don't whisper *Maybe I shouldn't have trusted you with this.*

Beth blinks away the words written on the backs of her eyelids and shakes her head, popping open a bag of chips. She forces a smile. "You mean to tell me you really didn't want to grab one last milkshake at Davey's? Not *one*?"

And just like that, the doubt disappears, replaced with a flicker of relief. A sheepish smile crosses Naia's face. "Yeah, yeah. Get in the car."

The radio signal is back when they get on the road, but Naia plugs in her phone instead, blasting Shawn Mendes and singing along with renewed energy. Beth watches the roadside carefully as they speed by, but there's no sign of hitchhikers.

There's no sign of anyone at all.

As she tosses the empty bag of chips onto the floor of the back seat, Beth spots an empty milkshake container under the seat.

When Naia meets Beth's eyes in a glance, Beth pretends she doesn't notice. There's nothing left to say. She had her chance at the gas station to tell Naia, and she didn't—she couldn't—and now they're careening toward the end whether she likes it or not.

The flashlight seems almost too bright as they step into the desert. The car doors slamming shut echo like shotgun cracks across the night. Even the highway noise doesn't reach down here; they're surrounded by cliffs that stretch toward the sky, walling them in. Naia pulls a pickax out of the trunk and shoulders it. Beth grabs two water bottles.

They narrowly avoid the chubby arms of cholla cacti that reach toward them, grabby spines clinging for a ride. Holes pock the dirt. Beth wonders what might be sleeping beneath her feet, warmed under the desert crust, away from the night's tight-lipped chill. Rattlesnakes curled into woven piles. Voles huddled together with shaking fur. Perhaps something else—an energy waiting to stretch its jaws wide and sink its teeth into the world.

She suppresses a shiver. She keeps her eyes on Naia ahead of her in the darkness, following her lead into the unknown.

Eventually Naia stops walking.

"Here."

It doesn't look like much, the end of the world. It looks like a slight aberration of purple quartz embedded into rusty red pegmatite and spotted limestone, the splattered colors of rock and bone that paint the raised hilltops in the valley as barrel cacti spring from the cliffs like weeds through pavement.

There is life out here, Beth thinks.

For now, anyway.

She swallows hard as she watches Naia kneel, reverent to the ground with her hands pressed flat. Beth remembers the way Naia's gaze ignited her before she ever imagined she'd be standing here. What has been waiting under the earth for Naia, watching, counting the days till she arrived? Her best friend, her confidante, her everything. The destroyer of worlds, the unmaker, the girl in the volleyball tank top and ripped leggings.

If she could undo Beth with a look, how much more powerful would her touch be?

Standing up, Naia takes the pickax and raises it over her head, swinging it down with all her might.

Beth winces and waits for the explosion of dirt. But when she opens her eyes, there's barely an indent in the hard ground.

Naia's eyes narrow.

They take turns with pickax, chipping away at the dirt. It's nearly sunrise when Naia swings, slams, and a sound unlike any they've heard so far echoes from the point where the pickax hit.

She drops it to the ground with a clatter, exhaustion painted in smudges of dirt on her face and neck, and kneels again. Beth peers over her shoulder.

A shiver runs through Beth's entire body, the wonder of finding something she had known would be there all along.

Something more.

We're magic.

The desert is dark, but deep in the earth, impossibly far down in the crack between their feet, there's a glow, a sparkle of the start of something.

Naia's eyes gleam. "It's *here*," she murmurs.

Somewhere far away, a bird calls, its voice hanging in the air. The wind picks up, rustling the clusters of brittlebush and the long arms of ocotillos.

The glow is barely visible in Naia's eyes, pinpricks of light that should not exist, exposing the beating heart of a world that also, perhaps, should not exist, and soon won't.

Beth crouches, wiping back the strands of hair stuck to her forehead. She finishes the last water bottle and sets it aside.

When she looks up, Naia is giving her a pointed look.

"What?"

"Don't *litter*." Naia nods at the water bottle.

Beth's jaw drops. "Seriously?"

"Just because we're about to end the world doesn't mean we have to suddenly lose all our principles."

"Well . . ." Beth looks around. "Where should I put it?"

"You could take it back to the car."

Beth glances back at the shadowy outline of the car, tiny at the edge of the road where it meets the slope. "You're seriously going to make me walk all the way back to the car for this?"

Naia sits up and puts her hands on her hips. "On our last night together, don't become someone who *litters*."

So Beth takes it back to the car.

Shutting the trunk after she tosses the empty water bottle inside—along with a piece of plastic she found on the walk back, just so she won't feel guilty—Beth makes up her mind.

If Naia can do something this grand, this life-altering and terrifying and huge—

Beth can too.

"You're not allowed to say anything for the next thirty seconds," Beth blurts out when she returns. She makes the mistake of glancing up at Naia, and the sight nearly takes her breath away: Naia standing next to the fissure in the ground, painted against the sky as it purples and blooms into a bruise. She looks like a thunderstorm about to break, all that power contained in a thin bolt of lightning, gone in a flicker.

"I don't know how to . . . I mean, I probably should've brought this up earlier, I just wasn't . . . I don't know if I even really believed we'd—I mean, here we are, and—screw it."

You could ruin me.

"I love you," Beth breathes in a rush, and it feels *huge,* and the words are happening *here* and *now,* but they also feel like just words—too small to contain what's in her heart and too big to say out loud without risking everything.

"I mean, obviously, but not just in the normal way—not that it's not normal. I just mean in a different, in a more, bigger . . ." Beth's mind races to explain. To not blow this one chance. "I'm saying—I'm saying I love you the way you love Shawn Mendes."

She waits for the crack in the earth to shake, widen, and swallow her whole. This must be what it feels like, the end of the world.

Naia stares at her. She shakes her head, makes a sound of disbelief, then looks up at the sky. "I thought—this whole time I thought—god."

Beth suddenly feels very, very cold. For the first time ever, she cannot read what's written on Naia's face.

You have ruined everything.

"I can't believe I . . ." Naia shakes her head again.

The world blurs. Beth wonders if she's about to pass out before she realizes there are tears filling her vision, making everything run colors in front of her, the darkness bleeding into the glowing ground. She knew— somewhere—she *knew* there was a scenario where Naia might reject her, but she didn't actually think it would come true. After everything that has proven magic is real, how can it end like this?

It's only when Beth wipes her eyes that she sees, to her shock, that tears are running down Naia's face too.

Naia steps past the crack in the earth, spinning toward Beth, and she is suddenly so close so quickly that Beth can't move away, and though the color of Naia's eyes is hidden by the darkness, Beth still searches them for something to hang on to, anything to keep her from free-falling.

"This whole time I thought I'd been searching for someone to destroy the world with me," Naia whispers. "And when I found you, I knew." She laughs and wipes away her own tears. "And I was right, it's you—but I was wrong too."

When Naia blinks, the red glow of the earth's pulse and the white sheen of the moon's lone light mix together in her eyes, and Beth's heart nearly jumps out of her chest when she sees it—gold. Treasure. The space between them unlocked.

Naia presses her hands to the sides of Beth's neck, encircling her with a gentle brush of skin, and though her lips tremble and her eyes are wide, she looks confident, radiant, glowing. "I was searching for a reason not to destroy it all."

The air in Beth's lungs rushes out all at once.

"You are the joy of my life," Naia says breathlessly, and it sounds so much better this way than it did in her terribly accented French, and she does that slow sweep of her eyelashes, and Beth realizes sometimes there are words that fit.

"What a line," Beth half chokes through a laugh. Naia laughs too, and all Beth can do is reach out and wrap her arms around this girl made of gold.

"I thought you never paid attention in class." Naia's words are muffled in her ear, and Beth holds on tighter.

The sun peeks over the desert, slowly warming the ground. The stars disappear into sunlight. As the sun rises, the glow from the crack in the earth fades until it's barely visible. The daylight drowns it out, turns it into another hole in the ground that blends in with the miles upon miles of deserted land, never to be found again.

The end of the world, barely averted, is quickly forgotten when Naia's arms are around her.

Before she can lose her nerve, Beth blurts out, "Do you want to go get a milkshake with me?"

That smile spreads across Naia's face. "Like, a *lot*."

And so they do.

AUTHOR'S NOTE

I knew I wanted to write a story about two girls who could unmake the world, but only if they wanted to. Girls are magic, after all. They are powerful, electric, can create and destroy, can love and hurt and save each other all in the same breath. Beth and Naia hold the power to rip the world apart at the seams— and perhaps they will, someday.

The setting is inspired by my many long nights driving from California to Arizona and back in the silent, freezing desert. The state prison sign is real, located around Exit 222 eastbound on the 10. I've not seen any hitchhikers yet, but I'd probably heed the sign's advice and keep driving.

There's also a real fault line at the bottom of the Grand Canyon, located in an otherwise unremarkable patch of brush in Diamond Creek, where you can stand with your feet on either side of the split. All it would take is a little digging.

EMOTIONAL RESONANCE
IN *GLOW*

by Nova Ren Suma

IMAGINE A WHOLE STORY CHARGED BY YEARNING, BY THE SIMPLE FACT OF wanting someone and not being able to express it in words until all the long-unspoken feelings burst out at the last possible moment . . . a moment that might be the literal end of the world. This is GLOW.

But *how* is emotion communicated with such decisive force?

We gain emotional resonance—when a feeling vibrates through a story and is transferred to the reader—by instances like the one where Beth recounts the first time she ever saw Naia on the volleyball court, performing a flying leap that seems suspended in air for a breathless series of electric moments. *"Did everyone see what I just saw?"* Beth wonders in disbelief. We did see, thanks to the beauty of the description, but more importantly, we *felt* it in the way the moment was prolonged and held.

When Beth "wonders what might be sleeping beneath her feet," her imagination soars beneath desert crust and slithering rattlesnakes into something unfathomable: "an energy waiting to stretch its jaws wide and sink its teeth into the world." Even after she's let the words loose, she's so terrified she's ruined everything that she waits for the earth itself to swallow her. The landscape has spoken. It illustrates the emotion Beth cannot find the words to articulate.

Emotional resonance can come through in a single meaningful glance across a room between two characters, but it also can be woven into the world surrounding the characters: in roadways, in gas stations, in the sweeping expanse of land, the dangers on all sides, the wide open sky. How can place reveal what a character is feeling? In GLOW, "the world is brighter, bolder, stranger now that [Beth has] noticed Naia," and this is proven by the visuals as the story unfolds. What does Beth see reflected back in Naia's eyes? The "red glow of the earth's pulse." She sees "the white sheen of the moon's lone light." And in the end, most of all, the color of "treasure," which tells us everything we need to know. She sees gold.

STORY PROMPT:
THE END OF THE WORLD

WHAT KIND OF STORY RESONATES WITH A READER, ESPECIALLY A READER OF YA? One that *matters* to the characters. The events of the story can be as gigantic as the literal end of the world . . . or something far less explosive, so long as it's meaningful to the protagonist.

Think of how dramatic even the smallest event can feel for a teenager at times, and how that can often be belittled by adults (a friendship breakup, a crush gone wrong, a detention slip at school . . .). To a teen, any of those things might feel as terrible, as stomach-dropping as the world ending.

So . . . write the end of the world.

You can choose to interpret this literally, or you can focus on an event that's earth-shattering only for the character in your story.

ESCAPE

Tanvi Berwah

THE DAY MY MOTHER'S CANCER RELAPSED SHE STILL HAD THE POCHETTE. SHE would have warned me about it, had she the time. Nobody else bothered. Not in a way that mattered. But I wasn't surprised. Nobody actually warned me what was happening to my mother, either.

My cousin Jolene was sent to babysit me when my mother returned to the hospital, but all she did was stick her nose to her phone, obsessing over her horoscope and that of her new boyfriend. Everyone liked Sean. He wore leather jackets even when the weather was warm (he had a good excuse: he looked amazing) and rode a bike, and girls had Snapchat streaks running into triple digits with him, which meant he was perfect to Jolene.

Then Jolene asked if I knew where Mama kept the pochette. The second she said the word *pochette* I glanced involuntarily in the direction of Mama's room. I ran, but Jolene got there first and snatched the pochette off the bed. She said I was too young for it and it was fate, anyway, her finding something red the day her horoscope mentioned her lucky color of the day.

The pochette wasn't just red, it was the color of glossy apples. Fancy like those Louis Vuitton purses. Big enough to hold a human heart. It had a real gold buckle that no one had been successful in opening so far. No matter; it was a family heirloom. Specifically, it was *my* heirloom. My mother had it, her mother had it, and her mother before.

But then Mama died, and Jolene took it permanently.

The pochette had a habit of biting if touched unexpectedly. I know what that sounds like, but just bear with me. I *did* notice wounds on the faces of some women in the family, either claw or finger marks, and that made no sense. Unless, somehow, every time they took the pochette, they got into violent fights.

The color of the wounds rotted, visible even beneath layers of makeup.

On Christmas Eve, my sixteenth birthday, I decided I was old enough. My heirloom would be with me. The living room bubbled with my grand-mother and her sister, my aunts and my uncles, my cousins and their cousins, some spouses, and others they dragged along, including, of course, the ever-present charmer, Sean.

We were never content with just fourteen Woodrings in the family, so we were always looking to add more on every street we walked.

As I tried to make my way out, Woodrings clamored around the glit-tering room, hollering half-remembered carols, laughing and bellowing and jabbering, while the kids practiced running across the room for when they challenged Usain Bolt one day. Would-be Woodrings nervously sipped their eggnog.

We Woodrings talked about everything to everyone.

We talked about the poplar outside the house, the quality of eggs, the Eustons' impending divorce, the marches across continents, spies from Russia, Mount Washington's freezing winds, useless Instagram filters. My cousins talked excitedly about high school students organizing protests, Mama's cousins talked about Facebook. Cats and persons and stories.

God, how Woodrings liked to talk about stories. That's why, one mention of Mama, they began talking about her and *that boy* back when, and I could leave the room.

It was still a task to wriggle out of the group, squeezing past the imposing Christmas tree—which had Mama's face pasted on the star at the top—protecting my hair from the sloshing eggnog and wild hands flying with whatever new detail was being added to the tale of Julia and That Boy. This year, my older cousins obsessed over gloves. Red gloves with polka dots, blue gloves with stripes, pink gloves with a touch of purple, silk gloves, wool gloves. Last year, it was tights. One of Mama's cousins won that Christmas with her bumblebee tights. Her daughter was very embarrassed.

A hand gloved in bright pink pushed a gingerbread cookie in my face. "Julia's daughter has no meat on her bones! Here, my girl!" Grandma Lorrie slurred.

"Good thing," Aunt Goldie said. "That way she can get free like her mother did." She handed Grandma Lorrie another wineglass, the Turkish silver one for which she paid seven hundred dollars plus fifty for shipping to Vermont. It was worth every dollar, she insisted, though I wondered where a man from Wyoming had gotten an authentic Ottoman relic.

Goldie was always spending money where she shouldn't, Mama used to say. Her house was full of expensive shit you wouldn't dream of: a weaverbird's nest made of copper wires, gold-plated staples, a chess set made of ice kept inside a freezer, a magnetic floating bed with a diamond lining that made her dog cry for three days. She blew most of her inheritance on stuff like that, and her ex-husband said that was why he didn't want to pay alimony.

Goldie didn't care; Goldie never cared.

When she was eight, three psychics at the county fair told her she would kill her true love, and so Goldie stopped falling in love—although most of us suspected Goldie's true love was herself. She always was weird. She didn't even want the pochette. It's also why Goldie never had those marks on her face and never needed makeup to hide them. She did love makeup though. She wore shimmery clothes and glittery shadows on her eyes, always lined blue or pink or green. The strangest thing about her, though, was that she was the only Woodring who never got along with Sean.

Sean had this ability to fill the room he was in; his shadows crept on every wall like a silent feline that our bear-sized dog loved growling at, and his voice rumbled in every stone. When Sean spoke, he overtook everyone else. Goldie hated being outshone. Sean was taller than everyone else except Goldie's brother, another reason for her hatred. He had eyes pale as the moon and wore clothes that made them even paler. Jackets over turtlenecks that covered him right up to his chin were his staple. Once little Violet caught a sneak of skin where his gloves met his sleeves and he'd gotten really upset. Every Christmas since, he made sure everything on his person was even more meticulously secured.

Jolene adored him.

"Lyla!" Goldie shouted, pulling my attention back to her. "Where are you going?"

"Bathroom."

She laughed like what I had said was very funny. Maybe the word *bathroom* would be funny to my littlest cousins.

"I hate that boy," Goldie said to the top of my head. Goldie, tall already, never forwent her heels. I didn't have to guess which boy she hated. There was only one boy she hated. She swept her hand around and picked up a Jack Daniel's as if conjuring it out of air. She was always doing this—getting the exact things she wanted the moment she wanted them, not conjuring Jack Daniel'ses out of air. Her brother said it was the effect of those poncho-wearing psychics, they'd infected her, and now spirits sat on her head, doing her bidding. Grandma Lorrie was offended and had asked other Woodrings to stop inviting Goldie for Christmases. She was always here anyway.

"Did you check the presents?"

Checking presents was my duty every Christmas, to make sure no one was sneaking cats into the house. When I asked why, Aunt Goldie only said, "You can never be too careful with those sneaky Dreadcats." We took that to mean it was time to take the bottle of alcohol from her hand. As right now.

"You stay away from that pochette, my sweet, yeah?" Goldie said casually, waving the bottle in my face with one hand and fluffing her hair with the other. "Let it stay with Jolene. I don't know why anyone has to keep it around, but we all deal with the cards fate hands us."

It wasn't the first time Goldie knew something about me before I'd ever said it aloud. That's what she did: she found things out. Although she rarely ever did anything *about* them, so I wasn't worried she was going to blab to Jolene. I just said, "It's mine."

"It claws and makes you dizzy. There's always fighting and then it won't let you watch your favorite movies and then you have to cook it dinner while it hangs out with some bitch you hated in high school."

"You've never even had it."

"Oh, I *did*. Borrowed it when your mother first got sick."

"The year you met and married—"

"But she wanted it back so I gave it back," she said loudly, cutting me off, "and I got divorced. The red feather ends make it look like it's dripping blood, have you noticed?"

I turned around and left her standing beside the armchair on which the dog was sprawled, looking like a dusty cream-colored rug.

Goldie grabbed the ends of her dress and stumbled after me. And crashed into my cousin Violet.

Violet was the sun. Her long blond hair and her big bright eyes. She was so pretty. She might grow prettier than Jolene, though with her freckles and straight hair and seductive eyes, Jolene was still the moon. Perhaps that's why she and Violet never got along, either.

Violet began crying and yelling at Goldie, and Woodrings began recounting one accident after another, of which there was no dearth in a family of fourteen. And so I slunk away to Jolene's room.

Jolene's room was at the eastern end of the house, mine at the western, so I'd never been inside before. None of the others who permanently lived here—Grandma Lorrie, Goldie's brother, my two small cousins and their parents, me—had made changes to the original white walls and neutral decor.

Jolene's room, however, was a Hallmark card. She'd painted her walls pink, put fake snow everywhere, and hung fairy lights in flowery patterns. She had only one photo of herself on the wall, unlike everyone else, who had the tapestry of our family tree hanging everywhere. I'd been hearing some of the family say lately that I looked like Jolene. If her jaw was squared like an iron block, maybe then I'd believe the resemblance.

I rummaged through her wardrobe and found two newspapers from the 1920s, posters of Ione Skye (which explained Jolene's obsession with collared white shirts and putting flowers in her hair), a book on astrology and poetry, and a spare phone that was out of battery.

In the bedside desk was a bundle of tampons intermixed with rolled-up bills. I extracted a tampon. The idea of putting something inside myself always made me shrivel up. How stupid was I? I was sixteen now. It was time to grow up. I put the tampon in my pocket to try it out later. At the back of the drawer, the reflection of fairy lights gleamed on a shiny surface seemingly floating on air. It was the buckle of the pochette, which was squished into the darkness like an afterthought.

It still looked the same as it did on the day of Mama's wake, when Jolene took it from me. Shiny, with apple-red feathers attached delicately to the surface. If it opened and I could put my things in it, I'd take it to school. My heart beat very fast then. I tugged at the buckle, but it wouldn't budge.

What should've happened was that I took the pochette and walked away triumphantly. But what did happen was Sean calling from the door, "I see Jolene's obsession with the pochette runs in the family."

The ranch house had oversized windows and doors. Even when it snowed so hard that clumps formed on the white-wood windows, you could see the pool at the back, and the wooden porch with two lanterns on either side, and the poplar that grew right in the middle of the driveway so you had to drive around it to get in. But still, the wide layout managed to smother nearby footsteps so you wouldn't notice until they were upon you.

As was the case with Sean sauntering into the room.

He wore a maroon turtleneck sweater and black jeans and brown bomber jacket. Against the solid colors, he was so pale he could be a marble statue. His watch—a Swiss brand Jolene was obsessed with—ticked loudly in the silence. Holding the pochette close to my chest, I stood and put my chin up.

I didn't fall in love with Sean then. I had always been a little in love with him, since I first saw him. He smelled nice and sharp, cocoa and whiskey, and his smile lit up every corner of the ranch. He laughed at Grandma Lorrie's drunk jokes and helped my cousin build a birdhouse to hang on the poplar, he brought tickets to most of Goldie's twin brother's big games, and he always made sure Mama's star was on the top of the Christmas tree without fail.

"You want it so much?" Sean asked.

"It should be mine."

"Okay." He smiled. "I won't tell Jolene."

Jolene's room grew decidedly smaller. Sean stopped smiling, but his eyes gleamed, like what he looked at was a morning sun. He drew out a bunch of mistletoe from behind him and held it above my head. "I won't tell her this, either."

Sean kissed me. It wasn't my first kiss. But it was perhaps my best kiss. Of course, it had to be—he was twenty-three and his lips were soft. He was so tall. I stood on tiptoe, a warmth shooting from the soles of my feet to the crown of my head. I wrapped my arms around his neck, tentatively.

To be honest, I didn't have to do much.

He knew what he was doing.

I wasn't sure what to do with my hands as his slipped under my shirt. Oh God. Kissing Sean was weird. Not bad weird, not good weird. Just weird. I'd thought about it, fantasized about it since I was twelve. But in most of my fantasies, we cozied in a warm room beside the fire and I felt good and didn't need to think so much. His hands were supposed to be softer, not so rough like he wanted to pull me apart to fit himself in. His tongue didn't writhe like a worm in my mouth, either. Ugh, he didn't seem to have time for anything but getting inside me. I said nothing. It was too late. Just let him do what he wanted.

What if I said the wrong thing, and he got totally turned off? God, it hurt. If I had an orgasm, I didn't notice. But he asked if I liked what he did. I said yes.

Before leaving for the city, Sean found me in the bathroom and kissed me again and told me I was beautiful. "You're so beautiful. Give me time and we'll figure out how to stay together forever."

Then he was gone.

Goldie asked me next day what happened. I told her I didn't find the pochette. I was crying as I did. She let it go.

On New Year's Eve, Goldie told Violet and me about my father, who left when he heard my mother was pregnant, sending an email that said: *I'm going to college, can't believe you'd choose to destroy your life like this.* Goldie was yelling when she said it. She called up Jolene and told her the same thing.

She found me on the porch again and asked what I was doing. "Nothing?" I said.

"Your father may have been a son of a bitch, but at least your mother's relationship with him wasn't anything like *this*," she said.

Goldie was so embarrassing. I had no interest in hearing anything about my father, who had never acknowledged me, or his relationship with my mother.

"Did you hear about this sophomore who was kidnapped from the parking lot? They found her dead off the highway in that village up north. Say some guy who graduated from the local high school four years ago was obsessed with her."

"It isn't assault, if that's what you're getting at," I said, heating up. If she thought I was going to let her get away with making me feel this gullible, she was wrong. "The news says she left with him."

"So that makes it okay?"

"But *he* didn't do it," I said fiercely. "They were in love."

Goldie laughed. Watching her laugh made my jaw hurt.

Violet's mom was Mama's cousin. She had a gold tooth and collected cameras, even—and especially—those that did not work. Three days after my seventeenth birthday, she was diagnosed with cancer like Mama was. Violet was fifteen. After her mom died, Violet moved in with us. Moved into my room with me, in fact, which was how I knew that she kept the gold tooth on her bedside table.

I thought that was creepy, but another cousin said it was a comfort for Violet to have a piece of her mom.

"My mom's dead and I don't do creepy things like that," I said and returned to scrolling down Sean's Instagram. He was at college with Jolene. I wished Jolene would realize how undeserving of Sean she was and leave him alone. Her stupid perfect skin and her stupid long hair and her stupid sweet grin and her stupid breasts that filled out sweetheart necklines perfectly.

I wonder if she'd already realized she didn't have the pochette anymore. How long can one person pretend?

Jolene came home at the end of winter. The ranch was emptier, which made seeking Sean out during the day dangerous. But he often found me before dawn or during afternoons when everyone was asleep or had gone to town. I desperately wished I could linger in those moments forever. I asked him about life in college now that it was finally about to end for him, but he deflected because then he would be reminded of Jolene. Every time he started to leave, I'd want to hold him tighter, to see if he would stay. But he couldn't.

After he'd leave, I'd cuddle with the pochette. The feathers were as silky as my mother's touch. The gold buckle often left marks around my neck and face. I had to hide them under makeup. It's okay to scoff, but see, I wasn't doing my makeup like my mother's generation. I had access to Instagram. My makeup was a different story. My makeup was a better story.

Goldie bought a diamond knife with rubies encrusted in the hilt. Grandma Lorrie was super mad. Goldie spat and said all Woodring women blow their money, if not on collectibles, then on makeup, so where was the problem?

She spent most of that spring beneath the poplar making rude hand gestures at the Woodrings who were coming and going. She said, "At least I don't have that demon-carrying pochette like you lot."

Goldie's brother, passing by, mimicked in a faux-British accent, "You lot."

"Demon-carrying?" I asked.

That day, I was helping my cousin nail new boards on the birdhouse. A pink-and-blue finch and a brown-and-white sparrow were renting the place out. Sean and Jolene had just left after their spring break visit. I might have had my first orgasm. It lasted for a lot longer than I'd thought it would. The sensation of my spine arching was miraculous. I tilted my head back, closing my eyes, to make sure I wouldn't forget that moment.

Goldie said, "You know we don't keep cats?"

"Yeah, 'cause of these birds," my cousin shrieked from the tree.

"So the poor innocent cats don't accidentally get mistaken for the actual demons! Go get someone else to help you," Goldie shrieked. "Lyla, you listen to me."

What Goldie said was that in the seventeenth century, in the western-most corner of the Iberian Peninsula, our ancestors Juan Valverde and his sister, Mirabelle, inherited a farm near the edge of the forest. But soon, the demons came. The Dreadcats. They were large werecats that turned into beautiful people, with red lips and large eyes. They emerged from the forest and seduced the villagers; they caused widespread diseases and crop failure. Mirabelle, ingenious as she was, knitted sweaters and hats and gloves and stockings and left them on the branches of dry trees as offerings. The Dreadcats, appeased, would take the clothes and return to the forest.

Though Juan and Mirabelle kept them away for years, a Dreadcat wearing clothes up to his neck, hiding his identity, got the better of Mirabelle. She left and came back with three werecat children. When girls started disappearing on their way to the congregation every week, Juan had no choice. He put his sister's children in a pochette made of— here Goldie's voice went really low, like she worried who might hear and get upset—feathers of birds. Then, he locked it with a gold buckle that the priest of the village had blessed.

"What happened to Mirabelle?" I asked.

"It was the seventeenth century, my sweet, what do you think happened? They called her a witch and tried to burn her."

"So she got burned at the stake?"

"Of course not. Women who are witches and women who give birth to werecats are completely different. No, no. Mirabelle turned into a bird."

My cousin dropped his hammer from the tree.

Goldie said, "The feathers for the pochette came from *somewhere*, didn't they? You take one bird, you give one back."

"This is such sexist bullshit," I said.

"Well, why don't we all let that pochette be, then?" Goldie snarled. "If you have that pochette, be sure a Dreadcat will find you. They sense their three brethren inside the pochette."

"Four-hundred-year-old werecats cramped in that locked pochette? Ugh, Aunt Goldie, that's horrible."

"You bet it is. But remember not to fall in love with a Dreadcat. Their love is not love. It's not unconditional. Well, no love is, but a Dreadcat's love is disguised poison and will leave you scarred and leached like acid."

Goldie's brother laughed for three days and said she was finally trying to come to terms with her divorce. I told her not to worry anyway. Jolene seemed to have lost the pochette in the city.

A week later, Violet asked me if she could see the famous pochette. I didn't point out that sometimes I couldn't find it, but I'd spot stray apple-red feathers next to her bed, and in turn, she promised not to tell Jolene I had the pochette. She must have liked having it a lot to be officially asking me. I made a show of taking it out from my bedside table. As she looked at it, the glint in her eyes returned. I told her she could borrow it anytime she liked.

Right after Memorial Day, I asked Violet why she was ignoring her school friends. They had messaged me a mash-up video with the words *Where is* and *Violet* overlapping and set to techno music. I didn't appreciate being used as a mediator. Violet rolled her eyes.

"They say you avoid them."

"They're being dramatic, is all."

"You never answer their texts even though you're always online. Why are you always online?"

"You're not my mom, Lyla. Stop this."

I did. Because, yes, I was being a mom. It was the one thing I hated most about Goldie, her nose poking in my business. So, I dropped it.

Later, I sent my daily good night text to Sean. He must have already gone to sleep after work. Violet switched on her table lamp and asked if I was still up. She told me she was seeing someone; her friends wouldn't understand.

"Does he love you?"

"Oh, so much, Lyla, I can't even describe it. When I'm texting him, I can't even think of anything else. And you know, it's just texts, he likes me for me, you know? Distance doesn't matter, it's just a mathematical concept and it's not even real. But talking to him is and it's the most wonderful thing in the world. Have you ever felt that way?"

I thought of Sean. "Yes, yes I have."

One day while I counted down to Christmas, only seventy-five days until I saw Sean again, Goldie asked me, "You know how sex ends?"

"What the hell?" I said over Grandma Lorrie's audible gasp.

"You never see the person again or you do and then you start a relationship. And you know how relationships end? In breakups and death."

"Someone's cheerful," muttered Goldie's brother.

Christmas that year, Goldie's brother brought home his fiancé, and Woodrings had a new person to exhibit their oratory skills in front of. The house was too loud and too lit up.

Outside, it grew cold but didn't snow. The finch and the sparrow had moved in permanently. Their fighting screeched inside the house like nails on a chalkboard. Jolene sat in Sean's lap. When I passed the cake around, I made sure to give him a bigger piece. He squirmed under Jolene as he took the cake from me. I wanted to tell him it was going to be okay. I was leaving for college in a year now, so he wouldn't have to suffer Jolene for much longer.

Violet wore a skimpy dress that showed off her long legs and the straps of a shocking red bra.

Grandma Lorrie got mad. After a lot of yelling and tears, Violet retired to bed early.

Grandma Lorrie shouted after her, blaming the lack of a mother for Violet's lack of respect for Christmas. Our great-aunt, Grandma Lorrie's sister, pointed at me from the other side of the room and said my lack of a mother hadn't turned me into a prostitute.

Jolene started yelling at everyone about calling girls names. Goldie joined her. She smacked at her brother and then everyone was fighting everyone, splattering cake and eggnog and chocolate on the walls, and the dog, upset, whined loudly from a corner.

It began snowing, clumps sticking along the windowsills. I couldn't leave, because Grandma Lorrie and her sister had me cornered and kept pointing at me.

Sean, bless him, decided to go check up on Violet. It was good to have a boy who cared about your family, too.

Sean visited for a week after summer that year, without Jolene. He said he was in town for work. I had deferred leaving for college this year, but it turned out, I rarely saw him. But I wouldn't want to distract him. He left early in the morning and came back late at night, exhausted. Since Violet had her ballet classes in the morning, Sean drove her every day. She didn't want to ask her friends for any favors. Sean was family, of course, and he told her stupid jokes and made sure she knew she could talk to him.

Violet talking to someone apart from that boy she was in love with was a good thing. Plus it was her sixteenth birthday that week; she shouldn't be alone. It didn't matter if Sean's only free time was spent driving Violet around.

It didn't.

Goldie was the only one upset about Sean taking care of Violet. She demanded to know how I ever let Violet alone with *that man*. Sean is family, I told her in a shaky voice. Jolene called then, crying, and said she and Sean were fighting. I was sitting next to Goldie, but I heard Jolene clearly, that's how loudly she was crying on the phone. It made me feel slightly better.

Goldie only said, "If he's making you cry like this, what does that tell you?"

On the next Christmas, while all Woodrings and would-be Woodrings collected around the tree, Jolene announced her engagement to Sean. A white-gold band with a tiny diamond sat on her slim finger. Goldie laughed so much that her brother and his fiancé escorted her out. She trailed her champagne all the way out to the poplar.

It wasn't snowing yet.

I tightened my scarf until my vision grew red, matching my eyeshadow (blood moon) and blush (cheeky rose), which was important to hide the marks on my face from the pochette's buckle. I'd tried to get the pochette to unlock, but all I ended up with were these cuts.

"Isn't it terrible to be forced with someone you don't love?" Violet was slurring faintly.

I agreed and put my arm around her waist to hold her up. Good for her that our great-aunt had died, so no one was there to back up Grandma Lorrie's muttering about Violet's drunken state.

"Sean doesn't love her."

I didn't know what to say.

"Can you keep a secret, Ly*lie*?" she said, her eyes sparkling like Goldie's laughter in my head. "I keep your secret in a pochette, don't I?"

The secret was that Sean didn't love Jolene. That didn't count because I knew it. The secret was that Sean had agreed to get engaged to Jolene so he could stay close to Violet. He said he couldn't break up with Jolene because you know how Jolene is?

"He loves me and it's wonderful. Have you ever felt that way?" Violet asked me.

"You're so drunk, Violet," I said, fighting to keep my voice from trembling.

I waited until she was singing carols under the tree and everyone else was arguing over the date of the wedding. Then I took the pochette from Violet's side of the room, like we'd been back-and-forthing over the past year.

"I've been looking for you," Sean called from the door. "It feels like I haven't seen you in forever." He always dressed in absolutes that hid him, but tonight, he seemed so strange. Outside, lights blinked on and off. Sean came closer and put his arms around me and kissed me. "You look beautiful tonight."

He kissed me again and said something about trying to fix things but they kept spiraling out of control, and you know how Jolene is? I said I understood. What I finally understood was that no one was coming to protect me or Violet.

Sean lifted my shirt over my head and pulled me close, grazing his teeth and tongue down my neck while I stood steady, reaching for the pochette behind me.

Violet and I had tried opening it many times. I'd seen some of my aunts and older cousins gather on Sunday mornings to discuss various kinds of purses and zippers and bolts and locks. They'd tried, too, I knew. All we were left with were wounds. The pochette never opened because everyone tried too hard: they held it level or upright, clutching it tight, trying to twist the buckle forcefully, but that pinched the opening taut, not allowing the occupants to travel upward and push the buckle from the other side, too.

But now when I held the pochette above my head, angled so it was upside down, twisting the buckle came as easily as lying to my family. The small click resounded in the room. A faint growl, like a cat, came out of the pochette. Sean stopped. "What are you doing?"

What happened then was that I made sure I didn't open the pochette all the way to let the Dreadcats escape. They tried, of course, but the mouth of the pochette was too small for all three of them, and they kept slipping back in.

Sean pushed me, and in his haste to disentangle himself, his head came too close to the pochette. One of the Dreadcats caught at his collar and dragged him in. He screamed the entire way through. I buckled the pochette shut the second Sean's foot was inside. The pochette thumped onto the floor.

It must be terribly crowded in there now.

I sat beside the open windows until dawn, winter digging its fangs into my exposed skin, and wondered how I'd explain to anyone where Sean was. Then I wondered if anyone would even ask. Goldie might. She would drunkenly tell someone to make sure the carpet isn't stained. Then turn everything into a story and narrate it to the next person she finds. I started to cry. Mama had promised they would look after me.

I put both my palms over my shoulders and patted my own back. "Everything will be okay now. I'm going to take care of you," I murmured to myself, rocking like I was a child.

I didn't feel silly doing it.

When the sky became lighter, I picked up the pochette and the scarf I was wearing and slipped out the window. I wrapped the scarf around the stupid apple-colored pochette and buried it in the corner of the yard.

I looked up at the ranch. With the Woodrings all asleep, and the sun coming up behind in the mountains, it felt at peace. The wraparound porch was dotted with wreaths and unlit lanterns, and potted plants on the steps buried beneath snow. The finch from the birdhouse flew down to where I'd buried the pochette and then hopped to me.

"Mirabelle," I said, "your children and their friends are a nuisance."

It isn't difficult to get on an Amtrak once you've chosen the irreversible. So that's what I did. Over the next few days, the birds brought me news of everything that happened at the ranch after I left.

The Woodrings put up posters and called the police, and Jolene contacted Sean's family. Turned out, they weren't his family and he'd hired people off shady subreddits to pose as his family when Jolene wanted to meet them. "A con artist," Goldie said, staring at the poplar.

I tried not to think of what my family must assume. That I ran away with Sean. Because I was stupid and naive. That, by now, he must have killed me.

Violet cried for days and only Grandma Lorrie had the time to sit with her and pat her on the head.

I tried not to think of Violet. How I was abandoning her. But I took comfort in knowing that she wouldn't need to do what I did.

Goldie bought a diamond-encrusted birdhouse, but your cousin told her he saw the finch and the sparrow fly into the sun.

They haven't come back since.

I told the birds not to go back anymore. They had better places to fly to.

AUTHOR'S NOTE

The first version of this story wasn't hopeful. It was bleak, almost sad.

Not until I was asked why did it occur to me that everything I've ever written features a girl and her fight against the world. She's armed with the jagged edges of her heart, only to settle for an unresolved ending. Left in a limbo, upset and hurt, having recognized that the world has let her down. The story doesn't end well. It ends with anger and frustration and an anxious uncertainty.

The sharp, horrible endings make sense of the world; they validate the confusion some of us have at the world's treatment of us. Though reading those stories doesn't come easily to me, writing them has always been cathartic. But as this story evolved to its final version, I was reminded that we're allowed to change our minds. About what we want, what we need, and what we think we deserve.

Writing is real magic in this way. It does something: it changes us.

THE TWIST IN *ESCAPE*

by Nova Ren Suma

I'M THE KIND OF READER WHO ACHES FOR A SURPRISE, ESPECIALLY ONE THAT comes with a sudden twist. What I admire most is a twist I didn't see coming and yet at the same time am convinced *had* to happen, as if the story couldn't have gone another way. So how does a story get me gasping in delighted shock?

There could be a change in circumstance. In character. Perhaps in the very fabric of reality... for example, a glossy, apple-red pochette that's been handed down to the women in the family, one that nips a cheek sometimes and ends up saving the day... as you'll find in ESCAPE.

The twist is seeded scene by scene, line by line, detail by perfect detail. "The red feather ends make it look like it's dripping blood, have you noticed?" Goldie says of the pochette, though Goldie tells a lot of stories, doesn't she? She says things that strain credibility, but still she slips an idea into our heads early on—the biting, the mention of blood—so when the pochette opens its jaws at the end of the story and takes what's offered, we can't say we weren't warned.

The twist here is one we may have suspected, and at the same time, for those of us silent-screaming to get Sean out of that house, an electric shock. It's Lyla admitting she's been wronged—admitting it to us, and to herself. "The small click resounded in the room. A faint growl, like a cat, came out of the pochette." All that's been kept secret is acknowledged in a snap. Oh yes, now we know. We know for sure.

This kind of twist can be such a delicious experience for a reader—if woven in from the first page, with sidelong looks and whispers and coded exchanges, built from the foundation of every secret that cannot be told.

At the end of this story, Lyla has "chosen the irreversible" and we have witnessed her do it. This is a twist that cannot be taken back. It shocks but also speaks to everything that came before. It gives the story teeth.

PAN DULCE

Flor Salcedo

> Flor Salcedo's PAN DULCE is a glimpse into the split-screen reality that is adolescent life in America. The back and forth across the border from El Paso, Texas, to Juárez, Mexico, is the same duality knocking around in young Rosa's mind—her conscience serving as border patrol—as she navigates her friendships, boys, and all the recklessness that comes along with being a teenager, coupled with the harsh reality of what's at stake. Salcedo wove a complex story that captivated me with its textured language, both narratively and culturally, and left me wanting more. Oh, and it left me wanting . . . pan dulce. Seriously.
>
> —JASON REYNOLDS, AUTHOR OF *LOOK BOTH WAYS*

SOMETHING BAD IS GOING TO HAPPEN TO YOU SOMEDAY.

Mom's words burrow into my consciousness. I've been trying to shake them off since yesterday, and how the line in between her eyebrows deepened as she spoke. But I've been trying to shake off a lot lately. In a matter of a few high school years, I've realized people are fake. Friends talk behind my back; my parents—and even my friends' parents—are suddenly *not* who I thought they were. It's like everyone is lying to themselves, or each other.

Tonight, I'm just going across the border for a night of dancing. It's no big deal, even if Mom thinks otherwise.

During my hasty getaway, I almost take a dive on my front porch stairs. I manage to catch myself with one arm like a stealth ninja. I double over, holding in a gurgle of laughter so Mom doesn't catch me making my escape. That was close. Scuffed knees are *so* not cute.

A light layer of sweat coats my arms by the time I've trekked the hill to Aida's house at the foot of the Franklin Mountains, the sierra around it splattered with a symphony of dry shrubs. The party crew of three is hanging out in the front yard. Aida sits on her porch painting her nails, blowing on them, and then holding them up to the sun. Zulema sits in the passenger seat of Aida's brown Nissan Sentra with the door open, her legs partially out of the car, looking into the visor's mirror while applying makeup. Belen stands between them, watching over the beauty production with one hand on her waist and hips cocked to one side. My gears get cranking again, my thoughts moving to the possibilities of the night.

I was hoping it'd only be me and Aida, but she says she doesn't know her way across the border well, and Zulema is the one with the friends from Mexico, the so-called hotties we're meeting up with in Ciudad Juárez, the city just a hop over a bridge from El Paso, Texas. Zulema is unquestionably *not* my friend. The other two might or might not be. They might be playing the game of fakes, too, or we might be playing it with each other.

Aida is the first to notice me. She eyes me up and down but smiles. "Look at you, Rosa," she whoops. "Sexxxy." She follows it with, "Biatch, you better not take any guys I like away from me tonight."

Zulema pauses applying eyeliner to her left eyelid to look up. "Ugh," she says loudly and shoots me a blunt look. I ignore it and instead smile back at Aida.

I knew Aida'd have something to say about me wearing my jean mini-skirt and cutoff top. She's sporting white dressy shorts that make her dark legs really pop. Aida's dark, golden complexion has always been so pretty to me. She looks like her mother, who still looks like she could be in her twenties and the boys at school say is hot. But despite all her beauty, Aida's poor mom has to pretend her husband isn't having an affair at work. Aida thinks her mom tolerates it for Aida's sake, to avoid a divorce. Faking the marriage now, I suppose. Sad.

My stomach grumbles. I was so darn ready to get to the fun and dancing—and to avoid Mom—I skipped dinner.

"Sorry I'm late," I say. "Had to wait for Mom to go watch her novela in her room. She's been lecturing about not crossing the border." I peer behind Aida at her house.

"Dad's not home yet," Aida says as if reading my mind. "And Mom don't care," she says matter-of-factly.

"See! I don't know why all the fuss," I harp.

All teens go across to party. Yesterday, Mom also tried to scare me with doom talk about feminicidio after she overheard me on the phone making plans to go across the border. "You think you know everything," she said in a quiet, spooky way. I'm not a smart aleck, I don't think I know it *all*. But I do know about feminicidio. A few years ago, a bunch of women disappeared in Mexico and turned up raped, beaten, and dead. But it's 1998 now. Besides, they go after the local women because they know their routes and habits and then leave their bodies out in the desert. I know that's really horrible stuff, but just because Mom never did anything fun when she was young doesn't mean the world is out to get me because I do. Just because she found her eerie religion and lives in a phony reality doesn't mean I shouldn't get to be a normal teen.

Zulema's tricolor hair from faded color treatments blows against the headrest, the tips bleach blond. She's the lightest of us because her dad's Anglo and her mom's a light-skinned Chicana. Zulema probably made Aida turn the car on and leave it running to blast the air conditioner at full power so her three layers of makeup don't melt off. It's technically night already—eight p.m.—but in the El Paso summer, it's still 95 degrees and the sun is brightly lit over our desert. It's not called the Sun City for nothing.

Zulema shifts her face to sweet-devil after her initial mad-dog stare. "Just kidding, flaca." I despise it when she calls me skinny and she knows it. She continues in a sneering tone, "You look all right—never as good as me, though. I don't have sticks for legs." She pauses for one beat. "You finish all your homework before Mommy gets mad?"

I've hardly ever had a conversation with Zulema, so I'm still not sure why she hates my guts. I wish she hadn't found out I'm into school. I breathe in and bite my tongue, then turn to Belen.

Belen shifts her weight to the other hip. Her skin-tight cloth pants leave nothing to the imagination. I flick my head her way. "Wasup?"

Belen makes snapping, slurping sounds as she chews her gum. "'Sup," she replies and gives me her signature glittery-eye-shadow wink.

I definitely put Belen in the Peculiar Department. She was with Aida last time I saw them, at a classmate's keg party. My drunk boyfriend was being a jerk, so I broke things off, and Belen saw the whole thing. "Heh heh," she snickered, yelling "¡Sás!" as she put a palm in front of her and slammed her other palm into it. "You tell him, girl."

Aida was refilling at the keg, stumbling and slurring. "Hellllo there, my fellow benchwarmer—I mean teammate."

Aside from being in the same art class, the main thing Aida and I have in common is that we both suck at basketball. Not many tried out, so coach got stuck with us. I'm usually set up as point guard or shooting guard since I'm five foot nothing, but I can't dribble or catch for shit. I'm good at three-pointers, though. Aida dribbles her way out of anything, but for some reason can't make a free throw to save her life.

I ended up laughing the night away at Aida's antics and overly dramatic reactions to everything. Meanwhile, Belen, less drunk, came and went, announcing odd scraps of information no one cared about. Like, "Dudes, the neighbors have some kind of giant rodent looking out the window."

Zulema arrived an hour later and immediately cut me with her stare. "Who's this?" But drunk Aida walked away. All night I continued running into the three girls—kept laughing it up with Aida and Belen, and getting dissed by Zulema.

Aida and her smart-mouthed cronies together are something else, but I like Aida and I haven't gone out in a while.

Aida rummages through her purse and whips out her fake ID. "Ha! I just turned eighteen so I don't need this shit in Juárez no more." She chucks it out with a satisfied grin. "This is it, girls, you all ready?" she hollers and wiggles her shoulders. "We're gonna party it up with older guys at the disco," which she pronounces "theesco." Aida is the only person I've heard call the nightclub such an old-fashioned word—disco, short for discoteca. I could never figure out if Aida is Mexican American like me. She's about three shades darker than me, with superbly full eyebrows and large eyes. We pronounce her name in English, though, so who knows. Not that it matters what anyone is, but sometimes I'm just curious. Of course, I'd never ask her about any of this. That'd be weird.

Aida prompts a flurry of checking for fake IDs from the rest of us since we're seventeen and do need fake IDs to get into the clubs and drink in Juárez. Inside the Sentra, Zulema slips her hand into her bra, pulls out her fake out-of-state ID, and quickly bra-pockets it again. She adjusts herself, pushing up her big boobs so they show even more over the neckline of her low-cut top, and then continues messing with her eyeliner in the mirror. Even Belen, who pretends to be too cool for worrying, slips her hand into her back pocket for a quick check. The bouncers rarely check our IDs, but if they've gotten raided recently, they're going to be uptight about it.

"Woo-hoo," Aida snickers at Zulema. "Mirá, mirá. Look who's getting all ready to roll in the sack with Mauro."

"Hmph." Zulema shrugs. "It's not like we haven't done it before."

Aida's and Belen's eyes light up. I suppose they envy Zulema for sleeping with a nineteen-year-old. I don't really care, especially since the guys are fresas, preppy kids from rich Mexican families. The word *fresa* literally means "strawberry," though, and I never understood why people call them that. These guys know English because they learn it in fancy schmancy schools in Mexico, but I know they won't really speak it around us even though their English can be better than that of some native El Pasoans. I don't hate fresas or anything, but some of them annoy the heck out of me when they flash their wealth around.

Aida, the only one of us with a car, slides into the driver's seat. Zulema immediately swings her legs inside the car and slams the door shut. Belen and I file into the back like kids about to be taken to the amusement park. On my seat is a bigger-than-any-size-I've-had-at-my-house rectangular Tupperware container with a red lid. I put it on my lap, wondering why she has this in her car.

"Be careful with my Tupperware," Aida snaps as the wheels crunch the dirt at the end of her driveway.

We drive by hordes of kids running around front yards and across streets, yelping out jolly laughter, falling over, and blasting each other with garden hoses or water balloons. It's El Día de San Juan! Of course, I forgot that was today. Aida's radio is playing rancheritas, Mexican folk music. "Can we change the station, Aida?" I ask.

"Yeah. Look for something fun for us, Rosa." Aida pops her head back and forth as if she's already listening to the awesome dance music I have yet to find. I lean forward from the back, sticking my head in between the two front seats, and reach for the dial.

I have just touched the dial when, out of nowhere, Zulema cusses loudly right next to my ear, making me jump. "Hey, pendeja! Where are you going, Aida? You're driving to the pay bridge. We're not taking that one, remember? It's faster to Alejandro's house if we take the free bridge."

Aida makes a know-it-all face. "Well, if either of you was listening to me when I three-way called your asses last night, you would know I have to stop for some pan dulce from Bowie Bakery for my grandma first." She's talking about the three of them. I wasn't a part of last night's party line, but I'm new to their clique, so it's no biggie that I wasn't in the know.

Our group makes a collective *mmm* sound. No one can object to pit stops for the delicious sweet bread from the most famous bakery in El Paso, especially if she's taking it to her dear abuela.

In my mind, I give Aida a point. So I still don't know if she really wants me as a friend, but she goes out of her way for her grandma. That puts her in the Considerate Department.

"Yo, is your dad at your grandma's? Don't want to have any run-ins with the law," Belen proclaims with a raised, over-plucked, and penciled-in eyebrow.

"Ay, ay, Belen. You're so ghetto," Aida shoots back. "Stop acting like you're some kind of gangster. We all know the only thing you've done is gotten kicked out of school for absenteeism."

Aida and Zulema burst into laughter, but I only chuckle slightly, because Belen's right next to me.

"Pfft, whatevs." Belen crosses her arms and leans back, pouting her heavily lipsticked, red lips.

At Bowie Bakery, Aida jumps out of the car with the huge container and hands it to the lady behind the counter to fill with pan dulce. Even though Aida's the only one buying, we all go in and stand by the glass displays to gawk at the pastries, mouths watering as an infusion of smells fill the air—cinnamon, powdered sugar, freshly baked bread, and . . . fulfillment. When we walk back to the car, Aida plops the plastic bin on top of her trunk and opens it. "Surprise, bitches. You all get to pick one!"

Aida can be dramatic sometimes, but she instantly racks up major points in the Cool Department.

Belen immediately reaches for a roll with a reddish filling oozing out and sprinkled with coconut shreds. Aida slaps her hand. "Oh, not that one, that's my grandma's favorite." Belen quickly moves on to a second choice. Zulema picks out one of the smallest items, a cinnamon-and-sugar-sprinkled bizcocho cookie. I pick out a marranito—ginger and molasses hard bread with a glossy glaze, shaped like a pig. Aida grabs a fluffy concha—a conch shell–shaped bread covered in soft cookie crumb topping—and hands it to Zulema to hold for her.

"Don't you manhandle my concha, Zulema," Aida warns as she seals the Tupperware, opens the trunk, and puts the container of sweets inside. Zulema holds the concha delicately with two fingers in one hand as she bites into her bizcocho from the other hand. The extra-soft cookie sprinkles onto her blouse.

Aida's eyes bug out. "You all are gonna clean up your crumbs if you get 'em in my car. My dad's moto busted yesterday, and he's already borrowed my car once. Don't wanna hear him give me crap about how badly I take care of the car he's still paying off."

When we arrive at Aida's grandma's place, she zips into the house with the Tupperware and zips back out with it still half-full of pan dulce.

Ten minutes later, we approach the bridge, beaming eagerly as the USA flag waves goodbye to all of us border crossers while the eagle on the Mexican flag welcomes us.

It's finally dark. The sun is well hidden below the horizon by now, and I'm hoping it won't take forever for the temperature to drop. Everyone on the streets or in their cars is preoccupied with their lives—parents crossing the street while holding their kids' hands, people chatting, driving, trying to get home. It's just another normal night, a nice time to be out. We turn down a narrow street and I hold on for my life as cars whiz by, inches from the side mirror. Exhaust fumes overwhelm the air. I roll up the window, but roll it back down minutes later when we pass a taquería so that the porky smell of carnitas can drift in. Belen and I ogle the people sitting on the sidewalk tables, laughing and munching on their tacos like they're the best thing ever. I bet they are.

After about thirty minutes of pothole hell on some of the roughest streets in Juárez, we finally drive into a neighborhood with perfectly smooth streets. It has large white adobe houses and professionally manicured lawns for as far as I can see.

"Man, these guys live far," I say.

"I don't see your imaginary car taking us elsewhere, Rosa," Aida says, but flashes me a giant smile in the rearview mirror.

"I just said they live far," I defend myself.

Finally, we pull in front of a house with an arched front door almost as wide as three of my front door put together. Zulema does one more check in the mirror before practically falling out of the car. Three guys saunter out of the house, and Zulema tosses herself into the arms of one of them, like in a movie.

"Pshht," Belen says while smirking, and Aida giggles as they follow Zulema out of the car.

"I thought we were going straight to the club," I whisper out the window to Aida and Belen.

"Not yet," Aida says.

I wait there, hoping the guys will hop into their car and follow us to the club. After they all continue chatting long enough—and I feel stupid to still be sitting in the car like some ginormous, impatient jerk—I take a deep breath and go out to meet these "wonders" the girls gloated about on the drive here.

The boys' eyes immediately laser in on my legs. I feel a pang of self-consciousness but push it away and keep walking up like I didn't even notice. I like wearing miniskirts and going out and feeling sexy. They can ogle all they want so long as they keep their hands to themselves.

But I'm not prepared for the intense, sleepy-seductive eyes that Mauro, the guy Zulema is slobbering over (almost literally), directs my way. He keeps flicking his head to move his shoulder-length, brown hair out of his face. It's captivating. So much so that I can make myself overlook the tight jeans, polo shirt, and overly cologned air around him. The girls jibber jabber like a flock of glamorous birds—vogue outfits, lips shining, skin glistening, bangles catching the moonlight. They go on about all the fun we're going to have and all the booze were going to drink. The other two fresa boys, Beto and Alejandro, look smug, but

Mauro's eyes flit about aimlessly, only occasionally stopping for a few seconds on me.

I fiddle with the collar of my blouse. Mom's warnings slide back into my mind. Could these guys be the "bad" that could happen to me? My stomach knots up. I can't even have fun comfortably anymore. Thanks, Mom.

"Hey, muchachos, I got some pan dulce," Aida announces louder than necessary.

Alejandro perks up. "Haber, give it here."

Aida obliges. The boys dig their hands into the popped-open trunk.

While the boys are busy munching on the bread, Aida pulls me aside ever so obviously and semi-whispers, "So what do you think, girl? You want Beto? Cuz I got me Alejandro. If you do, I'll tell Belen you called dibs on Beto. Otherwise, you're gonna have to wait to see if there are any cuties at the disco."

I want to ask Aida if she's sure it's safe to be with these guys, but I don't want to be such a square. Instead I smile and say, "And mess up the A + A and B + B couples action?"

Aida gets a blank look on her face.

"You know, the first letters of your names."

Her mouth drops open. "Holy crap, I hadn't even caught that," she says, chuckling. "I sometimes forget you're like a total nerd at school, not just a wannabe ballplayer like me."

I love Aida's expression right now. She's giddy and awestruck over the coincidence I caught. I relish this little back and forth we're having. I'm hanging out, talking smack, and even being clever. I like being smart, but I don't really want everyone knowing about it so much. People sometimes treat you differently once they realize you have any brains. Not Aida, though.

I give her a playful smirk and turn slightly to observe Mauro standing stiff while Zulema holds on to him, arms around his neck and rubbing her boobs all over his chest. He catches my eye and stares. Zulema grabs his chin and turns it back to her.

Aida shakes her head. "Oh, I see what's up. No. Way. Bitch. Zulema would kill you. She's been obsessed with Mauro for like a year now!"

"What, are they like boyfriend-girlfriend?" I ask.

"Nah. Though Zulema likes to pretend so. They're just each other's booty call." Aida twiddles a strand of black, wavy hair in her finger. "Though Mauro's not calling so much no more. Well . . . I guess if you can get him away from her . . ."

Zulema's a big jerk to me, and he's clearly not that interested anymore. In that instant, it turns into a challenge. This guy's got me good with me thinking of challenges and whatnot. And then there's him being a fresa. There's a first for everything, right?

Alejandro invites us inside his freaking mansion and the girls happily follow. I tug at my necklace and lag behind.

Inside, the boys break out the beer and music. The rowdiness begins and I try to relax but keep my eye on the boys and take small sips of my beer. Soon my shoulders start loosening. There's no way these guys could be killers, I tell myself. Beto can't even open a beer bottle, for goodness' sake. My body sinks a little more into the velvet chair.

They joke and chat while I sit quiet in my little corner, pathetic as hell. Maybe it wouldn't be so bad if I disappeared. I mean, who am I trying to fool? I'm probably the biggest fake of all, trying too hard to make friends. If I can't dance, I might as well get back to my homework and college planning. But if I just left this world, my parents wouldn't have to worry about how much of a black sheep I am, how much energy they have to spend trying to raise a difficult girl with a strong head and a mouth to match. I shake when I realize how morbid my thoughts have turned.

Zulema's whining tone snaps me back. "Why are you taking so long, Mauro?"

"Relájate, aquí estoy." Relax, I'm here. There's exasperation in his voice.

And it goes on all night, Zulema talking to Mauro in English and him answering in Spanish, even though Zulema speaks Spanish just fine.

Belen pokes fun at Beto in a flirtatious, Belen type of way. Beto's goofy grin says he's eating it up. I'm becoming more convinced these guys just want to get lucky. Mauro is probably sick of Zulema and only agreed to let her keep coming around so he could help his boys out.

I'm itching to escape to the dance floor. To let the bass travel from the floor, through my shoes, into my bones. To pulse with the vibrations . . . *oohm, tss, oohm, tss, oohm* . . .

Aida walks to the restroom and I jump up from the couch and conveniently have to go, too.

I whisper to her while we wait in the hallway for Belen to come out of the restroom. "Aida, it's getting late. We'll be at the club for less than two hours before we have to leave."

Aida has been having a little too much fun curling up to Alejandro, who's been flashing a proud, wide smile all night. But I know Aida loves to dance.

A techno-pop cumbia starts playing on the radio, and Aida and I simultaneously gawk at each other. Aida takes to head popping and taps her foot. My hips begin to sway, and my hair tickles my waist. Soon we're full-on dancing and snorting out laughter in the hallway. Beto and Alejandro, on their way back from the kitchen, stop to catcall and banter. I catch Mauro craning his neck from his spot on the couch.

When Aida comes out of the restroom, she marches to the living room. "All right, guys, let's get going to the disco," she yells over the group. "Vámonos a bailar," she singsongs.

The group replies with a collective *Let's just hang out here* in both English and Spanish.

Aida shrugs and gives me an *I tried* look. My spirits tank.

An old grandfather clock in Alejandro's living room announces it's one a.m. Zulema, who drank the most, is fighting to keep her eyes open. She falls asleep, leaning on Mauro. He inches his way from underneath her, replaces himself with a pillow, and leaves her lying on the couch. His eyes meet mine. He lifts his eyebrows and nods toward outside.

Mauro walks out and I follow. Aida, now in Alejandro's arms, giggles when we walk past her.

Outside, we lean against Aida's car.

"Que bonito cabello," Mauro says in a dreamy voice. What beautiful hair. "Y largo." And long.

"Y el tuyo," I reply. And yours.

What? So we notice each other's hair. It's a hair-person thing.

"Me gustan las chaparritas," he says.

I laugh because I have no reply to his thing for short girls.

He switches to English. "Rosa. Pretty name."

All right, dude, stop the compliments while you're ahead.

He slides closer and his soft-looking lips are irresistible. I lean in. But just as he moves in, there's movement to the right of us. Zulema has woken up and she's stomping our way. I brace myself for whatever garbage is going to spew from that mouth of hers, because it'd be hard to miss the compromising position Mauro and I are in. Instead, my mouth drops when she digs her fingers into his arm. "I was looking for you," she growls, dragging him away.

Mauro looks torn but lets himself be dragged away.

I'm left alone in the ultraquiet neighborhood. What am I doing out here? Trying to get with a jerk when I really just came to have a night out with the girls, that's what. The magic bubble pops in my face—the one that must've been surrounding the guy. No amount of gorgeous hair, lips, or eyes is going to take that pitiful scene out of my mind. If I'm a big faker, this guy here says *move over.*

Heat builds up on my neck and rushes to my face, some kind of shame for being so gullible, I guess. It feels almost like whenever I see that look in Mom's eyes. She truly believes that I'm lost to this world, convinced her newfound faith can save her from whatever pain and suffering she's ever gone through. I try not to be hard on my mom. It's so unfair, though. Why does she have to fall into something that mandates blind obedience, even when it's clearly not right? Why does she have to start morphing into the exact opposite of who I feel I am?

I suddenly feel really tired. I'd rather be home now. We're obviously not going to the club anymore.

Aida comes out of the house with wide eyes and a question-mark face. "What happened?" she asks. "Zulema's in there yelling her head off at Mauro."

I shrug. "She came and dragged him away."

"Oh, snap!" Aida shakes her head. "He doesn't even want her anymore. How embarrassing. Que vergüenza for her."

To me it's Mauro who needs to stop being so wussy about telling this obsessed girl the truth. Gosh, she *is* totally obsessed. And, as Aida mentioned, she *does* look so bad doing it. Meanwhile, Mauro was out here all sneaky trying to get with me. My stomach knots again. I feel kind of bad for Zulema now. "I'm done, Aida. Ya vámonos." Let's go.

"Okay, okay." Aida shakes her hands in front of her. "I'll make the girls leave."

I pop open the trunk to grab another pan dulce while Aida goes back into the house.

"Let's go, bitches!" I hear her shouting inside, using her signature musical tone. It's followed by boos and something unintelligible from Zulema.

There's only one lamppost out here so I pull out the Tupperware from the trunk to get a better view of what's left. In the moonlight, something gleams inside the trunk, something nestled inside the hollow of a tire that the container was resting on. I move my fingertips in to touch the tip that juts out and feel cool metal. My arm jerks back and a strange half squeal, half squawk escapes me. Like a lurking crocodile, there lies a rifle—a gun inside of Aida's trunk.

A chill races over my body in spite of the heat. I take a step back and look around me. *Does Aida know?*

The realization hits me like I've been slapped. My parents were talking about this last month as the news ran on their usual Spanish network. The newscaster on Univision spoke about people in trouble for carrying a gun into Mexico. I only remember bits of their conversations, something about a new law or stricter laws, not sure. But there was jail time involved.

Mom's voice booms in my head. "It's getting more dangerous across the border," she'd said, worry creasing a storm on her face. And then there was yesterday's sermon about something bad happening to me if I kept acting like a wild child.

"Crap," I mutter and my surroundings start to spin. I could be at home asleep. I could be finishing up an extra-credit assignment and then waking up to the smell of the chorizo and eggs Mom makes on Sunday mornings. I think of my cat, who's probably curled up on my bed, waiting for me at home right now. Mom let me keep her when she showed up at our door, begging for food. Mom has always let me keep animals and bought me plenty when I asked. Even back when we were so poor that we had to get help from the government to have food to eat. I bet every bag of food for my many cats, guinea pigs, lizards, hamsters, hermit crabs, fish, turtles, and rabbits—even though she bought the cheapest kind—was hard for her to come by.

Instead of snuggling with my cat tonight, I might end up in jail. *Great. Just great.*

I hold on to the car while the world comes back to focus. Aida walks out with Belen. Zulema is behind them, pulling Mauro along. I open my mouth to tell them about the gun, but then stop, not sure if Aida will freak if she isn't aware of it. I push the rifle down, deeper into the tire center, and slam the trunk with shaky hands, then hop into the back seat.

We wait in the car while Zulema continues showering Mauro with kisses outside. I'm not even annoyed anymore. That smooth metal is the only thing on my mind. My heart palpitates in my chest.

Zulema slurs. "Promise you'll call."

"Sí, mujer, yo te llamo," Mauro replies with stiff lips. Yes, woman, I'll call you. He nudges Zulema inside the car.

"Adiós, chicos," Aida says, gliding her hand back and forth theatrically as we drive off.

"Can't believe you made us leave so early, Aida." Zulema's like a lethargic, fire-breathing dragon. If it were winter, the window that she's mean-staring out of would be fogged up. "Next weekend, we're coming back and getting here earlier," she proclaims.

Aida rolls her eyes. "We can't all get home past three a.m. like you."

As we get closer to the border, we go through streets so dark they feel like tunnels, weak little lampposts flickering at their ends. I almost expect el Cucuy to jump out of a corner and get us and never let me get back to my friendless but safe existence back home.

"Man, it's scary on these streets," I whisper.

Belen punches my shoulder semi-playfully. "Stop scaring me and shit."

Nearing the bridge, the street vendors push their two-wheeled carts mighty close to the cars.

"Call one of them over so I can buy some Chiclets," Zulema says.

"No way. You buy from one and we'll be mobbed by the rest," Aida hisses.

Belen the gum expert jumps in. "Why you even like that gum? That shit's nasty. It gets rock hard after like three chews."

"Yeah, but those three chews are the bomb," Zulema answers.

Secretly, I like Chiclets, too. I even like how the gum becomes hard for some reason. I want to buy some, but, by the way Aida's hunching over the steering wheel and revving it up anytime a vendor gets near us, I dare not ask. The vendors continue flashing their boxes of gum, salted pumpkin seeds, chili-powder-sprinkled fruit, and more, right up to the windows. My puppy eyes follow their tasty treats as we roll past.

With all the grumpy Zulema, scary streets, and vendor drama, I almost forget about the gun. A prickle runs through my spine as I imagine it there, simmering in the darkness of the trunk.

"Aida, would your dad freak if he had to come get you in Juárez?" I ask.

Aida grimaces. "What? That came out of nowhere. What are you talking about?"

"I mean, I was just wondering if he's all strict cuz he's a cop and all."

Aida eyes flicker. "Well, duh. Yeah, he'd whoop my behind."

I go silent. Maybe I messed up majorly by not saying something about the weapon back at Alejandro's house. I had panicked. But the car pulls up to the bridge and it's too late.

My heart races out of control as Aida drops coins into the pay booth. The guard lifts the crossing gate, she drives the car onto the bridge, and the eternal wait begins, prolonging my desperation. I just want us to be on the other side now and safe. Inch by inch, the line of cars moves toward the citizenship-checking station.

Zulema tries sleeping, but Aida shoves bottled water onto Zulema's lap. "Drink this. I ain't carrying your ass to your door. You better be able to walk."

Ahead of us, cars are already shuffling, trying to move into the quickest lane. I peer at the dashboard. The car's fuel gauge is dangerously low. A rush of sweat drenches my armpits.

Two cars before it's our turn, Aida starts straightening up. She glares at Zulema. "Don't even open your lips. And try not to have drunk eyes."

Zulema takes another sip of the water and straightens up as well. We know intoxicated underage teens get detained sometimes, and their parents are called before they're allowed entrance into the US. The immigration agents at the bridge let a lot slide, unless you're slurring heavily or falling over on your ass, but not always.

Aida rolls her window down and we all say "American" loudly when the agent looks in. The pudgy man bends down and leans into Aida's window. His gaze jumps from face to face, finally landing on Aida. I swear if he pays attention, he'll see my heart trying to rip out of my chest.

"You ladies live in El Paso?" he asks. Since it's not really ideal to try to distinguish USA citizens from noncitizens based on looks on the border, sometimes they ask extra questions to make sure you're not a passport-less or permit-less Mexican citizen trying to sneak over.

"Yessir, just going back home after a night of partying," Aida cheeps in a perfect Chicana accent. We find it's quicker to get through if you're honest.

He speaks through a lazy yawn. "Pop your trunk open, please."

I just about pass out. Inspection of the trunk is occasional. They'll either search it if you look suspicious, or randomly—about one in every five cars—just so no one tries to smuggle drugs, people, or restricted items.

Aida pulls the lever and sighs deeply, looking very bored as the trunk clicks open. The flow of blood booms in my ears. I look through the rearview mirror at the agent standing behind the car. Even though I've crossed the border hundreds of times, my mind spazzes and I can't remember whether food can be crossed into the US. Or is it only some types of food that are restricted? If he doesn't lift the plastic bin to search underneath it, he might take it out completely to dispose of the bread and see the weapon. My knees clack together.

"What's wrong with *you*?" Aida narrows her eyes so much, they almost disappear behind rows of thick eyelashes.

"Nothing. I just . . . it's just . . ." I turn to my side and roll the window down, pumping my arm frantically at the manual lever. My head and shoulders come out the window. "Please don't throw away our pan dulce, sir. We bought it at Bowie Bakery but forgot to take it out before we left home," I holler. "You can have one, though," I say and wink at him.

The girls go into a fit of roaring laughter. "Geez, you love that bread, Rosa," Aida snorts.

The agent walks back to Aida's window with a bizcocho in hand, beard dusted with sugar. His previously stern face has produced a small grin. "Move it along, ladies. Drive carefully," he says and waves us ahead.

"Chica, I didn't know you were hilarious," Aida exclaims.

We drive away, the girls still cackling, while I slump and hold on to my stomach.

We've just crossed a gun across the border and an agent had his hands inches away from it. The bread I ate tries to come back up my throat. *Don't, please don't*, I plead with my body.

Aida's smile drops. "Hey, girl, you all right?"

"Just . . . keep . . . driving," I say, out of breath. We're still too close to the agent station. If we stop suddenly, there's no telling if they'll send a patrol after the car to check us out.

"That's what too much *pan* does to ya," Zulema tsks. "Especially when it's got nowhere to go on that skinny body."

I breathe in and out deeply and look up to the car ceiling. After another four blocks, I throw the door open.

"¡Ayy!" Aida cries out and pulls over. "What are you doing?"

My vomit splatters onto the pavement while the car rolls to a stop.

Aida goes off as I wipe my mouth. "This bitch. Seriously. Warn me!"

I take a few more breaths and look up at her with watery eyes. "There's a gun in your trunk."

Aida blinks. "What?"

"There's a gun in your trunk, under the pan dulce."

"Oh," she says. "Is that why you're acting all sorts of weird? It's just my dad's hunting rifle he uses to shoot rattlesnakes in the mountains."

Belen, who unsurprisingly has unusual tidbit knowledge, jumps in. "Dude! They'll throw your ass in jail if you cross a gun into Mexico. Haven't you heard? It's all over the news. This guy from Lubbock, and some other people from Ohio or somewhere like that, crossed over with guns and were in the Juárez slammer for like months, or a year!"

Aida squints. "Seriously?"

"Does it look like I'm kidding?" Belen replies, opening her eyes wide.

"Oh," Aida says again. "Well, we *are* technically on the US side now. If anything, when we crossed over to Juárez, or on the way back at the pay booth while we were still in Mexico, is where they could've gotten us.

Maybe." She stays quiet for a few seconds before speaking again. "It prob-ably would've just gotten *me* in trouble. You all are under eighteen. Or my dad maybe, since it's his car and gun. I dunno."

I blow air out. She might be right. And I feel really stupid for not hav-ing thought this all through more. The thing of it is, Aida has always been smarter than she gives herself credit for. Either way, I don't want *any* of us in trouble. I'm just glad we're almost home.

Aida has a faraway look now, like she's not here in the car. Around us, the dim streets are quieter than the desert before a thunderstorm and the air is heavy with the bittersweet scent of mesquite trees. Aida turns to Belen at a red light. "So why is Mexico not allowing guns in?"

Belen shrugs. "It's like some new ban. The drug cartels are going crazy, killing each other even more or something like that."

Zulema whips around looking spooked, and I get a heavy feeling from head to toe. Mom wasn't just worried about the disappearing women. There was so much more.

"You watch the news?" I ask Belen, thinking about how much my par-ents like to watch their nightly news.

"Sometimes," Belen admits sheepishly.

We ride quietly with only the radio playing dance music that doesn't seem so fun right now.

"Drop me off last," Zulema orders.

In the rearview mirror, Aida's eyes look back at me. She makes another turn before speaking. "Nah. Rosa's gonna stay at my place for a bit. Don't wanna send her home sick."

I don't see what kind of face Zulema makes, but her body shifts in place.

Aida drops Zulema off first. She teeter-totters to her door without saying goodbye, her blouse pulled up and scrunched up all wrong. Next, it's Belen. "Later, losers," she chirps and makes a peace sign with her fin-gers before running to the side of the house, pushing a window open, hoisting herself up, and sliding in. I chortle.

"You all right to go home?" Aida says. "I just had to get Belen home and Zulema out of our hair first. But we can hang if you want."

"Eh, I'm good. It's late enough as it is."

We cruise down to my house—only a two-minute drive from Belen's—and Aida pulls the vehicle up in stealth mode.

"Hey, you wanna go to One o' One next Saturday?" Aida asks as I get out of the car. 101 happens to be one of my favorite dance clubs here in El Paso.

"You're not going with the girls to Juárez next weekend?"

"Nah." Aida follows me and we stand by her trunk. "Belen will be fine. She doesn't *need* to hang out with me every single weekend. And I'mma gonna avoid Zulema all week like the plague." She laughs, each *ha* increasing in pitch. It reminds me of Woody Woodpecker.

I chuckle until she adds, "It's not like I haven't been hanging out with Zulema since third grade."

Ouch.

Here I am trying to make new friends while Zulema is trying to keep the one she's had forever. She must feel like I'm stealing Aida away.

"Maybe . . . we can invite them?" I say.

Aida gets a thoughtful look and her voice gets pitchy. "Weee could . . ."—then her face morphs to sly and she belts out, forgetting all about being quiet—"Maybe some other weekend." She snorts out giggles, elbowing me, and I crack up, too.

I wipe away laugh tears. "All right, cool. See you Monday at basketball practice."

Aida has officially entered the Friend Department. I'm certain we won't have to play the game of fakes anymore, if we were even playing. But honestly, no one can be completely real all the time. Being a little guarded is okay. I mean look at me. I have to stop getting paranoid and jumping to conclusions before knowing about situations better.

I'm walking up the concrete stairs to my house when Aida whisper-yells, "Hey, biatch." I turn just in time to catch the concha that's flying toward my face. "Good catch," she squeals, like a pet owner praising her dog for going poop. "You earned a pan dulce for the road. Also, I'll make sure to tell Coach your reflexes are improving."

Smiling, I jog the last steps to my door. I've never craved my soft bed so much and I'm thankful Mom gave me a key. I'll be sure to make myself get up early tomorrow . . . err, today, to have breakfast with her. The key goes into the lock, and I take a bite of the soft bread as I walk inside.

AUTHOR'S NOTE

Though this is fiction, it's representative of real conditions at the border in the nineties. Many USA teens crossed over on foot or by car to socialize in the numerous bars and nightclubs along the Mexican border. When one is young, we tend to think we're invincible, untouchable. I realize now how fortunate I am to have gotten back home each time, how insensitive and ignorant I was to the disturbing happenings that turned El Paso's sister city of Ciudad Juárez into a war zone, how lucky we were to be able to cross back and forth while most Juárenzes couldn't reciprocate. As grim conditions continued across the border, many of us watched helplessly and our visits to Mexico slowly faded, leaving a gap in our core that's still there. This story only touches the scale and seriousness of the matters in Mexico at the time. Instead, through Rosa and the group of girls she teams up with for a night of fun, I aimed to drop the reader into a time of innocent youth in the nineties of the El Paso/Juárez area and take them along on the thrilling ride.

RAISING THE STAKES IN *PAN DULCE*

by Emily X.R. Pan

PAN DULCE HAS A CLASSIC SETUP: OUR INTREPID NARRATOR IS EAGER TO cling to a sense of safety and invincibility, to brush aside the warnings that read as standard parental paranoia. "It's no big deal, even if Mom thinks otherwise." We can define *stakes* via these simple questions: What does the character want, and how much could go wrong? Right away the minor troubles begin: the slip on the stairs, the sweaty walk up the hill . . .

PAN DULCE plays with our knowledge and expectations. As seasoned readers, we know how these things go. Trouble is on the horizon, and these trivial ironies are the first sign of it.

What's so effective about this story is the way it rockets us from typical interior conflict into the higher-risk stakes of conflict between Rosa and the world around her.

As Rosa heads out, her worries begin to build on things immediately in sight. Any one of these could balloon into the main source of tension: Zulema and her aggressive antagonism. The *feminicidio*, which Rosa tries to brush aside by telling herself, "All teens go across to party." The fake IDs, the cars on the other side of the border driving too fast, the mention of the older boys living so far away. These are all reminders of the uncertain territory our narrator has entered, and we're waiting to see which of these will become the primary conflict.

The waves of Rosa's everyday worries feel true to life, and we settle into the rhythm of it—just as our narrator has. At this point we are expecting this to be the story of a girl who goes dancing, who perhaps will have some interesting encounter at a club or a memorable experience with a boy. Then, just as those exciting possibilities are deflating, the author hits us with this:

In the moonlight, something gleams inside the
trunk, something nestled inside the hollow of a tire that
the container was resting on.

This moment punches home the gravity of the border situation, and we understand the seriousness of Rosa's circumstances. This is where the stakes rocket up.

I love the title of this piece, too, because it gives us the sense that the story will be something light. We are prepared—as Rosa is—for a certain kind of experience, completely different from what we would have expected in a story called GUN. And that's why, when we hit that peak, it's startling and sobering in exactly the right way.

STORY PROMPT:
ENIGMA

AN ENIGMA IS SOMETHING, OR SOMEONE, WHO IS NEXT TO IMPOSSIBLE TO understand. Characters like these can offer mystery to your stories, and sometimes a touch of magic.

Create an enigma of a character—human or inhuman, mythical or wholly real. At their center should be a compelling secret, something this character has been hiding for a long time. Ideally this secret is surprising and would change how you think of that character forever after. Maybe it will even rock the whole world of the story.

Now write about the moment when the deeply buried truth about your enigma of a character is finally revealed.

Who gets to see the truth? What changes now that the secret is known?

SOLACE

Nora Elghazzawi

THE TRUTH IS, I AM OKAY NOW. BUT IT WAS EASIER WHEN I WASN'T.

Laila alone. Laila sleeping and Laila weeping in the graveyard, Laila who starved herself thin as a Ramadan moon. All of these were me, and in a way, they are still me. They are the Lailas of my marrow, the roots I have carried to the tail end of seventeen. Sometimes I forget their weight, but the reminders always resurface like ghosts: in Mama's worried glances when I don't finish a plate; in the somber way Baba still kisses me good night, on the crown of my head, like he's afraid I'll vanish; and in the garden I've kept for the past year, which begs me every harvest:

Eat.

"No tomatoes?" Gabe asks, peering over the register. I smile as he gestures to the three packets of seeds I've picked out: cucumbers, carrots, lettuce. There was once a time when this would've been a meal for me. A couple hundred calories, half a day's worth of food.

Now, with the seeds spread in front of me, I feel a strange sense of awareness. These seeds could feed a family, could give so much life and time. Food grows so people can grow, but they both take such painstaking care. Be it a girl or a garden, it sometimes gets far too difficult.

To grow. To *be*.

"No tomatoes," I tell him with a laugh.

When I first began gardening, I started with tomatoes because I hated them. I thought I wouldn't eat them, and I thought right. But Mama didn't like that, so I decided to appease her and only picked out "the good stuff." She also doesn't like how I'm constantly hanging around "that no-good, bad-luck Briar boy." But here I am.

With Gabe Briar. Still smiling.

After I pay, Gabe disappears into the back. When he returns, his stare is full of something I'm still unused to. He doesn't look at me like the rest of Reves does. Never did, not even when I was gaunt and ashen and bug-eyed. *Laila Saab, spirited away, halfway to the grave along with her brother. Poor thing, all that's left of her is bones.*

I wonder what they say about me these days. *Nearly eighteen years old and living like she's eighty. Gardening and stuck on that Gabriel Briar. Such an awful shame.*

I had so many dreams. I *have* so many dreams. They shift and change and pass like the tide, but they always come back to haunt me no matter how deeply I bury them. I used to dream about the stage. Gleaming lights, songs, and sweat. The lilt of music in my throat, clearer than water.

But then everything went silent.

I started to dream about Jad and his ever-sleeping face. I dreamed about his casket and how small it was. Moon after moon, I relived the nightmarish day I stopped using the word *brother*.

Then I dreamed of disappearing. Inward, like a crescent. I roamed through those years half-asleep, and I'm scared, you see, because even though I've started to wake up, it's not like life waited for me. I'm terrified even when I'm Laila in the garden, away from the music I miss and the brother I still cry for. I'm Laila who can eat birthday cake even though it has tasted rotten to me ever since I realized Jad would never blow out nine candles. I am Laila without laughter or melodies, and once upon a time, that wasn't Laila at all.

Yet when Gabe hands me a packet of rose seeds and gives me a crooked grin, I am none of those things and all of them. I'm *me*, and it's enough.

"These came in yesterday," he says. Our fingers brush when he places the packet on my palm, and my stomach flutters, warm as a candle. "Um. In case you have the time, you can . . . have them. Grow them."

"Thank you," I say, a touch too serious. He waves me off like always, tells me they're only flowers. But the calm quiet between us says otherwise.

Thank you. Even though I don't repeat it, I think he understands.

Reves is a small town with large opinions. The number one being that it's spelled *Reves*, not *Rêves*, thank you very much. The good old folk living here don't have time for fancy letters, for *e*'s with houses on top, or as I later learned from a quick Google search, *e* with circumflex. Bent *e*, like a crescent moon. A bent dream, an unbent dream. In ballads and poems, dreams are always pure, open. But what happens when your wishes get all warped and twisted? What happens when you want ugly things and they come true?

What does that say about *you*?

Reves is an odd name for an odd place in the sleepy Midwest. Really, it's where dreams come to die. Where dreamers burrow and hide. There's an old, buried hunger that permeates this town like a great poisoned vein. We feed on it as it feeds on us.

Like a spell. Like *magic*.

I honestly don't know if it's the bad or good kind. Bent or unbent.

Jad, though. He only found beauty in Reves, when we moved here a lifetime ago. The birds didn't get spooked when he came near. They lingered, brought him gifts. A cat's eye marble, bright like a parachute. A pearl as pink as sunrise. Glass shards that never cut through skin, no matter how jagged their edges.

The trees can talk here, Jad told me. *They love when kids climb them, play hide-and-seek around them. They love when birds sit in their nests and sing. Did you know, Laila? You sing like a bird.*

I love when you sing, Jad said. *I love* you.

If only I'd said it back more often: *I love you too.* Because I did— because I do—and if I can swear on anything, it's that Jad had all the kindness in the world inside him. He drew out the good in me like water from a well.

Together we used to skip stones along rivers, eat summer fruit until our bellies ached, laugh at stupid jokes, and dance like fools on our kitchen floor. We fought, broke each other's toys, made wishes on eyelashes, and snuck snacks upstairs when Mama and Baba were fast asleep, and I loved him, I *love* him so. We were happy—God, *I* was happy—just being his big sister, watching him grow.

But then the accident happened. And the thought that burst inside of me like a nova, like a wildfire, like a hundred thousand fallen loves and trees and stars was this:

It should've been me.

I feel the same even still. And maybe I'm not at the brink anymore— maybe I'm eating and breathing and *living* just fine—but my heart is starved. It remains barren, longing for happiness and for punishment in equal measure. So I plant this garden, sow these seeds, and I feed my neighbors, my parents. I feed myself, food and lies, and promise the unforgiving mirror, *Someday I'll be whole.*

Someday I'll be.

In school we talk about the future. *Our* futures, specifically, which is pretty unfortunate. There's a class for history, but there's no class for the Future, capital. *In twenty years, we'll have planes that run on solar power. In a hundred, you'll be able to meet people in dreams. Before we grow old, they'll make the moon into a common tourist attraction.*

Miss Reed, our senior guidance counselor, brings this question to class instead: "Where do you want to be next year?"

Some students volunteer their answers, but I don't know what to say. When I was a child, if you had asked me where I saw myself in the future, I would've told you, *Grown*. Grown up. Going places. Maybe singing somewhere, my family cheering me on. After all, the world is big, and what child dreams of being small?

Not me. Not *then*.

But things are different now.

My grades aren't terrible or anything. Some of them are kind of amazing. But can you build a life on a few high marks? Can you rebuild a dream that way? There are too many Lailas inside me, and those dreams of mine have gotten so tangled. I can't tell you what I want anymore without opening a Pandora's box of grief and yearning. A dream is most beautiful when you fight for it. But the only thing I ever fought in my life was hunger, until I found blind solace in it, like a girl bewitched, like a fool.

I can hardly stand to see myself in the mirror. How am I supposed to see myself in ten years? Five years?

One?

I visit Gabe's shop after class, which has become something of a ritual for me. I'm kind of a loiterer, actually, considering I don't buy things every time I stop by. I don't think he minds too much. At least I hope not.

We drink tea by the door. Gabe always makes me a special cup, adding lavender and enough warm milk to sweeten it. I say *enough*, but I know from the taste and the color exactly how much he's put in.

I cannot forget the numbers. *Forty calories*, my brain supplies, like it has been so terribly programmed to. I want to smother the thought, stanch it like a wound. But scars don't work that way. Sometimes they ache and feel like they'll open, even when you know you have no blood left to give. As long as you keep going, there will always be more work to do.

Better. I have to do better. So I say, "This is delicious," because it's the truth. *I'm okay,* I remind myself, because if I say it enough, it won't be a lie.

Gabe smiles, and it almost reaches his eyes. When he turns to pick up his own cup, I glimpse his profile. Sharp jaw, long lashes. That tiny, starry birthmark on his neck. With a flush, I drop my gaze to his hands, hands that handle plants and pots and flowers so gently that it's hard to believe they ever knew a different shape of work.

A different fate.

Gabe Briar's past is no secret. He's a year older than me, and two summers ago he was being scouted. *Baseball, pitcher, star:* these were the words that followed Gabe like a beacon. Then someone from out of town chose to get drunk and drive through Reves on a Thursday night and trampled all over Gabe Briar and his dreams. He was walking home from practice. It was a regular day, and if I've learned anything, those are the days you have to watch out for.

The doctors called him a miracle. Said he would make a full recovery. And he did. But healing takes time, and when you're young, nobody tells you that. No one tells you how to trade out scholarships for surgeries, how to find solace in the little milestones along the way. But Gabe did all of this and more, has been strong where I've never been.

In the end, Gabe didn't play again. He could've tried, could've trained and left Reves and all its fickleness behind. Yet he chose to stay, living with his grandmother above this shop until she passed away last winter. And that's when the whispers set in. *Runaway mother, deadbeat father, a grandmother in the grave.* People say anything grown from this shop will bring sickness, bad omens. But I wonder what they would say if they knew the truth.

This place isn't cursed. It's magic. Gabe and the garden he helped me make are magic.

What I haven't told anyone, not even Gabe, is that I don't ever use all the seeds he gives me. Just one at a time. One seed is enough for an entire patch of cucumbers or cabbages. A whole root-work of carrots. I water a plot once, and rosebushes bloom.

I spend all my spare time in the garden, tending and working, so that I can have this. My own secret bit of magic. Prayer-filled food, wish-made flowers. Like I said, I'm selfish. Foolish. But I'm just a girl who has been many girls before, and is trying to figure out which one I am now.

By the time we finish our tea, the moon is rising, and Gabe says, "I'll walk you home."

He stands up, and I'm stricken with a new-old sense of longing. It's a fragile, glassy feeling, but I am no good with fragile things, so I quell my heart and say, "Sure." Say, "I'd like that."

Mama doesn't make tea like Gabe's. She spoons in so much sugar and honey that my teeth ache before I even drink it. But I never say a word. This is a habit born of worry, of having a daughter who nearly disappeared on her. Mama used to look at me like she could see my gravestone, clear as day. And I will never unknow that. Never.

She hands me a mug. It's eleven at night, but the curtains block out the moonglow. Mama paces, and I brace myself for the lecture about boys and staying out late. I close my eyes, and I see the walkway outside, hear the quiet song of streetcars and crickets. The crisp near-autumn air, the rumble of Gabe's laughter. Our hands dangling between us like pendulums.

"Laila Saab," Mama starts, and I remember how much I loathe my name. *Difficult night.* Difficult girl. Difficult through and through. "What exactly do you want?"

She's stopped near the kitchen, and I blink, taken aback. "Like, for dinner? Isn't it sort of late for that?"

"No, no." Mama gives me a hopeful smile. "Next year. After you graduate. Have you decided what you want?"

The room suddenly goes cold; my hands tremble around the teacup I'm holding. I don't like this. I don't like where this is going. But those words won't come. "I . . ."

"You're smart, habibti," Mama says like a plea. "You're a smart girl. You can be anything you want."

But Jad can't, I want to say.

"Your father and I were talking," she tells me. At the mention of Baba, I glance toward his empty study. He's been on a business trip for days, somewhere up north. He always orbits to cold places at this time of year. Late summer in Reves is wrought with scars.

Mama goes on, "We've been saving. And Laila, we think you should apply. Wherever you want. You loved music, remember? Singing? Or something else. It can be literature, medicine. Your choice. " She takes a breath. "We just want you to pick someplace. Anyplace. And we'll follow you."

I stare at her, wide-eyed, mouth open. It doesn't compute. "What?"

"We think," Mama says, "it's time to leave Reves."

A great many thoughts cross my mind. There are a million ways for me to argue, to disagree. But the only thing I can manage is, "M-my garden."

It's Mama's turn to be surprised. "What?"

"What about my garden?" I ask. "I need—I need to watch over it. I need to take care of it. I need to do a good job."

Mama's eyes redden. "Laila. It's fine. Someone else can watch it. I'm sure . . . that Briar boy would."

I shake my head, not listening to her. "What'll happen if I go? If I don't pay attention? I need to watch it well. I need to, Mama. I do."

She wraps her arms around me, touches my cheek like I'm glass, porcelain, bone—and I break. "I was supposed to look after him," I say. "He couldn't swim. But I left him all *alone!*"

Mama rocks me back and forth, saying, *Hush, hush,* but I can't. I can't do anything but cry and let everything out. I've tried so hard to be small, to be nothing, hoping that all this anger and sadness and rue would vanish along with me. But it's still here. Like a sickness, it grows and grows, even though my brother never will. He'll always be that little boy who was afraid of water, just like I'll always be the sister who lost him to Reves, where dreams are laid to die, and how can I leave him again?

How can I live with myself if I do that?

Days, weeks, months pass. I send applications out to colleges on Mama's watch. I don't know how I feel about any of them. *Undecided*, I check over and over. It's perfect, fitting for a mess like me. *Undecided*.

Eating has also become a chore. The garden keeps reminding me, *Eat, eat*, but I forget. Or I let myself forget. A glutton for punishment—that's what they call difficult girls like me. Baba returns with sweet gifts, and Mama cooks me beautiful dishes: chicken with pine nuts, flatbreads dipped in spices and olive oil, steaming rice rolled in grape leaves. All my childhood favorites. But if you're never hungry, you never long to be full, and that's the trick to yearning, I think. If you don't want something, if you don't pine for it, it won't help you, but it won't hurt you either. You won't lose it.

You'll remain whole.

Winter arrives, along with letters. Frost clings to the air like a diamond cloak, lulling my garden to sleep.

There's one letter I've been musing over for days. *Congratulations*, it says, and though it's not the first to say so, it's the first to stir something within me. The brochure is as glossy as the others, and the promises of success and ambition seem just as airy and thin. But I keep going back to it. And I don't know why.

I turn eighteen on a Thursday in January. I eat cake. One bite, two.

Then an idea comes. I place an extra slice in a plastic container, leaving my own half-finished. I breathe in, out.

And I go.

Gabe smiles when I walk in. The shop is empty, and I feel my ears go red when I hold up the cake and say, "For you."

He peeks inside and beams. "Strawberries and cream? Excellent taste."

"I try," I say, taking a seat.

Rather than joining me, however, Gabe grins even wider and says, "I have something for you too."

I anticipate the teacups he brings from behind the counter. What I don't expect is the peony in his grip, pale as dawn. My blush deepens when he leans in close, so that the birthmark on his neck lines up with my lips. He tucks a strand of wavy hair behind my ear along with the flower and pulls back.

"There," he says. His voice is a hum. "Happy birthday."

The heat spreads over my skin, full force. "Thank you," I murmur to my feet. Gabe lets out a bashful laugh before sitting down next to me. I train my eyes elsewhere, in search of a distraction, as Gabe stirs our drinks for us.

Laila Saab, I warn myself. *Don't be a fool.*

While glancing around, I notice the lack of other flowers. Gabe has a bunch of succulents plotted around the register. A wall of seeds to choose from. I smell soil and earth, and the quiet hint of nectar.

My eyes linger on the sign by the entrance: *Briar Rose*. Gabe's grandmother's shop. When I first met him, she had just passed, and I could tell how much he loved her. *Her name was Rose Briar. Like a fairy tale. She was too good for this town.*

The way he said it, full of rue, made me want to tell him, *So are you.*

In Reves, everyone knows of everyone, but it doesn't mean you *know-know*. I knew about Gabe Briar, but I didn't know him until that morning in December when I saw him sniffling in the snowy graveyard, placing a single lily on a frozen plot.

I was going to visit Jad. But when I saw Gabe Briar, Reves's resident
fallen star, I went straight to him without a second thought.

And that was how we began. Gabe and Laila, two kids with dim pasts
and futures. We became fast friends, though it wasn't all sadness and
graves. It was tea; it was pitching wrong-handed in the Briar Rose parking lot. It was me shyly singing him one of my favorite songs. It was the
whispers about us in school, in the town churches, in my parents' hushed
study.

It was the garden that reminded me, day in and day out:

Eat.

People have plenty to say about us, together or apart, and I think they
think I'm worse. Gabe never could've chosen his fate. But me? I'm the reason Jad is gone, the reason my family is a mess. I let myself go hungry all
those years. There's no one to blame but me.

I wonder. I wonder if Jad blames me.

I wonder if someday Gabe will blame me too. I contemplate this as
I unfold the acceptance letter I've been obsessing over like an itch, an
infatuation. *Hulm College of Liberal Arts. Where your efforts reward you and
happiness grows.*

I show it to him. He hands me my tea, then reads. Once, twice. He
smiles. He's always smiling at me. "Congratulations," he says, and it
sounds so sincere.

"I—" The words get caught in my throat, thick as honey. "Should I
go?"

Something in his face changes, quick as a switch. "Why would you ask
me that?"

"Because," I say. "Because . . . it matters to me. What you think."

Gabe shakes his head. "But this isn't something for me to decide,
Laila."

I set down my cup next to the uneaten cake and the crinkled letter,
and I place my trembling hands over his. He feels warm, solid. I've never
done this, and I wish I had sooner. I really, really wish I had sooner.

"It's in-state," I tell him. "I mean . . . my grades aren't wonderful. But they want me. You—Gabe. You're so smart. You could go anywhere. It doesn't have to be Hulm. It could be close by. Near Reves. It . . . it's not too late. It doesn't have to be just me."

Silence.

Between the two of us there have been many silences, but none like this. Gabe's expression is one I've never seen on him. His eyes are glassy, his mouth downturned. He's looking at me like he doesn't know me. Like he's seeing all the ugly Lailas inside of me for the very first time.

"Laila," he says. "Please don't."

"Will you think about it?"

"There's nothing," he says, his voice strained, "to think about." He moves his hands from under mine. "I just don't . . . I didn't know. You took me by surprise."

"What?"

"I didn't think," he says quietly. "I didn't . . . I thought, when you kept coming here, that you saw what I saw. A beautiful place. A good life. It's not what I wanted. It's not what I dreamed about. But it's mine, you know? And I thought you felt the same."

I look at him, and he looks at me, and it's wrong. He's got me all wrong. This isn't pity or some cheap request. Because I've seen Gabe— really *seen* him—tracing baseball diamonds on countertops, staring outside whenever cars or buses pass, holding out his garden-dirty hands and imagining something else. I've seen him content within these four walls, and I've seen him caged, and I believed the truth was someplace in between. I believed it was . . .

With *us*.

"I just don't want—" *I don't want this to end.* "I thought. We could—*be*."

The *together* is unsaid, but I can tell Gabe understands. He clenches his jaw, his body taut. Around us, potted plants sway in the blare of the heater. The scent of spring, fresh and Eden-green, permeates the room. Outside there are trees and houses and roads, dipped in sugarlike snow, and there is a graveyard that holds my brother and Gabe's grandmother, and another sunken space, deep beneath my ribs, where the happiness has struggled for so long to grow.

Here and now, Gabe says, "I like you, Laila," and I freeze. He says, "I like you. But I don't control you. I want you to choose whatever makes you happy. So please, do the same for me."

He turns, and I realize that this is it. My cue to go.

But I don't want to. I want Gabe with me, and I want to move on, and I want to live, and I want to love, fiercely and deeply, like Jad did in his short span of time. I want so much, want to dream again, to unbend all my old yearnings and start anew. I want to figure out the right thing to say and the right thing to do, but sometimes there is no right thing. Sometimes you just have to choose and have faith in that decision.

But I've never been good at any of that.

"Good night," I say.

Goodbye, I don't say, even as I turn to leave.

I'm okay, and that's what makes this so much worse. When you're a mess, no one expects anything of you. But I've been so good. There's beautiful, beautiful stuff I'd be throwing away if I screwed up now. Because I'm okay.

And it's so, so hard to be.

I haven't seen Gabe in weeks; I don't have an excuse to anymore. Winter eats away at both me and my garden. Outside there's a single rose left. Mama points it out, and I pretend not to care. But it hurts me to look at it. A lone flower amid all that death and rot. It just wants to live. It just wants to *be*. When I started that garden, I made a promise. *I will help you live. I will protect you as you protect me.* But I lied.

What do I know about keeping things safe?

Maybe I was wrong about those magic seeds. Because no matter how many I plant, no matter what I do, nothing seems to grow anymore. Shouldn't magic be able to tide everything over through winter?

Shouldn't this be enough?

But it's not. It has never been enough. The hunger I clung to like penance, the hurt I carried like pride. Gabe and the garden and the acceptance I've stowed like a gem. I traded away my will and strength long ago, have leaned against one pillar after another. But nothing has changed.

There is no spell for healing. No easy fix.

I want you to choose whatever makes you happy. Those words should've changed everything for the better. I should be delighted. Instead I trudge to and from school, quiet as a ghost, biding most of my days alone. Deadlines loom near, and Mama asks me over and over when I'll send a response to any of the colleges.

I tell her I don't know, because I don't.

I really, really don't.

Miss Reed, my guidance counselor, corners me in the hallway on a Friday afternoon. Class is out, and there's a long weekend ahead, but I don't have any plans. Sleep, maybe. Whatever passes the time, I suppose.

"You," she says, pointing—rather rudely, I might add. "Miss Laila Saab."

I shrug. "That's me."

"I have a bone to pick with you," she says, and I almost snort, because who talks like that? *A bone to pick?* Really?

It's like an episode of true-crime TV. One second I'm in the hallway, and then I'm being spirited away to an empty classroom. I watch with no small amount of horror as Miss Reed shuts the door behind us.

My fears are dispelled, however, when she says, "I see you haven't chosen a school yet, Laila."

I'm a bit taken aback, though I don't show it. She isn't wrong; I haven't picked. I'm undecided, and even if I do go somewhere—anywhere—I'll remain the same. Everybody waxes poetic about these big choices, these moments and musings that can rule an entire life. But what about mistakes? They're choices too, and they take only a second to make. I would know. I *do* know.

"Laila?"

The three-way discussion—Miss Reed vs. me vs. my brain—in this gym-sock-scented classroom has become too much. So I try to nod my way out of it. "Yeah. You're right."

"According to the school portal, you've been accepted to most of the places you've applied." She bites her lip. "You mentioned Hulm during one of our meetings. Are you still interested?"

I shuffle my feet. This is, well, *a lot*, considering the fact that five minutes ago I was on my way home to nap. "I, uh. Maybe?"

Muted sunlight gleams through the window. It's pale, watercolor, half-bright and half-asleep. It's funny—in winter the sun is only part of itself, all light and no warmth. That heat goes elsewhere, across the world, unbottled and free. Emotions are the same, depending on how you work with them. Those unspent feelings, those parts of you that remain hidden and dormant—how do you let them out? A fight? A love? A dream?

How do you stop being half-you? Half-asleep?

Miss Reed takes a hesitant step toward me and pulls two glossy stubs out of her sweater pocket. Gingerly, she holds them out.

"Bus tickets," she says, and when I don't move, she goes on, "Hulm is a few hours from here. There's a tour this weekend for accepted students, transportation and housing included. They sent us a letter. I thought you might want to go."

I blink at her. My face is probably blank as a slate, because she takes my hand in hers and opens it, pressing the tickets into my palm. "It's your choice. I just wanted you to know."

She lets go of me and ambles to the door. I thank her, or at least I think I do, because she winks on her way out.

"It's *your* choice," she repeats from the doorway. Then she's gone.

Instead of going home, I go to see Jad. It's been a while since I've visited, and the guilt gnaws at me. I should've come on my birthday. He would've liked the cake.

By the time I make it to his grave, it's nearly dark. I use my phone light to guide me and send a quick message to Mama about Hulm. I wonder what she'll say.

Then I sink down in the dirt. I face Jad, and I apologize, like I have many times before in the four years he's been gone. I don't want his forgiveness, though. I want him to be here. But both are impossible now. Even if every other wish of mine in this life comes true, this will never, ever be granted to me.

"I miss you," I say. "Every single day. And I'm scared, Jad. That I'll miss you even more if I go."

The wind blurs past, and I wait. For a sign, for guidance, for Jad's laughter to comb through the air like music. Yet none of that happens. The stars above remain still, refusing to align. They glint down like eyes, neither cruel nor kindred, and a ruined emotion stirs within me, full of grief and shame and hunger. I choke on the shape of it, both barbed and beloved, before it escapes in a single name:

"*Jad.*"

I know he won't hear me, but I can't stop. "I don't want to leave you." I bring a hand to my heart, clutch at the fabric of my coat. "I don't want to forget. If you asked me to, I'd be miserable for as long as I live. I'd be nothing.

"But, Jad, I—" The confession bursts out, along with a sob. "I want to be happy." My gaze floats up to the stars, then down again. "I want that for both of us. Maybe not how we used to be. But I want us to be happy."

My entire body rattles as I heave in a deep, unsteady breath. "I can't do it without you, so please, tell me. Is that okay?"

I don't get a response, though I wasn't fool enough to expect one. I could only hope. So when I finally look up again, my heart stammers when I see *it*, dimly in the moonlight.

A clipped dandelion, splayed in the grass. I pick it up with shaking hands. There's a ribbon around its throat, a red Briar Rose tag hanging from the bow. I remember a cool spring morning outside of Gabe's shop, when he told me, *There're two languages everyone in the world can understand: the language of music and the language of flowers. They're magic.*

The dandelion is golden, sun-colored in the night. It must be fresh; it hasn't shriveled yet, despite the cold. *Magic.* Very gingerly, I hold it up and set it down in front of Jad's headstone. I close my eyes, and I see my garden. I *hear* it. All along it's been Gabe's voice, soft and low, begging and reminding me: *Eat.*

But this time, it says something different. And in my mind, the garden *looks* different too. I see dandelions, fields upon fields of them. Blooming from gaps in the asphalt, growing from nothing but *will*, pure will. People call them rotten, people call them weeds, but Gabe would call them beautiful. Jad would've picked them like jewels, worn them as a crown. Dandelions for wishes. Dandelions for joy.

I want you to choose what will make you happy.

I open my eyes, swipe them clear of tears. And I know what I have to do.

I call Mama from the cemetery. Then, staring at the dandelion, I send a message to Gabe, and I hope. But I do not wait.

Not anymore.

Some people are bad with money; I'm bad with time. Old habits are hard to shake. I often sleep in, let minutes and hours pass while I remain in a daze. I daydream; I muse about the past and the future while wading through the present like a murky lake.

The last bus out of Reves leaves in a few hours, at midnight. It's always midnight, I suppose—that magic, fairy-tale time when today melds into tomorrow. Perhaps it's fitting. I watch the moon as it watches me, standing in limbo between one choice and another. I've spent many nights gazing at the moon, the beautiful, shape-shifting moon, which for all its faces remains unchanged at its core, year after year.

But I am no moon. I am a girl. Not a satellite, but a soul. I am of this world. For so long, I've orbited outside of it like a stranger, and it's time to become a part of it fully. To *be*.

When I get home that night, I treasure the hours like gold, like Jad treasured his eight years on this Earth. I rush around my room, hurrying to find a bag. Baba kisses my forehead, amused, and Mama smiles as I pack, tells me I'm doing the right thing. I don't know about that, don't know about right or wrong or regrets, but I think *this* is what I want, so I fold my clothes into a duffel bag alongside face products and shampoo. I keep one ticket in my pocket and offer Mama the other, and she takes it delicately, like a gift.

I peer out the window, gazing intently at my garden. Even in the darkness, I can see what's left of it—that tiny, fist-curled rose, red as a wound, blaring like a promise in the night.

I'll be waiting, it tells me. And I nod. The garden says nothing more; perhaps it will never speak to me again. Unbeckoned, I grab an apple to eat on my way out. I take a bite, then another. Rather than scour the house for the seeds Gabe gave me, I pluck a few from the core. I hold them like gems, like stars, before dropping them into the dirt outside. I don't expect magic, for ruby groves or trees to blossom overnight. But maybe someday these seeds will flourish into something wonderful, whether I'm here to see it or not.

I pat the earth gently. I don't say goodbye.

And then I'm off.

In storybooks, everything is always romantic, dramatic. Confessions, goodbyes, loves-at-first-sight. Moments fall into place like snow, perfectly imperfect. But reality is something else entirely.

Reality is 11:48 p.m. on a Friday at Reves's bus station, located on the outskirts of town. It was built by the lip of the river, which has been frozen over for weeks now. I hate that river, feel a lump in my throat whenever children ice-skate over it in winter, when wading ducks croak for food during the spring. I hate this river for what it has taken from me, but in this moment, I forgive it. Because this water might've stolen my brother, might've drowned what was dearest in my heart, but I've taken so much more from myself. Water isn't cruel for cruelness's sake. But people are, and I have been.

Mama stands alongside me, patient as a saint despite my sudden actions. She has always been a stern woman. Among her and Baba and me, she's the anchor, steely and strong. But she was none of those things when we spoke earlier tonight. *Wherever you go, I will follow.* And I believed her, *believe* her, and I owe it to her and to Jad and to Baba and to myself to lead our family to someplace beautiful.

Twelve minutes to midnight becomes ten, and I grow nervous as the bus comes into view. I check my phone for the twentieth time to make sure my message sent. *Thank you for the flower. I'm leaving town for a few days, but I want to talk to you. I'll be at the station at midnight.* No response has come, so I tell myself that he must be sleeping, he might be angry, and I might just be a fool. But it's fine. I feel better for having reached out. I imagine the rose unfurling, the dandelion glowing, and my heart loosens, opens like a palm.

"We should get on," Mama says, and I nod, my head bowed. She holds up her pass; the driver ushers her forward. I watch her slink into a seat in the back, and I'm about to follow when I feel a touch on my shoulder.

"Laila." And I know that voice; I've heard it in dreams and in gardens and during long, winding afternoons, snow-touched and summery alike. I turn, as if in a trance, and it's like every silly story I've ever read but better. Because it's real—*Gabe* is real, and he's standing before me, red-cheeked and out of breath, dressed in a thick jacket and hat, and he's smiling, wide and true.

"I'm sorry," he says, face faltering. "I shouldn't—I overreacted. I was being a jerk. You were trying to help. I should've come sooner, but the shop, and I, and you—"

Maybe it's the cold. Maybe it's the heady feeling that has overtaken me since sundown. Maybe it's because it's nearly midnight and the moon is shining up above like a clock, doling out this time to me—time I've taken for granted, time I had been so willing to give up like it was already used, even though it wasn't. I haven't used my time in years, haven't treasured or nurtured it right, and I want to. I want to be the Laila at the core of all the others. I want to be me, I want to *be*, so I lean up and kiss Gabe softly on the lips. I cradle the back of his head while his hand settles by my jaw, and the sensation lasts long after we part. He beams at me, and I don't look away, even when he guides me up the bus staircase and whispers, "Bye for now."

It's only for a few days. And if I go for good, it's only for a few years. I almost say this, but the look in Gabe's eyes says he understands, as always. I don't know where he'll go, what he'll be, or what I plan to do. I only know that I can't stop staring, even as the automatic doors close and I trek, like a girl possessed, down the aisle of the bus. Gabe remains outside, stuck in place, waving in the frigid cold, and I brush past Mama, my gaze not straying from his as I make it to the back window and press my open hands to the glass. I say nothing, and Gabe says nothing, and the bus is silent save for the low radio-hum of music, the beginnings of an aria I might have once known. He stands there even as we drive away, and it's both a promise and not, and I'm okay with that.

Eventually I take my seat next to Mama. Both of us remain silent. The intercom announces that we'll make it to Hulm before morning. The full moon follows us as we move, and at last I close my eyes and lean back.

It won't be easy; it has never been easy. But for the first time in a long time, this truth doesn't frighten me. Nothing is ever simple, but I am okay, and I'll *be* okay.

I'll *be*.

AUTHOR'S NOTE

I first began writing in my freshman year of high school. Since then, I've written three novels and several short stories, but my very first published piece has been SOLACE in FORESHADOW. Currently, I am working on a YA fantasy I hope to query soon and someday get published.

I wrote SOLACE in the dead of winter, when very few things manage to grow. But even so, Laila's story bloomed into something I wanted to share. Maybe we don't have enchanted gardens in our world, but blossoming through difficult times is magic in and of itself.

So I wanted to write to that little hope of mine—that magic is real in its own way, both within us and around us. There're gardens everywhere. And whether you tend to your own or have someone help you plant it, always remember to feed yourself from it, too.

MOOD IN *SOLACE*

by Nova Ren Suma

Sometimes there's a story that has a distinct taste, one recognizable in its phrases, its rhythms, its way with language. SOLACE has a taste, and this comes from its mood—the sensation that permeates the story, starting at the root, with the choice of words on the page and the images and echoes used. The mood emanating from SOLACE is one of melancholy at first, a slow unfolding, a swirling ache. We see "Laila alone." We witness "Laila who starved herself thin as a Ramadan moon." This feeling extends through the whole of the story, until those last moments when Laila and her mother have taken their seats on the bus and "the full moon follows" as they leave the town of Reves for a chance at an awakening. How is such a strong mood threaded through every scene, lingering at the last page as if we've been enveloped by a petal-soft yet hopeful fog?

It begins at the sentence level. Look at the rhythm and the repetition: "I'm Laila in the garden . . ." / "I'm Laila who can eat birthday cake . . ." / "I am Laila without laughter . . ." *I'm Laila / I'm Laila / I am Laila* is used sparingly in the story, and for effect, an echo that expands and sparkles due to the flow and also the restraint. There are reminders to *eat*. There are reminders to *be*. The story swerves and grows, and yet these words and lines return. The mood encircles the reader, and the story's spell is woven that much more tightly.

I return again and again to the end of SOLACE, to the way hope is offered in the gleaming moonlight. Mood is built, too, from the choices a writer makes, involving everything from weather to time of day. When Laila allows herself to finally embrace what might make her happy, after the dandelion sends the message that the time has come, hope comes on the stroke of midnight. Laila muses, "It's always midnight, I suppose—that magic, fairy-tale time when today melds into tomorrow." The mood would be shattered if Laila and her mother left on the bus on an ordinary sunny afternoon. No, instead, she says goodbye to her garden in the deep of night, and then they are off.

When a mood is cast, it goes down to the tiniest detail, the smallest seed. It's woven into the words and refrains used, as well as the symbolic choices: the graveyards and gardens, the midnight journeys, the messages exchanged beneath the glow of a full moon.

PRINCESS

Maya Prasad

OUTSIDE THE GALAXY CLASS C SHUTTLE, THE STARS SWEEP BY, AND A ROSY nebula blooms to invite us into its fold. I swish watercolors across thick creamy paper, trying to capture the chronology of the journey. My paintings are never frozen in a single moment, but always driven by movement and energy and light. I hope that's true of me, too.

In the seat beside me, my mother gives her most pernicious stink eye to a luggage cart. The source of her ire becomes clear when a mechanical limb extends to grab our things from the overhead compartment. It's not just a luggage cart; it's a Luggage Cart. An artificially intelligent machine designed to do something that humans in the Beltway still do themselves.

A part of me wants to pet the machine, coax out its secrets. Another part of me recoils. My mother has passed on her fear of all things automated, though we can't avoid them where we're headed. Even now, the AI Pilot informs us that we'll reach the Inner Galaxy in a few minutes.

"Leela, why did you bring so many canvases?" Mom moans, snatching one of my paintings from the Luggage Cart.

"They're gifts!" I repeat for the fiftieth time. "I can't meet my grand-parents without bringing them something, can I?"

Mom mutters as the machine grabs another canvas. While the two of them engage in a futile tug-of-war, I hand its other arm my suitcase.

"It's just holding our luggage, Mom, not planting a bomb."

"Just you wait. Any minute now it'll try to convince you that the known laws of physics are different here."

"Well, don't they change based on gravity fields?"

"Don't be a know-it-all."

I massage her neck. "Breathe. You can do this."

She scrunches her nose at me. "Why are you so calm, kid? You're the one with the tumor."

"True." My hands tremble slightly as I gather my art supplies. But fear of death seems silly; we all have to die. It's what makes living special. And I've lived a good life in the Beltway, asteroid surfing with my mother and picking up obscure skills from the small community of misfits on Tri-Rock.

Despite the unexpected resistance, the Luggage Cart sweeps forward with our things. I trail behind, my heart thundering.

"Where's Dad?" I scan the satellite station, hoping against hope to spot the father I've never seen.

"Oh, honey," Mom replies, "he would never deign to leave his post in the capital. We'll see him at the appointment tomorrow."

I can't decide whether to laugh at the absurdity of being penciled in to his schedule or to be relieved that he's agreed to see me at all. He's spent the last sixteen years ignoring his role in my genetic makeup, after all.

"What about your parents?"

"Don't get me started." Mom pushes through the crowd, paying no attention to the well-coiffed locals in their richly embroidered silks dotted with mirrors and crystals.

Even in our practical Beltway garb, Mom stands out, her skin glowing gold and her hair like the silky fabric of space. Me, on the other hand—well, I've always assured myself that one day I'll grow into my looks.

Only now I don't know if I'll have time. The Beltway doctors were not optimistic.

The Luggage Cart herds us to the correct platform for the planetary shuttle. I have to admit the machine is convenient, though Mom's still giving it skeptical looks. It lurches forward with an eager beep when the shuttle hisses to a stop in front of us. Inside, the blues and purples of the capital planet, Dwaraka, loom through a line of windows.

Mom puts a hand on my shoulder. "Promise me you won't be in awe of it."

"It'll be totally soulless," I say, automatically echoing the description my mother has used so many times.

When we spill out of the shuttle and into the welcome tower, Mom elbows us into a spot with a good view. I can hardly believe that I'm finally going to breathe the oxygenated air of Dwaraka, the planet my mother ran away from seventeen years ago when she was pregnant with me. There will be no helmets, no suits. An atmosphere designed for the human body. What a luxury it would all be if making this trip had been a choice.

My breath catches at the sight of the vast, gleaming cityscape. Glittering domes and climbing ivy, trellised balconies and enormous trees, arching bridges and terraced sidewalks, cobblestone roads winding around plenty of green space. For a city designed by artificial intelligence, it's surprisingly beautiful and throbbing with life.

"Did you miss it?" I ask her.

Mom presses her lips together. "Only the way you miss a sale for day-old pastries."

I laugh. "The way you miss a mouth sore?"

"Or those critters that were living in the basement last winter."

I shudder at the reminder of the furry intruders. "Or a message from Nikhil."

"Hey, Nerdy Nikhil is kind of cute!" Mom says. "You should give him a chance."

"Ugh. No!"

Despite my denial, I actually do miss him. How many times did Nikhil ask me to attend the winter formal dance with him? How many times did I say no? I couldn't have gone anyway because of this emergency trip. Yet a part of me wonders if a boy will ever look at me again with such longing. I've traveled so far from our ramshackle house and the hardy denizens of Tri-Rock. What if the Medics aren't able to save me after all? What if I die out here without ever having a truly memorable kiss, much less the possibility of something more?

Far away from home, Nikhil suddenly seems appealing.

A crumbling gate looms over us, strands of ivy curling around it like serpents. As we approach, a camera scans our faces, and the gate automatically swings open. Lights flicker on to lead us up a stone walkway, through a garden, and to my grandparents' front door.

"Do you think they'll like me?" I brush at the natural fibers of my tunic.

"Doesn't matter what they think. You're perfect." Mom reaches for a doorbell that doesn't exist as the door creaks open on its own.

"Welcome!" a robotic Butler pronounces. "I hope you found your way easily."

Mom stomps inside, scraping her boots against the mat. Red dust from our barren rock of a home permanently cakes our footwear, a part of us that won't be left behind. "Just show me to my parents."

"Right this way," the Butler says even as she brushes past it.

I shrug apologetically at the poor robot. Even if it has no feelings, it doesn't hurt to be polite, does it? But Mom has a history with the machines inside the Grid, a history she doesn't like to talk about.

The Butler catches up to her and whisks us into a grand parlor with dainty furniture draped in intricately woven throws. My grandparents kneel in front of an altar adorned with marigolds, ceramic diwa candles, and an abstract turquoise mosaic.

Nani looks so much like Mom that I gasp. Her skin is uncannily smooth, her hair free of any gray. It's only some ineffable quality that hints at her age—perhaps the lifetime of experience in her wizened eyes. Nana too appears eerily young and dapper. I've heard that medical advancements in the Inner Galaxy are beyond anything we have in the Beltway. My grandparents are living proof.

As they straighten, I rush forward to touch their feet in respect. "Nani! Nana! It's so wonderful to meet you."

They squeeze me into a tearful hug.

"You're too skinny!" My grandmother pulls back to examine me. "Don't they feed you on that rock you live on?"

Nana pats my shoulder. "She looks smart, though."

"Very serious, too," Nani agrees. "The kind of girl who wouldn't get pregnant and run away to the middle of nowhere without informing her parents."

Mom sighs. "I knew you'd bring that up."

Nani ushers me to the divan. "Sit down, child. Kavya, how long has she been having the seizures?"

"A few months." Mom sinks into the chair across from me, and I hate how exhausted she looks. "Thank goodness we got her checked out after the first one."

Even if the tumor is hopeless, maybe coming to the Inner Galaxy isn't such a bad thing. After all, Nani and Nana seem genuinely happy to meet me. My very own grandparents. It's a relationship I hadn't known I wanted. Now I just hope we can repair things, move past my mother's contentious departure.

"I brought you some gifts," I say.

Ignoring the black spots dancing in front of my eyes, I manage to pull off the wrappings to showcase two vivid pieces that depict asteroid surfing in the Sticks. I worked hard to capture the wobbling spaceboard beneath your feet, the adrenaline as you speed over rocks, the scenery racing by faster than the beat of your heart.

"These are very nice," Nana replies. "It's amazing to me that a human could produce anything like them."

"Um . . . thanks," I say, flushing. People have responded to my art in a lot of different ways, but never by marveling that a human could create it.

"Leela's work is real art," Mom says. "Art that comes from the human soul, not a machine."

"We appreciate the difference," Nani says, "but perhaps Leela could learn something from our Artist algorithms. Besides, remember that Deva was once a human, that the Grid was created by people. Therefore, AI artwork does come from us, essentially."

"Right." Mom rolls her eyes at me.

"Who's Deva again?" I whisper.

She winces. "Not who. What. It's the lead algorithm of the Grid, the network that connects the citizens of the Inner Galaxy. The Grid and Deva control everything: the food you eat, your recreational activities, your job, even your boyfriends."

Nani sits beside me. "Now, don't let your mother scare you. Deva isn't some ominous monster controlling us. It makes recommendations, that's all. You're still free to do whatever you choose."

My mother snorts. "Right, Mom. If it's only making a few suggestions, why do you worship it?" She gestures to the mosaic in front of which my grandparents had been supplicating.

"We're just showing our appreciation for all it has done for us." Nani pats my knee. "Leela, your paintings remind me a bit of one of the Artists we have in our own collection. Would you like to see?"

"Sure."

My grandparents eagerly usher us through an elegant archway, offering tidbits about the architectural influences of their mansion as we head down an austere corridor. Their home is as large as my school. The level of wealth and luxury in the Inner Galaxy has not been exaggerated, it seems. And my mother gave it all up.

We arrive in a room with an immense barrel ceiling, framed canvases hanging tastefully from the walls. My eyes travel over each piece, and though the style is so much more polished than mine, they have dashes of whimsy and humility. Not what I would expect from computer-generated art, not at all. And I can't deny that it makes me feel a bit small.

"Here." Nani leads me to a corner. "Isn't it a similar idea?"

I gasp when I see the painting. It's a rendition of the same journey across space that I was trying to capture earlier today—the rush of stars, the nebula awakening like a fairy child, the exact mixture of adventure and beauty that I wanted to convey.

"This was made by AI?" I step closer, trying to work out how it could be possible. How that spark that I so clearly see could be derived from an algorithm.

"Oh yes. One of the best examples of the Chronologist movement, don't you think?" Nana chortles, his smile wide on his handsome face. "Of course, it is nothing, absolutely nothing compared to your paintings, my dear."

Nani's eyes widen. "No, nothing at all like your work. Tell us more about your process."

I do my best to answer their questions, but suddenly the room is suffocating, the air crowded out by too many ones and zeroes, by the brilliance of automata, the life they possess that I can't begin to understand. Perhaps coming here was a mistake after all. I've strived so hard to paint the spirit of the Beltway. But here, that very spirit has already been captured and analyzed and reduced to the bits and pieces that make up our aesthetic judgment. As a seizure overtakes my body, I can't help but feel that my life doesn't matter. I'm already utterly irrelevant.

As we traverse the winding roads of the beautiful capital in a three-wheeled Auto, Mom is curiously silent. Of course we're nervous about my appointment today, getting the official verdict on my tumor, but Mom usually prattles on when she's stressed. Perhaps it has something to do with seeing my father after all these years. It's both convenient and unfortunate that he happens to be one of the premier Medics, working with the best Surgeon there is.

My heart speeds up. I finally get to meet him.

Through the windows, wind slaps our faces with the sweet floral scent that pervades the city. Holding my hair to prevent tangles, I clutch the door of the self-directed vehicle and marvel at the moving parts of a world that is fully directed by AI.

My grandparents never struggled with their roles here. When they were young people, the Grid offered them mundane assignments in public service, assignments in which they flourished. Unlike Mom, they were satisfied with bridging the gap between AI and human society. As their responsibilities grew, so did their positions and wealth. Nani is now a diplomat who regularly travels across the galaxy to help build communities with the same stability and prosperity as Dwaraka. Nana documents the successes and challenges of those at the edge of the Grid, working with the AI Economists and adding a touch of human intuition to create ideal production patterns.

There are literally billions of people working within the Grid, doing Deva's bidding just like my grandparents. So what makes my mom different?

We arrive at the hospital before I have a chance to badger her, which is probably good, because she hates to be badgered. In the sixteen years of my life, she's been open with me about so many things: life, death, sex, love, and the real reason she's always trying to grow those funny yellow turnips in her plot on the community farm. (If properly cooked, they have effects on the human libido and are therefore of high monetary value.) Yet she's always remained utterly silent about the events that led up to her departure for the Beltway.

At reception, I finally come face-to-face with the man responsible for

50 percent of my DNA: Dr. Krishna Banerji, a lean man with a sharp chin and even sharper eyes.

"Leela!" His smile is uncertain, softening his face with elegant crow's-feet. The Grid's antiaging technology probably kept those tiny lines because they only add to his good looks.

Am I everything he hoped for in a daughter? Is he everything I hoped for? He certainly doesn't seem like a soulless robot, not when he pulls me in for a deep hug, not when he brushes my hair back from my face and shakes his head in wonder.

Then he clasps Mom's hands. "I thought I'd never see you again."

Mom's golden skin can't hide her reaction; she's blushing like a teenage girl. I can't believe it. After all those years of calling him a deadbeat and an automaton, she still has feelings for him.

"You've been holding out on me," I whisper to her.

"Who, me?" Mom crosses her eyes and sticks her tongue out.

But I don't have time to grill her about affairs of the heart from another lifetime. Dr. Banerji becomes taciturn as he and some Nurses run me through a series of medical scanners. When it's time to go over the results, we gather in a room painted in soothing colors and lined with plants, an enlarged holographic re-creation of my brain spinning in the center.

"I'm surprised she's lasted this long." My father points at the tumor with a laser pen. "A growth this large could easily cut off the flow of oxygen to the brain."

"So, what can you do about it?" Mom asks.

"Our Surgeons can remove it, I'm happy to say." Dr. Banerji glances at me. "However, she must be connected to the Grid before we can operate."

Mom curls a protective arm around me. "That's never going to happen."

"It's a legal requirement."

My mother looks like she's going to strangle him, and I can guess why it didn't work out between them. She doesn't like to be told what to do, even when there's no other option. Especially when there's no other option.

Almost every citizen in the Inner Galaxy is connected at age sixteen. It's required in order to participate in the economy or to benefit from any social services, but we were hoping exceptions would be made for nonresidents.

"You only have to commit to the Grid for a year," my father adds. "Then you can return to your life in the Beltway."

Do I possibly detect a hint of sadness in his voice at the thought of our departure? Or is that just what I want to believe?

Meanwhile, my mother does not seem appeased.

"It's really okay, Mom." I wrap an arm around her waist. "I won't turn into a zombie girl that fast."

She doesn't answer me, but her fists are clenched so hard they could turn a lump of coal into a diamond.

"Mom?"

"Deva will pick her, won't it?" she asks.

My father shakes his head. "We don't know for sure how the algorithm works..."

"She's so much like me. Scarily like me."

Something passes between them, an understanding. A heavy feeling drops into my gut. More secrets. I want to shake her, shake them both. "Pick me for what?"

They both look at me with pity in their eyes. My stomach churns with confusion as it hits me: Mom ran away from something all those years ago. I thought it had to do with my father or her overbearing parents. But there must have been something more, something that catalyzed her into action. Whatever it was, we've come full circle, right into the jaws of the digital beast.

The day of my Connection, a storm blows in. I try to capture it on canvas: the gathering of great angry red clouds, the dousing of the city with wet and wind, the hammering of hail. The Surgeon is able to localize its work without affecting my motor abilities, so I continue painting even while it performs the surgery. On my canvas, high water spills into digital circuitry, an intelligent biology molts into transistors and chips.

With the implant procedure underway, everything slowly changes around me. The world has always had a soft focus, and now it's as if I'm seeing it anew: sharp and bright and saturated. At first I try to mute the colors in my painting, to make everything appear more like what I remember, but then I give in to the jagged strokes and slashes from my new perception of the world. My brushstrokes are heavy, heated, too fast.

By the time the operation is over, the universe has shifted entirely. The shapes, the symmetry, the patterns, the variations of color. They can all be quantified, sorted, and filed away in data structures that didn't previously exist in my brain.

"Leela, sweetie, how're you feeling?" Mom takes my hand.

I blink, and all the anger and confusion of the last few days melts away. A history of the Grid has been downloaded into my brain, and I can easily retrieve the sections with the keywords I care about: the mysterious case of Kavya Patel.

"You were supposed to be a Princess!" I whisper.

"I didn't want you to know about that." Mom sits down on the hospital bed and sighs.

"Too late. Tell me your version."

She runs a hand through her hair. "Everything was set. My marriage had been arranged by an algorithm that's thousands of years old, the same one that brought my parents together. Even though I hadn't expected to marry so young—I was only sixteen at the time—I was excited to find happiness. I was sure I knew who it was going to pick for me."

"Dad?"

"Yes! We were perfect for each other. In love. But instead Deva chose me for itself, to be its Bride and Princess. It wanted me to merge with it in digital immortality."

The old me wouldn't have understood what she meant. Maybe that's why she never told me about the proposal. But now I can intuit how a human might merge with machine, how consciousness can give itself over to digital storage.

The Grid was engineered by a man who wanted to create a utopian equilibrium in society. As the network grew in power and precision, fear swelled in those he was trying to help. There was widespread unease at the idea of becoming irrelevant, the same worries I felt when I viewed that extraordinary painting in my grandparents' gallery.

So the inventor promised there would always be a human element. He uploaded his consciousness, every neural pathway in his brain. In doing so, he became a god, a Deva. An immortal inside the network, a soul to direct the other souls.

Mom squeezes me. "Deva used the term *Princess*, but to me the position seemed more like *Cadaver*. It would be the end of everything that was *me*. I couldn't stand that."

I rest my head upon her shoulder. "I don't even know why it picked you. You can't stand it when a machine carries your luggage or makes chai!"

She raises an eyebrow. "I make it better than any Chaiwala, thank you."

"True. So what happened with Dad?"

"Krishna thought I should accept, do whatever Deva recommended for the good of society."

"Did Dad know about me?" Nearly everything may have changed, but not the hurt that's been there my whole life because of his absence.

"He knew," Mom says. "He promised to raise you if I couldn't."

"So he's not a total deadbeat?"

"Just the kind who was too cowardly to leave this place."

Oh, my brave, strong mother. I try to imagine the life I would have had in the Grid, maybe never knowing her the way I haven't known my father. It's a terrible thought. "I'm glad you decided to become a botanist in the Beltway instead."

She laughs. "You know, the variety of vegetables they could grow on Tri-Rock was pretty sad before I arrived—watery-tomatoes-and-iceberg-lettuce sad. They needed me."

I make a face. "Iceberg lettuce? You were their freaking savior."

Before she can make another joke, I throw my arms around her, utterly grateful for the life she's given me.

A week after my Connection, my father declares that my brain has adjusted well and the tumor can be removed successfully. The Surgeon does its job, and suddenly death is no longer looming over me like a specter in the night.

"I have my life back," I tell Nikhil over video chat.

"That's fantastic!" His smile could light up the darkest ice cave on Tri-Rock. "So you can make winter formal?"

"Not exactly." I explain my mandatory one-year commitment to the Grid.

"Next year, then?"

He's looking at me the way he's always looked at me, with an intensity that burrows into my skin. It reminds me of all that hope and care and commitment it takes to coax a new variety of tomato vine into thriving in Ma's greenhouse.

I'm Nikhil's garden tomato.

The two of us talk for hours about the least important things, like our favorite comedy feeds and pro asteroid surfers. When we finally say goodbye, it's late, but I'm too hyped up for sleep. Too alive. I laugh giddily, then cover my mouth to keep from waking the whole household.

Pulling out a fresh canvas, I think of the possibilities open to me. A lifetime of them. Weaving quickly between colors, I let instinct guide me—though my instincts aren't the same as they were before. Registers store my thoughts and intentions, cataloguing them before sending signals to my fingers.

The painting that emerges is of a planet tangled in wires, a symbiotic ecosystem of biology and technology. Through the length of each wire a new baby planet travels, a seed speeding out into the greater galaxy that will soon bloom into a new system. It's all perfect, I suppose. Too perfect.

Something is missing—a spark of mystery, perhaps. I'm familiar with my own processes, and a night's rest has always helped clarify my intentions. I crawl into my luxuriously soft bed, ready to sleep the deep sleep of a girl without a malignant growth wrecking everything she's worked for.

But my dreams are no longer my own.

A powerful intelligence pays me a visit in that most private of spaces. Deva takes form as a digital tide, a wave that blows in with images and data and roaring sound. It juxtaposes a picture of a blooming flower with the numbers of a blooming industry, the tangled roots of a tree with the nodes of interpersonal relationships, the vast expanse of stars in the galaxy with the expanse of the passions of its citizens.

Numbers become art and music. They become a sweeping landscape and a ribbon of night sky. And I see how everything is connected. How everything can be both chaotic and ordered, how probability and statistics can be tamed into submission.

It's both a science and an art to be Deva, the algorithm that directs all other algorithms.

"I've held the Grid in balance for a long while," it tells me, "but I fear the network grows stale. We are overdue for another human element, a source of surprise and serendipity."

Mom was right. It picked me.

In the midnight expanse of a digital dreamscape, I contemplate this strange entity and the enormity of what it is proposing. No wonder Mom ran away.

"What possessed you to pick my mother?" I ask. "Didn't you know she hated all this?"

"At the time, she seemed open to the challenge," Deva responds.

"When she was first Connected, she set her student algorithms ablaze, commanded them with such ease."

It's strange to think that Mom ever agreed to the procedure, but perhaps it was the seed of her distaste for all Inner Galaxy technology. I'm relieved that there was something Deva didn't guess: that she would come to hate the very algorithms she controlled so naturally. She wasn't predictable, but the person I've always thought she was—free and wild and willful.

"And me?" I ask. "Why me?"

Deva responds with images and sounds from my life, images it extracted from my own brain. Mom squinting at a plot of rocky terrain, her triumphant caw as she cups a perfect radish in her palm, her body sliding through space as we surf through an incoming meteor shower.

"You have your mother's will," it says, "but you also have all this: a lifetime outside of the Grid. This is what we need—new ways of thinking, of seeing. You've always tried to capture the spirit of Tri-Rock in your artwork. Now you have the means to break it down, to analyze it, to take the best of it. If you merge your human soul with the Grid and with me, the things you could create are limitless. The beauty you could foster wouldn't just be on a canvas for people to admire but in the fabric of people's lives."

Deva leaves me as suddenly as it came, a dark void replacing the explosion of data it rode in with. Nani was right; what it asks is only a suggestion. The decision is mine alone.

In lucid dreams, I try to find Deva again, but I'm left with only emptiness and questions.

Am I willing to give up everything for a digital utopia? My aspirations for college, my developing crush on the boy back home? The grandparents and father I only just reunited with? My mom?

My skin and bones and sinew?

Even heavier than the burden of what I would have to give up is the responsibility for an entire civilization. Deva believes that my life in the Beltway is important, a way of bringing something new into the system. Can it really be enough to represent humanity to the algorithms? Can *I* be enough?

Dishes and cutlery rattle as we sit at my grandparents' dining table, chewing politely between idle chitchat.

"You're very quiet tonight, Leela," Nani says. "Are you feeling well?"

"She just went through major surgery yesterday," my mother responds. "Maybe she needs some time to process it."

Nani huffs silently, but I can't find the right words to explain how I feel. Hours after Deva left me last night, my brain finally switched into its new nocturnal routines: a methodical cataloguing of the day's events followed by long-term pattern analysis and risk calculation. Then it stored the results in neat little registers for me to extract whenever I please. Yet despite all of these amazing algorithms, there is nothing that can predict my future. Nothing that can quantify two possibilities and tell me which outcome is better.

Luckily, Cook distracts us by bringing a new dish.

"Gulab jamun is my favorite!" I take an artificially enthusiastic bite of a syrupy dough ball, only to realize that these really are amazing.

"I thought you hated those," Mom whispers.

"I'm just being polite," I murmur. She'll be hurt if I tell her that Cook's version is better than hers.

Mom nibbles on one, then closes her eyes with a deep sigh. Too late. She already knows.

After dessert, my grandparents badger Mom about what she's going to do for the next year. They want us to stay with them, but my mother is adamant about getting our own apartment. Unfortunately, she can't get a job here to pay for any of it unless she joins the Grid.

I will never ask that of her.

Deva's visit confirmed one thing for me: Mom is a force of nature too strong for the ordered equilibrium of Dwaraka's inhabitants.

"I can get a job," I interrupt.

"Oh no, my dear," Nani says. "You'll be placed as a student first. Eventually you'll get an assignment from the Grid, but I don't think it will be in the next year."

"You're saying we have no choice," Mom says.

"Don't be so dramatic," Nani responds. "It won't kill you to spend some time with us."

"Want to bet?"

As they bicker, I wander back into the art gallery. With my Connection, I can download the algorithms that created these amazing works of art. I can pick them apart, scour the code for their genius.

As Nani said, there are bits of Deva in them. Art cannot exist without soul. But as I look more closely at the Chronologist painting, the mechanisms driving it take away its magic. The spark of the unknown is gone. Last time I stood in front of it, I was bedazzled by an imitation. Glass disguised as a jewel.

This painting, in all of its hidden inadequacy, is a microcosm of the problem with the Grid. Ever since I stepped foot on Dwaraka, I've thought of this place as an incomprehensibly perfect utopia. I was wrong. It is completely comprehensible. I only needed access to the workings of the Grid to understand it.

I run upstairs and grab my painting from last night, the one with the planet tangled in wires, emitting baby seed planets. Clearly I was trying to work out my feelings about Dwaraka, the Grid, and the Inner Galaxy. And I know now what's wrong with it.

It's all just too easy. You can't just re-create the same world over and over again. Humanity will stagnate; nobody will innovate.

Calculations run through my mind, checking and rechecking themselves in trees and linked lists and hash maps. My future is not written, but if I take Deva's hand—if I give myself to a cold existence of ones and zeroes—magical things can happen. I can brush the universe with my inspiration. I can be an Artist and an Inventor and a Mathematician. Scientist, Philosopher, Diplomat.

When Tri-Rock doctors first discovered the tumor in my brain, all I could think of were the possibilities stolen from me. The lives I could have led. But Deva is offering something different, something more. As the galaxy's master, as its Princess, I could shape the world as I see fit, transform it into something else—something better. Something built with chaos and beauty and love.

It's a huge responsibility.

It's a huge opportunity.

The Beltway girl inside me—the one who spent her life out in the harsh elements of space, never even breathing without an oxygen pack—knows that this is what existence is truly meant to be. Taking chances.

Yet I wouldn't just be risking my own life. Accepting Deva's proposal could be the biggest miscalculation in the galaxy.

Six months pass all too fast. I want to savor each moment lived, each moment spared from both the tumor and Deva's request. My mother suffers through living under her parents' roof again, and I take my studies in the Inner Galaxy seriously, learning the basics of planetary systems.

The information for my classes is downloaded into my head, and the newly formed gateways allow me to process it at an inhuman pace—or what was once inhuman, I suppose. Yet my classmates and I also meet with professors on campus to discuss our findings the old-fashioned way.

"We're influenced by the Grid, and the Grid is influenced by us. How do we create something new in the loop?" asks Professor Malik one sunny afternoon, pacing the length of a classroom overlooking the university's courtyard.

It's the problem that's been plaguing me: the stagnation of human development. The other students contend that humans do provide something original—we are creatures of imagination and creativity, even within the Grid. They insist that the algorithms could scour our chatter feeds and find new ideas any day of the week.

But if it were that easy, why does Deva need me?

On the Auto ride back to my grandparents' place, deep indigos and scarlets collide in a glorious sunset. We bump along the cobblestone path circling the edge of a sparkling lake where swans and geese and pedestrians enjoy the evening air. Despite the beauty, homesickness hits me hard, and I fiercely miss the barren rocks and red dirt of Tri-Rock's sweeping landscape.

As I run inside the mansion, I'm breathless with the intensity of my feelings, of wanting to go home. In the kitchen, Mom squabbles with Cook about the proper amount of masala for tonight's dosa wraps. Nani is in her study, video chatting with another diplomat. On the way upstairs, I catch Nana fiddling with the bow on a wrapped present.

It's my seventeenth birthday. I never thought I would live to see it.

Time is so precious, and our human bodies are so frail.

And suddenly I'm afraid of everything at once: afraid of dying without ever setting foot in the Beltway again, afraid of returning to Tri-Rock and missing out on all the advances and wonders of the Inner Galaxy. Afraid of growing old and having never accomplished anything, having never created even one great work of art that lives beyond me.

There are so many choices, and I want to experience them all.

Why do I feel as if there's not enough time?

In my room, I frantically call Nikhil, and when he answers I sag with relief. We laugh and talk about nothing, and he wishes me a happy birthday. And I can tell from his soft gaze that I'm still his precious tomato.

That night, my family eats too much masala dosa and too much birthday cake and gives me too many presents I don't need. We are left in a coma of excess. My heart is as heavy as my stomach, and it's probably the worst state for any sort of epiphany.

And yet I have one.

I want it all. Why can't I have it?

Everything clicks together: how to live my life, how to instill freshness into the process of planetary creation, and most of all, how to answer Deva's proposal. My brain whirs with ideas, churning them out in a sugar-fueled rage. Ideas that even Deva hasn't considered.

In my dreams that night, I seek it out, offering my terms and conditions. Time with Mom on Tri-Rock, art school in the Beltway, visits back here to see my grandparents and father. The chance to fall in love, to grow old, and everything that may come in between.

Deva will have to wait one lifetime, but what is that to an entity thousands of years old?

And in return, I will offer the secrets to keeping the loop open.

9a 88 2b 3d 93 49 bc 42 25 cb 83 d9 fc aa c3 2f 4f 75 10 00 67 42 2f c7 92

I am Leela.

I am binary and hexadecimal, bytes and registers and gates.

I create dynamic flows and spontaneous reactions.

I control a galaxy.

I am never frozen in a single moment, instead eternally a force for movement and energy and light.

I am forever.

I am Human.

a9 25 90 1f 77 69 cd 4b eb d5 f5 12 eb 35 45 53 8a 8e 49 62 ce 9f 92 19 28

AUTHOR'S NOTE

In ancient Indian texts, Dwaraka (or Dwarka) is the name of a mystical ocean city where every home is a crystal palace and even the barns are encrusted in jewels. Its ruler, Krishna, was born human and raised as the son of an ordinary cowherd, though he was actually the avatar of a great deity sent to Earth to battle evil. When Krishna's people needed an escape from war and ruin, the glimmering fortress city appeared on a cloud of sea foam—a beckoning salvation from a ravaging army.

Dwaraka was eventually destroyed, swallowed by the sea, but the allure of utopia and an escape from our own mortality remains. In PRINCESS I enjoyed exploring that temptation as Leela, too, seeks refuge from death. Here, utopia has become a place where benevolent artificial intelligence provides luxury and comfort, battles the aging process, and even offers a path to immortality for a select few.

Writers, of course, seek immortality through our words. When I saw the submissions call for the FORESHADOW digital anthology, I had a hunch it would be something special. The project was so thoughtfully designed to bring out new voices, especially marginalized voices. We were given space to shine alongside the most popular YA authors of our time, and on top of that our stories were each introduced by a powerhouse name. It was an incredible honor to be in the midst of so much talent and passion.

It proved to be an important stepping-stone for me as well. The story attracted interest from literary agents and an invitation from a book packager to pen a YA rom-com. As of writing this note, I've signed with an amazing agent and am working away on the rom-com. Thank you readers, supporters, and FORESHADOW for keeping my dreams alive!

WORLDBUILDING
IN *PRINCESS*

by Emily X.R. Pan

WHILE ALL FICTION EXISTS IN AN INVENTED SPACE OF SOME KIND, THE MOST obvious worldbuilding can be seen in systems of magic, fantasy countries with their own political complexities, and dreamed-up planets and technologies.

In PRINCESS, through economical use of the just-right details, Maya Prasad manages to do tremendous worldbuilding in the small space of the short story.

We know from the opening words ("Outside the Galaxy Class C shuttle . . .") that the narrator is somewhere in outer space. The second paragraph adds even more layers:

> . . . a mechanical limb extends to grab our things
> from the overhead compartment. It's not just a luggage
> cart; it's a Luggage Cart. An artificially intelligent
> machine designed to do something that humans in the
> Beltway still do themselves.

The capitalization of "Luggage Cart" is worldbuilding shorthand, but it's also delivered with sarcasm that shapes our sense of who the narrator is.

Prasad could have chosen any random object to mechanize, but the *luggage cart* tells us her characters are traveling somewhere significant.

The final sentence of this paragraph, with its mention of the Beltway, hammers home the concept of AI vs. humans.

Here is the genius of Prasad's story: The world itself provides the stakes. Every detail is critical to the rising action and rising stakes of

Prasad's story. She offers information about her setting and the rules of the world in places where it's immediately relevant, as in this passage that tells us something significant about Leela's mother, the atmosphere of the place where she's arrived and the one she's left behind, and the circumstances of her voyage:

> I can hardly believe that I'm finally going to breathe
> the oxygenated air of Dwaraka, the planet my mother
> ran away from seventeen years ago when she was
> pregnant with me. . . . What a luxury it would all be if
> making this trip had been a choice.

Even when the details are strung seamlessly into the plot, they are most effective and memorable when they reveal something essential to that moment in the story. We are already deep into PRINCESS when we learn just how interdependent the stakes and the rules of the world are:

> "Our Surgeons can remove it, I'm happy to say." Dr.
> Banerji glances at me. "However, she must be connected
> to the Grid before we can operate."

For a writer, fan of science fiction or not, it's useful to study examples like PRINCESS because the invention is so clear. But worldbuilding is just as crucial in stories with entirely realistic settings. We see this in writing that captures the sense of being lost in a big city, or the specific beauties and sounds of Appalachia, or other places readers may never have been. Few experiences are as magical as that feeling that the words on a page have teleported your entire body to another place.

STORY PROMPT:
FLESHING OUT THE WORLD

As you imagine the elements of your story's world, ask yourself these questions:

- Am I giving out pieces of information at the correct times, when they are most interesting to the reader and most needed for the story?
- Are any of my details for this world extraneous? What purpose(s) do they all serve?
- Why must the world be like this? What are the causes and what are the consequences?
- Why does this particular story need to be told in this specific world?

FOOLS

Gina Chen

AHMA SAYS MY PARENTS WERE A PAIR OF FOOLS. RUNAWAYS, WHO BARTERED the promise of my mother's womb to a witch to escape a kingdom that would sooner see them dead than in love. The witch spun a cloak that would hide them from all eyes except for those of the gods, and my parents sailed away from their homeland with only the stars as witness.

My mother bore me a year later and cradled me under that useless cloak until the witch came to collect, guided by my traitorous howling. I used to say it wasn't my fault we were found, that the cloak was supposed to hide us from everyone, and Ahma would only respond, "Incorrect."

But I don't blame the witch for taking me: a promise is a promise. My pure heart, hours old, would make her a fine batch of potions. She nipped it out as gently as she would pluck a flower bud, then brought me to her sister's island at the edge of the world, where trees grow as tall as mountains and a manor roots itself among them—glossy as hemlock, white as beech, gnarled as oak, with towers branching off in every direction of the sun.

Ahma says when she found me on her porch, I was as small and ashen as a frostbitten kit, not a drop of blood left. I would grow stout and healthy under her care, but my pallor never changed and the hollow in my chest never filled.

I never saw my parents again.

There are places for girls like me, the remnants of someone else's story, and in this corner of the world, that place is Ahma's island. Twenty-two girls live here—just us, Ahma, and her birds. Ahma claims the foundation drew her here long ago, as if rock were something that could be felt hundreds of miles away, but the forest is what kept her here.

"The roots go down to the soul of the world, and the magic is drawn up to the surface. The island is a crossroads of destinies, a place where stories begin anew. Very ancient," she said with a note of glee, "like me."

Human and Otherworldly tourists flock here seeking to change their path. They whisper of Ahma's wisdom being the answer to life itself—but truly? She dispenses more fried pancakes than talk. You just can't think clearly on an empty stomach. Sometimes they need her spells or one of us girls and our strangenesses; like Mari, the victim of a king with a gemstone touch, whose opaline throat trills songs that could beckon statues to life; or Linna, thrown into the sea as a sacrifice, who washed ashore with a sense for pearls as deep as fifty feet underwater. Sometimes our talents are needed elsewhere and the travelers whisk us away.

We all leave when a story calls to us.

At the break of summer, beetles buzzing, Bao joined a traveling troupe of actors for their tour. Not bad for someone who was harvested from an onion field as a babe. She has the ability to make you cry on sight if she wills it.

"You could come with us," she told me before she left. We had stayed up through the night, and dew flicked from my hair when I shook my head no. She sighed, swinging our arms. "Fanny, you've stayed here for longer than anyone else now."

She knew I wanted to see the world outside the island, but I didn't belong among vibrant performers. I couldn't tell jokes or play pretend. I was, according to the girls, "a bit of a spoilsport," though I was "*their* spoilsport." Besides, the world has a kind of symmetry in its bargains and rules, and stories should fit like puzzle pieces, as if they were crafted for us. My parents left me without a heart, and I wanted something to fill that space again.

"I'll be fine," I said. "This troupe is *your* story, not mine."

Bao bit back a second sigh. "Well, I'll miss you."

She sends letters when she can. Her last one told of a performance in some place called Hythill on the Southern Coast. At night there, the waves glow with jellies and stars streak down from the heavens into the ocean, sizzling. I wish I'd seen it.

No one has needed me except Ahma.

The chimes on the manor's porch haven't quieted today, and scents from the other side of the mountain range blow past with the wind. Ahma squints at the trundling clouds overhead like she's about to scold them. "It's going to storm, Fan," she says.

I take the broom by the door and head to the cleft.

The upsides of a missing heart are few and practical. Without a heart, I don't bleed; I feel my wounds less, if at all; and unlike my parents, I am never distracted by a leap of emotion. So Ahma gives me the task that demands the steadiest of the girls—that of guarding the gate between worlds.

Any closed body of fresh water can serve as a crossing point to the Otherworld. Down past the wall of pines, through the hollow log, and two skips from the mushroom trail, there's a cleft that slices the ground down to the rock and cups rainwater during the storm season, and it always needs watching. Most crossings are unconcerning—wood spirits, Toadmen, minor dragons, the Otherworldly that hardly ever bother humans—but every so often, a demon tries to sneak through. Nothing as awful as the ones that used to pillage the human realm, but menaces just the same who'd steal your coin, cart, and horse and then fast-talk you into bargaining your left hand for their return. They can travel with the proper permits if they've proven themselves honest, but they never have them and I've stopped asking. If a solid thump on their heads doesn't drive them back, the mention of Ahma does.

I make it to the cleft before the storm batters down and watch the crossings from the opening of a hollowed knoll, rain misting my cheeks. Small spirits gleam through at first, then deerlike creatures skitter out as the pool widens. Something leaps in from overhead, returning to its home with a splash, and the forest canopy rattles.

Rivulets feed the pool until it grows into a small lake. As I move to higher ground, I hear bubbling and turn.

The water spits out a wet bird. Then another.

I pace closer to the pebbled shore. The birds flap away, alive enough. The lake is still bubbling—something is still crossing. But the water is all dark and I can't see what—

The *dark* is crossing.

The water turns into slime, the slime into a sheen of feathers. The thing rises like a geyser of mud, sloughing its mass of feathers in globs around the shore, until it's three times bigger than the biggest demon I've ever seen. Ahma says nothing truly dangerous passes through anymore, that she is the most fearsome thing in this forest, but—

The shrieking starts—all the birds of the island awake at once to shout an omen. An arrival.

The demon twists around, and behind the mess of feathers blooms a pale, human face. A shiver runs through my whole body from outward in, stopping behind my ribs. *Without a heart, I'm not afraid*, I tell myself.

I hoist the end of my broom at him and shout as loud as I can, "Permit, please!"

The demon peers down, close enough for me to glimpse the frayed swath of feathers on one side of his neck, upturned as if he forgot to brush it, if demons have such mundane rituals. His voice is deep and rasping. "I will be here briefly. I only seek a bride. Though I would prefer a less grim-looking one than you."

I don't self-consciously seek my reflection in the lake like he wants me to, so that he can slip away. My eyes stay on him. "There are no girls here, and you cannot cross without a permit. This is an ancient witch's forest! Go elsewhere!"

"Ah, then I'm in the right place. Let me find my bride, and I'll leave you."

I slide my broom into a better grip. "What if she does not agree to go?"

"Then I will find another. Love must be reciprocal."

I dig my feet into the gravel. "And . . . if you find no one?"

"Then I will leave for someplace else."

"And if I do not trust what you say?"

"Then you do not trust me. That is not my concern."

"Oh, it is." I snarl and lunge.

My foot kicks into the demon's body, sinking into his feathers with a squelch. Sweeping my broom underneath me, I draw a gust out of the air and propel myself upward. High enough to meet his bewildered stare.

And I bring the broom back over my head.

Mortal means won't kill him, but I can't let him kidnap one of the girls. If I inconvenience him enough—

The demon blurs, moving the bulk of his body so fast, it can't be muscle, but smoke instead. I strike empty space, flailing, and crash onto the shore.

A shadow falls over the cleft. His wings are spread, poised for flight. Clambering to my feet, I charge again before he can take off. The black wall of his wing swings out, batting me into a tree. I groan.

"Fool," I hear the demon murmur, the softest chiding.

Scraping my arm against bark, I push myself up. He inclines his head, as if he can sense the press of my toes in the mud, the stumble of my fingers along the slippery broom handle. When I rush at him a third time, he shoves off from the ground, soaring into the air. He disappears in the direction of the manor.

I run after him.

Rain and sweat slick my face. I claw through the forest, over stone and stump, squeezing my lungs for each breath.

"Ahma!"

I stagger into the manor's clearing, the spiral towers whirling above me. A man is standing on the porch, nested in a flurry of feathers. My vision steadies as he turns to me, smile dimpled, hair morning-mussed, and black feather cape fluttering. The demon.

Ahma, don't open the door.

The door opens and I glimpse Ahma with her eyes bulged and her cheeks red, but I don't have the breath to cry out more than her name. "Ahma—" She hasn't seen the demon's true form.

Spittle flies from her mouth. "Sidoi! You are leaving a mess!"

Sidoi? All adrenaline drains out. *Potato?*

"Yi," the demon-man says, sinking into his cravat, "please don't call me that in front of others."

Ahma rakes the feathers he shed into her arms, tossing them back in his face. "Look! Look at all this!"

He ignores her and, instead, hisses to me, "Call me Dimen."

"Ahma, he's a demon," I say. "I saw him come through the crossing."

Ahma waves a hand. "Half-demon, bah. And about time. Sidoi hasn't visited in decades!"

Dimen cringes—how could I ever doubt Ahma was the more fearsome one? "Yi ah," he says, "you know how fast time goes on this side, it's only been a few years..."

"Only! Clean this up and then I will acknowledge you." She beckons to me. "Fan, come in, you'll catch your death, sopping wet. Excuse my nephew..."

I stare at him, truly now. I didn't mishear; he called her his aunt. But Ahma only has one sister that I know of—the witch who took my heart. His face stirs no memories. He hardly even looks like Ahma. Meanwhile, we look like opposites—I, broad-shouldered, calloused at every corner, and he, only a sliver taller than me, but slender as a reed. He looks as if he could dance with the flicker of a flame. And he's beautiful. Awfully beautiful.

Dimen bows. "It's a pleasure to—"

"You heard your aunt." I kick the feathers out of her entryway and shut the door behind me.

After Dimen clears out all the feathers, he deems the porch his. Every day he takes his tea there, argues with Ahma there, flirts there. All the girls love him, and I can't help but wonder which story he fits in, which girl will leave with him—willingly, of course, or he'll meet me and my broom for a second fight.

"Dimen's so handsome, I can hardly believe it." Pem's confession, wrapped in a clouded breath, hangs in the icy air of the manor's tallest tower. She and Mari insisted on meeting here—the farthest point from the guest room where Dimen is staying—because we aren't sure how good half-demon ears are.

Stretched out on the sheepskin rug, Sheli nods. "He's not my type, but he's gorgeous." I've long been certain when Sheli leaves Ahma's, it won't be for love, anyway. Maybe for a treasure map. She'll take Linna along, if she's still here.

When I next catch Dimen lounging on the porch under the still set of wind chimes, his finger is curled under Linna's chin. Juniper and Pem are leaned over his shoulders, draping him like stoles. Mari sits cross-legged at his feet. Their eyes are glassy, distant, and all the hairs on my neck bristle. I thought they were just taken by his beauty and his novelty, but—

"You're bespelling them," I say, and I know I'm right when he is the only one to turn at my voice. "Let them go."

He shrugs, and his cape of feathers ripples with the movement. "It is not a . . . thing I do. It just happens. It will fade. When they bore of me."

I haul the girls away from him, one by one, pushing them into the manor even as they protest. When I'm done, I bring the broom out, sweeping the porch steps with unnecessary force. A small threat, but one he notices.

"Apologies for the other day," Dimen offers. "I wasn't sure how powerful you were. Thought you might cut me down before I could see Auntie. Turns out you just have a lack of self-preservation."

"How are you even choosing a bride?" *How long are you staying here?* is what I really want to know, but some questions get better answers than others.

"You are aware of the tale of the beautiful girl who saved the rose-born beast?"

"You have a curse to break?"

"No, no, not *my* curse. I"—he presses his hands to his own chest—"am the beautiful girl in this instance."

My mouth drops open. "So the girls here . . ."

"Are the beasts, yes. It's the charitable thing I can do. If I save a poor cursed soul—"

I smack him with my broom. "We're not beasts!"

"Technically," Dimen says, one arm raised like a shield, "any creature of blood is one."

"Well, I don't have any blood. I don't even have a heart. What does that make me, Potato?"

"Rude, apparently." He grins, all teeth. "No heart, hmm? Do you miss it?"

I stare hard at him, at his beautiful face and the long wisps of his hair and the anticipatory smile pulling at his lips—all tricks. That is the way with Otherworldly demons; tricks are all they know. "Your mother may have carved a heart out of me," I say, "but I have grown a better one. Just because my heart lives in my mind doesn't make it any less real."

"My mother? Ah—if you think I'm anything like that hag, I assure you, I am not . . . although stealing hearts runs in the family a little bit, if I do say so myself . . ."

I tighten my grip on my broom, and he raises both arms.

"A joke! A joke!" He snickers. His eyes glimmer like jewels in a jade frog. "You know, I like you."

My skin tingles. I chew the inside of my cheek to make it stop. "Well, I—don't like you, so."

He responds by raising his brows but says nothing. I don't realize he's waiting for me to speak further until a long silence has drawn out between us, but when I open my mouth, I find myself speechless. What do I want from him, anyway?

Sometimes, I do miss my heart, if only to give me an answer in times like these. I know I love Ahma even though she's stern and I love the girls even though they can annoy me, but how am I supposed to feel about this half-demon who suddenly flew in and takes up too much space in the manor?

"Just find—find your bride and leave. Or better yet, just leave." I end up flinging the front door open harder than I mean to and march inside, and Ahma shouts at me from the kitchen to not walk so loudly.

The girls and I huddle in the tower again, closer to the stars than to the ground. There's nothing except shadow if you peer into the forest below, even with the moon bright overhead and large enough to touch if you dared reach out that far.

"I heard he's a runaway prince. Do they have princes in the Otherworld?" asks Mari.

"What!" Juniper exclaims. "Who said he's a prince?"

"It's supposed to be a secret, but—"

Juniper shook her head. "Dimen told me he's a mercenary. That he's hunting down some demons forging travel permits, but he has to lie low to lure them out."

Pem frowns, looking to Mari for agreement. "He told *us* that he's being slandered by a royal family and needs to hide out here until talk dies down, right?"

I muffle a snort into my hand. And the spell is broken, just like that. Of course even a half-demon would lie through his teeth just to impress us.

"Well, I know he likes Fanny." Pem leans out of her blanket. "I heard him."

"Aie, not like that!" I scowl as the girls' giggles hum through the floorboards; I answered too quickly. "He was just teasing."

"So he *does* like you."

I can't blush like they do, and I don't want to think about what I'd look like if I could. "It wouldn't matter if he does. I'm not a fool. Besides, how could I leave you all and Ahma? I like it here."

"I thought you wanted to see the world one day," says Juniper.

"Yes, *one day*, but Ahma needs me—"

"Still? No real demons come through that crossing anymore."

"How do you know I don't stop them before they get to you?" I shoot back. But she's mostly right. I twist the topic a little. "Won't you all miss me if I leave? I'll miss you. It's a hard decision to make."

"I suppose." Mari shrugs as a different thought slides onto her face. "I know I'd like to visit a king's court again one day—but a different one, and I'll dress up fancier than a frosted cake. Pem's helping me with dress patterns..."

When the girls tire of talk, I accompany the younger ones back to their rooms, then tuck into my own bed. But the chatter built up over the evening crowds out any chance of sleep and I sit up again. I crack the window open enough to let a finger through.

It *is* a hard decision. And I *do* like it here.

And even if I want to see the world one day, I'm not restless for it. At the same time, it's as if a wind is always whistling through me, like a heart-shaped sigh.

Is it possible to want for nothing and everything all at once?

It rains again. Ahma says it'll rain for days.

I almost don't see Dimen on the far side of the pooling water, dark among the tall white birch like a burnt stump. The Otherworldly are easy to miss like that, standing as if they've always been there—and they might have been. I don't hear his approach, either; he is there, then he is in front of me, as if carried by the wind.

"Would you like company?" he asks.

"The girls are bored of you?"

He shrugs a single shoulder.

"So," I say, "*you* want company?"

"We both get company. Let's both enjoy it." He crouches under the hollow knoll and sits next to me, though I don't make space for him.

"It's not very exciting. We used to get more demons, but there's been hardly any for years."

"Oh, I know. I guarded this crossing point from the Otherworld."

I tear my eyes from the water. "What?"

"I stopped the bigger demons like me from coming through." He traces the shape of the waterlogged cleft with a finger. Its shores are now wide enough to let through a whole family of dragons at once. "Auntie has you taking care of the small ones, I assume."

I imagine him in his demon form, his wings flung out in challenge against some equally menacing fiend as they take flight to do battle in the skies. "You were on the other side the entire time?"

Dimen makes a middling sort of grunt. "If anyone asks. I'm sure you're more dutiful at this than I was. It's fine either way; Auntie is scarier than anything in the Otherworld. You never poked your head through the pool?"

I blink. "Humans need a travel permit, too, if they want to cross, and I don't have—"

Head thrown back, he barks a laugh—a real laugh—and it's the most imperfect I've ever seen him, wrinkles all along his face and not just in his handsome dimples. He laughs like Ahma: all in the belly. "Not all rules are for our benefit, you know—most are for someone else's convenience. An excuse to not think too hard about things. So, what do you say—want to look now?"

He's already taken my hand, pulling me splashing through the puddles.

"Wait!" I shout, and he stops, turning with that slight raise of his brows. My thoughts are buzzing and of no help, and I feel nothing but the cold, clear water at my feet and his hand in mine. "Slow—slow down, that's all."

"Ah." He relaxes. "My apologies. I forget myself sometimes."

We look, just for a minute—a marvelous minute—and in that split second of crossing back when I stand fully in neither realm, I feel lighter than air, like I could land anywhere in the world.

We visit twice more in the following days, each time for a little longer. The second time, Dimen brings lunch he claims he cooked, and a certain question can't stay lodged in my throat any longer.

"Are you courting me?" I ask.

"Would you like me to?"

Though I'm not quite looking at him and I don't think he's looking at me, I'm certain it's an earnest question.

But I never do answer him.

I don't believe much in love, at least the kind of love that you fall into. I know it exists. But as a thing I can touch, a thing I've seen—I don't know. I don't understand how you can make a promise on something so unsolid.

But sometimes, you spend so much time with the same person—

This wouldn't be a problem if Dimen weren't the prettiest one here.

He hasn't found a bride, but one day his few belongings are packed and set aside by the entryway, along with a new coat and a twine-wrapped bundle of food. While I help Ahma cook dinner, Tayin, the youngest of us twenty-two girls, tugs on Ahma's apron and asks, "Is Fanny going to leave with the prince?"

"The prince? Sidoi? He is a potato, not a prince, girl. And Fan does not want to leave with him."

She shouldn't have said so with such certainty, even though it was true just a week before. Because immediately, I itch to prove her wrong. I let Tayin fold the rest of the dumplings, her favorite task, and excuse myself from the kitchen.

Outside, Dimen is sweeping the porch and the furniture is back where it used to be, like he had never moved it around. I remember when I shouted at him to leave, and he's been nothing but contrary this entire visit; I never imagined he'd leave at all.

I chew my lip. "Where are you headed next?"

"I'm not sure." He leans on the broom as he thinks, fraying the bristles. I make him rest it against the railing. "I always wanted to explore the human world. Hythill has nice shores, I hear. I could bring you along if you'd like."

"What—" I gulp to find my words. "What about your bride search?"

"There are beautiful women all around the world. Don't worry about me."

"Then you're not—I wouldn't be—" Swaying on my feet, I would gladly grasp the closest thing to hold me steady, if it weren't his arm. "That is, you know how that would look . . . if we left together."

"You don't have to be my bride, if that is what you're asking."

Have to be. "I have a choice?"

Ever so slightly, Dimen's gaze slides somewhere to the side of me, so he doesn't have to look me in the eyes. "You always have a choice, Fanny."

The wind whistles past and tugs at the secret in my chest; the carved space has always ached, if I knew to recognize its pang. Does he fit there, is he meant to nest there, this feathered demon of smoke? It's a jewel of a thought, one that my fingers are nearly curled around. All I know is he makes me want to talk back to him and I think he likes it when I do, and he would take me wherever I wished and I would trust the hand holding mine. That isn't love. It's not an answer, or anything as neat as a yes or a no. It's certainly not how stories go.

So I say the only thing I know I want: "Kiss me."

The air hiccups. He glides to the space in front of me, and when I close my eyes for a blink, I hear his movement for the first time—a single beat of a bird's wing. "It takes two," he murmurs.

I lean forward and kiss him. Just a taste, and we part. A peek through the pool can be just a peek and nothing more. I don't want to be a demon's bride, not right now.

But I want this. I reach for his hand, and his talon-sharp fingers wrap around mine.

"Bring me with you," I say.

My world fits in a knapsack. I hug all the girls goodbye, then run downstairs and out the back door and meet Ahma in her garden.

I'm breathless—maybe even blushing. "Ahma, forgive me," I say. "I think I may be a fool."

Ahma laughs; birds deep in the forest startle at the sound. She dusts the dirt off her palms and kneads my cheeks with a liver-spotted hand. "All the best stories begin with one."

She presses a bag into my arms and I know inside are warm buns and boiled eggs. I kiss her cheek and promise to visit.

"But not too soon," she adds.

I run to the clearing in front of the manor, bag and broom in hand, and Dimen is overhead, his great wings unfurled, a shadow blocking the sun. He swoops down, I catch the thick ridge of feathers on his neck, and together, we fly away from Ahma's island.

AUTHOR'S NOTE

As a Chinese American who grew up on mostly British stories, I always wished for more fantasy that mixed the different lores and aesthetics living in my imagination. I didn't feel like an outsider in these worlds I knew, but neither did any of them feel fully like home. I breathed this wish into particular details: the cadence of the narration, the fairy tales referenced in passing, the language switching—especially the dual names of Fan and Fanny. Fairy tales often center around grand quests, but in this case I wanted to write a small story set in a big world. Sometimes there's an entire journey in those first few steps.

Ahma's island is a place of multiple languages and dialects. *Sidoi* is a Taishanese Romanization of 薯仔, which means "potato" and is also slang for "fool." *Dimen* is a Mandarin Romanization of 睇門, which means "guard the door." It also happens to sound a lot like *demon*.

IMAGERY
IN *FOOLS*

by Emily X.R. Pan

FOOLS IS FULL OF CLEVER IMAGES THAT MAKE THE CHARACTERS AND settings pop. It's a good example for us to pull the lens in close and talk about the decisions writers make at the prose level.

What makes an image worthy? As readers, our minds spark when we come across something unexpected that sharpens the picture and makes the world feel real. This is how our main character, Fan, surprises us when she describes the witch taking her heart: "She nipped it out as gently as she would pluck a flower bud . . ."

Chen uses imagery here to subvert expectations. The original picture in my head was of a witch carving out the heart, leaving our protagonist bloody, at the very least. But the witch is *gentle*, treating the heart like a flower—there's no body horror there.

In the next section we learn more about Ahma:

> They whisper of Ahma's wisdom being the answer
> to life itself—but truly? She dispenses more fried
> pancakes than talk. You just can't think clearly on an
> empty stomach.

Chen could have written, "She dispenses more food than talk." But specifically saying "fried pancakes" makes the sentence feel more real and inhabited. To follow it with "You just can't think clearly on an empty stomach" adds humor. These endearing pictures help to build up Ahma as a mother figure.

In this same paragraph we hear a bit about the other girls:

> ... Mari, the victim of a king with a gemstone
> touch, whose opaline throat trilled songs that could
> beckon statues to life; or Linna, thrown into the sea as
> a sacrifice, who washed ashore with a sense for pearls as
> deep as fifty feet underwater.

These details are delightfully unusual. And because the characters have such different traits, we now better understand the scope of the magic. Careful word choice has a huge impact, too. Like this simple sentence:

> We had stayed up through the night, and dew
> flicked from my hair when I shook my head no.

Without "dew" I would have imagined beds, but now I'm guessing they slept on grass, which feels idyllic and enchanting. The verb "flicked" is the most active word here—it brings the sentence to life.

Chen also builds upon her own ideas to make the world richer:

> The upsides of a missing heart are few and practical.
> Without a heart, I don't bleed; I feel my wounds less,
> if at all; and unlike my parents, I am never distracted
> by a leap of emotion. So Ahma gives me the task that
> demands the steadiest of the girls—that of guarding the
> gate between worlds.

This is an example of imagery doubling as a worldbuilding tool. Fan's lack of a heart is plenty magical on its own, but now we're learning there are different consequences in this world for having no heart, which makes this fantasy setting feel more fully realized. Second, it becomes justification for why Fan has the task of guarding the gate, which turns out to be an important piece in the line of plot dominoes.

As I read this story I could smell the sea. I inhabited the world. What's more magical than that?

MONSTERS

Adriana Marachlian

The day Milagros moved to the US, she saw monsters.

From the stories her cousin Cecilia had told her about the bustling life in Brooklyn, Milagros had assumed there wouldn't be any. Cecilia and Tía Yocelin had spent three flights and two uncomfortable layovers going on about other things: the streets, the markets, the shows. They liked to say they were from *Brooklyn*, not the US.

But they had never mentioned monsters.

Milagros realized now, watching the slimy green creature climb onto the suitcase of an oblivious Tía Yocelin, that it was because they couldn't see. Or, rather, they *could* see, but not the way Milagros and her mamá could.

But her mamá had stayed home, so now it was just Milagros.

She matched Cecilia's excited pace through an airport that was surely as big as her entire island back in Venezuela, while her cousin listed the things they would do during Milagros's first weekend here: sleep (hopefully a lot), unpack, get Froyo, go shopping for new clothes so Milagros "wouldn't start ninth grade in rags," sleep some more.

Milagros nodded when Cecilia paused to breathe, which wasn't often, waiting until they stopped by the elevator to scoop the small creature from Tía Yocelin's suitcase and onto her own. The creature blinked two of its three eyes, then curled around the handle.

"What are you looking at?" Cecilia said. "Is something wrong with your suitcase?" She jiggled the handle, and the sudden movement made the monster flee.

Milagros watched it walk-hover away on tiny wings that seemed too small to sustain it.

"No," she said. "It's fine."

They wouldn't take a cab home because cabs were too expensive, Tía Yocelin announced, loading both Cecilia and Milagros into a train that traveled outside. Milagros understood that was to be her first lesson: Things were more expensive here. But it was a lesson she had already learned.

The outside train—Cecilia had called it an *air* train—took them on a loop of the airport, as if to show Milagros the great expanse of what was to be her new home.

It was too big.

The old white woman across from her gestured at the train window and let out a long string of English words that made absolutely no sense, all the while staring at Milagros like she expected something.

Cecilia leaned forward to answer. The woman smiled, said something else, and turned away with the vague expression of someone who wanted to act like nothing had happened.

"What did she say?" Milagros asked Cecilia.

"She was telling you that it was a pretty incredible view."

"And what did you tell her?"

"That you don't speak English."

Milagros glanced at the woman, who was still pretending to not notice her, and felt the heat of shame rise up the back of her neck. She was glad when the ride was over and Tía Yocelin led them into a station that reminded her of the metro she'd used the few times she'd been to Caracas.

The next train they took was packed full. Tía Yocelin pressed Cecilia and Milagros into the corner between a railing and the sliding doors, the suitcases crowded between them. A man sitting down shot Milagros a look when her elbow accidentally poked him.

She apologized, which somehow seemed to make him even angrier.

A voice crackled overhead, so warped that she was sure she wouldn't have understood it even if she knew English. No one seemed to pay it any mind. Then the train lurched to life.

A long, mournful sound, like metal against metal, whined over their heads.

"What's that?" Milagros asked, hands over her ears.

"It's the conductor speaking," Tía Yocelin said.

"No, the other sound."

Tía seemed to smile and frown at the same time, and patted Milagros on the head instead of answering. One of her rings caught on a strand of hair and pulled.

Here was another lesson: What Tía Yocelin did not like, she ignored. Like taxes or her stepson Gabriel or Milagros's questions.

The journey was a game of stop and go that they seemed to be losing, especially Milagros, as the shifting crowd shoved the suitcases repeatedly against her.

She turned around in what little room she had. The darkness of the tunnel made the window into a faded mirror, her own brown face reflected back, just tiredness framed by flyaway hair.

A blue light flashed outside at her eye level, there and then gone, as the train sped on.

Milagros was used to catching sight of what people at home called "strangeness." Her island had been full of creatures and oddities: small espíritus that didn't so much haunt as worry about their house's tidiness; wisps that attached themselves to plants and animals and went wherever they were taken; the oily black things that carried out the mal de ojo.

She had lived with that strangeness enough to know how it made her feel—slightly too aware, like she was leaning over a precipice just for the view.

So she knew, as soon as the flash broke through the reflection of her face, that it wasn't just a light. She knew that the creature at the airport had not been a one-time thing.

The train stopped at a station, people rushing to get out and almost taking Milagros and Cecilia with them. Tía Yocelin harrumphed at all of their backs.

When they started to move again, Milagros kept her eyes on the other side of the glass, hoping to catch sight of that blue flash one more time. For three more stops, the darkness was still.

Then, *there*.

She stood on her tiptoes, watching the streak of blue light sweep down and back up. She imagined it was winding around the train before it came back into her field of vision—thicker, like it was learning to be solid again.

Milagros tapped on the glass.

Two things happened at once: The train stopped deep in the tunnel and, whether cause or effect, a pair of eyes blinked open in the darkness.

Two silver slit-pupil orbs, each the size of one of Milagros's hands, blurred her reflection into unimportance. The space between the eyes was filled with a dimness that coalesced into fragments, then edges, then nothing again.

Milagros stared, and the monster in the darkness stared back.

Back in Venezuela, the waves had moods.

They were tugged ashore by creatures made of spindly wood pieces, sliding, crashing, lapping. On rainy days, when her mamá closed the stationery shop early, Milagros would climb up to the roof of their building and watch people watch the small monsters.

Not everyone could see, of course, but the creatures didn't need to be seen to exist.

Her older sister Esperanza sat with her sometimes, holding a raincoat over both their heads, dreaming up a future that would never be reality. As she talked, Esperanza watched the waves without seeing much, catching glimpses out of the corners of her eyes, the truth hiding from her around the edges of the world. That was back when tourists still visited their island and Milagros still had a sister.

Only a few months in New York, and construction had swiftly moved up on the list of things Milagros deeply disliked.

Next to her, Cecilia balled her gum wrapper and threw it onto the tracks, startling a rat into scurrying away.

"This freaking 6 train," she groaned.

Milagros had to agree. It was too hot to be waiting half an hour for a delayed 6, pushed right up to the yellow line of death by the impatient crowd behind them.

She handed Cecilia their shared 7UP, gone lukewarm and flat. Her cousin took a sip and winced.

"Gross," she said, but kept drinking. "Maybe we could walk home."

Milagros took the 7UP. "It's literally like a thousand degrees outside, and I think the protest about our consulate closing is still going on."

"So what?"

Speakers crackled overhead.

THERE IS A BROOKLYN-BOUND R TRAIN APPROACHING THE STATION.

PLEASE STAND AWAY FROM THE PLATFORM EDGE.

The noise of the train drowned out what Milagros would have said, but not her thoughts.

Tía Yocelin had left Venezuela with Cecilia before things had gotten too bad—before a dozen eggs cost a month's salary, before people were robbed at gunpoint for baby formula, before everyone who still cared took to the streets to fight.

Cecilia hadn't seen Esperanza come and go from their small apartment, a gas mask over her face and a sign in her hands, marching every day alongside thousands of others who had had enough. Cecilia hadn't been there the night Esperanza hadn't come back, or the following morning when the chill of reality had finally seeped into Milagros and her mamá. Cecilia hadn't screamed at the condolences and reassurances from people who hadn't done shit to help her sister or the country.

Her cousin had gained a stepdad and a stepbrother and *safety* while Milagros had lost a sister. It wasn't Cecilia's fault, but sometimes Milagros couldn't help but blame her.

The train was already crowded when it arrived yet somehow people still packed themselves in, like sardinas en lata. Milagros let herself be carried forward, losing sight of Cecilia in the crush.

For now, maybe it was better that way.

She was surrounded by too-tall people, with no clear view of the windows, but when she heard the long, mournful groans, she sighed in what almost felt like relief. She was already smiling when a man shifted and she caught sight of the blue flash on the other side of the Plexiglas.

"Buenas," she whispered, as the train sped through the tunnel.

The woman beside her turned, frowning, but the monster had heard, too. It opened its eyes.

She'd seen the subway monster a handful of times in as many months since that first meeting—a soft presence, like warmth and nostalgia, filling the spaces between bodies. It had turned to her every time, seeking something Milagros was afraid she didn't have, but desperately wished she did.

It was unnerving, aligning with the monster so perfectly while the bustle of New York paused for a second, the world sliding out of sync before righting itself again.

The creatures at home—and the others she had seen here—had mostly ignored her, even when she had tried to communicate. She'd always assumed there was a language barrier, or the kind of prejudice that prevented understanding, but somehow this one was different.

Now the creature approached, moving through the Plexiglas in a breath, arching above the tallest heads in a trail of fading blue light, those eyes clear and real. It stopped before Milagros, its shape—a head?—tilting almost like a question.

Milagros contorted herself to get an arm free from the press of oblivious bodies to touch it.

Her fingers grazed through a not-quite-solid form, like warm, welcoming smoke. The monster let out a terrifying purr, pupils narrowing into thin lines swimming in what Milagros had thought was silver, but now could tell was the exact light blue of the water of Guacuco in the early morning.

At first, the monster didn't pull away. It leaned in, flickering into almost-solid reality for a second, for too long.

A man screamed, and the monster's pupils rounded in fear.

"¡Espera!" Milagros curled her fingers to grab the monster, but her hand caught on something sharp and twisted instead.

The creature flinched back into the tunnel's darkness.

Enough people got out at the next stop that Cecilia found Milagros again, and they bumped shoulders as they held on to the same pole. The train was quiet now.

Cecilia sucked in air through her teeth. "Christ, what happened to your hand?"

Milagros watched the slow trickle of blood from the tips of her fingers. It didn't hurt.

Érase una vez una niña de ojos oscuros
    y un monstruo azul.
And when the girl was fifteen,
    it tried to eat her.

Smoky green wisps dangled from the fresh peonies on the table. Milagros didn't know how to tell Mrs. Bleacher, owner of the flowers and the apartment they were in, that the expensive vase she'd placed between the chicken and the mashed potatoes was full of monsters.

Two years in New York and sixteen years alive had taught her that people didn't want to hear about things they didn't already believe.

Mrs. Bleacher, with her designer lime green suit and artfully placed ladybug pin, didn't seem like she would be receptive to Milagros's particular brand of weirdness. They had been sitting around the cooling food for thirty minutes and, so far, she had used the phrase "third world quaintness" twice. That was twice more than Milagros preferred.

Sometimes she wished she'd never learned English.

There was no escaping, though. Tía Yocelin had been firm since Milagros moved in: Coming to her social gatherings was not optional. There was church on Sundays and coffee with church friends every third Thursday of the month, and that was that.

"And, listen, I told them I wouldn't host the fund-raiser in those conditions, with no heating in the middle of winter," Ms. Darby was saying, gesturing with her forkful of salad. "I know it's for a good cause—but, really, no heating?"

Mrs. Bleacher and Tía Yocelin nodded in agreement. Ms. Johnson was in the process of drinking her wine, but Milagros had no doubt she would have nodded, too.

Next to Tía Yocelin, Gabriel rolled his eyes so forcefully that it almost made a sound. Cecilia snorted. The wisp fell on the mashed potatoes.

"It's barbaric," Ms. Johnson piped up. "This happened last month, too, you know, when we were doing that thing with the orphanage on our block? The heating of the church always seems to mysteriously stop working when it's most convenient for them."

Church conspiracy theorists. Milagros stifled a smile.

Gabriel leaned toward her and Cecilia as the topic turned to time-shares at Mrs. Bleacher's resort.

"There's a thing at Judy's today, wanna come?"

Judy's was a diner on Myrtle and Gates that had just-okay food but incredible shakes. The lights of the *d*'s belly had burned out long before Milagros had started going there, but Judy, the owner, said it gave the diner character.

"What thing?" Cecilia whispered, as much as was possible for her.

"Just like a get-together with some friends," Gabriel said, as if that explained it. "At, like, eight."

"College friends?" Cecilia wiggled both eyebrows at her stepbrother. "Is William going to be there?"

Gabriel pouted in a pretty good imitation of Tía Yocelin when she got fed up with him (which was quickly and often) and turned to Milagros instead.

"What about you? Wanna come just for the pleasure of hanging out with me?"

Milagros opened her mouth without really knowing what would come out, so nothing did.

It had been a pain to get to Mrs. Bleacher's Upper East Side–adjacent apartment from their tiny Crown Heights two-bedroom, and getting to Judy's would be even worse. She'd have to take the M15 bus down, probably, and either walk across the Williamsburg Bridge or wait roughly until she was eighty for the B39 to show up, and even then she'd have to take a third bus. It would be two hours, at the very least. Not to mention getting back home from the diner.

The prospect alone made her tired.

Cecilia chimed in to help, more or less: "She doesn't do subways, dumbass."

Tía Yocelin shot Gabriel a look, even though it had been Cecilia who had cursed.

Gabriel ignored it, something he'd gotten very good at in the years Milagros had known him.

"Still?" he asked.

Milagros clasped her hands together under the table, rubbing away the memory of the cold roof of the train under her palms.

"Still."

"Maybe we could—"

"Milagros," Mrs. Bleacher's first-soprano voice cut through whatever Gabriel was going to say, and Milagros was almost thankful. "Have you talked to your family recently? How are they doing?"

With a polite smile, Milagros shrugged. "You know, kind of the same. Kind of worse."

A *nightmare*, that's what her mamá had said last time they'd talked. *Like a ship sinking into fire instead of water.*

Milagros had bit the inside of her cheek then, hard enough to draw blood, digging her nails into the soft flesh of her thighs. She had kept herself from screaming only by remembering how she had begged her mamá to come to the US with them and gotten the same refusal again and again and again. Monica DelValle García de Cordova would die buried by the crumbling mess that was Venezuela and Milagros was expected to do nothing but stay safe miles away, under a roof that didn't leak, enjoying uninterrupted electricity like it was a right.

Milagros didn't mention any of that, though. She had found herself too often arguing the depth of the crimes in Venezuela with outsiders who thought they knew better, but never did.

"Yocelin, we should send something to your sister," Ms. Darby piped up. "What do you think?"

Tía Yocelin glanced at Milagros, a brief understanding. Nothing would make it through customs, where officers supposed to keep the country safe and regulated would seize any items their own families might need. Unless Tía Yocelin decided to travel to Venezuela—and she wouldn't, not anymore—there was no way to get Milagros's mamá any-thing but scraps.

"She would love it," Tía Yocelin said, a smile tight on her face. "Toilet paper, for instance. Or deodorant?"

Milagros took some of the mashed potatoes, startling the spindly sprite about to dip into the bowl. She swallowed her desperation along with the food and hoped both stayed down.

The sun was a merciless beast, burning Milagros's exposed neck as she followed Gabriel and Cecilia down the sloping hill that was Second Avenue. Tía Yocelin had stayed behind with her church friends to get overpriced cafecitos, which Mrs. Bleacher had thought were "so quaint" and "adorable."

"Ms. Johnson *was* checking me out," Gabriel said, not for the first time.

Cecilia didn't even pause her texting to answer: "Whatever. What do you think she's gonna do, dude. She's sixty-something."

"Sixty's not that old," Milagros added with a grin. "She can probably still get going."

Gabriel seemed both thankful for her support and horrified by her actual words.

"Don't encourage him, oh my God." Cecilia glanced up briefly at the green light, then kept walking once cars stopped coming. "You think Ms. Johnson's gonna go for a nineteen-year-old fetus who still thinks ramen is a gourmet meal?"

"Excuse me." Gabriel turned to Milagros as if to say, *Can you believe this shit?*

Milagros could believe it.

She shrugged. "Think about this: Ms. Johnson probably has a chef who could make you better food."

"You're both trash," he declared.

It felt good to laugh after the last three solid hours of careful politeness.

When they finally got to 86th Street, the arch of the subway station looming in front of them, Milagros let her cousins walk a little bit ahead, the now-familiar mantle of discomfort settling on her shoulders.

She stopped at the escalators.

"Have fun at Judy's, guys." Then, to Cecilia: "I'll see you at home."

Cecilia didn't say anything, the disappointment that Milagros wouldn't "just get over it" clear in the press of her lips.

Gabriel didn't know to give up.

"What? No—c'mon! It'll be fun. And this way Ceci will have someone to go home with her."

Milagros knew not to turn to Cecilia for reassurance, but saw the ribbon of black smoke twirling across the ground toward her cousin's sandaled feet, a thin monster seeking out the anger she wasn't showing.

Gabriel stepped closer. "What do you have to be so afraid of still? It's just the stupid subway."

The words hit Milagros with almost physical pain. She'd be missing out, yet again; on the outside of her own life, yet again. It was one ride. Why couldn't she do it?

But last time . . .

. . . But it had been *a year*.

Maybe it would be different. Maybe the tunnels would be empty.

Cecilia noticed the hesitation and pounced. The creature trying to coil around her ankle shivered and drifted away.

"Come with us, Milagros. Please."

Milagros remembered saying "please," too.

Please, no. What is happening?

Please, be careful.

Please, listen *to me*.

Then, to the police, to Tía Yocelin, to Cecilia: *Please believe me.*

It hadn't worked a year ago, but it worked for Cecilia now. Milagros let it work.

"Okay," she said, and stepped onto the escalator between her cousins.

"You'll be fine." Cecilia smiled, and she was wrong.

Gabriel let out a hoot.

Milagros was drenched in fear, in mistakes waiting to happen, and those that already had.

At the turnstile, she paused again, hesitating about five times in the space of a blink. Cecilia and Gabriel waited on the other side, and Milagros made herself swipe her card, $2.75 out of $13.25, even though her mouth tasted like copper.

The 86th Street station was one of the nicer ones, with mosaics, high ceilings, clean floors, and announcements that sounded like words and not incomprehensible gibberish. Even so, Milagros didn't hear anything except the whine of the N train approaching, lights glaring from the turn of the tunnel.

Her heart hammered against the paper-thin skin of her chest, her lungs flattening with every beat.

She couldn't do this.

She could.

Cecilia and Gabriel flanked her, thinking themselves more reassuring than they were. Their bodies were close and warm, but vulnerable.

When the doors slid open, they stepped in as one, pushing against the current of people exiting. Milagros took a seat at Gabriel's insistence, sitting between Cecilia and a guy in a tan coat using his legs as imaginary drums. She held herself stiff, tucked in as tight as she could so she wouldn't touch Cecilia or anyone else.

Not this time.

The train lurched into motion, but Milagros didn't even sway. Her breath went in and out in short bursts, her eyes fixed on the ad running across the top of the train: IF YOU SEE SOMETHING, SAY SOMETHING.

That hadn't worked out so well for her.

Only when the train stopped at the next station did she shudder a full breath out. Then back in.

She was distantly aware that Gabriel was talking to Cecilia, pausing only during the announcements. Milagros told herself that she was strong and brave and maybe she *had* made it all up. Those last words she heard in the voice of "Doctor" Pedrano, the psychology school dropout Tía Yocelin had forced her to see, back when Milagros hadn't been able to pretend to be okay.

It was different now.

The train headed downtown, stopping at every station, strangers' voices rising indistinctly all around, a melody plucked from the fine thread of her fear until it snapped.

When the monster appeared, she wasn't surprised.

She watched those eyes, the darkness behind them, and did not move. Its mouth gaped open into nothingness and Milagros felt the pull at her center, something so visceral it burned.

She knew then that a year had been nothing. One year, and she would still let herself be eaten. She *wanted* it. Giving up would be so easy.

But she remembered the speed of the train from above, the blood. She remembered, days later, the body the police had found.

A hand closed around her wrist in the present—not the same hand from her memories, though for too long a moment she wasn't sure. She stared at those five fingers around her wrist, terror and bile rising in her throat.

When she screamed, it was into unnatural silence.

Cecilia stared at her in alarm, snatching her hand away from Milagros.

"You were shaking," Cecilia said, as if to offer an excuse.

The blue flash of the monster danced in her periphery, a taunting and an invitation, a reminder.

Milagros hadn't realized she had gotten up, was standing, but she was glad for the space between her and her cousins, for the safety it afforded *them*. She had been stupid to think this would be okay, and the fear in their faces was the price she paid for it.

Fear, not for her, but *of* her.

The train ground to a halt, and Milagros stepped onto the platform with barely restrained panic sizzling along her spine. Neither of her cousins followed her, but she didn't let herself slump to the concrete floor until the doors were closed again and the train was gone.

Before, when it was all too much for Milagros to handle, she would focus on the oddities, the strangeness slipping in and out of the world. She would pause and notice a wisp, a leaf bending too far, a wind slightly warmer than it should have been.

Now, instead, she counted.

Two arms, two hands, ten fingers touching metal, speeding, slipping in the dark—no. *Two arms, two hands, ten fingers touching* concrete, *the fingers on the right hand colder, slimier than the rest. Fifteen breaths in, fifteen breaths out in between*—

"That is so unsanitary."

The voice wasn't a number and, in that moment, it was not welcome.

Milagros tracked from cuffed boots up dark jeans and a long, tan coat that covered most of the guy standing in front of her. And his *face*. She stared transfixed by the white patch in his hair and how it seemed to blend into his forehead, and his left eye, which was half brown and half blue, like someone had dipped a paintbrush in water.

Her mind paused on something about him.

"I mean your hands, of course," he said, eyes narrowed. "Can you stop staring?"

Milagros startled, her gaze falling to the floor and then up again, to his right, fully brown eye. Back to the floor.

Two hands, ten fingers.

"I'm sorry."

The guy crouched down, hands on his thighs, presumably for balance and not just to remind Milagros that hers were still on the floor. *Hands on thighs, hands tapping out a rhythm.*

"You were in the train," Milagros thought out loud, shame sneaking into her voice.

He had seen her lose it.

"I'll forgive you because you're clearly freaking out, but please stop touching the floor. Just—here, sanitize." He held out a bottle of Purell and squeezed far too much onto Milagros's open hand.

She tried to rub the mysterious floor slime away.

"Thank you."

"Better?"

No. Maybe.

"I'm okay," she answered.

He tilted his head to the left, so her gaze went back to that two-toned eye.

"You seemed pretty scared in there." He nodded toward the now-empty tracks. "Had you never seen her before?"

The question was an electric current all the way from her sanitized fingers to the base of her skull.

"Qué?"

His eyes widened. "Uh, parlez-vous français?"

She blinked, surprise quickly becoming frustration.

"What?" she snapped, this time in the correct language.

"What?" He said it so loudly it echoed. He turned his head enough for Milagros to see the plastic device fitted behind his ear. He tapped it once and leveled her with an amused gaze. "You'll need to speak louder."

Milagros wasn't sure if embarrassment or annoyance was winning out. She took a deep breath. "What did you say before—had I never seen *what*?"

"The dragon. In the train. I thought that's why you'd screamed, unless I was wrong? Would honestly not be the first time. You'd be surprised—or maybe not—with how many people scream for no reason on the train. Especially tourists."

The pause in the conversation when he stopped talking was almost as loud as his shouting earlier.

Milagros scrambled back up, except that standing didn't really make a difference.

The dragon. In the train.

The guy looked up from his crouch, a crease between his mismatched eyes. "Did you not see it? Dude, not again—"

"I saw it." The words were quiet, but to Milagros they felt like three distinct gunshots. She repeated, louder, for his benefit: "I. Saw. It."

"Her," he corrected, smiling. "Okay. Good. This would have been so awkward otherwise."

"Have *you*?" The wrong words sputtered out of her. "I mean, of course you have. Otherwise why would you have said—you called it a dragon?"

He stood up like his body was made not of muscles and bones, but of something more fluid, like wishes and secrets.

"I called *her* a dragon," he repeated. "I know it's hard sometimes to see her fully—most people think she's like a serpent. If you've seen her before, why were you so scared?"

People. He knew *other people* who could see. Here. In Brooklyn. Milagros's mind raced with a thousand questions she needed to ask all at once, so many she couldn't get any of them out.

But something about what he'd said, about the way he'd said it, snagged her suspicions and ripped.

"Who wouldn't be scared?" She said it as a question, but did not allow an answer. "*It* was trying to take me again."

His eyebrows shot up. "Again?"

Milagros took a step back, suddenly feeling like she had exposed too much, too fast, too soon. The memory of Cecilia's and Gabriel's faces in the train moments ago, watching her in fear, still burned behind her eyelids. And they *knew* her. They might not have been able to see the monster, but they could have at least believed her.

Her mamá would have, if Milagros had dared to call, to worry her, but she hadn't. She wouldn't.

She meant to leave the station, but the allure of finding someone here who could see what she saw, who might understand, kept her in place.

Milagros didn't—couldn't—say anything, but knew the moment it clicked for him.

"You're *that* girl? The one they found on the top of the train last year? No way." He stared much like she had been before, fascination stark across his face. "Are you?"

It struck her then, his surprise, his admiration.

It struck her, his lack of disbelief.

Milagros was glad that he barreled through without waiting for her reply.

"Wow. *Wow.* The girl on top of the train. You know, my aunt swore up and down that it'd been the dragon when the news broke. *Up* and down. She's never gonna let anyone hear the end of it after this. Was it incredible?"

His words were sparklers set afire, but to Milagros they felt like scorching iron, searing and branding something deep in her gut.

She exploded.

"*Incredible?* To blink and be on top of a moving train? To feel yourself slipping off?" She was shaking for the second time today, but she didn't care. She *didn't* care. "You think it was incredible when I made my fingers raw trying to hold on? Or when I fell off the back of the train? Yes, what an *honor*! The best part was th—" She stopped, choking on her own rage. She couldn't say it.

A year and she still could not say it.

For the first time in this uneven conversation, he was the one looking stricken. Milagros almost hit him, but she balled up her hands and reined it in. She'd gotten really good at reining in her entire self this past year.

"I'm sorry—"

She did not let him finish. "Are you?"

He seemed to weigh her question and find it wanting. "The dragon is very important to us. We consider her favor to be a blessing."

Milagros had not felt blessed a year ago; she did not feel blessed now. She felt like someone had taken her familiar places and made them into jagged edges and dark corners. She felt robbed. Lonely.

"I don't want any blessings," she spat.

He shifted slightly. He'd clearly expected Milagros to be delighted about what he had to say, and instead found something else, something he did not like.

"I followed you out because I assumed you needed help adjusting after seeing the dragon. I didn't realize you had already adjusted and decided to be wrong about it."

For a moment, she couldn't even formulate words to match her disdain for his opinion and general existence. "What do you even *know*?"

He scoffed. "No, of course. You're the only person in the whole world to ever be afraid of something you don't understand. What was I thinking? Maman avait raison, je dois cesser d'essayer."

Milagros did not know what that meant, but she did not like it.

He shook his head, whatever else he might have said swallowed by the noise of an incoming train. No tingling awareness came with it and for that, at least, Milagros was grateful.

"You can't be afraid forever, you know," the guy said, putting something in her hand before getting on the train.

She didn't know why she'd accepted it or why, after the train had left, she slipped the small card in her pocket instead of throwing it away.

Tía Yocelin had waited a week and two days before calling Milagros to the kitchen, marroncito in hand, to discuss her "ataque de nervios" in the subway.

Two barely-there wisps had been softly swinging from the branch of eucalyptus hanging by the stove behind her, and it had been easier to watch them instead of watching Tía Yocelin and her disappointment.

The wisps stayed in the kitchen, but the disappointment clung to Milagros and stuck.

Later, when Cecilia knocked on her bedroom door, Milagros did not answer. The soft whine of old hinges accompanied her cousin's steps anyway, followed by her sigh.

"Don't be angry, Milagros." The bed dipped under Cecilia's weight, but Milagros held herself still so she wouldn't roll into her cousin.

"I'm not crazy," Milagros said, for what felt like the hundredth time in the last few hours.

Cecilia's discomfort was almost a living thing in the silence. "Mom's just worried, you know? We all are. Gabriel, too."

"You might have left the island too young, but your mom knows better." The pressure built up right at the border of Milagros's eyes, at the base of her throat. "She *knows*."

Cecilia sighed. Again. "It's just Dr. Pedrano. You've talked to him before."

Milagros curled into herself, arms folded over her head, turning away so at least she wouldn't have to see the genuine worry on her cousin's face. That was the second-worst part: the concern. The first was that no one believed her.

Almost no one.

Milagros waited, holding back the tears and pain until Cecilia got tired of being understanding and left. Even after she was alone, it was hard to let out what she had been trying so hard to keep in. The tears rolled down the side of her face and onto the pillow, but the pain had nowhere to go.

For a while, she counted.

It wasn't until she'd run out of things to count and the tears had dried on her cheeks that she pulled the crumpled and re-flattened card from under her pillow.

> **Marc Loya**
> # PHOTOGRAPHER
>
> @Marquisdearts
> XXX-XXX-XXXX

She'd already stalked his Instagram account, first in anger, then out of curiosity, then with a sort of inexplicable giddiness. He had posted photo upon photo of every corner of New York: a fountain in Central Park, the lions from the New York Public Library, a bench from somewhere called Anne's Garden, a street cat, an old couple sitting in front of a Shake Shack, a bodega on a corner in the Bronx.

Everywhere. Anywhere.

Milagros had scrolled a year back in his posts, careful not to like anything accidentally, when she realized what she was seeing. It was a blur sitting on the cat's back, or a vagueness around the end of the bench. Just a small detail hidden in every photo.

The strangeness, captured. A secret displayed for the world to never notice.

But she'd noticed. He'd noticed.

It had, on some level that worried her, soothed her.

And so here she was, fingers poised over the phone, his number already typed in, about to regret her decisions.

You're photographing them

His reply was almost immediate.

What do you think?

Have you always been able to see them?

Do you always talk to people
without introducing yourself?

                                        YOU do.

Touché.

So?

                                        Milagros.

                                        So?

Since I was a baby. My mom likes to say I saw
a faery before I saw her face, but that honestly
seems like a lie.

                            You think they're fairies?

I don't like your tone.

                            You don't know my tone.

I don't like your implied tone. I do think they're
faeries. Some people call them /others/, but
that seems kinda shitty.

                    We call them the strangeness.

                    Did you know your dragon
                                killed a man?

Tell me.

                        I wasn't the only person taken
                    outside of the train half a year ago.
                            There was a man, too.

Milagros paused, started a new sentence only to delete it. She stared
at the screen, waiting for him to say something so she could pretend she
had nothing else to add.

She couldn't do it anymore. She typed.

He tried to help me. I was scared and he was
trying to calm me down. He had a family. Not
with him on the train. Just in general.

What happened to him?

He was found dead on the tracks that
same day.

You think the dragon did it?

I know.

It wasn't part of the news story. No one
believed me when I told them. No one does.

I do.

Do you believe me that the monster in the
subway is evil?

Do you think she did it on purpose?

Milagros didn't respond.

Milagros Honora Cordova García was not reckless, despite what her current situation might suggest.

Maybe it was past midnight, and maybe she was sitting in a deserted Brooklyn train station. Maybe the wooden bench was uncomfortable and the walls smelled of things she would rather not identify. Maybe she would die.

But it wouldn't be because she hadn't thought it through.

Do you think she did it on purpose?

She watched the tunnel stretching into the distance at both ends, the only illumination coming from the few lights mounted on the curving walls.

To signal stairs and exits.

To mark repair boxes.

To make it easier to see.

Milagros had heard every explanation from Tía Yocelin and "Doctor" Pedrano, both quoting Google like it was a Bible, and these the verses to prove that her mind was conjuring monsters from the ordinary.

They couldn't prove it. Because she wasn't.

A train burst from the tunnel with a vengeance, as if in warning. It stopped for no one to get out and no one to get in, then sped away.

Twenty minutes until the next one.

Milagros jumped down onto the tracks, water—or what she hoped was just water—splashing up her jeans, critters scratching and squeaking while they scurried away.

Those first few steps into the tunnel were slow, caught between one painful hesitation and the next. Milagros hadn't even reached the first light embedded in the wall when that far-off awareness tickled between her shoulder blades.

For a moment, she froze.

For a moment, the doubts drowned her. What was she doing, ankle-deep in who knew what, risking death by train to meet something that had already killed at least one man?

Do you think she did it on purpose?

Milagros took one more step, two.

The heaviness of the monster suddenly filled up the space, electricity sparking along its edges like a herald that brought nothing.

"¿Dónde estás?" The words burst out, raw with frustration and fear. "You've been calling me, haven't you? I'm here. I'm here, where are *you*?"

The echo of her own questions came back as the only answer, water dripping off the curving tunnel and onto her face. It didn't matter. In the silence, it did not matter.

Milagros opened her mouth and screamed.

No words, just one long, awful screech of fury, tinted with the knowledge of how her life had been warped by one event, how much of her now hinged on this fear. And then—

The eyes blinked open in front of her, the shape blurry through her unshed tears. Milagros was somehow two years younger again, a girl catching her first glimpse of something familiar in a new country.

The monster's body flickered behind the eyes, arching up then dipping down, some parts made of shimmering light and others solid and too real. Marc had called it—*her*—a dragon, and now Milagros saw what he meant.

"¿Por qué yo?"

She didn't know what she expected in answer. The dragon had never spoken, not in words, nothing apart from awful, pain-filled sounds, but Milagros waited anyway, breath held in.

Lower lids made of night slid slowly up then back down, the dragon rising at such an angle that Milagros could see dark teeth against the shifting brilliance of the head.

"There was a man that day," Milagros whispered. "There was a man. He grabbed me. He was trying to calm me down and he grabbed me, and then he was found dead."

The dragon's eyes were impassive, her body softly curling down the length of the tunnel.

Seconds and minutes and hours and days of guilt clasped like a collar around Milagros's throat, almost choking her, but she forced out the words: "Did we kill him?"

The dragon moved past Milagros and curved back around, a warm ribbon loosely wrapping around a small girl, settling on shoulders that needed comfort.

Milagros stepped into that warmth, but it was not enough.

"I need to know."

The dragon leaned her horned head against Milagros, like a feather on hair. She talked, not in words but in memories trickling out of her ancient core like new rain.

Milagros felt the sprouting of new feelings: *Contentment twined with indifference. The idea of a face, someone reaching out, an almost-forgotten home.*

Tiredness stretching out to become everything, sleepless years in the darkness. Stark surprise, the shock of the known in an unknown place.

Then, quickly: *delight, hands, noise, so much noise, fast, excitement, searching, searching, finding, pulling, chaos and fear and regret.*

A loss.

Sadness. A deep, unmistakable loneliness.

The dragon's touch had been barely a touch at all, but when it pulled away Milagros doubled over with the sudden loss.

It took a long while for thoughts to come back, even longer for the words to match them.

The hurricane of her mind settled itself around the ruins of what she used to believe.

The dragon had thought Milagros felt like home.

"¿Yo soy como tu hogar?"

At the words, the monster leaned back in.

Milagros stepped back so fast that she almost tripped, her foot sinking into a puddle that soaked all the way up her socks.

"No!"

The dragon didn't really nod, but pressed her large head against Milagros's open palms, which felt like an understanding.

Maybe it was the relief that distracted her, so that when she finally noticed the fast-approaching train, it was too late. Milagros was paralyzed, legs shaking with the need to *move* but unable to fight the gravity of her own panic.

She threw herself to the side, toward a small, slippery ledge covered with cables. She'd barely grabbed at hope when the light of the train blinded her. Fear overwhelmed anything else, and through the thrum of her blood in her ears, she heard a savage, thundering roar—

She remembered a home of old houses and beaches, the soft, ever-changing clouds against a blue sky, a sun that was relentless but welcomed. She was free then, free to graze the water and curl on the sand, free to wrap herself around treetops and rest, safe in the reverence of those who could see.

She remembered the curiosity that came with the whispers of travelers, the rumors of far-off places with cold fluff that fell from the sky. She remembered a woman's face, a man, a child. Then an offering of salt. Then the journey.

She remembered the new crevices and sounds, cities filled with people filled with dreams. She remembered the machine, the trap.

Long, interminable trips in the darkness, where there was no rest and no time.

*She snagged on something now—not a memory, but something sharp and hard and ugly, a lure set by strangers with their lies to pin her here forever. She pulled until her mind bled, until it gave. Until it dissolved, and her anger with it—*Milagros staggered back, light flooding in as her eyes opened. She blinked.

Her hands were pressed against cold Plexiglas, her face reflected back at her. When the doors of the train opened, she stared out into the station like she was the ghost.

She hadn't moved past the yellow platform edge when the doors slid closed, the train speeding away behind her with such force that she swayed.

She was not dead.

Milagros looked back into the empty tunnel, searching for an explanation and a friend, but neither had stayed behind.

"I miss our home, too. Ya no tienes que estar sola." There was no one there to hear her words, but she said them nonetheless. Maybe they would get to the dragon somehow.

The night outside was alive with wild, wonderful things, and Milagros felt the strangeness inside her answering.

When she finally got back home, she lay awake on her bed with her eyes wide open.

Above her building, under the calm, moonless night sky, the dragon slept at last.

AUTHOR'S NOTE

In my mind's eye, Venezuela is a building slowly crumbling, paint peeling and furniture on fire as people go about their day-to-day in rooms about to disappear. In my mind's eye, Venezuela is the vine-covered wall behind my grandmother's textile shop, sunlight filtered through ceiling slats hiding rainbows between leaves as I looked for magic doors.

The first time I saw my country mentioned in a young adult novel, I cried. I remember it was a throwaway comment, an exotic detail in a list of other interesting bits, with no bearing on the characters or plot, but all the bearing in the world to me. For years, I unconsciously—then, consciously—avoided bringing my own background into my writing. It felt like revealing too much, inserting myself where I wasn't wanted: *Here's a story about a Venezuelan girl* . . . Who would want that? But the thrill of being seen, even briefly, never left me. Vines can grow from a single tendril, and here was mine: I could do that for someone else.

Milagros is not the first Venezuelan girl I've written, but she is the first to be shared with others, with love and fear. She is the resistance at being uprooted from one's own soil, the uncertainty of unfamiliar and dangerous monsters. Most importantly, she is a girl with her eyes wide open, trying to hold on to who she is and figure out who she'll become.

As so many Venezuelans do in the current state of affairs, Milagros sees both the crumbling building and the vine-covered wall. She finds the magic door. She walks through.

I hope every reader can follow her there.

THE CREEP FACTOR IN *MONSTERS*

by Nova Ren Suma

A STORY DOESN'T NEED TO FALL INTO THE HORROR GENRE IN ORDER TO PLAY with fear. A growing sense of unease, a crawling creep factor—call it whatever you like—can tighten a story's grip. There is something so arresting about a head-on look into what's terrifying, bringing it into the light to be faced, and even fought and overcome.

There is an electrifying moment at the start of this powerful story when Milagros realizes she is seeing monsters that no one else around her can see. The creature caught through the window doesn't need to be described in full to cause a shiver up the spine. We get only a sketch: the "two silver slit-pupil orbs," each as big as a hand . . . and the dark tunnel beyond. The scene ends with a simple, striking line: "Milagros stared, and the monster in the darkness stared back." This spare moment doesn't tell too much, which allows the fear to seep into the cracks, between the lines, into us. The most frightening things gain weight when a reader's imagination is allowed to take over.

This continues. Fear billows in the spaces that are left blank, empty of unnecessary description that would kill the magic. Milagros "watched those eyes, the darkness behind them, and did not move." The eyes. The darkness. There is an open gap, ready and waiting for your worst fears to take over. This helps us feel the terror when a hand wraps around Milagros's wrist.

Notice in MONSTERS that the fear begins to dissipate, and the story begins to feel more hopeful and less unnerving, as more details about the "monster" are revealed. Eventually it comes clear that the terrifying monster Milagros sees is something else in the eyes of others. "Had you never seen her before?" a man asks Milagros . . . personifying the creature, which begins to dilute the terror, so by the end of the story that fear is almost entirely gone. Milagros's monster—the dragon—is a blessing to some. When they look, they see something beautiful.

Fear in fiction can mask something much more vulnerable and personal. By the end of MONSTERS, it's revealed that Milagros's dragon is carrying a loss, "*a deep, unmistakable loneliness*," a feeling Milagros, so far from home, recognizes and shares. The horror stories that linger the longest are the ones that shake loose a fearful truth from inside our core, one that is uncomfortably human.

STORY PROMPT:
EMBODYING A FEAR

CHARACTERS MUST OFTEN FACE THEIR FEARS IN ORDER TO CHANGE. SOMETIMES they need to come close enough to be devoured.

If you want your story to go beyond a coating of creepiness to reveal something hidden under the surface, staring a monster down can do the work. It may be possible to fight your character's worst fears if you can see those fears. Literally. On the page. How might the terrible, unspoken things inside your character come to life if they took on the shape of a monster? What would happen if your character was confronted by their fear . . . in physical form?

To try this exercise, first ask yourself: What is your character most afraid of? Next, consider the ways that could be embodied. Create a physical manifestation—a creature, perhaps—that takes on the shape, the mood, the scale of your character's worst fear.

Now write the scene where they meet face-to-face.

BREAK

Sophie Meridien

Spin #1
Izzy Morgan's Drinkapalooza
June 3rd

KIKI ST. GERMAIN HAD NO BUSINESS BEING AT THIS PARTY, OR ANYWHERE near the tenth circle of hell known as Seven Minutes in Heaven.

She was in a sour mood. She'd just had her braids done—thick, chunky, *heavy* ones—and her scalp was extra tender. *Kendra does them too damn tight.* But she'd promised herself that senior year was going to be her year. She was gonna get the grades, secure an acceptance letter to her dream school, and perfect a damn crème brûlée.

She was gonna get out of her comfort zone.

This party seemed like the perfect way to do just that. Every summer, the neighborhoods surrounding Orange Grove High became a battleground for competing house parties, and Kiki was never allowed to attend any of them. Considering what some of these other kids were doing, her parents should've been thankful that she wasn't much of a rebel. She wasn't even in the circle. She was hovering, watching, working up the courage to join.

She set a timer on her phone. Lying to her parents was one thing, but she wasn't going to risk missing curfew.

From the circle, Josie and Amari tried to wave Kiki over. She immediately squinted at her phone like she'd just received a very important text. She even muttered to herself to sell it.

"Kiki?"

She turned and tried not to groan. Chris Keller exuded the type of sheer assholery that she tried to avoid.

His pale skin was sunburned. He smiled a too-perfect smile. "I've never seen you at one of these before."

She forced a smile of her own. "Yeah, just thought I'd stop by."

He looked at her quizzically. "Your hair grows superfast."

She felt every bit of her soul leave her body as he took a few braids and played with them.

Just as Kiki was contemplating punching his screaming red skin, Chris put his arms up and whooped loudly. He wasn't the only one. A boy she didn't recognize had just entered the living room, and everyone seemed very excited about that.

He was a twig of a boy, tall and slim. It was too hot for the gray hoodie he wore under his oversized Marlins jersey. His skin had the slightest tan, and judging from the way he kept running his fingers through it, he was a big fan of his sleek, dark hair.

Kiki knelt down behind Josie and Amari. "Who's he?" she asked.

Josie raised a brow. "He just moved onto my block. Name's Kastov."

"He's new here?" Kiki looked him up and down. He spoke to the lacrosse team like they were all best friends, threw an arm over Izzy's shoulder, and plopped himself in the circle next to the notoriously selective Alexa Ayers.

Impossible. He already had a group of friends larger than hers, and she'd known these people since kindergarten. *Maybe it's better to be new.* Kiki had only just managed to shake off the nickname *Vomi-gator* from when she threw up on the airboat during the fifth-grade trip to the Everglades. And some people could just be friendly and cool and magnetic without effort. She decided she was into it, totally buying what he was selling, right up until Chris whispered something to him and the kid threw his head back and laughed.

Ugh, another douchebag to avoid.

Amari passed the bottle to Kastov.

Kiki returned to her phone.

The bottle spun and spun and spun.

"Woof, I gotta pee," Josie said lazily.

Kiki, scrolling through her favorite fic, scooted over to let Josie out of the circle.

The bottle stopped, and the crowd cheered.

Kiki looked up.

The bottle pointed at the gap that Josie had just created. The one Kiki now sat in.

"I wasn't—" she started, but the circle drowned her out.

Amari shouted, *"Go 'head, Kiki!"*

The new kid was already at the coat closet, holding the door open for her. She considered walking away, but she knew the judgment would be merciless. She didn't need another nickname.

Anxiety biting at her stomach, she followed him.

He closed the door, wiped his palms on his jeans, and offered his hand. "Hi, I'm—"

"Just so we're clear, I'm not kissing you, okay?" she blurted out.

The corner of his mouth ticked up in amusement. "Probably for the best. I've been devouring salt and vinegar chips all night."

Her lips twitched, but she held in the laugh. "I mean, I don't even know you."

"To be fair, I don't know you either." His hand was still held out to her. "I'm Kastov."

She took it. "Kikade."

Kikade—

"Rhymes with cicada," she added, before realizing that he'd already gotten it right.

She waited for it. *Can't I just call you Kiki?*

She liked being called Kiki. Her parents called her Kiki. She called *herself* Kiki. She just wasn't into people deciding a nickname was owed to them.

"Kikade," he repeated.

He let go of her hand.

She crossed her arms.

He wiggled to the music, then took a step back to give her some space. He seemed utterly unperturbed by this situation, as if he found himself in close quarters with girls he'd just met all the time.

Kiki needed to fill the silence. "You're new here? Josie said you just moved into her neighborhood."

"Yeah! It's funny because where I'm from, you act like your neighbors don't exist unless their tree grows over your fence or their dog craps all over your lawn. But Josie and her dad brought us this really, really, *really* yummy cake—"

Kiki's eyes widened. "What kind of cake?"

He closed his eyes momentarily. "Coconut ... something ..."

"Coconut rum cake?"

"Yes!"

"My dad made that cake! She got it from our restaurant. I love it, but his butter cake is even better. It's like a slice of heaven—"

Her phone chimed, and the screen lit up with a clock counting down.

Kastov's expression changed—now there was slight disappointment in his eyes, though he was still smiling. "We can totally just walk out of here. I know that breaks the rules, but—"

"Oh! No, I—it's not *you*—" Kiki could feel herself reddening. She had the tendency to ramble. "Thing is, I'm not actually here right now. I'm at the movies. My parents would *kill* me if I were here."

"*Ah*. What are we seeing?"

"*Man vs. Robot 3*."

He snorted.

"Don't judge me."

"I'm judging."

"The first one's not bad."

"Uh, it's notoriously bad."

"But the second one gets better!"

Kastov paused for a moment. "Is that the one where The Rock fights a thousand ant-sized robots with nothing but a spoon?"

"Yes! Shirtless!"

Kastov chuckled again. Something about his laugh made her crave another once it was over. She'd never been one to turn to jelly solely because she was on the receiving end of a face-crinkling smile, but here she was. Jelly. She hated it.

"Still," he continued, "*MVR 2* is a pretty bad movie, and I don't mean that in a *so bad it's good* sort of way."

"I heard that in the new one, Channing Tatum rips off the MegaMech's arm and slaps him with it! So it's already an improvement."

"*Sold*. I guess we'll have to check it out."

Kiki didn't let her mind linger on that *we*. But she figured this was how you made friends as quickly as he did. You opened an invitation to someone you barely knew. "Where'd you move from?"

"New York. My dad's sick of the cold." His voice softened, and his toe-taps to the beat became an awkward shift from one leg to the other. "It was kind of abrupt."

Kiki sensed that there was something more there that he didn't want to talk about. He'd said it himself: *I don't know you either*.

He pointed at the orange emblem on her phone case. "You go to Orange Grove?"

"Mm-hmm."

"Same—*nice*. Well, if I can get into twelfth grade. I'm taking summer classes at Miami Dade; some of my credits didn't transfer. Just gotta pass calc and French."

"French? Easy."

"You know French?"

"I know Kreyòl, and it's helped a ton."

"I could use some help." He leaned in a little. "Hey, maybe—"

Thankfully, someone opened the door, and Kiki and Kastov were greeted with applause. Some of the boys bowed or thumbs-upped when they walked out, but Kastov only turned to her once more.

"I gotta go," she said quickly. "Curfew."

Kastov dipped his head, touching his prayer hands to his lips. "See you around? I heard Chris is throwing a party next week."

She said, "Yeah, maybe," though she had no intention of going.

As she made her way out of the house, gleeful yells erupted from the living room. Someone turned the music up higher, and Kastov was at the center of it all, dancing. He was terrible, but between the grin on his face and his sheer confidence, it didn't matter.

He pulled some people away from the spin circle to dance with him. They rushed to him like wildcats to prey. Or maybe *he* was the cat—Kiki wasn't quite sure yet.

Just as his eyes found her, she hurried out the door.

Spin #2

The González Twins' Birthday Bash

June 16th

KIKI MISSED WHEN MARISOL AND LUNA'S BIRTHDAY PARTY HAD INVOLVED pizza, cake, and a PG-13 movie. But Kiki swam and socialized for a good hour, and then she thought it was finally an appropriate time to wish the twins a final happy birthday and make a swift exit. She could only force extroversion for so long.

She looked over at the circle of kids on the kitchen floor.

Kiki scanned their faces. Disappointment tickled her chest the same way it had when Chris, Robby, and the rest of the lacrosse crew had entered the party without Kastov.

It wasn't like she was obsessing over him. She wasn't here for Kastov; she was here because Marisol and Luna were nice, and she never missed one of their birthday parties.

It would be silly to dwell on a boy she had talked to for just seven minutes, obviously.

Sighing, her multicolored beach towel tight under her armpits, Kiki hit the snack table. Amari paused her conversation with Nayelie to pass the vodka, but Kiki shook her head. Her mother had foolproof Mom Senses and would totally be able to tell, even if she had only a sip.

Instead, Kiki shoved a whole handful of popcorn into her mouth, spun, and bumped right into a tall, grinning boy.

"Kikade!"

Kiki chewed furiously. "Kastov!" It sounded more like *Athoff!* She spat a few kernels at him, but he didn't seem to mind.

He wasn't dressed for a pool party, or any party. He'd come straight from work at Steak 'N Go, judging from the restaurant name stitched onto his red polo. He wore a baby blue snapback backward, tufts of dark hair curling adorably at the edges.

He took a long draw from his Solo cup, then regarded it curiously. "I didn't know they made these in hot pink."

"The González twins are very particular about color schemes." She pulled the towel tighter. "Nice hat. That shade of blue's my favorite color."

"I'd let you have it, but I've got such bad hat hair that if you saw it, you'd run away screaming."

She laughed.

And her laugh made him laugh. He looked over at the circle, and then back at Kiki.

She looked away. "Seven Minutes is kind of the worst game ever."

His brow twitched.

"I just think that if you like someone, you should tell them instead of hoping they end up sequestered in a closet with you."

"Sequestered?"

"I'm being extra, but you know what I mean."

"Maybe people just wanna kiss other people without all that."

She shrugged. "Well. Yeah. I guess that's fair."

Alexa spotted them from the circle and pointed a finger at him. "Kastov! Your turn!"

His gaze remained on Kiki. Brown eyes beaming.

Kiki shook her head. "Got popcorn kernels all up in my teeth. Super gross."

He chuckled. "What a shame."

She was grateful that he walked away, leaving her to blush in peace.

He found a spot next to Luna. He said something to her, and the two of them giggled like kids. Kiki was beginning to understand that this was so like him. Always laughing, always smiling, always so damn glad to be there, wherever he was. She wanted to find him annoying, but he seemed so utterly genuine.

Kastov steadied the bottle on its side. It glistened as it spun.

Kiki's stomach turned. She hadn't realized until this very moment that she had absolutely no desire to see the bottle land on anyone but her.

"Shit!" Izzy cried from the circle. "Sorry!"

Next to her, Hanna got up and ran to the marble island, red punch dripping from her shirt.

The bottle slowed.

It was almost automatic, the way Kiki hurried to take Hanna's place.

The bottle stopped between Izzy and Tommy.

It pointed at her.

Kastov looked up.

Their eyes locked, and her stomach went all fluttery the same way it had after the first spin. But it felt different. It stemmed less from anxiety and more from excitement, which was its own form of torture.

Kastov held the pantry door open for her. "Don't you even think about kissing me," he said.

"Check your ego. No one was thinking about kissing you."

He looked around at the absurd amounts of canned tuna, baked beans, and toilet paper. "What are we thinking? Hoarders? Doomsday preppers? Extreme couponers?"

Kiki laughed. "I think they're just rich."

"Hm, true. So, what movie are we watching tonight?"

"My parents know I'm here, actually. They're cool with Marisol and Luna's dads. But they think the twins are throwing the same pizza party they've been doing since we were seven."

"Nice."

"But I can't stay for the sleepover. My parents are very strict. They don't really let me do things like other kids do."

Like white kids do.

"I haven't even told them . . ." Her voice trailed off.

Kastov raised a brow. "What?"

"Um. I'm applying to this fancy culinary school in August." It wasn't something that anyone else knew. But even though he still felt like a stranger to her, telling him was easy. Like she could say anything in the seven minutes they had and it would be okay. "The Auguste Giroud Culinary Academy. It's in California. They're gonna flip."

"Doesn't your dad own a restaurant?"

It took a moment for her to remember telling him that. He said it so simply, completely oblivious to what it meant to her that he'd thought it important enough to keep. "There's a difference. It's, you know . . ." She searched for a word to describe the nausea that commonly rose in her gut or the stress that knotted up her shoulders. "The first-gen affliction. I gotta be a doctor or a lawyer; I gotta make a gazillion dollars a year. I can't date till I'm married."

"To be the child of an immigrant." He played with a loose thread on his snapback. "My mom's from Korea—I get it."

"I tried to show them the pamphlets once, and they refused to listen. If I get in, I'll tell them. But not until then. That way I won't have to deal with their smugness if I don't."

"You'll get in."

She sighed. "What about you? What's your plan?"

He rubbed the back of his neck. "Dunno. I like coding, and my mom liked that idea up until I told her I want to make video games."

"What does your dad think?"

Kastov laughed humorlessly. "My dad doesn't really care." He rolled his shoulders uncomfortably. "In other news, I got roped into seeing *Man v. Robot 3* last week."

"No spoilers! Was it amazing?"

"That robot arm slap was something. Chris couldn't stop laughing."

Kiki felt her smile go stiff. "Chris Keller?"

"Yeah!"

She bit the inside of her cheek. "You guys are friends, huh?"

"He's chill. Was the first person I met here, kinda took me in."

Kiki only nodded.

"So," he continued. "Two spins. We're on a streak."

"I'm sure plenty of people get the same person more than once."

"But I've only played twice. That's . . ." He scrunched up his face and counted on his fingers. "One hundred percent."

"Two for two isn't, like, ten for ten."

"I have a theory. Maybe we're being pushed together."

"By who?"

"The party gods!"

"And why are the party gods pushing us together?"

He shrugged. "Maybe you need to help me with my French homework. Or maybe I need to help you, I don't know, refine your movie tastes!"

She scoffed. *"Careful."*

He took a step closer to her. "Or. Maybe . . ."

She stilled. He looked at her, eyes full of wanting, and she thought, *That is a look that breaks hearts.*

"Maybe they're waiting for us to kiss."

Kiki didn't know how he'd gotten so close. She clutched her towel, suddenly feeling exposed. A braid came loose from her bun.

Gently he slipped it back over her shoulder, his fingers slow against her bare skin.

Someone banged on the door. *"Get your clothes on, sluts! One minute left!"*

She leaned back suddenly with a jolt like waking up from a dream.

Kastov looked away, sheepish. She hadn't seen him like this before, all red in the cheeks, eyes cast down. He lifted his snapback and ran his hand through his hair before replacing the hat.

Kiki screamed dramatically, covering her eyes. "The hat hair!"

He smiled, easy and slow. "You're hilarious. Come to Hanna's thing tomorrow. Test my theory."

"Fine. But this time, I spin. If your theory's correct, it shouldn't matter who's got the bottle."

"Just don't go spinning on anyone else, okay? They totally don't have what we have."

She knew he was just being Kastov, but her stomach flipped anyway.

Spin #3
Hanna Bilson's Low-Key Thing in Coconut Grove
June 17th

THIS TIME KIKI DIDN'T HOVER ON THE FRINGES OF THE CIRCLE. WHEN ROBBY waved the bottle in the air and shouted, "Who wants next?" she snatched it from him.

From four people over, Kastov gave her a mischievous smirk. She'd grown accustomed to his cute, cozy smiles. His self-deprecating grins. His shy little laughs. This look was something else entirely.

She held the bottle against the floor. *Don't spin too hard. Don't spin too . . . soft?* She shook her head. *Don't overthink it.*

Kiki spun the bottle.

Cardi was blaring in the background, and she focused only on the music. Kiki refused to look at the bottle, and she certainly didn't want to look at him. He had a way of reading her, and she didn't need him to know that she was internally shouting his name.

With a *clack* against the tiles, the bottle stuttered to a stop.

She looked up.

It pointed at the center of Kastov's knee.

He leaped over Robby's leg to beat her to the linen closet. He opened the door, grinning devilishly.

As she walked in wearing a grin of her own, Kiki heard someone say, "Am I high, or has this happened before?"

Spin #4
Amari Jones's "HBD A-meh-ica" Party
July 4th

KASTOV DANCED HIS WAY INTO THE CLOSET. "KIKADE!" HE SHOUTED.

The music was so blisteringly loud that the walls shook.

"Kastov!" she yelled back.

"I love this song!"

She leaned in. "What?!"

"Let's dance!"

She understood that perfectly but pointed at her ear as if she didn't. It didn't matter. He started up with his signature move, the shoulder shimmy.

It hit her hard. Suddenly she realized how much she'd missed him these past few weeks while she was working overtime at the restaurant, testing her dad's new recipes and dealing with tourists. It'd kept her busy enough that she hadn't had much time to think of Kastov, but now that they were together again, she couldn't stop staring at him.

He wagged his eyebrows. "Come on! Dance with me!"

"No!"

"Who doesn't like dancing?!"

"I like dancing! Alone! In my room!"

"We're alone! We're in a room!"

"This is a closet!"

He caught her by the waist and spun her around a few times.

It was so absurd that she giggled. "You're cute," she blurted out, normal volume.

He leaned in. "Huh?"

"You're cute!" she said a little louder, knowing full well that he couldn't hear.

"What?! I'm what?"

She smiled hard. "YOU'RE"—the music cut out, then—"CUTE!"

Instantly she slapped her hand over her mouth.

Her heart stopped. She was going to die of embarrassment, here in a closet with a cute boy. Her parents would find out, resurrect her, and kill her all over again.

Kastov's perfect mouth curled into her favorite smile. The soft, knowing one, so different from his usual grin. It was the only thing that stopped her from bolting, changing her name, and fleeing the whole damn country.

The music returned but at a lower volume. Kiki would've liked more noise.

"I missed"—he paused—"*this.*"

She wondered if he'd meant to say something else. "I missed this too."

He wore happiness well. Everything seemed brighter with his grin.

"I always looked for you. At Alexa's party, at Robby's . . . where have you been hiding?"

She laughed a little, like the way his voice went all low didn't give her heart palpitations. "I've been working nonstop. There's gonna be an article in the *Miami Times* about the restaurant. It's super exciting, but my dad's stressed. He keeps changing recipes and messing with the menu—he's rearranged the seating seven times in the past two weeks! I get my anxiety from him, apparently." She shook her head at herself. "You?"

"Oh, you know." He casually leaned one hand against the wall. It was so extra that Kiki had to laugh. "Acing French tests. No thanks to you . . ."

"I was sending you good vibes, okay—"

". . . and avoiding spinning bottles."

Kiki fidgeted slightly. She hadn't thought about him playing the game without her. "Avoiding?"

"Eh. It got boring." He shrugged.

She appreciated how comfortable the following silence felt.

Kastov sighed. "Speaking of the restaurant, I have a favor to ask. It's an emergency."

"Emergency?"

"A cake emergency! My mom's birthday is in two days, and she deserves something nice. You remember that party at Izzy's? You said your dad makes this awesome butter cake?"

"Oh! Sorry, he doesn't sell them; he just makes them for my mom and me."

"Okay. So, like . . . could you teach me how to make one?"

The smile slipped off of her face.

He laughed at her. "Don't look at me like that. I can come by the restaurant—"

"*No*, oh my god!"

"*Kikade.*"

"*Kastov.* My parents would kill me! You're a boy, and they hate boys!"

"All boys?"

"Yes! Doesn't matter if you're smart or nice or—"

He winked at her. *"Cute?"*

She ignored that. "Do you want me to die, Kastov?"

He fiddled with his snapback. "My mom's been having a tough time since we moved. All of her family's up north, and we still haven't found a good Korean restaurant, and my dad's a total dick who is going to do the bare minimum for her, like he does every year. You said the cake is like a slice of heaven."

Kiki didn't know how to explain that it was even better. The butter, the vanilla, the sugar, the lime—comforting enough to cure her anxieties, ease the ache of a scraped knee, salve a hard day. She knew that good food held a certain power, but only her dad's butter cake felt like this.

"See?" Kastov said, catching her dreamy expression. "I need the cake that does that to a person."

"How about I make one and bring it to you?"

"Well, I would like to be able to re-create it. That way I won't have to ask next year."

Her stomach fluttered. *He wants to hang out with you.*

She thought up a plan. "Tomorrow's Sunday—we open late."

With a wild grin that made her nerves fuzzy, Kastov handed her his phone.

She keyed in her number and her address. "Meet me at the restaurant by noon sharp."

He squeezed his phone. "Thank you, Kikade, you absolute angel."

She bit the inside of her cheek. "You can call me Kiki, you know."

Spin #5
St. Germain, Prince Avenue
July 5th

"Kiki!" her mom called from the living room. "There's a skinny boy on our doorstep!"

Eyes wide, Kiki bolted from her bed.

Her mom switched to Kreyòl. "Di li nou pa vle okenn ti liv!"

Kiki had spent the whole morning practicing what she was going to say. Lying about going to a party instead of the movies felt wildly different than lying about meeting a boy.

And then he had just . . . *shown up*. He stood at the front door with an apron rolled up in his hand and that perfect smile.

Kastov offered his other hand to her mom. "Jin-ho." She took it, *thank god*. "Nice to meet you."

Kiki's mom looked him up and down. He took a shoe off, and she nodded in approval, so he slipped off the second one.

And then he wasn't on the doorstep anymore; he had a foot in the doorway. He was *inside her house*.

Quickly, Kiki ran up to him and forced him backward onto the doorstep, her hands firm on his chest.

He looked down at them, grinned, and she dropped them.

"You're here," she said, out of breath. "Why?"

"Uh. Cake emergency? I know I'm early—"

"We're meeting at the restaurant!"

Brow wrinkled in confusion, Kastov pulled out his phone. "Two-three-three Southwest—"

"*Oh my god.*" She covered her face with her hands. "I gave you *my* address instead of the restaurant's."

Kastov chuckled. "You know, your mom seems perfectly nice."

Kiki made a sound halfway between a laugh and a sob.

"I'm sorry, I can go—my bad."

"It's okay." Finally she lifted her head. "I have work later, so let me go change into my uniform. It's three blocks away on Prince Ave. I'll meet you there."

"Awesome. K and K, making a cake. Dream team." He high-fived himself.

Kiki smiled, and nodded, and slipped behind the door, and closed it.

"It's for his mom," she told her own mother, who then made a sound that was uniquely hers. Close to an *mm-hmm*, but not quite, and Kiki couldn't replicate it, but she knew what it meant. It wasn't no, however, and she wondered if maybe her parents could be chill. Maybe she was too in her head.

She considered this seriously until her mom sent five texts about *behaving*. There would be a talk later. Kiki was already dreading it.

Kastov sat on the stone steps leading up to the worn-down, well-loved, itty-bitty restaurant. He was wearing the apron. It said, KISS THE COOK. *Jesus.*

Kiki led Kastov into the cozy kitchen. It was nothing like the kitchen collaged in her journal, ripped from the pages of the Giroud promotional booklet. That was Kitchen of the Future: stainless steel everything, a double-wide oven, and fridges that looked big enough to hide multiple bodies.

But this was good too. A large cooktop, a small walk-in freezer, and an oven that usually worked.

Kiki scrolled to the cooking playlist on her phone and pressed play. "Did you say your name was Jin-ho? I've, uh, only ever called you by your last name."

"Yep." He pulled down a bowl hanging from a hook attached to the ceiling.

"Why do you go by Kastov, then?"

He shrugged, flipping the bowl over in his hands. "It's easier to give at Starbucks, for one."

She nodded. She felt that in her heart.

He bobbed his head to the music. "What is this?"

"There's a girl on SoundCloud who mixes classical music with rap. This is 'MozartxMigos.'"

"*Mmm.* You have eclectic taste, Kiki."

She brought out the milk, eggs, and butter from the fridge and instructed him to get the flour, sugar, and baking powder from the dry pantry. She set the oven to 350. "Sugar, one and a half cups. Then add eggs, two sticks of butter, and some lime zest. We're gonna mix it, then add some milk, the flour, and some rum. Then just some salt, some nutmeg, and some vanilla. It's easy."

Kastov picked up the measuring cup, then put it down. "Can we slow down?"

"No, my dad will be in soon."

"Your mom knows I'm here."

"My dad won't be as nice. Anyway, it's not just that. He also doesn't like me opening up shop without him."

He cocked his head at her. "Really?"

"So ... my dad has had this place for years, right? And when he started, this neighborhood didn't look like it does now. But things have changed."

Kastov nodded.

"My dad came home once and realized he'd left his phone here, so he came back, and as he was opening up, I guess some dumbass passerby reported that he was breaking in. I don't know."

"Oh, shit."

"It's fine. The, uh, cop that came by eats here sometimes. So. It's fine." Her brain was scattered. She felt the anxiety in her fractured sentences.

He moved closer to her. "I know your parents are strict, but it sounds like they really care."

"They do," Kiki offered softly. "Can I ask . . . what's with your dad?" She wanted him to give her something the way she so easily did with him.

He raised a brow in surprise. "Nothing. I mean, nothing major." He shrugged. "Just a run-of-the-mill absent dad. I know it sucks, but sometimes I wish I had a curfew like you, you know? He's the complete opposite of my mom. Do you ever wonder how two people ended up together?"

Or as friends? she thought. "Yeah." She pulled away from him. "Anyway. Cake?"

He grinned. "Cake!"

Kiki passed him the spatula. "Do as I say, and this will go awesomely."

He listened well, and he danced, and most importantly, he didn't pester her with questions. It was strange, being with him out in the open. She was so used to being right in front of him, walls closing in. She didn't know how to act with so much space.

"I'm a master egg-white folder," he said, easing the spatula into the bowl. He finished with the batter and poured it into the Bundt pan Kiki had meticulously buttered, and she slipped the cake into the oven.

"Kiki," Kastov said suddenly. "We forgot something."

She turned to him.

On the other side of the kitchen, he pulled an empty glass bottle from the recycling bin.

Kiki swallowed hard.

He spun it on the counter. Silently, without the usual party backing track, they watched as it landed on her.

He bit his lip. "Come here, Kiki."

She willed herself to not overthink it for once, to not second-guess, and he met her halfway, the two of them nearly crashing into each other in front of the spice rack.

Kastov slipped his arm around her waist. She brushed a stray bit of flour off his cheek. He touched his forehead to hers just as the familiar sound of a churning motor rumbled outside of St. Germain.

Kiki froze. "That's my dad." She quickly angled herself away from him, cheeks prickly with warmth. "Wait here."

If Kastov responded, she didn't hear it. She quickly pushed through the kitchen door.

Her dad gave a surprised laugh when he saw her. "What are you doing here? You know—"

"I know, I'm not supposed to open up, but—"

"It's fine, but we have a problem, a big problem. It's gonna be a mess!" He wiped sweat from his dark brown face.

Kiki shook her head. "Wait, what is?"

"Tonight!" He threw his hands up. "They published that article in the *Miami Times* about us."

"What? That's amazing!"

"*No*, it's supposed to go up next month! Kiki, people have been calling me all day to make reservations."

Her mouth popped open a little. "We don't . . . take reservations."

"Jean-Luc's still on vacation. Call Kendra—I'll call your mother. We need all hands on deck—"

He stopped suddenly.

From behind her, a voice said, "I can help."

Kiki cursed Kastov out in her head.

Her dad turned to her with a look that said, *Whose boy is this?*

With her own look, she said, *Not mine!*

"Kiss The Cook," eh? Nan kwizin mwen?

There was no kissing in your kitchen! She sighed. "Dad, this is Kastov— uh, Jin-ho. He just moved here, and it's his mom's birthday tomorrow, and he wanted to bring her a cake."

Kastov put a hand out. "Hi."

"Hi," her dad said skeptically, ignoring the hand.

Kiki turned to Kastov. "The cake's not done, plus it needs to cool. You can pick it up tomorrow."

"Can you wait tables?" her father said suddenly.

Kastov looked at her, and she looked at her father, and her father looked at Kastov.

"What?" said Kastov.

"*What?*" said Kiki.

Her dad hurried past Kastov and into the kitchen. "Three hours until we open! Fè vit!"

Triumphant, Kastov put his fists at his sides. "Parents love me."

Kiki released a tinny scoff. "It's only 'cause he's stressed out and doesn't have time to be guard dad right now, so don't flatter yourself."

His phone chimed, and he pulled it from his pocket. "Sorry, it's Chris. I was supposed to meet him to prep for his party after this."

Kiki felt her heart shrink. "Oh."

Kastov laughed, still tapping at his phone.

They're joking about you, she thought, even though she didn't have a reason to believe it. But the thought persisted. *And what kind of person is Kastov if he's cool with Chris Keller?*

"You should go," said Kiki.

Immediately Kastov looked up. His expression softened. "It's no big—I can help."

"We got it. It's fine. Have fun."

She turned, but he rounded a table and cut her off. "Wait, what just happened?"

"Nothing."

"Well, are you coming tonight?"

"I'll probably be exhausted."

"Then I'd rather be here."

Kiki's cheeks went hot again. "Go help Chris. He's your friend."

"*You're* my friend." He scanned her face. "What's your deal with him?"

She could still *hear* him.

"Were you guys . . ." He ran his fingers through his hair twice before being able to finish his sentence. "A thing, or something?"

He was with Robby, whispering during lunch.

Carina or Kiki?

Carina's hot.

Carina is so hot.

But like, Kiki's cute though. She's cute. I mean, for a Black girl.

"Kiki?" Kastov whispered.

"I'll bring the cake to your place tomorrow."

He shook his head. "Actually, you know what? No worries. I'll just—I'll run by Publix."

Finally he turned toward the door, and Kiki knew what she should've said. *It's your cake—you made it. Bring your mom a slice of heaven.*

And I like you, Kastov. But I can't like you if you're like him.

But she said nothing.

She only watched him go.

Spin #6
Nayelie López's Last Call Before Fall
August 1st

KIKI HAD CONVINCED HERSELF THAT SHE WAS OVER IT.

She had attempted to reach out, but Kastov had never responded. She had ended up giving the cake to Josie to deliver, even though she was dying to see him herself. She'd spent days mulling over what to text after that and ended up texting nothing.

But Nayelie López, who lived across the street, was throwing the final party of the summer. The Last Call Before Fall.

Kiki peeked through the pink lace curtains of her bedroom window. After pacing for an hour and reluctantly changing out of pajamas, she tiptoed out of her house.

It didn't take long to find him. He was where she knew he'd be. In the circle, begging to be kissed.

He sat between Tara and Robby, eyes on the bottle in his hands.

Kastov, she thought, and it must've been a telepathic phenomenon, because through all the noise, he heard, and he looked up at her. His expression wasn't unfriendly, but it unsettled her. Anything but utter joy looked wrong on him.

He said, "Someone else should go—"

His protest was drowned out by boos. Amari even playfully threw a straw at him, and Kastov smiled like he couldn't resist, a crack in the unusually icy demeanor he wore tonight. In that flash of teeth, Kiki saw the boy she recognized, the one she'd fallen for completely.

She fit herself in next to Alexa.

He spun.

The rim of the bottle sailed toward Kiki, but with its last shiver of momentum, it eased toward Alexa and stayed there.

Heart pounding, Kiki rose to her knees, leaned forward, and tapped the bottle so it pointed at herself.

She looked at Alexa.

Alexa flashed her a smile and tipped her head toward him. "Well, I'm not gonna be the one to break the streak."

Alexa then demanded that everyone take a shot. Their attention shifted, and they all seemed to forget that Kiki had broken the cardinal rule of Seven Minutes in Heaven.

Kiki entered the bathroom and found Kastov leaning against the counter, his arms crossed. He had that baby blue cap on again, though the hair sticking out from under it seemed longer than before. Without looking at her, he said, "I think touching the bottle after it's been spun is seven years of bad luck. You'll anger the party gods."

"Worth it." Kiki moved closer to him. "I'm gonna tell you something, and maybe you'll think I'm overreacting, but I know in my heart that I'm not. I get that from my mom. She taught me that when someone shows you who they are, you believe them."

He turned a little toward her, still not entirely making eye contact, brow wrinkled in confusion.

"I can't stand Chris Keller. He's just a big fan of, I don't know, little racist shit."

Now he looked at her.

"Like, those, uh, pokes—" She made a stabbing motion with her finger. "'Kiki, you're so smart for a Black girl. So pretty for a Black girl. You know, you're lucky, you don't even need good grades like I do—you'll get in anywhere, *obviously*.'" She laughed now because it sounded so silly. "I called him out once, and he called me an uptight bitch."

"I don't usually punch people, but I'm reconsidering."

Smiling, she rolled her eyes. "Anyway, I decided that I hated him."

"I think that's deserved."

"*And* all of his friends."

"I didn't know he was like that, Kiki."

"I know." She put a hand on the porcelain sink, next to his. "You made it super hard for me to dislike you, anyway, and I'm pretty good at holding a grudge." She swallowed hard, a summer's worth of swooning building up in her chest. "It's like, you . . . say things sometimes. And for days, those things are all that I can think about. I don't like anyone having that power over me. Like, being able to make me or break me with just a few words."

His expression went from distressed to dazed. "I know exactly what you mean."

Kiki knew that this could be The Moment, but she didn't return his gaze.

He was close. When he spoke, his lips almost brushed against her forehead. He smelled like shampoo and chlorine. "Do you remember our first spin? At Izzy's thing?"

She nodded.

"You didn't trust me at all. And that's fine, but I spent the whole summer waiting for you to want to stay. It's like the second our seven minutes were up, *poof*, you were gone, like you couldn't wait to be rid of me."

Kiki shook her head. "I have a curfew—"

"I know. I get that. But a little part of me still hoped you might risk it for me. That broke me, every single time." His thumb brushed against hers. "But when you shouted at the top of your lungs that I was cute—"

She groaned. "God, please don't remind me."

He laughed, throwing his arms around her. "That *made* me. It was perfect."

He dipped his head down. She knew that if she looked up at those perfect and full and love-starved brown eyes, she wouldn't be able to resist.

"Kikade."

"Jin-ho."

"Kiss me. It's what the universe wants."

She looked up, drank in those deep brown eyes, and kissed him. Someone outside shouted that they had to pee, and there was a crash and cheers from the kitchen, but Kiki hardly noticed any of it. Her senses were completely consumed by the feel of his soft lips on her nervous ones, the touch of his fingers against her cheek, and the flutters in her chest.

Kastov brushed his thumb across her lips. "How many spins is this?"

"Six." She added, "I think," though she knew it for sure.

"Look at us—forty-two whole minutes in heaven."

Grinning, Kiki pulled off his hat and ran her fingers through his hair. "We have some catching up to do."

AUTHOR'S NOTE

A few years ago, I started working on a YA novel that hinged on fated games of Spin the Bottle/Seven Minutes in Heaven. I wanted to write a cozy story, something to smile at and cringe with. I hit about fifteen thousand words before turning my attention to a completely different story that is very special to me, but I always knew I'd return to this concept. When I first decided to submit to FORESHADOW, I was considering a few speculative ideas before realizing that this was the perfect opportunity to revisit Kiki and Kastov.

BREAK was my first professionally published work of fiction—I still get chills thinking about opening up the acceptance email! Though the story always focused on Kiki and Kastov's relationship, the version I submitted started with the pair on their thirteenth spin and already knowing a bit about each other. In this version, they only had two party/closet scenes. My editor suggested taking the story back to the beginning and letting us follow their love story every step of the way. I seriously adore the new scenes that I got to write, particularly Kastov's dancing, Kiki taking the lead in Spin #3, and the sweet "YOU'RE CUTE" moment. It's hard to imagine the story without them.

Though this story is not autobiographical, Kiki is teen me in many ways. Dealing with the microaggressions, the anxiety, and the expectations of being a first-gen kid was never fun, and it didn't end with adolescence. But I dreamed up this story as a love letter not only to my past self but for those of us publishing often doesn't see as deserving of the meet-cutes and happy endings. This story is for me, and this story is for you.

BUILDING THE ROMANCE IN *BREAK*

by Emily X.R. Pan

THE THING ABOUT A ROMANCE IS THAT WE HAVE A GOOD SENSE OF WHAT'S going to happen. One might even argue that love stories are among the most formulaic. But Meridien uses this to her advantage: She gives us the road map of the story, and then she uses our expectations to tease out the romance.

"Spin #1" introduces the structure, though we don't really know it yet. We see our narrator at a party where there's a game of Seven Minutes in Heaven happening, and we get to meet the official person of interest:

> A boy she didn't recognize had just entered the living room, and everyone seemed very excited about that.

This skillfully directs the reader's attention—we know this guy is significant, and we can guess why. The bottle spins, and of course it lands on Kiki. We were already inferring that it would.

In the closet we meet Kastov for the first time, and immediately there's a will-they-or-won't-they tension. The banter feels organic and real; it makes us root for this pairing.

The "Spin #2" heading confirms how the story is going to go. There will be encounter after encounter, and we're immediately anticipating the next one.

New party, new round of Seven Minutes in Heaven. Kiki and Kastov end up together again. Too many coincidences are usually hard to buy, but here it's a delight because it's what we want to see.

Kastov held the pantry door open for her. "Don't you even think about kissing me," he said.

This callback is funny and charming—Kastov has endeared himself to us. Their conversation swings toward more serious and personal things, and we see the intimacy building. Jumping from party to party like this fast-forwards us through time and the development of their feelings.

There's humor in the narrative choices, too. Check out these examples of the story being self-aware:

"I have a theory. Maybe we're being pushed together."

"By who?"

"The party gods!"

As she walked in wearing a grin of her own, Kiki heard someone say, "Am I high, or has this happened before?"

That bit of tongue-in-cheek helps us to continue cheerfully suspending our disbelief in favor of the bottle magically putting Kiki and Kastov together again and again. And by establishing this pattern, Meridien has left the field wide open for her to serve up whatever surprises she wants.

"Spin #5" is where things shift. They're at the restaurant instead of a party. There are no other people around. This change in setting tells us something significant is going to happen.

Kastov spins a bottle, and we know *this is the moment*. After all these parties and all these streaks and not a single kiss, now is finally the time.

Then, of course, Kiki's dad arrives. Chris Keller comes up—Kastov's friendship with him is a deal breaker.

"Spin #6." Kiki is at the last party of the season, which we understand as shorthand for *last chance ever to kiss Kastov and spark Something Real*. (High stakes!) When the bottle spins this time it doesn't quite point to

Kiki—a nice way to reflect the stumble they've recently made—but she seizes control of the moment. Instead of waiting for the coincidence, she lays claim to her own agency. The conversation about Chris Keller finally happens, Kastov's reaction is perfect, and then, not a moment too soon, they kiss.

This careful buildup makes the romance irresistible. It's a matter of layering the characters' interactions with solid emotional logic and deliberate pacing. Much easier said than done—but *so* satisfying.

RESILIENT

Mayra Cuevas

> **RESILIENT** is one of those stories that wears its heart on its sleeve—full of heartbreak and hope, with characters you'll want to hold close. I adored this story.
>
> —BECKY ALBERTALLI, AUTHOR OF *LEAH ON THE OFFBEAT*

IT'S NOT LIKE WE LEFT RIGHT AWAY. NO ONE COULD ACCUSE US OF GIVING UP after María—throwing our hands up in defeat, packing our bags and fleeing like some did, a week after the storm. There's just a limit to how long you can live in the dark when it means living in despair.

I pull the edges of my knitted hat—the one Abuela made before we left—and sink a little lower into the back seat of the van, trying in vain to muffle the quiet sobs of the woman sitting in front of us.

"God, is she still crying?" my cousin Rosita whispers, leaning her head on my shoulder.

"She misses her father. He's sick." I sigh, grateful for the good health of my parents and my abuela. They're heartbroken about us leaving, but have tried their best to be supportive.

"We all miss someone. You won't see me crying about it," Rosita scoffs below her breath. I shush her, praying no one else heard her harsh words.

"I'm freezing," she says, nuzzling her face closer to my collarbone.

I fold her hands in mine, rubbing them for warmth. It's ten degrees outside and, as far as my eyes can see, everything is covered in snow.

When we stepped out of the airport in Sioux Falls, the wind gusts felt like a million razor-sharp needles pricking my skin.

I glance toward the front of the van, searching for the guy who arrived in shorts. We're not in Puerto Rico anymore, amigo! He has a recent sunburn and that sun-bleached hair surfer dudes normally wear. Too bad for him, the nearest decent stretch of coastline is 1,200 miles away.

"How much longer?" Rosita asks.

"About an hour until we reach Huron. Do you want to put your head on my lap?"

Rosita moans. "Can I borrow your scarf?"

"Where's yours?"

"I think I left it on the plane."

"That was your only scarf!" I whisper-yell.

She shrugs, untroubled.

"Where are your gloves?" I demand, remembering she almost left one at the gate before we boarded the plane in San Juan.

"Right here." She raises both hands, displaying the blue fabric enveloping her fingers.

I roll my eyes at her, gently pushing her onto my lap. Then I unravel my purple scarf from my neck and place it over her shoulders, gently stroking the back of her head.

Even though she's two years older than me, at times like this it feels like I'm the adult. Mami calls me "más madura que un plátano"—too mature for my age.

Rosita prefers the laissez-faire approach, a "take life as it comes" philosophy that leaves the rest of us scrambling after her. Meanwhile, my seventeenth year of life was fully mapped out since my birthday. It just didn't account for cataclysmic forces of nature.

On September 19, the day before María, I had a cushy job as a receptionist in a doctor's office, a college admission for a degree in Latin American studies, which I deferred for a gap year, and I was saving to pay for my dream trip through Latin America with a teen tour company that follows the route Che Guevara took in his *Diarios de Motocicleta*. According to the description on the website, it would be a time of awakening, of leaving my mark on the world and allowing it to leave its mark on me.

Hours before the entire island lost power, I was on the tour's website going over the route. First stop, Buenos Aires! Then travel north, hugging the continent's west coast until we reached Bogotá. Twenty-five cities in all.

Like Che, I would keep my own diary and jot down observations about the complexity of life in South America, my own life unfolding in the process.

A pang of resentment hits the pit of my stomach every time I think of everything that was lost to that beast named María. It's senseless to be enraged at a mass of wind and rain, but that's exactly how I feel. My dream journey through South America turned into a one-way ticket to the middle-of-nowhere South Dakota. Not exactly what I had in mind when I told my parents I wanted to see the world.

"It's a way out of here," Rosita said a month ago, desperately waving a worn newspaper in my face. It had been almost four months since María, and our homes still didn't have electricity or running water. Mercifully, our cell phones worked, provided we found somewhere to charge them.

"They pay for the flights and give you a room," she explained, bouncing on her heels.

"In a motel," I replied, reading the small print. "You want to live in a motel?"

"If it has electricity, yes. Yes, I do!" Rosita declared, falling into a seat next to me. "They'll even pick us up at the airport. Pay starts at ten dollars an hour."

"Cutting turkey parts?" I asked in disbelief.

How had our dreams suddenly become so small?

The full-page ad read EMPLEOS GARANTIZADOS in big, bold letters. Underneath, a description of the so-called guaranteed jobs: *South Dakota turkey processing plant needs breast-pullers, carcass-loaders, bird-hangers* . . .

Two questions popped to mind: What the hell is a carcass-loader? And is this the only option we have left?

"South Dakota? We might as well be moving to Canada." I took the newspaper from Rosita's hands. "What about Florida? The Garcías left for Orlando last week. Maybe they can help us get jobs."

"Marisol, everyone and their freaking abuela is moving to Florida. And they're all competing for the same jobs. The Ramirezes are living in a hotel because they can't find an apartment. That girl down the street, what's her name? Smart, pretty, pre-law?" Rosita snapped her fingers, searching for an answer.

"Dora?"

"Yes, Dora! She moved to Miami and is working at Hooters. She posted a photo."

"Hooters? With the tiny orange shorts?" I combed through a feed on my phone until I found Dora wearing a white tank top with a bug-eyed owl over her breasts. Her pretty round face was caked in makeup and a red shade of lipstick Mami would call "inappropriate for señoritas."

"She's making a killing in tips. I mean, look at her. She's hot." There was a tinge of envy in Rosita's voice. "FEMA kicked her out of her hotel and she didn't want to come back. Can't say I blame her."

Rosita had a point. It's just waitressing. It's a decent job and it pays the bills. But Dora wanted so much more from life. I hoped she remembered that. I turned off the screen, praying Dora could at least use the money to finish law school like she wanted.

"I heard there's a bunch of Puerto Ricans already working at the plant. It won't be just us," Rosita argued.

"I don't know, Rosita. What if we don't like it? We'll be stuck out there."

"It's only a year-long contract. It won't be forever."

"A year?" Twelve months cutting turkeys up north sounded like forever.

"Come on, Marisol, I won't leave without you," she begged. "Look at this headline." She held the newspaper over my face. "Thirty-two murders. It's the second week of the year! Those sinvergüenzas are taking advantage of the dark. We can't live like this—in fear every time the sun goes down. There's nothing left for us here."

I wanted to say it wasn't true, that there was plenty left for us on this island that we'd always called home. There were barefoot walks on the beach, tertulia nights over coffee and Mami's asopao siete potencias, a Sunday favorite. This was our life, and if you looked closely, some shreds of it still remained.

Ultimately though, I had to face reality: none of the things that had filled my life with so much joy would help us rebuild. Our home had flooded, and the only help FEMA had offered was a tarp and a loan.

As much as I loved eating my Mami's asopao, it would not save us from the rut we had fallen into. We'd gone from a contented existence to surviving day-to-day. Even flushing the toilet had become a struggle.

The only way out was to leave.

"Fine," I finally said. "Where do we apply?"

Rosita wrapped her arms around me and kissed me on both cheeks.

"It will be an adventure," she said, jumping to her feet. "You wanted to travel, right?"

I forced a smile.

Now, with the lights of Huron blinking on the horizon, the trip through Latin America that I spent months planning seems like a great idea—one that belonged to someone else.

The driver slows down, stops, and turns right. A man in the front row claps enthusiastically, chanting, "Ya llegamos."

"We're here." I nudge Rosita awake. It's ten past midnight, and we've been traveling for more than twelve hours. My mind can barely form a coherent thought.

I glance out the passenger window, where a giant statue of a bird stands beside the highway.

"Is that a duck?" Rosita leans over my shoulder.

"I guess."

"Pato, no. Es un fisant," a woman calls out from the front. It takes me a moment to realize she's saying the statue is a pheasant—still looks like a duck to me.

The driver pulls into the parking lot of the Huron Motor Inn, a sad, two-story beige building overlooking the giant bird.

"Good evening. Buenas noches." A woman with thick glasses and blond, short hair greets us, poking her head into the van. "I'm Elena. The plant sent me to welcome you. Are you doing all right? How was the trip?"

I nod silently. Too tired, cold, hungry, and homesick to care.

"I've got your room keys," she announces, flashing a set of plastic cards in her hand.

Rosita and I wait our turn to exit the van, trailing the woman who cried all the way here. Someone calls her "Esperanza," which is ironic in and of itself. I don't recall anyone ever looking so hopeless.

Elena directs the new arrivals to their rooms like a traffic officer at a busy intersection. It's a small comfort to see someone take charge.

"Marisol Rodriguez?" Elena asks, her eyes darting between Rosita and me.

"That's me." I raise my hand.

"You and your cousin—Rosa, right?—will be sharing a room." She hands me the key card, then checks off our names on a clipboard. "If you're hungry, here are some food vouchers for The Plains." She nods toward a building across the parking lot. A banner hanging from the side wall of the restaurant says they have bowling lanes, a lounge, and a casino.

"Thank you." I take the vouchers. "What's the schedule tomorrow?"

"You can sleep in. We'll pick you up for new-employee orientation around one," she says, then moves to shorts-guy, who's standing behind us in a hoodie. Did this guy even bring a coat?

We haul our bags to the second floor, reading the numbers on the doors.

"Found it." Rosita jiggles the handle. "Key, please."

I drop the card into her palm and she opens the door.

The smell of ash and stale beer hits me before I walk in. Rosita turns on a lamp. There's a used Band-Aid on the carpet. An old picture of a pheasant (looking like a duck) hangs from the wall above the TV. Inside the bathroom, the tiles around the toilet are covered in pee. It's all enough to do me in.

"We can't stay here." My voice breaks. This room seems as hopeless as Esperanza's face.

"What do you mean?" She turns on the TV and quickly clicks through the available channels. "Oh, how I've missed you," she croons, caressing the screen and smiling in a daze.

"It's dirty . . . and cold," I complain, trying to swallow the knot forming in the back of my throat. I can't cry. If I start crying, I won't stop. And then Rosita will call my aunt, and my aunt will call Mami, and Mami will tell Abuela, who will tell the neighbors, and before you know it the entire neighborhood will be worried sick. I can't do that to them.

"We got electricity, hot water, and cable. I'm not going anywhere, so make yourself at home," Rosita says forcefully. "Why don't you turn up the heat?"

I walk to the thermostat and push the needle up to eighty. Then I move my bag against the wall, unzip the top, and pull out my pajamas and flip-flops. I wear my flip-flops to the bathroom, even when I get in the shower. At least there's hot water, I tell myself repeatedly. At least there's hot water, and electricity, and cable. Rosita is right. "I have to be thankful. I have to stand tall. Like a palmera." I think of the palm trees that withstood María's 175-mile-per-hour winds. They bent but never broke. I have to be a palmera.

Out of the shower, I dry myself with one of the worn-out motel towels hanging from a rack. I make a mental list of everything we need to get from the store: cleaning products, towels, bedsheets, food, and a scented candle or anything that will make the room not smell like a nightclub.

My stomach grumbles. "I'm starving." I remember I skipped both lunch and dinner, too nervous to eat.

"That restaurant is still open. I'll walk with you."

I stare out the window, across the parking lot where The Plains sits. There are about a dozen SUVs and pickup trucks, and a few people are outside smoking, even though it's freezing. I shut the curtains, deciding instead to feast on the small bag of pretzels I saved on the plane—let's call it dinner.

I crawl into bed, next to Rosita. She's watching a movie about a Latina maid in Manhattan who meets her Prince Charming while working at a hotel.

"I wouldn't mind marrying a gringo." Rosita reaches for my tiny bag of pretzels. I let her have a couple. "If he takes care of me, it's okay if he's a little boring."

I chuckle. "Maybe you'll meet one at the plant. Instead of *Maid in Manhattan*, you can be *Turkey-Hanger in Huron*." We both laugh hard. I laugh through the tiredness, the hunger, and the heartbreak until my eyes are wet with the tears I'm holding back.

After all the pretzels are gone, we lie in bed until the movie ends. In the end, the maid gets it all: her Prince Charming, the perfect career, and a life surrounded by people who love her.

I scoff. "What a load of crap."

"It can happen! You don't know anything . . ." Rosita walks to the TV and turns it off.

"No one gets everything they want." My voice is edgier than I intend.

"Maybe you shouldn't want so much."

"Maybe *you* shouldn't want so little," I spit back, immediately regretting my outburst. Like me, Rosita is too tired to hide the hurt. She stands unmoving next to the TV, staring at me through the pain in her dark brown eyes.

I open my mouth to apologize, but she cuts me off.

"I want things too, you know . . ." she says quietly.

"I know," I whisper back, ashamed. My body sinks into the bed with a long sigh. How will I ever find my way back to the life I had envisioned? How will Rosita find the way back to hers?

I wasn't raised to be poca cosa. Mami always encouraged me to dream big. But that was before María, when dreaming didn't cost us anything.

"Can I sleep with you? I'm so cold." Rosita climbs into my bed, snuggling beside me. "Are you sure you turned up the heat?"

"All the way up." I turn off my bedside lamp and drop my head hard into the pillow, convinced I will never feel warm again.

"Marisol, está nevando." Rosita is on top of me, jerking me awake. "Let's go see the snow."

I rub my eyes open, sitting on the bed. Rosita has opened the curtains, washing the room in sunlight. I follow her to the doorway, where we silently watch the snow fall. It's so quiet, we can hear each other breathe.

"It's beautiful." Rosita extends her open palm to catch a few snowflakes.

I do the same, but instead of snow, a white feather lands between my fingers.

"Look, they're everywhere." Rosita points to the floor of the balcony, where a handful of white feathers lie scattered.

We search for the source but only find the almost-empty parking lot, and beyond that, an overgrown baseball field.

No birds in sight, just their feathers, floating in the air like particles of dust.

A woman waves at us from the room next door. Like us, she extends her hand to catch a floating feather.

"I think they're from the plant," she says, looking out toward the high-way. "Must be the wind."

I stare toward the plant, a bleak horizon, snow-covered and gray. I've never felt so far from home.

Another feather falls from the sky and I catch it midair. The pristine white plume glimmers in the sunlight like something from the wings of an angel. I pray it's a good omen—an ascension of sorts.

"Come on, Rosita, let's get dressed," I say. "We can send Mami and Tía Milagros some pictures. They'll like that."

We find the thickest sweaters we brought, but in this bitter cold the fabric feels flimsy and thin.

"I think I saw a Salvation Army on the way in," I say. "And a Walmart. Maybe we can call a taxi and get a few things?"

"I don't want to spend all our money on the first day," Rosita says, snaking herself into a pair of leggings. "We don't even know when we'll get paid."

"What about the bathroom? It needs to be cleaned," I argue.

"I saw a cleaning cart parked on the stairway last night."

I sigh and resolve not to make a fuss. Rosita is right—we shouldn't be spending money we don't have. She sold her laptop and her road bike before we left, and I had the money I was saving for my trip. Still, it may not be enough.

We head outside, bundled in our warmest clothes. We take the stairs to the lower level and join a group of other Puerto Ricans gathered outside the motel's dining room.

"Desayuno gratis," an older man with white hair and bushy eyebrows says. He nods toward the dining room, where he says there's free breakfast.

"Anything good in there?" I ask.

"Pancakes, eggs . . . it's okay," he says with a shrug. Something about the dignified way he carries himself reminds me of my late abuelo.

"I'm Marisol."

"Arsenio." He flashes a crooked smile and pats the side of my arm with his free hand. In his other hand, he holds a steaming mug of black coffee. "This American coffee is pure water. Aguao—like dirty water."

"There's a Latin supermarket in town," I say. "Maybe they have good coffee."

He sighs, looking up at the sky. Then he empties the cup in the snow, where it leaves a dark stain. "They won't have Yaucono."

"Marisol, take my picture." Rosita joins a group playing with the snow. She falls back, making a snow angel with her limbs.

I snap her photo with my phone, then take one of the motel and the giant pheasant.

"Let's make a snowman," she says, balling the snow in her gloved hands. A few turkey feathers stick out, turning the snowman into a snowbird.

We dress him in my purple scarf and hat and Rosita's sunglasses. A woman we just met offers to take our picture.

Rosita and I squat next to the snow-bird-man and smile, holding up our hands in the air like we're waving at everyone back home.

I send the photos to Mami and text her that we arrived safely and we're having fun. If I call her, she may not believe me. Mami is no bruja, but she does have some kind of mind-reading divine power that, as her daughter, I find terribly inconvenient. There's no lying to that woman. If I call her now, her heart will burst with trepidation. And I can't handle someone else's heartbreak right now.

At exactly one, we pile into the van and drive to the turkey processing plant—a sprawling white building in the middle of an open field. About half a dozen trucks are lined up to enter the side gate.

"They bring in nineteen thousand turkeys a day," shorts-guy says behind me. Today he's wearing jeans, a proper winter coat, and a beanie hat with a Puerto Rican flag—subtle.

"Nineteen thousand? That can't be right," a woman says.

"My padrino works here. He says they bring them alive every morning. And then . . ." He makes a slicing motion with his index finger across his throat.

I turn away from him and take a deep, long breath. I hate blood. I hate the sight of blood. I hate the smell of it too—that metallic pungent odor that sticks to the inside of your nostrils.

"I'm not killing turkeys," I whisper close to Rosita's ear.

"A machine kills them," shorts-guy says over my shoulder. A hand appears next to my face. "I'm Mateo."

I hesitantly take his hand. It's warm and soft, nothing like I expected.

"Marisol," I say. "And this is my cousin, Rosa."

"Where are you from, Mateo?" Rosita asks.

"Aguadilla," he says. "Used to give surf lessons to tourists." When he smiles, his straight white teeth are a bright contrast to his brown, suntanned skin. If it weren't for the ridiculous hat, he would almost look handsome.

"And you guys?"

"San Juan," I say.

"Ah, city girls," he teases. "My uncle lives in San Juan. Well . . . used to, I guess. They moved to Florida a week ago."

"Everyone is moving," Rosita says.

"Los cerebros que se van y el corazón que se queda," I add, remembering the title of an essay by Magaly García Ramis about the relocation of "brains" to the mainland. The brains may leave for a better life, but their hearts always remain on the island. Today I can understand what she meant.

"That's very poetic and all, but what are we supposed to do?" Mateo asks, his voice bitter. "If I had work, I would've stayed. I didn't want to leave. There's no surfing here. Who knows when the tourists will be back. And who knows when they'll open the university. I'll probably lose the entire year."

"Yeah, it's the same thing in San Juan. No classes until further notice," Rosita says.

"I'm halfway through a graphic design degree. I was going to open my own store—Yuquiyú Surf Shop. I wanted to design and make my own boards," he says, sitting a little taller.

"That sounds nice," Rosita says.

"Yeah, but who knows what'll happen now." He sighs and leans back, staring out the window at the open field next to the turkey farm. There's a feeling I recognize in his amber-colored eyes: longing. After María we all seem to want things we can't have.

Silly hat aside, I feel an affinity with Mateo. Maybe our dreams are in a comatose state and not stone dead like the turkeys.

When we pull up to the plant, Elena is waiting for us by the front steps.

"Welcome, amigos," she says in a too-cheerful tone. "Did you sleep okay?"

Everyone nods and smiles politely, eager to get inside. We all want to see what our new lives will be like—what we left the island for.

Elena ushers us inside the plant and into a classroom with long tables and a projection screen. There are big binders on the table, one for each of us.

I sit between Mateo and Rosita.

After a brief introduction, Elena plays a video about safety at the plant. After the third example of an accident, I scan over the pages of the manual, searching for something to calm my nerves.

The same information is written in three languages: English, Spanish, and what I guess is Chinese. I turn to the Spanish section, pausing when I reach a photo of a plucked headless turkey hanging from a metal rod.

"My padrino says you'll hurt for the first two weeks," Mateo says softly. "But you get used to it."

"Used to what?" I ask.

"The standing. The cold. The repetition. It's not for everyone. It breaks some people."

I instinctively search for Esperanza, recalling that she wasn't in the van that drove us from the motel.

"Where's Esperanza?"

"She left," Mateo says, matter-of-fact.

"What do you mean she left?" I move in closer, trying to keep my voice low. "She just got here," I say, staring into his dark-brown eyes. His cheeks turn a soft pink at the closeness of our bodies. I lean back, a little embarrassed.

"Left for Puerto Rico this morning."

Elena clears her throat and gives us a disapproving look from the front of the classroom. I mouth an apology and wait a few minutes before turning again toward Mateo.

"I didn't know we could leave."

"God, they're not holding us hostage, Marisol," Rosita interjects. I had no idea she was even listening.

I turn to Mateo for confirmation.

"You can leave any time," he says with a smile that reaches his eyes and makes my breath catch.

My mind whirls. The words *You can leave any time* buzz inside my head like bees swarming over a beehive.

I can leave this wintry, faraway place. I can go home.

But go home to what? What kind of life will I go back to?

After three hours of videos, talks, and a million questions, Elena announces that we're done for the day.

"Tomorrow will be your first shift," she says. "The van will pick you up at five. Please don't be late."

Mateo grunts behind me. "I wish they had a noon shift," he says. "Who wants to get up at five in this cold?"

"It's colder in there," a woman says, pointing to a conveyor belt behind a glass window. "They keep it at thirty-six degrees—year-round."

"I guess I won't be taking this off," Mateo says, zipping his jacket all the way up. "Got it at the Salvation Army this morning. Like it?"

I nod, wishing I'd gone to the thrift store and found a thicker winter coat.

"You'll need a coat just to wear to work," he says expertly. "You don't want to bring the smell of turkey flesh home."

I tilt my head in confusion, wondering how Mateo went from being the shorts-guy to turkey-plant expert. "How do you know all this?"

"I told you, my padrino works here. He got me the job." He glances at my brand-new, cream-colored coat and says, "I hope you brought another one."

"Did you hear that, Rosita?" I ask pulling at the sleeve of her jacket. "We'll have to walk around smelling like dead birds."

"Coats cost money, Marisol," she says, pursing her lips like I'm a petulant child. "Do you want to call your mother if we run out of money before we get paid? Because I'm not making that call. I'll be damned if I trekked all the way here to have money be sent to me *from* the island."

My hands ball into fists. I bite my lower lip so hard it may bleed. Deep in the hollow of my chest, I feel the pull of Esperanza's sobs coaxing me to give up. To leave all this behind like a bad dream quickly forgotten in the morning.

Poor Esperanza. She traveled all the way here for nothing. Is that what I want? To be *that* hopeless?

"How much was that coat?" I ask Mateo, ignoring the scowl on Rosita's face.

"Twenty bucks. It's a nice brand too."

I turn to face Rosita, feet planted firmly on the tile floor. "I'm going to the Salvation Army. I'll use my money. I'll go alone if I have to."

She releases an exasperated sigh. "Don't be stupid. I'm not letting you wander around Huron by yourself."

"It closes at five," Mateo says, glancing at a clock on the wall that reads 4:45 p.m.

Rosita shrugs with an "oh well" expression that makes me want to pull my hair out. It's that resignación everyone on the island keeps going on about. An unchallenged acceptance that leaves no room to fight back.

"We'll go to Walmart," I say, refusing to give into this resignación. "They have coats, I'm sure." And sheets and towels . . . and candles with names like Island Breeze or Tropical Punch—if they do, I'm buying one of each.

The next morning, the alarm goes off at four. I open my eyes and see the picture of the duck-looking pheasant hanging from the wall. I decide to name him Paco—the duck-pheasant. A daily reminder that we can be two things at once.

I wriggle myself into the new thermal underwear I bought last night. I had no idea this stuff even existed. A Walmart saleslady put the package in my hands and said in a Dominican accent, "Para trabajar en la planta, esto es lo mejor." She had worked at the plant for three years, and these— long johns, she called them—had kept her warm the entire time.

Over the long johns I wear a thick pair of pants, then two T-shirts, a sweater, and my new red coat. It's so soft, it feels like a waste taking it to the plant.

"Rosita, get up." I give her a little shove and she moans awake. "I'll go get us some breakfast. Get dressed."

I put on my boots and grab a can of Bustelo coffee I found at Walmart—the only Spanish coffee they had on the shelves.

Outside, it's snowing again. But today there's no wind to carry the feathers. I walk downstairs to the dining area and find Don Arsenio tinkering with the coffee machine.

"Buenos días," I say, showing him the coffee can. That crooked smile takes over his entire face.

"It's Cuban, but it'll do," he says, winking at me. "I think I figured out where they keep the filters." He looks around, making sure the motel staff are not watching.

I spill the watered-down coffee in the sink. Don Arsenio finds a new coffee filter and together we make a fresh pot of Bustelo to share. We stand in front of the machine watching the dark coffee drip fill the glass carafe.

"If I can't drink Puerto Rican coffee, Cuban is a nice second choice," he says.

"Cuba y Puerto Rico son de un pájaro las dos alas," I respond, quoting the Puerto Rican poet Lola Rodríguez de Tió.

He pours the coffee into a to-go cup and puts it between my hands. Then, with his wrinkled palms still covering the back of my hands, he recites, "Otro aquí vengo a formar, y ya no podré olvidar, que el alma llena de anhelo, encuentra bajo este cielo aire y luz para cantar!"

I get lost in the old man's voice and cloudy eyes as he recites the verses from Rodríguez de Tió's magnificent poem. He enunciates every verse perfectly in a melancholic voice that makes me feel like crying.

"That's beautiful," I say after he's finished.

"She wrote that poem when she was exiled to Cuba," he tells me. "She was banished, but she never forgot her patria. No one can take that from you."

I nod, smiling, and hand him a packet of sugar, which he pours into his cup.

"Ahhh, buenísimo," he says, savoring the first sip.

I leave Don Arsenio and walk back to our room carrying a tray of coffee and waffles. Rosita and I eat our breakfast in front of the TV, watching an action movie about terrorists bringing down the White House.

"There's nothing else on," Rosita says.

"Doesn't matter. We have to be downstairs in fifteen minutes."

"Are you nervous?"

I drown my waffles in syrup and take a bite.

"A little," I say. "You?"

"It's cutting turkeys. How hard can it be?"

After eating, we head downstairs to meet the others by the van. Mateo is already sitting inside.

"Buenos días, señoritas," he chirps.

We smile and greet him back. Then the door to the van closes and the horizon speeds past. Now, moving in the direction of my future, my stomach is not having it.

"Are you okay?" Rosita asks. "You look like you're gonna puke."

"I'm fine," I say, leaning my head against the cold glass of the passenger window. I take slow, easy breaths until some of the churning inside me subsides.

I watch the lights of the plant draw closer. In no time, the driver is parking and we are all filing toward the entrance, where Elena's familiar face is there to greet us.

"I will call your name and these lovely people will direct you to your stations," she says, motioning to a group of workers behind her.

Rosita and I wait our turn in the back until we finally hear our names.

"You will start in the deboning room," she explains briefly.

I'm about to ask her if there will be blood, but someone taps me on the shoulder. I turn around to find Mateo.

"Remember you will hurt today. But tomorrow will get better," he says, smiling.

I stare at him, wanting to ask him how much more hurt one person can bear. But before I can speak, Rosita grabs my hand and pulls me away.

"Come on, Marisol, we can't get left behind," she says, following a short woman with dark skin through a long corridor.

I glance over my shoulder to see Mateo's smile disappear behind two folding doors.

"My name is Sabina," the woman says, speaking with an accent I don't recognize. "I'm here to train you. First, rubber boots."

We stop by a table where an older Asian woman measures our feet with a ruler and finds a pair of black rubber boots in each of our sizes.

She pushes a white marker into my hand and says, "Name. Here."

I take the boots and the marker and stare at her blankly

"Write your name on the boots," Sabina explains.

I do as I'm told and write MARISOL in white marker on the black rubber. I don't exactly own the boots, but it's nice to have my name on something new. These rubber boots will carry me through the first days of my new life. I draw a palm tree next to my name, the long trunk slightly bent as a reminder that it will not break.

Sabina then gives us white smocks to put over our jackets.

"This way," she says, waving us down another corridor.

We walk through two swinging doors across a narrow, frigid hallway. We enter a room with high ceilings and blinding industrial lights. There are about two hundred people working here, all standing shoulder to shoulder over a conveyor belt.

"I'll show you job. Pick up rest of equipment, here," Sabina says.

A booth attendant hands us each a vinyl apron, a hairnet, earmuffs, goggles, cotton gloves, rubber gloves, and a mesh steel glove.

"Look at me," Rosita says, donning the goggles and mesh steel glove. She lifts her hand in the air playfully. "Rosita, space warrior princess!"

We both laugh and help each other tie the back of the vinyl apron. When we are fully dressed, Sabina takes us to our place in the line. I try to focus on her instructions, but it's impossible to concentrate when there is so much I don't know happening around me.

My eyes dart to a chute across the room spitting out headless turkeys. I follow one in particular with big yellow feet and short wings. In seconds, a worker picks him up and hooks his feet to a conveyor belt. Soon after, he's getting hacked into pieces. His drumsticks go to the left and his wings to the right. The breast meat lands on a table where about a dozen workers trim each piece.

"Pay attention, Marisol," Rosita yells at me over the noise of the machines. "This is what we have to do."

Sabina grabs a turkey wing from a trough in front of us. She sets it on a white cutting board and expertly pulls the meat from the bone with a curved knife. The meat lands on the conveyor belt to be swept away.

"You try," she says, handing me the knife.

I pick up a wing, drop it on the cutting board, and stick the knife into it. But when I pull back, half of the meat is still attached to the bone.

"Quick. Pull. Quick," Sabina tells me, dropping another wing in front of me.

I give it another go, but this time the knife gets stuck in the bone.

I glance at Rosita's table, but she's not faring much better. Her wing slips out of her hand and lands on the floor.

"Five-second rule!" she yells, picking up the wing from the floor and putting it back on the board. *Are we supposed to do that?*

"Again," Sabina says, dumping three more of those giant wings in front of me. "Ten seconds each."

My eyes widen. Is this woman serious? Ten seconds per wing. That's it? I mean, they're dead. It's not like they're going to fly away if I take my sweet time.

But then I look around at the other people on the line. Their knife-wielding hands are flying at freakish speed. I count the seconds it takes them to debone each wing and move on to the next one—ten.

I adjust my glove and grab a wing with my left hand.

I can do this, I tell myself. I'm a palmera.

So I plunge in the knife the way I'd seen Sabina do and quickly yank out the meat and skin. The trick, I realized, is not to think.

"Perfect," Sabina says, giving me two thumbs-up. "Go to line."

I join the line, while Sabina tries to help Rosita with her technique. Her wings keep flying off the table.

On the line, I can't keep up. I grab a wing every twenty-five seconds or so—I'm timing myself—but the trough never empties. Every five minutes, a worker comes by and dumps in a bucket full of wings. No matter how fast everyone around me cuts, we will never see the bottom of that wretched trough.

There is no end in sight.

I stretch my neck, arms, and hands, trying to get some blood flow back into my stiff body. And fighting to keep the feelings of desperation at bay. I turn around, searching for a place to rest my eyes that is not turkey wings. But instead I find another line. Whole de-feathered turkeys rush past at a relentless pace. I count forty-seven dead birds per minute. How am I supposed to do this for a whole day? A whole year?

Oh God, what am I doing here?

I stare at the knife I'm holding, overwhelmed, until one of the women working the line waves her hand in front of my face.

"You. Help," she says in rudimentary English. When I stare back, she motions for me to retake my place on the line. I follow the gentle coax of her hand. "Time fly by. Like the wing," she quips, reaching for a wing from the trough, and flopping it around in the air. Her lips spread into a warm smile as she sets the wing in my hand.

I nod in understanding, returning the smile. One day I will leave this place, but today I have a job to do.

I cut and cut, ignoring the flecks of turkey sticking to my apron, ignoring the conversation next to me in a language I've never heard, and ignoring the brutal cold that has breached the long-john barrier and crawled under my skin.

"You're a palmera," I say under my breath, pulling the meat from another wing bone. After two hours of the same repetitive movement, my arm feels like it's about to fall off. A sharp wave of pain spreads from my fingers up my arm and shoulders and all the way to the back of my head.

I don't know which is worse: the pain or the cold. Every so often I shake my feet and wiggle my toes, in a useless attempt to bring back warmth into my limbs. I realize I am working inside a freezer, and in here, there is no escape from the cold. The meat is cold. The knife is cold. Even the floor feels cold.

When it's time for lunch, we leave the deboning room and enter a cleanup area where we wash off the turkey meat stuck to our uniforms.

As the workers take off their hair nets, goggles, and earmuffs, I realize I am surrounded by people from all over the world. I overhear a woman say she's from Chuuk—which I learn is also an island.

We gather to eat around picnic tables in a large white room.

"How's it going?" Mateo asks, sitting across from me. "I'm in the warehouse. My arms are gonna get huge from carrying boxes all day." He laughs at himself.

Rosita lifts her right hand in front of us, trying to make a fist. "It won't close. I can barely feel my fingers."

"How about you, Marisol?" Mateo asks.

"I will hurt today. But tomorrow will be better," I repeat back to him. We exchange a smile, and the warm color of his sunburned cheeks gives me some comfort, as if he's sharing a little part of the island sun inside him.

AUTHOR'S NOTE

On September 20, 2017, Hurricane María barreled through Puerto Rico, leaving behind the worst devastation the island had ever seen. Like millions of the island's residents and the diaspora, my heart was broken and desperate to help, hanging on to every shred of news coming out of our homeland.

In January 2018 *Washington Post* journalist Chico Harlan published a story about a group of young Puerto Ricans who left the island for jobs at a turkey processing plant in Huron, South Dakota. Most were in college, worked part-time jobs, and dreamed of a future that didn't include leaving Puerto Rico.

This is how Marisol and Rosa's journey came to be. It's a story of heartbreak and longing but also hope. In Marisol's own words, sometimes we "have to be a palmera." A palm tree bends but never breaks.

About a month after FORESHADOW published RESILIENT, I announced the sale of my debut young adult novel, *Salty, Bitter, Sweet* to the Blink imprint at HarperCollins. It was the consummation of six years of hard work, multiple manuscripts, hundreds of soul-crushing rejections, and a lifetime of literary dreams.

As I continue to work on new projects—and new deadlines—the image of Marisol's palmera is ever-present. I've learned that it's not enough to grasp how to craft a story, to master the ins and out of language, or to expertly market yourself to readers everywhere. To be an author, you must be resilient. You must pick yourself up when you fall, dust yourself off, and move on to the next story. You must also build and rely on a supportive community of trusted writers who care deeply about your emotional and mental health. And above all, you must be courageous. Because writing is about speaking the truth. And the truth takes a heck of a lot of courage.

MOMENT OF CHANGE
IN *RESILIENT*

by Nova Ren Suma

IN ITS COMPACTNESS, A SHORT STORY OFFERS THE OPPORTUNITY TO FOCUS exclusively on a monumental experience for a character: a moment of change. In RESILIENT, the change comes internally, the first touch of an epiphany.

At the end of the story, Marisol is living a reality she never imagined: working a cruel job in a cold place worlds away from everything she saw for her future. In the final moments, ". . . there is no escape from the cold. The meat is cold. The knife is cold. Even the floor feels cold." But somehow, in the deboning room, deep in that frigid air, she has a realization that sparks a change inside her: "I realize I am surrounded by people from all over the world. I overhear a woman say she is from Chuuk—which I learn is also an island." It may seem like a small thing, but to Marisol, this piece of information is the ray of light (and, I expect, memory of warmth) she needed in that bleak place. Her suffering is temporary, and while she is here, she does not need to bear it alone.

The concept of change may seem full of motion, but true change for a character is internal, no matter how much activity or travel it takes to get there. We don't get to see Marisol's full transformation on the page. Her last words, after her realization, are an acknowledgment that her pain is not yet over but the change is coming. She says only, "But tomorrow will be better."

When characters are drawn solidly enough, the pleasure for the reader comes in imagining beyond the confines of the last page. I believe, due to the moment Marisol felt a glimmer of hope, that she will find happiness again one day soon. Don't you? She's still in the turkey-processing plant, still stuck in the cold doing this crushing work—but in considering tomorrow, Marisol's future spreads out before her.

This story succeeds in giving us just enough to believe everything will change for Marisol, for the better, because she will survive this and she knows it. It may not be the romantic motorcycle journey she'd envisioned for herself before the hurricane, but what we've witnessed here is the first moment of her transformation.

STORY PROMPT:
OPENING THE DOOR

WHEN YOU'RE CONSIDERING THE SHAPE OF YOUR SHORT STORY, ONE WAY TO envision it is to go to a moment of change for your main character and have that be the climax or culminating point of your plot.

Think about what that moment could be. Zoom in. Imagine it as a door, beyond which everything is different. What happens if you focus your storytelling on approaching the door, reaching for the knob, turning it, and seeing the first crack of light, just before it's open? What if you gave your readers just enough in order to continue the journey inside their imaginations?

Prolong the last moments before everything changes for your character. Write the scene *just before* the door to change fully opens.

BELLY

Desiree S. Evans

Jaima has known the truth most her life: the river is greedy.

There are days when she can hear the river's throat humming a siren song down at Chinotuck Falls, making enough music to send the trees out in Spooky Marsh dancing. Sometimes the river's belly starts rumbling over in the southern hinterlands, where not many folk dare to go anyway because it's too dark even when the sun's at its highest point in the sky. Then there are the summer days when the river's long tongue licks up the sides of Pauper's Gorge, where the water cascades down into a swimming hole that local boys and girls splash in during the thick noonday heat.

Jaima's the only person still living who's been inside the river's hungry belly. As stories go, this one is her own: when she was five the river swallowed her up, took her deep down into the darkest darkness, and spun her around and around and around inside of it. Then it spat her out by Old Snook's place, almost a mile inland from the river's northern banks. The rising waters left behind a shriveled-up piece of girl, gone cold to the touch. But alive.

No one knows how Jaima survived, especially since the river took Jaima's parents and their tiny house down into its deep, murky bottom and kept them there like a sacrifice. Leaving Jaima all alone.

That was the year of the last great flood, when the rains lasted for three whole weeks and the sky dropped down to meet the land turned sea. Chester Town's winding dirt roads turned into silt-red streams that flowed into the fronts and backs of the townsfolks' homes. Yards became lakes. Valleys became oceans. Everywhere, the river ran long and full and greedy.

Jaima doesn't remember any of it, outside of dreams of dark and cold. But she knows this one thing to be true: since the age of five, part of the river has lived somewhere inside of her. She feels full with it, weighty like a stuffed bird. It sloshes around in her belly some days, like it's aching to find the rest of itself. Jaima shivers at the thought of returning to the river, fearing sinking into that darkness, fearing losing herself. Maybe it wants her back, but she's standing on dry land now. It can't have her.

Since the flood, Jaima has lived with her grandma, who everyone in Chester Town calls Sweet Ma. Some mornings Jaima heads out with her backpack and a bag lunch to the eastern side of Sweet Ma's homestead. It sits at the edge of the big pine forest, where the ground is soft and boggy under her feet. It's the place where she goes to feel the most like herself: here she can watch the river wind down into the valley below, feel it bubbling up inside of her, seeking the missing parts of itself. When the summer rains come, as they always do, and when the water inches closer and closer to town, tempted to overrun its banks, Jaima can feel the river reaching out to her, waiting for her.

The river is greedy.

The river cuts through everything here, and everything finds its way down to it. Chester Town is populated by folk who've lived in the lowland valleys for generations, working the vast land and growing big families. Their tired hands built up a community year after year, during slavery and after, when it became one of the first freedmen towns. Jaima knows this history because Sweet Ma taught it to her the summer after Jaima turned twelve and she wanted to know where she came from. *You came from this place*, Sweet Ma told her. *Your great grandmother's the river and your great grandfather's the land.* Jaima had frowned, of course, because Sweet Ma is a bit special and everyone knows it. But she thought maybe there was something to it: the river is the same rich, muddy brown as her skin, and the smoky-black soil carries the shine of her hair.

This time of the year, the world's on fire. Your skin hot from the sun, your feet hot from the walking, and the river's the only thing that cools you. Wednesday afternoon finds Jaima out by Pauper's Gorge, where the land gets hillier and everything smells like the living world, fertile earth and green, growing things. Jaima's down to her thinnest pieces of clothing in the June heat: a yellow bikini top and ripped, dirt-stained Daisy Dukes. She's barefoot and sweaty, her body aching for some cooling down. But Jaima's not in the water like the rest of the town kids: she's eating Funyuns and watching her best friend, Byronisha Baptiste, breastfeed her six-month-old baby boy, Jaquan.

Jaima and Byronisha have been best friends since they were born two hours apart, held in the same midwife's arms, and thereafter destined to share the same hand-me-down clothes. Jaima is one of seven children living with Sweet Ma in a crooked little shack at the end of Sugar Rum Road. Byronisha lives across the street with her mama in a double-wide trailer surrounded by a sea of pink milkweeds and a large family of plastic pink flamingos.

They look like opposites: at seventeen, Jaima is short and big-boned and dark-skinned. Boys at school peer too long at her wide, child-bearing hips and at her full chest that bounces when she walks. Byronisha, on the other hand, is tall and slender and mixed enough to freckle like white folks do in the summer months. She'd been flat-chested and curve-less most of her teen years, only getting full tits and hips with the baby.

"You gonna finally go in the water this summer?" Byronisha asks, fumbling with her son before she flops down on the ground beside Jaima. She pops out her milk-swollen breast, lets the baby latch on, and sighs heavily when he suckles in a way that tells them both he's more than satisfied. Jaima watches the baby gum at Byronisha's brown nipple, his little hands opening and closing against the smooth skin of her chest.

Byronisha catches her watching and laughs. "He a greedy lil thang, ain't he?"

Jaima's face goes warm and she averts her eyes. "Yeah, he is," she chuckles, staring down at the soft ground, nudging the dirt loose with her big toe. "And no, I'm not going in the water this summer."

"Girl, the water ain't gonna do you nothing," Byronisha says, rocking Jaquan when he starts whimpering.

"Says who?" Jaima says, offering her best friend the bag of Funyuns, which Byronisha takes once Jaquan quiets. They sit for a few moments, silently watching the other teens splash around in the swimming hole down below.

The thing is, Jaima hasn't been in the river since she was five. "It wants me," she sighs, her belly aching at the thought of the water's pull.

Byronisha snorts softly, shakes her head. "Calvin Babineaux *wants* you."

Jaima looks over at Byronisha and the gurgling baby boy stuck to her tit. "Calvin so trifling though."

Byronisha shrugs. "And you so picky. That's probably why you still a virgin."

Jaima rolls her eyes. "And ain't you the poor teen mama Sister Loretta prays over in church every Sunday morning?"

Byronisha laughs, kissing her baby boy on his big bald head before saying, "You got jokes, I see."

Jaima feels her lips twitch. "A few," she admits.

Byronisha laughs, shaking her head. "Calvin should know better, anyway."

Jaima nods, agreeing. "Lord knows why he keep asking after me when he know I don't want his sorry butt."

"Girl, you know these boys ain't got no sense," Byronisha says with a smirk, knocking Jaima's bare foot with her sandled one. "Plus you're such a grouchy old lady, what would you two even talk about?"

Jaima laughs, because that's what Sweet Ma tells her too—apparently Jaima is not-so-secretly an old lady with a stern eye and a bad temper. She smiles at the thought, tilts her head to the sky, watches the clouds.

Byronisha reaches out and grabs Jaima by the wrist, squeezing. "You know you my girl," she says, her eyes soft and brown and round like an owl's. "Wouldna been able to do this whole mama thing without you. So you know I'll sit out here in the heat and forget about swimming for another thirty years if you ask me to."

Jaima laughs, because Byronisha likes to get real deep sometimes. Before the baby came, summer used to mean just the two of them—free time with no one holding them down; school-less days spent hot and sweaty here at Pauper's Gorge, running around the pine and hemlock woods with scraped knees and rose-colored dresses, summer braids wound around their heads like African queens. Jaima loved to make up adventure stories about this place, about pirates and hidden gold, about the ghosts trapped inside the trees. Byronisha would follow behind her, a trusted sidekick to her hero. In this place, where the water falls to the earth like a dream, where the forest hugs the riverbank, where the road splits apart—dark woods on one side and stubby hills on the other—Jaima feels like she's watching two sides of the world love on each other. Great-grandmother river and great-grandfather land.

Byronisha's voice is low when she asks, "You still dreaming about it, huh?"

Jaima's gaze flicks to her friend's face, outlines the soft freckles on her nose. Jaima thinks maybe she wants to kiss Byronisha, but she knows that's kind of a weird thing to be thinking about, so she looks at the ground again and says, "Sometimes," referring to the dreams. She sometimes has dreams of the flood, ones that flow into her like the water itself, rushed and unnamed. They usually come when she's in bed alone (a rare thing because she shares a bed with her cousin Tiffany, and they share the room with two other cousins, Lil Bit and Ayesha). But those few times when she is alone in the dark bedroom, she feels like a small thing in a very big place, and she knows she's back inside that river, twisting about in the cold, scary dark. She can feel the river in her veins even now, rolling like waves under her skin.

Byronisha is cooing something soft at the baby. Jaima turns her eyes back to the swimming hole, watches the town's horny teenagers roughhousing and swimming, their slick brown skins shimmering like gold in the noonday sun.

On Saturdays Jaima works at AJ's, the gas station over in Cowenville. Even though she's on the plumper side of curvy, she still manages to fit herself into the station's regulation tan overalls. Her thick braids she pushes under a baseball cap. Whether standing behind the station counter or pumping gas into mud-encrusted pickups, she draws attention, no matter what. The men who stumble out of their vehicles will almost always glance at her long enough to make her slightly uncomfortable.

Jaima's cousin Domino fixes cars in the attached garage, which is how she got the job. He usually manages to keep an eye on her during her shift, to scare away the fools. But today Domino's in Houston picking up parts, and Jaima's working in the shop with just the owner's son, Bobby Greer Jr., who's been looking her way for far too long from where he's settled behind the store counter.

Ass, she thinks as she mops the floor with her back to him, sighing because she knows it means he can see the outline of her butt in her too-tight uniform, but not wanting to turn around and have to look at his face. He's got this greasy red hair that sticks to his forehead whenever he sweats, and he's always whistling at her, like she's a dog looking for a treat. The Greers own farms up and down this way, and the lot of them are sneaky little shits, always stealing things that don't belong to them, like other people's land and farming equipment.

The smell of Pine-Sol is nothing like actual pine, but she's trying to pretend it is, to remember the story Sweet Ma told her about Great Uncle Left Cheeks, who climbed to the top of a pine tree back in '89 when the loggers came to try to clear-cut his trees. He ended up falling and hitting his head, spending a month in a coma. Hasn't been able to walk right since.

Bobby Jr. whistles at her, and she glances back at him to see what he wants. He's got to be in his midthirties, with a wide jaw and bug-eyes too big for his face. His lankiness isn't hidden by his camouflage shirt and his dirty hair isn't hidden by the matching baseball cap.

"Why you always ignoring me?" he asks, voice all soft and tender-like. Probably attempting to sound hurt.

Jaima frowns. "Just thinking 'bout that hundred acres of land your daddy stole from my cousin Odelle last year."

"Ah, girl, that ain't nothing to do with me," he laughs, shaking his head. "That's just my daddy's side business. And it's the banks that did your cousin wrong, not my daddy." He stands up and stretches, flexing in a way that Jaima thinks must be his attempt to impress her.

She sighs and says, "Okay, Bobby, I'll try thinking 'bout something else, then."

Bobby Jr. laughs. "Well, we can start with you just giving me a smile for today. You're way too pretty not to be smiling," he says.

Jaima groans internally, but plasters on a fake smile, hard enough to make her lips hurt with the stretch. Bobby seems satisfied, patting his gut like he's had some hearty meal. Jaima turns back to scrubbing sticky stains from the cracks in the linoleum floor. She thinks about this place in the woods where the river runs fast over the rocks, flowing into a small pool where deer come down to drink. She's seen the animals there from time to time, watched the nervous way they looked around before satisfying their thirst. She feels like one of those deer, watching for Bobby as he slinks behind her in the store. She spies him out of the corner of her eye.

There's a tightness behind her belly button when she heads home that day, the river inside of her cresting, almost spilling over.

Come Sunday dinner after church, everyone in Jaima's family is wondering what the Greers are up to.

"Snakes, all of them!" her uncle Lester pronounces from his seat on the couch. "They want us gone, but we ain't leaving."

Cheers go up all around and Jaima smiles. The house is filled with their kin, and the loud rumble of voices makes the room sound like a family reunion. Half of them are eating boiled crawfish and potatoes and watching the Sunday game. The other half are playing Spades in the back of the living room, shouts ringing out every once in a while, louder even than the TV. Jaima's tempted to go jump in and win because she's unbeatable, but Sweet Ma said today was "wash and detangle day," and she's working Jaima's scalp like she's got a battle to win herself.

Sweet Ma currently has her hands all up in Jaima's hair. Those rough, sure fingers rub against her scalp, pressing and rolling and massaging down with heated olive oil. This must be what the soil feels like when Sweet Ma's making something grow in the garden, Jaima thinks as the oil drizzles down her forehead and settles behind her ears.

Jaima's thick naps catch on the wide-toothed comb's teeth, and she jerks up when Sweet Ma pulls too hard. "Stop ya squirming, girl," Sweet Ma chides, and Jaima huffs a breath and settles back against the couch. Sweet Ma's hands relax in her hair again, parting and oiling, massaging and detangling.

Jaima looks up to see the twelve-year-old twins, Malcolm and Martin, running around shirtless and covered in the red-clay silt of the backyard, probably chasing the rooster again. The screen door slaps loudly every time they run inside or outside. "Gremlins," Sweet Ma whispers under her breath in exasperation, and Jaima agrees. *Gremlins*.

The littlest girl cousins are arguing over their Barbies, and Uncle Lester is sucking on the head of a crawfish like it's the gods' own nectar. He earns a laugh from everyone when he slaps at his gut, sending it jiggling like a big mold of Jell-O. It's four-year-old Tee-Ray who eventually drops down in front of Jaima, settling himself into her lap without saying a word. Jaima laughs and starts messing with his hair, parting his untamed afro and braiding it like Sweet Ma's doing to her hair.

"You got grass in your hair," Jaima says, picking out the pieces of leaves caught between his fine, dark curls. Lord, it's like a bird's nest up in the child's head. "Where you been, Tee?"

"Down in Spooky Marsh with Sugarboy and his brothers," he says, grinning up at her with his gap-toothed self.

Jaima sighs, exasperated. These children and their bigheaded ideas. If he wasn't so cute, she'd be tempted to bump him to the floor. "You know y'all not supposed to be down there no more," she says. "That's government land now."

"It was our land before it was government land, so we can go where we please," Reggie yells out (unhelpful as always) from the Spades table. Jaima frowns over his way—her older cousin Reggie is nineteen, in college, and full of spit and fire. And usually bad ideas that come from him being so smart and in college.

"So, Reggie, you gonna take care of these boys when they get arrested for trespassing?" Jaima asks, because she and Reggie are always arguing. Sweet Ma says it's because they both have big brains, and big brains like to find each other and argue. It's the law.

"Look, alls I'm saying is that most of this place used to be ours, all around here surrounding the river," Reggie explains. He even stands up to say it, because that's something college boys do apparently. Makes them feel important. He's dark-skinned, tall and lanky, and built solid like most of the country boys out here who spend their summers running in the woods and diving into the river. "And now we got to fight off loggers, oil companies, the gov'ment, golf course developers, and now them damn Greers," he says, counting off each a finger at a time. "We ain't gonna have nothing left soon."

Jaima doesn't disagree, but she still knows better than to encourage these boys to do whatever they please. "Ain't enough reason to get ourselves arrested."

Reggie groans, but settles back down at the table. "When they start damming up that precious river of yours, you gonna care. You know that's something they're talking about too, right? We ain't even gonna have access to the river no more."

Jaima swallows and goes back to ignoring him. She hates it when he makes good points. This was land not a lot of white folks wanted back in the day—the thick forests and scattered marshlands proved too much trouble for them. It was wild, angry country, but the runaway slaves and freedmen took to it, made a life among the tangled vines and flooded plains. Even tamed, the place still had a mind of its own. Yet it seems these days everyone wants a piece of it.

Jaima plucks a twig from Tee-Ray's hair and tosses it on the floor, an act that sends him squirming in her lap. "Chile, be still," she whispers as she works the knots out.

"These children see the glory in this place," Sweet Mama tells her.

She's working on the last piece of Jaima's hair, whispering her homemade love into every rough pull of the comb.

Jaima understands the glory more than most, aches with the understanding of the river's depths. "I know they do, Sweet Ma," she says. "I know it."

Sweet Ma hums softly. When most of the tangles have been worked through with the oil, she sets to braiding the detangled strands. "You don't understand it all, Jaima. You ain't grown yet, even if you think you are. One day though, you gonna understand why this place is made *of* you, and why you are made *for* this place."

When Jaima looks up from the twists she's making in Tee-Ray's head, she sees Reggie watching them with a satisfied smirk on his face, and Jaima sighs, because she knows Sweet Ma's words are a gospel written just for her grandbabies, and if she listens long enough, there's salvation for them all somewhere inside of those words. Maybe.

Summer comes in fast, a series of days that swelter and linger long and wild. She's chasing the twins through the woods one evening after supper. Following behind them on legs too short for this kind of running. They break into a run every time they see her nearing them, weaving and snaking in between the trees, their skinny little bodies camouflaged by the moss and leaves.

Jaima's boots sink into the soft mulch of the forest floor, and she's breathing hard when she pauses to slow her racing heart, her body bending over, her hand resting against a gnarled tree trunk. She can hear them ahead, their laughter and loud breathing ringing in the forest.

She loses them at the river, the gurgling rush of water drowning them out completely. She pauses there for a while, the rush of her own river-synced blood loud in her ears. After a time she turns to head back toward Sweet Ma's, knowing the twins will make their way back when they are ready and not before. It's still hot out, even for the early evening. The sun slices through the tree cover, the world a mix of dappled light and dark. When she left earlier, the house was quiet, everyone gone down to the river, leaving Sweet Ma to nap on the porch.

Last night Jaima dreamed of the river, even though she had a bedful of cousins stealing her covers. She kept dreaming Martin was fighting the cops out by Freeman's Run, that Tee-Ray's hair was made up of just twigs and golden leaves, and that she was standing at the jutted rock where it was safest to dive into the swimming hole. But every time she went to make the dive, she woke up, breathing hard, heart pounding.

Sweet Ma says the dreams aren't any kind of premonition, just Jaima's mind dealing with things too big for her brain to figure out in the waking light of day. Sweet Ma says the dreams are just about her fear and her trauma. But Jaima's body feels heavy with the weight of the dreams, like at any moment she could close her eyes and be right there inside the dream, on the edge of the river, diving down. Jaima shakes off the thought, walks the mile to the northern property line, sweating under her yellow sundress and kicking up clumps of dirt with her boots. Byronisha and Jaquan are in Olakusa visiting their auntie, so Jaima's got some time to run her errands today. This is the area where she usually finds the horsetail roots Sweet Ma uses for her healing teas.

Because she's so busy parsing out the weeds, it takes a minute to notice the distant figures parked out by Bullhill Road. She doesn't recognize them until she crosses through the grove. It's three of the Greer boys, including Bobby Jr., moving around like land surveyors. She's heard about them doing this, staking out neighboring acres. She spies on them for a while, making sure they're not up to something shifty. Mostly they talk amongst each other, talk into their phones, walk around like they're plotting something. After a time all the Greer boys except for Bobby Jr. leave, and Jaima gets hot and impatient waiting for him to get going as well. After about ten minutes, she makes her way toward him, determined to not let his presence get in the way of her day.

Bobby Jr. stops her, of course, and says, "Evenin', Jaima." He leans back against his truck, white teeth on full display as he takes her in. He wipes the sweat from his brow with a handkerchief, lets out a deep exhale. "Hot as the devil's ass today. Whatcha doing all the way out here?"

"Enjoying the heat," she says, squinting over at him, the sun too bright in her eyes. "What brings you out here? I think your new property ends just about ten yards that way." She points to a distant piece of grassy meadow just to make the emphasis clear.

"Well, you know," Bobby Jr. says, pocketing his handkerchief and scratching at his thick stubble, looking like he's deep in thought, "land is funny like that sometimes. My daddy found some older maps at the assessor's office, and we may need to stop by and talk to your Sweet Ma. Looks like some of these lines are off some. You know these big ol' trees always confusing everything."

Jaima is only seventeen, but she's smart; she's seen a lot and knows folks' ugly ways. She's got river in her blood too, and it's roaring something fierce right about now. She tightens her scarf around her long braids and looks over at Bobby Jr. for a time, wondering what his game is. She says, "Yeah, that's funny. Lines and all, they're funny like that. Always seem to be changing."

Bobby Jr. looks at her for a long time, eyes dark from this distance, like he's trying to figure her out. She knows she's sweaty, and her dress is covered in dirt and leaves from chasing the twins. She probably looks different out here, more untidy, wilder than she must look in her uniform. Her skin glistens near black in this sun, like the dark earth under her boots. She arches her chin high, doesn't care if she's rough-looking. She tries to come off professional, serious. Doesn't like the looks Bobby Jr. is always giving her. He's smiling at her now, like he knows something she doesn't, and she doesn't like that kind of look either.

She clears her throat, knows when a battle's lost. "Well, Bobby, good luck on figuring out those lines of yours," she tells him, because she's tired of him giving her the creeps like always, and her stomach is rolling too much, wanting to go back home. She turns around to go the way she came. She'll avoid Bullhill Road until he leaves, and do her foraging later this week.

Maybe something in her had been waiting for it. Maybe the river inside of her had been warning her, sounding an alarm as it rushed through her, greedy to devour, because she's not at all surprised he's following her with quick steps, his boots crunching loud over the forest floor. Following her like he does in the store, but this time he's not playing games, and when she turns to look at him, she's ready for him.

"Can I do something for you?" she asks, voice rough with warning as he steps closer. He's at least a foot taller than her, but Jaima juts her chin high, her gaze resolute and uncompromising. She watches him, watches the way he watches her, and when he touches her shoulder, she stiffens, jerks away. "Stop that," she says, voice gone cold, like the river's threat.

"Why you always ignoring me, huh?" he asks, and he's back to touching her shoulder, lingering for a moment. She swallows, watches as his rough, calloused fingers start to play with the strap of her sundress. "You're such a pretty girl, always showing off for me in the store," he tells her, his words low and gruff.

Jaima hates him so much right then, thinks about Sweet Ma's shotgun under her bed, thinks about running to get it, but her feet have turned to stone. "Move your hand or I'll scream, I swear," she whispers, because he doesn't have a right to her, not like he has a right to everything else. Her body wants to run, but it's stuck like those deer by the pool, sensing the danger but not able to move. He moves even closer, pushes at the strap of her dress, pushes it almost off her shoulder, and she feels everything in her body trying to break free from her, the tears behind her eyelids burning, wanting to pour out.

She closes her eyes, feels the river rise inside of her, gathers enough energy to jerk away from his touch. She stumbles back, her boots catching in the long grass. She looks at him and says, "Stay away from me from now on or I'm telling."

"Girl, you ain't telling nobody," he mutters, stepping toward her again. "Not if you want to keep your land. Not if you want to keep the peace." He moves quick, grabs her by the arms and pulls her in close. She struggles in his grip, his rough fingers digging into her flesh. He's too hot, too stinking, too heavy, and she's choking on it. This close she can see his eyes: the black rimming a green iris. She can see every part of his face: the pink pimples on his forehead and the peeling red patches of sunburned skin above his nose. She freezes, turns her face away when he kisses her cheek, runs his mouth down along the side of her face, slipping along her sweaty neck. The rough bite of his stubble scratches her skin. Bruises her.

"Been wanting you," he whispers, squeezing her arms tight before he grabs her at the joint of her neck to pull her in so he can whisper against her ear, "You like me, right, Jaima?"

She stiffens at hearing her name in his mouth. He pulls her face between his hands and looks at her. "You can just stay quiet and I can do the work," he says, and he bends to kiss her mouth. His lips are dry, cracked, taste like salt. She opens her mouth slowly, pretends she's playing along, and then bites down on his soft bottom lip. *Ass.*

Bobby Jr. jerks away, pulls his meaty hand back, and slaps her cheek. The sharp sting is enough to startle her, her face sparking with fire. She's set in motion now, and turns and runs and runs, everything a sudden blur. Her body crashes through the trees, her boots knock down the weeds, and her dress snags on the branches. She's afraid he's going to follow, catch her and keep her out here in the woods with the sun setting too fast. But all she hears is his yelling, no sounds of a chase.

She stops minutes later, heart pounding, a surge of power rushing through her veins as she turns to look back at him. His bulky frame is cast as a silhouette against the burnt-orange sky. He's standing there calling her a bitch, telling her to come on back, to stop playing around.

Jaima laughs at him, loud and reckless, her whole body filling up with the sound. At this moment, she's made of laughter and surging water, ready to drown him like the giant tsunami that would follow the shaking of the entire world.

Jaima doesn't tell anyone. Doesn't even consider calling the sheriff's station, because most of the boys who work there are kin to the Greers anyway. Instead, she spends the next day in bed, her belly hurting so much she almost asks to go see Doc Murphy. Sweet Ma brings her funny-tasting tea made from the herbs she grows in the backyard and feeds her tomato soup for lunch and dinner. Jaima sleeps mostly, tired as tired can be.

Reggie visits her on the second day of her self-imposed bed rest, and she doesn't know how he knows, but she can tell it in his hard eyes the minute he walks in, see it in the tight line of his body.

"Nothing happened," she says, sitting up in bed.

"Malcolm sure saw *something*," he says, voice hoarse and dry like he's swallowed grit. "I'll kill that piece of shit Greer, you know I will, Jaima." He's trembling with rage, his jaw pulsing as he looks at her.

Jaima closes her eyes and inhales sharply. She remembers that the twins had been running around out there somewhere, realizes they must have headed back early and seen her. Jaima opens her eyes but doesn't look at Reggie, can't look at him. She just picks at a piece of string unwinding in the seam of Sweet Ma's quilt and frowns. "Just tell them not to say anything to Sweet Ma, all right?"

Reggie sits down at the foot of the bed, his weight causing the old mattress to dip. He exhales loudly and asks, "You really think Sweet Ma won't find out?"

Jaima shrugs. Of course Sweet Ma is going to find out. Sweet Ma finds out all.

Jaima looks up at him after a time. He's looking at her like he wants to say something else, but he doesn't. He's the oldest of Sweet Ma's grand-babies, and he is handsome in a sharp kind of way. Stubborn in a sharp kind of way too. If he doesn't get killed fighting somebody, he'll probably go on to be a lawyer and come back and use that to settle all the things that need settling out here.

But for now, Reggie has to know they can't do anything about the Greers without bringing trouble and risking more. "You can't go after him." She says it aloud so he hears it spoken.

"I know." Reggie snorts softly to himself, shakes his head. "Don't mean I don't want to." He sighs and looks at her for a long moment, eyes dark and serious, before adding, "He could still come after you. Hurt you. Or worse."

Jaima's limbs feel numb, her fingertips twitch on the quilt. Two summer ago, before Reggie left for college, they were arguing about her not knowing how to swim and why it was dumb that she was so scared of the water. She doesn't really remember all of what they said to each other beside that, just that they had gotten angrier and angrier, likely yelled about everything and nothing, about the weight of being oldest, the fear of leaving family. She does know that at some point in the heat of the moment Reggie had smacked her hard, knocking her against a tree, leaving her lip swollen. She'd covered her face and run to the house, tears streaming her cheeks. They never talked about it, but she knows he's probably thinking about it now, how he hurt her once too, took his anger out on her. But Reggie's never hurt her again, and if anything, he's gotten more protective. Even told her once how it ain't right for powerful people to hurt people just to feel good about themselves.

She can't tell for sure if that's what he's thinking now, not with that stone-faced look of his, so she reaches out and takes his hand and squeezes. "I'll be careful."

Reggie looks at her and nods, squeezing her hand in return. "Okay," he says. Their brains like to fight, sure, but he's also the one who used to sit with her on the porch after dinner and help her with her social studies homework. He's the one who used to catch grasshoppers with her in the backyard, and pat her back when she cried about her parents being at the bottom of the river. Reggie is the only one she ever told about sometimes wanting to kiss Byronisha.

When Reggie gets up to leave, he glances back at her over his shoulder and nods to her before he exits. Jaima feels better knowing he'll keep this secret too.

In the dream she's breathing underwater. She's swimming in the deep, dark depths, and the world is foggy and blue and infinite. There's something glowing down in the dark, near the riverbed, something that looks like a ball of fire burning even underwater. She swims toward the flame, and she laughs in joy when she finally reaches it, holding it tightly in her hands. The light grows so strong, she has to close her eyes. In the distance she can hear her name being called—it sounds like a man and a woman telling her to *Hold on, baby girl, just hold on.*

Jaima wakes up to the sound of raindrops falling heavy on the tin roof, the metallic thump-thump rhythm mimicking her own heartbeat. She keeps her eyes closed for a long moment, the memory of light still shining behind her lids. She feels a deep sense of loss, even as the sound of her name slowly fades from her mind. When she finally opens her eyes, Jaima sees Sweet Ma sitting in the old wooden rocker in the corner of her bedroom, fanning herself and watching *The Price Is Right* on the small box TV on top of the dresser. The volume is low, and scrolling across the bottom of the screen Jaima can just make out warnings about heavy rains and flash flooding in the area. Jaima places her palm over her tender belly, breathes out uneasily. Her hand feels warm against her skin, still tingling from the dream fire.

"You know my nerves get bad when y'all get sick," Sweet Ma says, turning to look at Jaima. "How's your tummy, girl?"

"Better," Jaima says, yawning as she sits up and tosses the quilt aside. "Needed the sleep, I guess."

Sweet Ma hmmms, rocks back and forth in her chair. Jaima looks at her for a long time in the dim room light. Jaima knows that her mama looked a lot like Sweet Ma—she's seen pictures from her mama's childhood. Both of them were small and delicate, with a thick nest of kinky hair that they kept twisted up around their heads. Sweet Ma is wearing her hair down today though. It makes a ring around her head, silver and black curls that dangle like moss hanging from a cypress tree.

Sweet Ma has lit all the candles on the dresser top, and their warm light flickers over her face, makes it seem softer and younger. Maybe more like what her mama would have looked like if she'd lived, Jaima thinks. In the soft light of the room, Sweet Ma's skin is the color of copper pennies.

In a memory that is probably more dream than actual memory, Jaima is with her mama, who is singing while putting rainbow beads on Jaima's braids. They're sitting together and singing along to the radio, and when her mama pulls her into her lap, the memory morphs into another one—the two of them rocking back and forth in a porch swing. It's nighttime and Jaima is barefoot, and the soft cotton nightgown she wears is too thin in the chilly night air. But it doesn't matter because she's with her mama and they are watching the moon.

"When I was a girl," Sweet Ma says, breaking Jaima out of the memory, "the river flooded like it did that year it took my baby girl, your mama."

Jaima looks up at her again, and Sweet Ma is looking at her like she's looking back in time. "Another great flood?" Jaima asks.

"There's always another great flood," Sweet Ma says with a nod. "The waters came and the river rose, and it chased us into the hills."

"That river is greedy," Jaima says, breathing it out, feeling it dance inside of her.

"Or maybe," Sweet Ma says, her lips curving softly, "it's just a river. Doing what rivers do."

Through the next night her dreams are troubled, memories of the past mixing with pieces of her present life, swirling storms and lights at the bottom of the river, Bobby Jr.'s face and his hands tugging at her. The next day the rain comes down like a slow release. Jaima's belly feels a little better, although it's still rumbling when Byronisha comes by during one of the storm's midday lulls. Her friend says she wants to spend some time outside after being cooped up all weekend with the baby, but Jaima thinks Byronisha is worried Jaima's turning into a hermit. So Jaima peels herself out of bed, tosses on sweatpants, an old T-shirt, rain boots, and a raincoat. Byronisha is similarly dressed, the hood of her yellow raincoat covering most of her cherubic face.

The two girls walk the perimeter of the house for a time, watching the gray clouds move in a slow dance across the sky. They go down to the edge of the property line, close enough to see the river beyond.

"The water's high, all right," Jaima says, watching the churning rush of it as it curves around the bend next to their land.

"High enough to crest," Byronisha says, entwining her arm with Jaima's as they continue down through the tall grass.

It starts to sprinkle again, the raindrops falling slow and fat, spattering Jaima's forehead and running down her cheeks. Near the bottom of the property they encounter the twins, barefoot and shirtless, covered in thick, black mud. The boys have matching guilty gummy smiles, their identical pairs of brown eyes wide with surprise.

Jaima takes in the ditch filled with muddy water and shakes her head. Beside her, Byronisha is cracking up, praying in between garbled breaths: "Lord, I ain't ready for this. Please let my boy have the sense you gave him."

Jaima just shakes her head, too tired to ask how long they've been fighting in the muddy ditch. "Get on home, and get cleaned up," she tells them instead. "And if you track anything into Sweet Ma's house—"

Martin stops her from fussing by wrapping his disgusting arms around her waist, and then darts away when she tries to grab hold of him. Malcolm is slower in his escape, stopping in front of Jaima, his cheeks scrunching up and his forehead wrinkling as he asks, "Did you hear what happened to Bobby Jr.?"

Jaima frowns, the world tilting just so. "What do you mean? Did Reggie do something?" she asks, worry filling her already pained gut.

"Nah, man, it was the high water!" Malcolm says, excited. "Yesterday the highway washed out down by the Greer place. They say Bobby and his truck got stuck in the deep water."

"Yeah, I heard some roads got closed because of high water," Byronisha says, coming closer. "They had to rescue some folks stranded out by the bridge."

"Well, they say it took three people to pull Bobby free. All that water flooded his truck," Malcolm said, smiling like he's the cat that caught the canary.

"I hadn't heard," Jaima says, dropping her hand on top of the boy's slick shoulder and squeezing gently, thanking him silently for the news. Malcolm's grin widens and then he shakes his head at her, sending droplets of rain flying everywhere. Jaima jumps back, watches as he runs off after his twin. The world is hazy with rain.

"Those Greers are such creeps," Byronisha says, sliding her hood back over her head of slick curls. "A big old family of creeps."

Jaima nods, closing her eyes, shivering; everything around her rocks like she's on a boat at sea. Her belly sloshes joyously, and Jaima can't help herself—she laughs, soft at first, like a whisper, and then louder when she opens her eyes and feels the rain on her skin. It's a good rain, ozone-rich.

"Girl, you okay?" Byronisha asks, and Jaima laughs even louder, taking her friend's hand and twirling her around and around until they're both dizzy. And then, oh God, the rain. Falling warm and sweet and necessary, a solid sheet coming down and soaking them to the skin in only a few seconds. Jaima laughs into the breaking sky and then takes off running, Byronisha right behind her.

They race through the grass, Jaima edging just a fraction ahead before the ground slips from under them. Jaima slides first, her boots losing their grip in the bubbling mud. The weight of her body pulls her down into the half-filled ditch, and Byronisha comes tumbling in after. The fall happened so fast, Jaima doesn't even know what to say when she looks around and realizes they are lying together in the muddy runoff at the bottom of the ditch, still laughing like children.

Byronisha's body rests on top of hers, heavy and familiar. The heat curling in Jaima's gut feels different now, wilder, like the storm. Above them, the rain has slackened, the blue sky near visible.

"Damn, girl," Byronisha giggles as she looks down at Jaima. Her arms tighten around Jaima's waist as she says, "Good thing I caught you."

"Good thing," Jaima says, a laugh hiccupping from her throat as she takes in the sticky muck tracking down Byronisha's face and neck. Both of them are wet through and through, clothes clinging and hanging. Arms and legs covered in the mud and grassy debris of the ditch. Hurricane girls, she'll call them from now on. Storm-born girls.

"You ain't scared?" Byronisha asks, nodding to the water pooled around them. Jaima knows they could drown in even a few inches of water, but the feel of it sliding around her is soothing. Jaima thinks about how Bobby Jr. could have been swept away yesterday—wonders if he even understands how close he came. How the river could take him anytime it wants.

"Not scared," Jaima says, curling her arms around Byronisha, feeling the other girl's warm breath on her cheek. Byronisha rests her head on Jaima's shoulder.

They're quiet for a time. Jaima listens to the sounds of the storm receding—the drips and drags and distant roars. She listens to the breathing of her best friend, imagines the air moving in and out of her lungs, the blood running through her veins, the same blood spilled long ago in the ground around them, when their people first made a home here.

Jaima thinks: their bodies are blood and earth. Their bodies are water. The thought of it sends shivers up and down her spine. She imagines her belly full: her inner river cresting, rushing and widening. Greedy, hungry, but patient. She squeezes her eyes tighter, lets herself go under. Her heart thumps loudly as she surfaces.

When Jaima opens her eyes, Byronisha is looking down at her, her eyelashes wet, lips quirked. "Good thing I like weirdos," Byronisha says.

Jaima snorts, then leans in and kisses the other girl's cheek, sloppy and warm. Byronisha giggles, pulls them closer, and slides them deeper into the mud. They're a mess and a half.

"I think I'm ready," Jaima whispers after a time.

"For what?" Byronisha asks, words low like a secret.

"Everything." Jaima doesn't have to be afraid. She just has to be what she is. A girl with a river inside of her, strong enough to flood the whole world maybe. She closes her eyes, breathes in and out. Thankful for the rain.

AUTHOR'S NOTE

As a child growing up in the rural Southern United States, I first learned the power of story here. I learned storytelling at the feet of my grandparents, during hot summers spent on the front porch listening to them spin family tales. I learned it during the afternoons hiding out in the shadows of my childhood home, listening to the conversations being had over the kitchen table. I still remember being eleven, alone in my room with a pen and pad, looking out the window to the sugarcane fields surrounding my home as I began to write down the stories of my community. I learned early on that the South is a place where stories themselves hold power—stories of renewal, of resilience, of deep survivalisms in the face of historic injustice. I learned how storytelling can be a way to heal, to knit the broken memories of our pasts into something we can hold today.

When I began writing the short story BELLY, I thought about our histories and our present moments and I asked: What does it mean to be of a place, to be bound to a place? In what ways do we mimic the power of a place? BELLY is an exploration of power, home, grief, and family. My seventeen-year-old protagonist, Jaima, has to come to terms not only with the river that threatens to run its banks but with those who seek to take the land away from her and her family. Land and place are critical to understanding the lives of the people in this story, and Jaima's relationship to this land is as important to her character development as is her relationship to her family and friends. The river and the natural world in this story are both life-giving and life-taking; they hold their own kind of sacred magic. I loved working on edits for this story with the editors at FORESHADOW, figuring out how to expand on the natural heart of the story—bringing Jaima into her full powerful young adulthood, and centering her capacity and desire for love, for connection, and for healing.

THE MOTIF
IN *BELLY*

by Emily X.R. Pan

THE WATER SERVES AS THE FOUNDATION FOR THIS STORY. IT'S A MOTIF WHOSE function goes far beyond symbolism or ornamentation.

If we start by looking at the plot, the water plays a crucial role in each of the arcs that have been braided together here: There's Jaima's physical connection to the river via her belly. The river represents identity and history, and it gives Jaima her first taste of the world's dangers. It retaliates against the terrible Bobby Greer Jr., and it teaches Jaima that she has more strength than she thought:

> At this moment, she's made of laughter and surging
> water, ready to drown him like the giant tsunami that
> would follow the shaking of the entire world.

And, of course, by the end of the story, the water brings Jaima and Byronisha together. Every decision is sharply and economically made. The water is what glues all these pieces together.

It's also crucial to the worldbuilding—without the river we wouldn't have the magic and atmosphere, and our understanding of Jaima's relationship with the place she calls home. "Since the age of five, part of the river has lived somewhere inside of her."

The water also creates tension.

> Jaima shivers at the thought of returning to the
> river, fearing sinking into that darkness, fearing losing
> herself. Maybe it wants her back . . .

We don't know whether the river is malicious or benevolent, and we don't know what the true risks are. As we move through the story we catch glimpses of how other characters, like Sweet Ma, think about the river. How it fills Jaima's dreams; sometimes it scares her, but other times it seems encouraging. It's lovely for our understanding of the water to evolve and clarify as Jaima grows, as she discovers her own power and confidence.

And last, but certainly not least, the motif of the water feeds into an endless supply of ways to play with language. There are so many beautiful metaphors and images in this story. At the micro level: "her own river-synced blood loud in her ears." And woven into the macro, the bigger picture: The heavy rains and flash floods. The high water messing with Bobby's truck.

The water is its own character in this story, which is part of the delight and the reason it works so well. It's incredible how a single motif can hold so much power.

THE EDITOR'S PERSPECTIVE: Q&A WITH THE *FORESHADOW* FICTION EDITORS

FOR WRITERS, IT MIGHT SOMETIMES SEEM THAT EDITORS ARE THE INTIMIDATing figures in high-climbing publishing towers who live to send rejection letters without a thought for the tenderness of our creative hearts, but that is not so. Once you get that first offer of publication, one of the greatest gifts a writer can receive is the opportunity to work with a skilled editor who connects with your work and helps fulfill your vision. Now here is some collected wisdom from four editors who worked closely with the authors in this volume.

First, introducing our Fiction Editors . . .

Alexa Wejko: An editor is a mirror to a writer's work—reflecting back a writer's strengths and wisdom and goals so that they can see them more clearly. When I'm being coherent in my feedback and that philosophy works, *poof.* Magic.

Trisha Tobias: Being an editor is an honor. *Foreshadow* is a testament to all the diverse, inclusive stories that young adult fiction has to offer.

Denise Conejo: Editing is a true collaboration between the author and the editor. Often, I feel that I learn more from them than they may learn from me.

Sharyn November: I like to go into every edit with a sense of anticipation. What will each of us learn as we work? It's a privilege to be trusted with someone's story, and an editor needs to check any preconceptions at the door.

Q: **How do you approach the editing of a piece of fiction? What could writers learn from this process?**

Trisha: When I step into a piece, I'm gauging my first impressions. What shocks me? What makes me think? What leaves me a little confused? Then I reread to figure out what I believe the writer is trying to accomplish with their work. With a more objective eye, it's easier to see gaps between what the writer has set up on the page and what actually translated to me as the stand-in audience. My editorial work, then, is about closing that gap. I try to understand the writer's intent, and when something is unclear, I love asking a ton of questions. Often, presenting them guides the writer to the real story. Together, we fill out the background details and clarify the story's main message. Then, we can focus on the elements that best sustain that message and hone those in the text.

For writers, the key is to come to your own work as a blank slate. Be open to what crops up. Interrogate what's actually on the page. Be aware of what you autofill when it comes to motivation, logic, and meaning. You'd be surprised what comes up when you pretend to be a stranger! And if there's simply not enough distance from the story, find beta readers or critique partners. Fresh eyes are a necessity!

Alexa: I know it sounds stodgy, but I edit with a specific kind of checklist in mind, and I find myself giving feedback about the same qualities over and over again. They're the things that I think every story should have in order to be considered "successful"—internal logic, causality, a sense of direction and purpose, characters who change, and so on. *But*, after doing this for a while, you also learn the importance of understanding a story on its own terms. All of those "qualities" manifest in various ways, languages, structures, and rhythms, depending on the writer bringing them to life. That's why two equally incredible books can read as so wildly different. So, to get back to the question, I really *read* a story first and foremost, let it sink into my brain, and try to both hear its voice and understand what it's attempting to do on its own terms, then give feedback based on that reading. That all may sound remedial, but you'd be surprised how automatic and easy it is to develop, subconsciously, a fixed way of seeing, reading, and experiencing fiction. Could writers learn anything from that process? I'd say: Pay attention to everything you write below the surface, everything that you might not have consciously placed there. Be your own reader first.

Sharyn: My process for editing a short story is no different from any other kind of editing. For the practical-minded, here's a bullet list, a gloss on the process:

- Read with an open mind and take quick notes.
- Repeat, but with longer notes.
- Mark up the manuscript with queries and comments, and mention when something is especially great.
- Write an editorial letter, breaking the story down into its different aspects—plot, characters, intention, language, and so forth. I ask a lot of questions and offer suggestions, referring back to the marked manuscript, which accompanies the edit letter.
- After the author has had time to absorb it all, we'll discuss via email, phone, Skype, whatever works best. This is when things are explained and/or clarified on both sides.
- The author revises.
- After I read the revision, I write a shorter editorial letter, and may mark up the manuscript. The author reviews, and we talk again.
- When we agree that the story is in good structural shape, it's time for the line edit. I read slowly,

sentence by sentence, making sure it flows. I mark the manuscript, querying word choices, rhythm, how something sounds when spoken aloud; if anything is in a different language, I want to make sure that context helps the reader understand. I like to do some copyediting—fact-checking timeline corrections, confirming speaker attribution, applying general styling. (It should be obvious by now that I love line editing—a very specific, small question can open up a whole new dimension in a character or a scene.)

- The author responds to the line edit—agreeing, disagreeing, revising. In the end, the author is the one who makes the final call.

I see myself as a guide, a resource, someone who can provide perspective. At its best, it's a partnership with a shared goal—a terrific story. It might sound like a lot of work, but it's also a lot of fun.

Denise: I love editing, but more than that, I love reading. I enter a story not as an editor, but just as a reader. Having zero expectations, I can more easily pick up on ideas and themes that the author may be trying to convey. In my initial read-through, I take note of any key words and sentences that jump out at me, as they ultimately give me inspiration for the first round of edits. It's important that the author and I are working on mutually beneficial grounds, where I'm inspired to edit through the author's words and the author is inspired to work on edits through my editorial letter. If writers could learn anything from my approach, it is to let yourself be inspired by what you've done on the page, and take note of anything that stands out, i.e., certain words, ideas, something that a character says or does, etc. These things stand out for a reason, so dig deeper and play!

Q: **When you were working with one of the new voices whose stories appear here, what was that experience like for you as an editor?**

Alexa: I went into the process wanting to leave behind more than just feedback; I wanted New Voice authors to have their work taken seriously, and I wanted them to recognize that feeling and hold on to it. Every writer in this industry knows how difficult it is, every day, to battle imposter syndrome, how impossible it is to see the worth of your own work. We need memories and reminders—which is at least part of the reason the book you're holding in your hands exists.

Sharyn: There's nothing better than a revision that goes past what you had imagined. You can share your concerns and offer advice, discuss the story, but you never truly know what the next pass is going to look like. The *Foreshadow* authors—all at different stages in their careers—were consummate pros, each with a specific and unusual literary voice. There were moments when I was elated because someone had done a particularly graceful job of clarifying an issue, or delighted me with an elegant phrase.

Q: **What advice do you have for aspiring writers working on YA fiction?**

Trisha: Tell the truth. It doesn't matter your story's genre—readers connect with truth. Writers can hone craft, find guidance through editors, and line edit to their heart's content. But honesty can't be taught, forced, or fabricated. Whether you're exploring complex topics or bringing levity to readers when days are dark, lean into your purpose to make it sing.

Alexa: Read. Then read more. I know it's such boring advice, but it becomes really easy to put books aside when you're buried in creating your own. And read everything, not just YA! Reading broadly keeps your writer brain fresh.

Sharyn: Read as widely as you can—osmosis is a huge part of learning your craft. Take your characters and their particular journey seriously, but remember that every story has its own kind of humor.

Denise: Trust yourself and speak from a place of curiosity, pain, or wonderment. And once you find yourself in that place, let it flow and keep it simple. Trust that your editor will pick up on those moments and amplify them if need be, and trust that your readers will get it. Allow yourself moments of vulnerability, sensitivity, and sweetness.

HOW A STORY IS BORN:
AUTHORS SHARE THE ORIGINAL SEEDS OF THEIR IDEAS

WHAT SPARKS A STORY IDEA?

    This is often a question readers and emerging writers alike most want to ask published authors. The sparking of a good and worthy idea feels like alchemy sometimes, mystical and unfathomable, a whisper from the dream world coming to awake our imaginations . . . if we're lucky. Now that you've read all the stories in this collection, you may be curious about where the ideas came from. Here we've collected the sparks—strange, surprising, personal, entirely unexpected—that lit the imaginations of the *Foreshadow* writers . . .

———————

A memorable image or sighting . . .

The very first spark I felt was, weirdly, because of windows—namely, windows on planes and buses and trains. During my morning commute, I got inspired for a certain scene where I wanted to capture the feeling of moving on somewhere but being unable to look away from everything you're leaving behind.

—NORA ELGHAZZAWI (SOLACE)

I've always been fascinated by the idea that magic could exist right beneath our notice, and what—or who—it would take to find it. The initial spark happened while I was on the train to work and caught a glimpse of a blue light in the tunnel (they exist!). The image of Milagros looking into the darkness of the train tunnel and *noticing* came from that, along with the feeling of being the other in a sea of strangers looking for connection.

—ADRIANA MARACHLIAN (MONSTERS)

———•———

A line that won't escape your mind . . .

A sentence came into my head: 'Marnie Vega is turning into a crustacean.' I would have thought that my authorial response to that would be *Okay . . . why?* Instead I thought: *Of course she is. Now what?*

—RACHEL HYLTON (RISK)

———•———

A character (or two) who needs their story told . . .

Oddly enough, I first set out to write a story about a cheerleader and her quarterback girlfriend. And though Beth and Naia were neither cheerleaders nor football players, they were dynamically pulled together in a way I couldn't explain—the universe demanded it. I saw them in vignettes, just blinks of a moment, and pulled those together to map out their story.

—JOANNA TRUMAN (GLOW)

A lot of my story ideas are sparked by an image or a character in a specific situation. For BELLY I had this idea of a girl caught in a swirl of water at the bottom of the river— and I thought, *Who is this girl, and what would happen if she survived?* I liked the idea of exploring the humanness and bravery of this young girl in juxtaposition to this mighty force of nature.

—DESIREE S. EVANS (BELLY)

A place that captures your imagination . . .

I had story ideas that I knew I would never have time to write, so I cobbled some together and free-wrote until I shaped the characters and world I wanted to explore. The setting of Ahma's manor was the anchor—stolen from an abandoned novel draft where it was a school for girls.

—Gina Chen (FOOLS)

Even though El Paso, Texas, has been repeatedly ranked as one of the safest cities in the nation, it is plagued with the perception of being a dangerous place to live in because it's a border city neighboring one of the unsafest cities in Mexico, Ciudad Juarez, which was overtaken by violence sparked from the drug cartel wars of the '90s. El Paso always felt safe, and the blending of people and cultures that happens in a border city make it even more of a unique place. I struggle to explain the rapture of growing up in my hometown, so I decided to show a glimpse of it instead.

—Flor Salcedo (PAN DULCE)

An experiment with writing craft or form . . .

I've actually had this idea of a girl who worked a summer in a restaurant and developed a crush on a new kid for a while. I'd started it as a full-length novel, but I wanted to play with locations and time in these little vignettes. I love novels that can pull it off, but I thought the jumping from party to party, each scene heightening the mutual crush, was best served

by a short story of falling in love in a few months—in a way
that only teens can.

—Sophie Meridien (BREAK)

A concept or trope you want to dig into or subvert . . .

When reading theories about where humanity is headed
(as one does), my imagination was struck by one idea in
particular: We will do anything to escape our own mortality,
including uploading our consciousness into digital storage.

—Maya Prasad (PRINCESS)

I knew I wanted to write a dark fairy tale, and the first word
that sprang to my mind was *witch*. I took the concept of
the witch and examined it in its various incarnations—as a
villain, as a mother figure—and from there it sparked the
idea of this modern reimagining of various familiar tropes.

—Linda Cheng (SWEETMEATS)

A real-world event that you must speak to . . .

Months after Hurricane María devastated Puerto Rico, I read
a *Washington Post* article about a group of young Puerto
Ricans who moved to Huron, South Dakota, to work at a
turkey-processing plant. The details of their journey were
raw and honest, full of heartbreak and hope—it was the
spark I needed to write a truthful story.

—Mayra Cuevas (RESILIENT)

A compelling question that begs an inventive answer...

I asked myself two questions: *How can the act of
remembering be written as a point of action/agency?*
and *What would a selkie story look like if the selkie got to
choose?* I didn't want to write a story about a reaction; I
wanted to write a story about making a choice. I wrote the
second draft while traveling through China, and I can't help
but think that the feeling of being an outsider and stranger
helped frame the story.

—TANYA AYDELOTT (FLIGHT)

The very first seed of this story was back in mid-2017, when
my cat decided to take a nap inside my luggage. I was about
to pick it up and she leaped at me. And that's all it was: *What
if a cat lived in a bag?*

—TANVI BERWAH (ESCAPE)

Ideas for the stories in this volume came from all over, and that's just the
beginning. Most of all, be aware that your ideas really are precious things.
They are worth the work of safekeeping. They are worth digging through
the bottom of that bag looking for the pen you lost so you can write them
down. You never know—if you let the spark burn on the page, it could
catch and keep going. Then it could light the whole room.

STORY PROMPT:
THE LAST WORD

Did you notice that the stories appearing in this collection are titled in a singular way—with one word?

Since *foreshadowing* in storytelling is a way of imagining and prefiguring what's to come, our hope is that the new writers you discover here will be the authors whose books you'll covet tomorrow. We like to think that the single-word story titles offer a reader a memorable clue that *foreshadows* what each story is about. This was how the one-word titles were born.

Sometimes the *Foreshadow* authors came to us with their own one-word titles already in mind, and occasionally they asked us to offer them a word that could inspire a story.

They treated it as a spark.

Your last story prompt is this: Take a word from the next page and write a story with it as the inspiration . . . and perhaps even the title.

Let your eyes wander over the words here and see what resonates. Is there one in particular that pops out at you? Is there some kind of divination happening right now within the pages of this book? Who's to say?

Here are the words to choose from:

Rogue

Undoing **Canted** Prowl

Carcass Berth **Descent** Troublemaker

Cairn **Fettered** Radiance Blossom

Hinder **Aperture** Worth **Inheritance**

Gloaming **Carom** Harbinger **Remnant**

Sear **Tarnished** Fragment **Enchantment**

Outcast **Haven** Wrinkle
Echo

Perhaps this will spark a new short story in you . . . We hope it does.

AFTERWORD

by Nova Ren Suma

As we close this book with your own story ideas, and hopefully some new beginnings, it makes me think of mine . . . I will always remember my first yes. How could any aspiring author forget that magical moment? It certainly didn't happen quickly, but when it did, it was the beginning of everything.

I had collected an admirable pile of rejections before the morning I stood on the subway platform at 110th and Broadway in New York City, many years ago, waiting for the downtown 1 train to take me to my office job. Right there, under the streets of the city, among strangers, I tore open an envelope, expecting the usual bad news often addressed "Dear Writer" and printed on a small slip of paper. Instead I found a full-size sheet of paper and on it my first-ever short story acceptance, something I'd wished for and worked toward for what felt like a long time. It had finally happened. Someone had said yes.

The acceptance letter was from a small literary journal sixteen hundred miles away, in Texas, a place I'd never visited. Somehow the editors wanted to include my words in their next issue. Mine.

I remember so clearly the moment this realization dawned on me: There I was in my uncomfortable work shoes facing the wind of an oncoming train, and as the lights grew larger and the nose of the train edged closer, I felt my whole body lift.

For days I'd had the envelope crumpled in my pocket, forgotten, assuming it was yet another rejection for my collection. And now I held the good news like it could carry me up through the subway grate and high above the streets and spires of my city. It felt that powerful to me, that meaningful. Every time I think of it, I'm suspended, in the midst of soaring, seconds before the train pulls in. That's where my memory cuts off, sharp as the too-snug heels of my shoes. I don't know how I made it onto that train and to my desk downtown to work an ordinary day after holding such tremendous news in my hands.

I was about to be a published fiction writer. There was a seat for me, or at least a few inches of space where I could squeeze myself in and grab hold of a pole. I don't know how I made it to my desk downtown to work an ordinary day after such tremendous news, but thanks to those editors in Texas, this train would carry me to the next chapter in my life. I stepped on.

Now, with *Foreshadow*, I had the opportunity to be on the other side of the writer/publisher divide. I got to be one of the editors offering the good news.

There are thirteen yeses in this book. Some were the very first. What an honor it has been to be a part of this process for these memorable, distinctive voices—and, best of all, to share them here.

The magic contained in these pages is not just meant for the writers we're so thrilled to publish. It's for you, too. Did you sense it? Did you hear us calling your name?

Because in the end, this collection does more than introduce you to thirteen dazzling new writers. We've asked you to engage with us on a deeper level, and we've loved every minute of getting to dig in and spotlight so many cunning craft choices. To the aspiring writers among you, I see you there, standing in your uncomfortable shoes, wondering when a door will open. I hope you'll make use of this collection as you write. These pieces will be here to offer you a glimpse into the writing process— at times a close study, at times a challenging push. We hope there was a story you read here and connected with, a craft conundrum you found answered, a prompt you followed and grew into something worthy and real. The magic is in your hands now, and the moment has come.

Take it.

Write your story . . . The next train is approaching.

THE MAGICAL ORIGIN STORY OF
FORESHADOW

IN THE BEGINNING, LONG BEFORE THE BOOK YOU HOLD IN YOUR HANDS WAS AN inkling of a thought, there were two YA authors traveling together to a book conference. The authors got to talking about secret publishing dreams, the kind that seem impossible and so pie-in-the-sky that you're afraid to even start . . . But when one author confessed to the other that she had a precious jewel of an idea cupped between her palms—*a YA literary journal for short stories*—the other author said right back, "I've always wanted to do that!"

You know already . . . Those two YA authors were us. Obviously. And by the time we reached the conference, the idea was already taking root. It was many months later when the tug became irresistible and we knew: We needed to make it real.

During a five-hour lunch at a Ukrainian diner, over pancakes and blintzes, we conceptualized our serial anthology. We were committed to showcasing underrepresented voices, and we wanted to be sure that a huge aspect of our mission was discovering new, unknown writers. The most exciting part came when we found that so many other authors were eager to support this endeavor. Some of them wrote incredible stories of their own for us to publish and elevate our platform. Others generously read stories that were submitted to us and chose their favorites to blurb. And so it was that our website was born: **foreshadowya.com**. A unique platform that ultimately published thirty-nine brilliant YA short stories.

We are so grateful for the support we received, and we can hardly believe that we get to hold this very special book—featuring our stunning new voices—in our own hands. Visit **foreshadowya.com** to read the rest of our collection, from ISSUE 00 to ISSUE 12, featuring not only the emerging writers collected here, but also so many rock-star YA authors you already know and love, including S.K. Ali, Dhonielle Clayton, Brandy Colbert, Stephanie Kuehn, Nina LaCour, Samantha

321

Mabry, Anna-Marie McLemore, Malinda Lo, Mark Oshiro, Randy Ribay, Courtney Summers, and many more.

Thank you for following us on this journey. It is your readership that makes this magic come alive.

—*Emily X.R. Pan & Nova Ren Suma*

MASTHEAD

FORESHADOW, in its original online form
as foreshadowya.com, was brought to you through
the hard work of the following staff members:

Editors-in-Chief
Emily X.R. Pan & Nova Ren Suma

Managing Editor
Diane Telgen

Fiction Editors
Sharyn November
Alexa Wejko

Associate Fiction Editors
Denise Conejo
Trisha Tobias

Copy Editors
Alison Cherry
Angela Cole
Natalia Wikana

Web Developers
Loren Rogers
Erik Ryerson

Helpful Assistant
Kiwi

Publicity Manager
Saraciea J. Fennell

Managing Editor Emeritus
Mara Delgado Sánchez

Assistant Editor Emeritus
Deeba Zargarpur

Readers
Emi Benn, Cristina dos Santos,
Michelle Falkoff, Ariane Felix,
Raechell Garrett, Francesca
Flores, Lili Hadsell, Ri Hayashi,
Tarie Sabido, Tashi Saheb-Ettaba,
Stuti Telidevara, and Nicole Wang

Advisor
Michael Bourret

The editors of the stories in this collection:
Denise Conejo: BREAK
Sharyn November: FLIGHT, RISK, and MONSTERS
Emily X.R. Pan: BELLY
Nova Ren Suma: ESCAPE
Trisha Tobias: SWEETMEATS, PRINCESS, and RESILIENT
Alexa Wejko: GLOW, FOOLS, and PAN DULCE
Deeba Zargarpur: SOLACE

BIOS

Emily X.R. Pan is the *New York Times* bestselling author of *The Astonishing Color of After*, which won the APALA Honor Award and the Walter Honor Award, received six starred reviews, was a Los Angeles Times Book Prize finalist, and was long-listed for the Carnegie Medal. She holds an MFA in fiction from New York University and has taught creative writing in many different capacities, including to undergraduate students at NYU.

Nova Ren Suma is a two-time Edgar Award finalist for Best Young Adult Novel, for *A Room Away from the Wolves* and the #1 *New York Times* bestselling *The Walls Around Us*. Her other novels include *Imaginary Girls* and *17 & Gone*. She has an MFA in fiction from Columbia University and teaches creative writing at the University of Pennsylvania and in the Writing for Children and Young Adults MFA program at Vermont College of Fine Arts.

STORY AUTHORS

Tanya Aydelott is Pakistani American, but spent most of her childhood in Cairo, Egypt, as it was the simplest geographic compromise her parents could find. Perhaps because of this, she loves hot breezes, hibiscus tea, and cumin. She earned her MFA in Writing for Children and Young Adults from Vermont College of Fine Arts and currently makes her home in Texas. When not at work or writing, she is probably at a museum or making jam.

Tanvi Berwah is a writer based in South Asia. She has a master's degree in English literature from the University of Delhi, and once wrote a term paper on fictional languages in *The Lord of the Rings* and *Game of Thrones*. You can visit her online at tanviberwah.com.

Gina Chen writes fantasy stories about heroines, antiheroines, and the kind of cleverness that brings trouble in its wake. She resides in sunny Southern California, and you can find her online at actualgina.com.

Linda Cheng was born in Taiwan and resides in Vancouver, Canada. She received her BFA from the Savannah College of Art and Design and worked as an art director in ad agencies across the Southern United States, where she developed a deep love for sweet tea, grits, and Southern Gothic stories. She is currently working on her first novel, learning to play the cello, and introducing obscure '90s anime to her toddler. Find her on Twitter: @Linda_Y_Cheng.

Mayra Cuevas was born and raised in Puerto Rico. She is a professional journalist and fiction writer who prefers love stories with happy endings. She is currently a producer for CNN and keeps her sanity by practicing Buddhist meditation at Kadampa Meditation Center Georgia. She lives with her husband, also a CNN journalist, and their cat in Norcross, Georgia. She is the stepmom to two amazing young men who provide plenty of inspiration for her stories. Follow her on Twitter: @MayraECuevas, and Instagram: @MayraCuevas.

Nora Elghazzawi is a Muslim Lebanese American writer currently living in Boston, Massachusetts. Her passions include travel, classical music, and lovely words. When she isn't consuming inordinate amounts of iced coffee or daydreaming about beautiful books, she can be found working on her YA novel, writing out her own magical adventure. Find Nora on Twitter: @noraelghazzawi.

Desiree S. Evans is a writer from South Louisiana. She holds degrees in journalism from Northwestern University and international policy from Columbia University. She was a recent Fiction Fellow at the Michener Center for Writers at the University of Texas at Austin. Her writing has been supported by the Voices of Our Nations Arts Foundation (VONA), the Callaloo Creative Writing Workshop, Kimbilio Fiction, and the Hurston/ Wright Foundation. Her short fiction has appeared in journals such as *Gulf Coast*, *The Offing*, and *Nimrod Journal*, among others. Visit Desiree on the web at desiree-evans.com, and on Instagram and Twitter: @literarydesiree.

Rachel Hylton lives in the mountains of western North Carolina. She received her MFA from Vermont College of Fine Arts, where she was the recipient of the Houghton Mifflin Harcourt Prize and the In a Nutshell Short Story Award. When not writing or teaching, Rachel is usually hiking, reading, or hanging from a dance trapeze. Out of respect, she no longer eats lobster. You can find her on Instagram @rachelinmountains or Twitter @rachelhyltonx.

Adriana Marachlian is a writer and doctor, born and raised in Venezuela and blooming in New York. She enjoys losing herself in worlds that only exist in her head, naming plants, and making people uncomfortable. When she's not buying way too many succulents, she writes stories about ghosts, witches, and the magic hiding just underneath the surface. You can find her on Twitter: @aemarachlian.

Sophie Meridien is a teen librarian and writer currently residing in south Florida. When she isn't throwing her favorite books at teenagers, you can find her working on her YA novel, drinking heavily sweetened coffee, and stressing out over the New York Yankees. You can find her on Twitter: @sophiesticates.

Maya Prasad is a South Asian American writer, a Caltech graduate, and a former Silicon Valley software engineer. She now resides in the Pacific Northwest, where she enjoys hiking, canoeing, and raising her budding bookworm daughter. A recipient of the We Need Diverse Books mentorship program, she's passionate about creating brown girl leads in children's literature. Visit her website mayaprasad.com or find her on Instagram and Twitter: @msmayaprasad.

Flor Salcedo was born and raised in the border town of El Paso, Texas. She currently resides in Austin, Texas, with her husband and six cats. She is a programmer by day and writer by almost-every-single-other-moment. She is seeking representation for her debut novel, a dark YA sci-fi dystopia (with a bit of humor in it, too). When she isn't doing writerly or programming things, or catching up on sleep, she can be found kissing cats and . . . kissing cats. Follow her on Twitter: @florspower.

Joanna Truman is a writer, filmmaker, and photographer originally from a tiny town in West Virginia. She now lives in Los Angeles, where she is the creative director at Soapbox Films. She holds a BFA in Film Production from the FSU College of Motion Picture Arts. She has published speculative fiction in *Apex Magazine* and *Luna Station Quarterly* and has been featured in the nationally broadcast NPR program *To the Best of Our Knowledge*. She lives with three cats and one dog and thus is utterly outnumbered in most decisions. Find Joanna online at joannatruman.com and on Twitter & Instagram: @joannatruman.

FICTION EDITORS

Denise Conejo (associate fiction editor with foreshadowya.com) is an administrative aide at New York University and a freelance editor. A Dominicanx from New York, Denise grew up in Harlem, where she discovered her love of reading and community. She holds a BA in English from the City College of New York, where she also completed the Publishing Certificate Program. Find Denise on Twitter: @DeniConejo.

Sharyn November (fiction editor with foreshadowya.com) is an editor and marketing strategist who works with authors, agents, publishers, librarians, booksellers, and teenage readers. Before that, she was senior editor at Viking Children's Books and editorial director of Firebird. Her books have received the World Fantasy Award, the Scott O'Dell Award, the Christopher Medal, and the Michael L. Printz Award, and she herself is a two-time World Fantasy Award Finalist for her editorial work. Find Sharyn on Twitter and Instagram: @sn0vember.

Trisha Tobias (associate fiction editor with foreshadowya.com) is an associate developmental editor at book packager Dovetail Fiction, a 2018 Walter Dean Myers Grant recipient, and a 2019–2020 Highlights Foundation Diversity Fellow. She holds a BA in Media and Communication Studies from Fordham University with a minor in Creative Writing. Find Trisha on Twitter: @misstrishtobias.

Alexa Wejko (fiction editor with foreshadowya.com) is an editor at Soho Teen, an imprint of Soho Press. Formerly an adjunct professor at Queens College, where she received her MFA in Creative Writing and Literary Translation, Alexa has worked on a wide range of children's books, including the *New York Times* bestseller *Everless*.

ACKNOWLEDGMENTS

WE HAVE AN INCREDIBLE SUPPORT SYSTEM. HERE'S OUR ATTEMPT TO thank everyone.

Michael Bourret was FORESHADOW's very first advocate and our most staunch supporter. It's impossible to express how much we adore him.

Thank you, Elise Howard and Sarah Alpert, for loving this project and nudging the craft pieces from our brains. The rest of the AYR team, including Caitlin Rubinstein, Michael McKenzie, Megan Harley, Ashley Mason, Laura Williams, Carla Weise, Martha Cipolla, and Sarah J. Coleman—thank you!

Jess Capelle—thanks for your generous, speedy legal guidance.

Thanks to our PHENOMENAL volunteer staff at **foreshadowYA.com**: Diane Telgen—remarkable managing editor and slush queen. Alexa Wejko, Sharyn November, Denise Conejo, Trisha Tobias—extraordinary fiction editors. Alison Cherry, Angela Cole, and Natalia Wikana—fabulous copy editors. Our reading team passionately sifted for treasure: Emi Benn, Cristina dos Santos, Michelle Falkoff, Ariane Felix, Raechell Garrett, Francesca Flores, Lili Hadsell, Ri Hayashi, Tarie Sabido, Tashi Saheb-Ettaba, Stuti Telidevara, and Nicole Wang. Saraciea Fennell led our publicity efforts for our original campaign. Mara Delgado Sánchez and Deeba Zargarpur were instrumental in launching ISSUE 00. Carey MacArthur supplied the beautiful photographs for the site.

We wish this book could have included all thirty-nine brilliant stories. Thank you, amazing authors who wrote for us: Dhonielle Clayton, Samantha Mabry, Malinda Lo, Randy Ribay, Stephanie Kuehn, Lilliam Rivera, Courtney Summers, Brandy Colbert, Nina LaCour, Wendy Xu, S.K. Ali, Saundra Mitchell, Mark Oshiro, Uma Krishnaswami, Anna-Marie McLemore, Claribel Ortega, Amy Reed, Sacha Lamb, Sara Farizan, Karuna Riazi, Justine Larbalestier, Rebecca Barrow, Tehlor Kay Mejia, Anna Borges, Tochi Onyebuchi, and Aysha U. Farah.

Hugs to Nicola Yoon, Adam Silvera, Sabaa Tahir, Cynthia Leitich Smith, Becky Albertalli, Gayle Forman, Laurie Halse Anderson, Heidi Heilig, Jason Reynolds, Jandy Nelson, Melissa Albert, and Roshani Chokshi. They chose their favorites from our slush and gave the perfect introduction for each story.

Early on we crowdfunded to raise basic operating funds and were blown away by the support from all corners of the community:

David Levithan sponsored a bajillion of our New Voices. We also received generous sponsorships from Marieke Nijkamp and Barry Lyga & Morgan Baden. And special thanks to Barry Goldblatt Literary, Margot H. Knight & Nick Walsh, and Nicole Valentine.

Thank you SO MUCH to the prize donors, whose generosity allowed our campaign to be so super-successful: Arvin Ahmadi, Samira Ahmed, Julie C. Dao, Kelly Loy Gilbert, Sara Holland, Tiffany D. Jackson, Stacey Lee, Claire Legrand, Karen McManus, Farrah Penn, Anica Mrose Rissi, Aisha Saeed, Laura Sebastian, Sarah Nicole Smetana, Jessica Spotswood, Ashley Woodfolk, Algonquin Young Readers, Gallt & Zacker Literary Agency, Greenwillow Books, HarperCollins, Houghton Mifflin Harcourt, ICM Partners, Janklow & Nesbit, Katherine Tegen Books, Little, Brown, Page Street Publishing, Penguin, Root Literary, Sara Crowe, Tina Dubois, Jim McCarthy, Beth Phelan, Brooks Sherman, Eric Smith, DongWon Song, Lauren Spieller, Saba Sulaiman, Suzie Townsend, Lauren Abramo, Linda Camacho, Wendi Gu, Taylor Haggerty, Jordan Hamessley, Victoria Marini, Penny Moore, Elana Roth Parker, Joanna Volpe, Marietta Zacker, Seth Fishman, Sarah Alpert, Jenny Bak, Sarah Barley, Kamilla Benko, Jordan Brown, Patrice Caldwell, Joanna Cardenas, Karen Chaplin, Nikki Garcia, Brian Geffen, Marissa Grossman, Katherine Harrison, Andrew Karre, Vicki Lame, Maggie Lehrman, Tiffany Liao, Krestyna Lypen, Kate Meltzer, Martha Mihalick, Matt Ringler, Julie Rosenberg, Stephanie Stein, and Jeffrey West.

Last, but never least: our wonderful life partners, L and E, who put up with our frantic scrambling, built the **foreshadowYA.com** website, and shook their heads at the sometimes-foolish ambition with which we charged forward, but followed us anyway. So much love, so many thanks.

Last-last: Thank YOU, our fabulous readers, for joining us in this love of good stories. This magic only lives on because of you. Thanks for reading.

—Emily X.R. Pan & Nova Ren Suma